Praise for *The Iron Assassin*

Los Angeles Times Summer Reading List 2015

"Greenwood weaves in several layers of political intrigue along with jaunty dialogue that adds a touch of humor to the story. A welcome addition to the ever-expanding steampunk genre."   —*Booklist*

"If you're looking for an imaginative and intriguing story within the steampunk subgenre, then this would definitely be one to check out."
—*SFRevu*

Tor Books by Ed Greenwood

Dark Warrior Rising
Dark Vengeance
The Iron Assassin

BAND OF FOUR NOVELS

The Kingless Land
The Vacant Throne
A Dragon's Ascension
The Dragon's Doom
The Silent House

THE IRON ASSASSIN

or

A Clockwork Prometheus

ED GREENWOOD

TOR

A Tom Doherty Associates Book
New York

THE IRON ASSASSIN

Copyright © 2015 by Ed Greenwood

Designed by Greg Collins

A Tor Book
Published by Tom Doherty Associates, LLC
175 Fifth Avenue
New York, NY 10010

www.tor-forge.com

Tor® is a registered trademark of Tom Doherty Associates, LLC.

The Library of Congress has cataloged the hardcover edition as follows:

Greenwood, Ed.
    The iron assassin / Ed Greenwood.—1st ed.
        p. cm.
    "A Tom Doherty Associates book."
    ISBN 978-0-7653-3846-4 (hardcover)
    ISBN 978-1-4668-3889-5 (e-book)
1. Inventors—Fiction. 2. Resuscitation—Fiction. 3. London (England)—Fiction.
4. Steampunk fiction. I. Title.
    PR9199.3.G759 I76 2015
    813'.54—dc23

                                                                2015012947

ISBN 978-0-7653-3847-1 (trade paperback)

Our books may be purchased in bulk for promotional, educational,
or business use. Please contact your local bookseller or the Macmillan Corporate
and Premium Sales Department at 1-800-221-7945, extension 5442,
or by e-mail at MacmillanSpecialMarkets@macmillan.com.

First Edition: June 2015
First Trade Paperback Edition: July 2016

Printed in the United States of America

0 9 8 7 6 5 4 3 2 1

**To Sal and Kyle
for opening the way**

DRAMATIS PERSONAE
in order of appearance

- **JOHN LANGFORD**, Dread Agent of the Tower (secret agent for the Crown) and Sworn Sword of the Lion (knight); loyal, trusted—and doomed

- **MISTER BLEYS HARDCASTLE**, a staunch and sturdy man of action; if this was a Holmes tale, he would be our Watson

- **JACK STRAKER**, Lord Tempest, a flamboyant and debonair nobleman, lean and hawklike inventor, and an Investigator Royal; if this was a Holmes tale, he would be our Holmes

- **QUENTIN AMBERTHWAITE**, Lord Staunton, a nobleman and the founder and sponsor of Lessingham's (an exclusive club in a fashionable part of London), within which establishment he bears the nickname "the Old Man"

- Chief Inspector **THEO STANDISH**, of the Yard; a dour, grim policeman fueled by fury

- **MISTER HALWORTHY BURTON**, a high-ranking Crown official of Whitehall, concerned with collecting taxes from gentlemen and lords; venomous and unpopular

- **HENRY ROLYNDSON**, Lord Hawkingbrooke, Lord Guardian of the Royal Household, "the Old Hawk," a formidable old warrior who is also serving as Lord Chamberlain of the Empire as our tale begins

- REGINALD THROCKMORTON, the Imperial Herald of the Realm; "Throck" to the Queen; old, loyal, and short, a man who knows very well how to glower

- His ROYAL HIGHNESS FREDERICK VILLIERS HANOVER, Lord Lion of the Empire, Prince Royal of England and Its Dominions Low and High, Sword of the Seas and Defender of the Two Faiths, and Most Dread Lord of London; better known to the Empire as just "the Lord Lion"; heir apparent to the throne, womanizer, and the possessor of very piercing blue eyes—dashing, very dashing

- IOLANTHE SHARPLEY, Lady Hailsham, a beautiful, spirited, well-armed, and loyal Dread Agent of the Tower (secret agent for the Crown) who is very good at what she does

- BERNARD BERINGER, Lord Gaunt, a scarred and gruff old nobleman who is loyal to the Crown, a member of the Privy Council, and a not-quite-retired old warrior

- LESLEIGH PEROWNE, Lord Winter, a nobleman and the current owner of Lessingham's who has a collection of secrets larger than is good for any man

- MISTER BENTLEY STEELFORCE, the prototype Iron Assassin, code-named "the Silent Man" and reanimated by Jack Straker from a dead London chimney sweep, Bentley Roper

- SIR JASPER RICHMOND, a loyal knight who happens to know the Iron Assassin's past

DRAMATIS PERSONAE

- ROSE GORDHAMMOND, Lady Harminster, an earnest young noblewoman of beauty and brains who lost her parents early and so is now the head of her house—and our heroine

- PONSONBY HARTWORTH, Lord Sefton, the elder nobleman of the Hartworth family to grace our pages, a fiery-tempered gruff and pompous old retired Rear Admiral and nonretired Dread Agent of the Tower (secret agent for the Crown) whose stiffest feature is his neck, and whose largest achievement is his mustache

- ALGERNON HARTWORTH, Lord Sefton, the hot-tempered son of Lord Ponsonby Sefton—and so, of course, also "Lord Sefton" (one can never have too many badly behaved noblemen in a gaslamp fantasy)

- WILLIAM BRENT (better known as "Willum"), an aging "beagle" (policeman of the Queen's High Constabulary), of the rank of Constable

- ADLER HOPWOOD, a young beagle (policeman of the Queen's High Constabulary), of the rank of Constable, and Willum's beat partner

- BERTRAM BUCKINGHAM, Lord Chamberlain of the Empire, a mild-mannered, polite, shrewd, and very capable man

- ALBERT HINDMARSH, holder of the rank of Commander in the Queen's High Constabulary, "Old Bert" to all in the force; scarred, ginger-haired, and heavily whiskered

- PERCY TRICKER, Lord Harkness, Commissioner of the Queen's High Constabulary, a fence-sitting diplomat notable for his fiercely drooping mustache

- NORBERT MARLSHRIKE, a vindictive and brilliant inventor bound to the Ancient Order of the Tentacles—who, as their name might suggest, are dark and dastardly villains. He likes his tea black.

- LADY CONSTANCE ROODCANNON ("Roo" to the Prince Royal); white of long leg and black of eyes and hair, a stunningly beautiful patron of cutting-edge art; a former lover of the Prince Royal who secretly bore his bastard son, Lionel; "Auntie" in the Ancient Order of the Tentacles

- ALBERT ALOYSIUS GRIMSTONE, known to all simply as "Grimstone," the sole surviving longtime family servant of the Roodcannons; now bodyguard and personal agent of Lady Constance Roodcannon; a formidably dangerous individual

- MILES WHIPSNADE, a dangerous man who has colorless eyes and a left hand of metal and clockwork that can thrust forth both weapons and tools; bodyguard to, and agent of, the mysterious "Uncle"

- DARMOND FFLOUKES, a rather anxious underservant of the mysterious "Uncle"

- ALSTON DRAKE, Assistant Commissioner of the Queen's High Constabulary, "the Commissioner's Hound," a stout, balding, massive man who is a disciplinarian and enjoys his work—that is to say, a bully

- "LONG" TOM BASTABLE, the scarred and battered publican of the Raging Lion pub in Whitechapel

- MISTER OSWALD SMEDLEY, a cracksman of Whitechapel

- **ADRIAN SYKES,** a fearful stablehand of Lord Barnstaple's country household

- **BURGESS CARTER,** a less fearful stablehand of Lord Barnstaple's country household

- **CHATWIN GOSLING,** a royal bodyguard (soldier) stationed at the gates of Foxden

- **MISTER KENDRICK MALMERSTON,** the butler at Foxden, a coldly correct and frighteningly competent "butler of butlers"

- **RODERICK DYSON,** better known as "Dyson the Knife," a snuffer (killer for hire) of Whitechapel

- **CONNELL FURLONG,** holder of the rank of Sergeant in the Queen's High Constabulary; a sad-eyed man assigned to the duty desk of the Tower Street police station

- **LEYLAND BLAKESLEE,** holder of the rank of Inspector in the Queen's High Constabulary; a good man

- **CHARLES BLUNT,** holder of the rank of Sergeant in the Queen's High Constabulary; a grim, competent veteran of the force

- **GERALD PRYCEWOOD,** Herald Pursuivant to the Empire (Throckmorton's assistant and understudy); thin, earnest, young, bespectacled, and loyal to the Empire

- **RODNEY OLIVIER,** a royal bodyguard (soldier) guarding the chain-gun in Foxden

- **LILY FRETWELL,** more commonly known as "Lil," a good-natured prostitute invited into Foxden by the Prince Royal

- MISTER SIMON MORROWPYKE, leader of the Crown Anarchists political party (who seek to set aside royal rule and to dismantle most of the offices and authority of government); a nervous and pompous man on the ascendant

- CLAYTON HAMMILL, a beagle (constable of the Queen's High Constabulary) of no particular note

- PAXTON MUNDY, a beagle; holder of the rank of Sergeant in the Queen's High Constabulary; a burly, cigar-smoking, cynical veteran of the streets

- "COUSIN ALFRED" in the Ancient Order of the Tentacles; a nobleman of the Empire, true identity unknown

- "COUSIN CLYDE" in the Ancient Order of the Tentacles; a nobleman of the Empire, true identity unknown

- "BLUSHING NIECE" in the Ancient Order of the Tentacles; a noblewoman of the Empire, true identity unknown

- "NEPHEW NESTOR" in the Ancient Order of the Tentacles; a nobleman of the Empire, true identity unknown

- JEFFREY ASHMAN, a young "beagle" (constable of the Queen's High Constabulary), assigned to the Tower Street Station

- THOMAS WILKINS, a beagle (policeman of the Queen's High Constabulary), of the rank of Constable; a good, competent man

- RUPERT SUMMERS, a beagle (policeman of the Queen's High Constabulary), of the rank of Constable; another good, competent man—yet the Empire still has too few

- **GARRETT OLDTREE,** a beagle (policeman of the Queen's High Constabulary), of the rank of Constable, who is more than he at first seems

- **ELIZABETH LALBROOKE,** more commonly known as "Bess," a prostitute invited into Foxden by the Prince Royal

- **SIR FULTON BIRTWHISTLE,** a magistrate of style, verbosity, and accomplishment

- **HELIOTROPE STONEBRACE,** Lady Armour, a young noblewoman of the Empire; Algernon Hartworth hopes she's "ripening for marriage"

- **MISS ALTHEA PEABODY,** a severe and tartly judgmental housekeeper to Norbert Marlshrike, whose looks reflect her character

- **AMELIA BRASSGIRDLE,** Lady Rathercoats, an old, wrinkled, respectable noblewoman; a widow with an indiscretion in her past

- **MISTER HAROLD JENKINS,** competent, loyal, and brave butler to the Rathercoats noble family

- **MONTAGUE PAUNCEFOOT,** a grotesquely fat and filthy-rich "twister" (crooked moneylender) of London, complete with ornate London mansion and an endless succession of fine meals

- **"OLD HORSLEY,"** in the Ancient Order of the Tentacles, within which his rank is high; a ginger-whiskered nobleman of the Empire, identity unknown

- **QUENTIN CHILDERHOSE,** Lord Amesbury, "Cousin Quillan"

in the Ancient Order of the Tentacles, within which his rank is high; a nobleman of the Empire

- "REDHAIRED NEPHEW" in the Ancient Order of the Tentacles, within which his rank is high; a red-haired nobleman of the Empire, true identity unknown

- AN ANONYMOUS MASKED ASSASSIN, who wears a top hat adorned with a descending column of diamonds, each stone marking a noble slain by him; Lady Roodcannon's visitor (and, it seems, her superior, but not in the Ancient Order); mysteriouser and mysteriouser

- ALICE LOUISA HANOVER, "the Dowager Duchess," widow of Duke Leopold (the younger brother of Queen Victoria), a grasping battle-ax and tyrant; also petty, spiteful, and lazy—and those are her better qualities

- VENETTA DELEON, maid to the Dowager Duchess and her sometime envoy; the Duchess thinks her "entirely too independent-minded and snippy"—and the Duchess is right

- NIGEL BURROWS, a beagle (constable of the Queen's High Constabulary)

- COMMANDER ROBERT ADAMS, holder of the rank of Commander in the Queen's High Constabulary, in charge of the beagles at Foxden in the absence of the Commissioner and Assistant Commissioner

- ABNER CANDLEPIKE ("Noseless" to Grimstone), a large and rather inarticulate thug who serves Clarence Sarkbottle; distinctive thanks to his missing nose

DRAMATIS PERSONAE

- **CLARENCE SARKBOTTLE**, a disgraced ex-doctor

- **RANDOLPH DRAPER** ("Fang" to Grimstone), a large and aging thug who serves Clarence Sarkbottle; distinctive due to his lone remaining tooth—a canine that juts down over his lower lip

- **CUTHBERT FURLOW**, Yeoman Warder at the Tower of London, charged with guarding its East Gate (that opens onto the street known as Tower Bridge)

- **AGNUS GLENCANNON**, a lowly member of the Ancient Order

- **ARCHIBALD MASON** ("Mase" to Glencannon), another lowly member of the Ancient Order

- **SEBASTIAN WATKINS**, a slightly less lowly member of the Ancient Order

- **HERCULES MULVER**, a sentinel of the Ancient Order

- **DAHLIA GALLISON**, another sentinel of the Ancient Order

- **BLAKE INSCOE**, a rather bloodthirsty member of the Ancient Order

- **TIMOTHY ILLINGWORTH**, a deckhand on the *Mary Rose*, a large freight airship out of Portsmouth

- **PHILBERT RUSHWOOD**, Lord Dunster, a conservative old nobleman of the Empire

- **HARBORD KENT**, an old beagle (policeman of the Queen's High Constabulary), of the rank of Constable, and the owner of an impressive mustache

- PHINEAS FAIRWEATHER, the Constable of the Tower of London

- ALEXANDRINA GLORIANA HANOVER, Queen Victoria the Third, Empress of the Lion Empire, nicknamed "Old Crowned Steamheart" and "Ironheart" (among less complimentary things); a feisty, aging woman kept alive by steam-driven lung and heart replacements

- QUADE JESSON, a beagle (policeman of the Queen's High Constabulary), of the rank of Constable, assigned to the detachment that serves at the Tower of London under the Yeoman Warders

- GILES PRITCHARD, a beagle (policeman of the Queen's High Constabulary), of the rank of Constable, who secretly serves Assistant Commissioner Drake before Queen and Empire

- GAVIN PARKHILL, a beagle (policeman of the Queen's High Constabulary), of the rank of Constable, assigned to the guard at Foxden

- HUMPHREY WYKES, a beagle (policeman of the Queen's High Constabulary), of the rank of Constable, who secretly serves Assistant Commissioner Drake before Queen and Empire

- HEATHCLIFF IVES, a beagle (policeman of the Queen's High Constabulary), of the rank of Constable

- GILBERT HARDYSIDES, the old, side-whiskered captain of the *Windlark* flitter airship of the Crown fleet

- KYLE TARKRIDGE, a masked member of the Ancient Order; assigned to guard the mill where Marlshrike was holed up

- **WALLACE BRADING,** another masked member of the Ancient Order; smaller than Tarkridge; also assigned to guard the mill where Marlshrike was holed up

- **KEENE GILRETH,** equerry (stablemaster) at Foxden

- **VERNON PARKINSON,** yet another masked member of the Ancient Order; a member of the boarding party that seized control of the *Mary Rose* airship

- **HECTOR BRACKLEBURY,** yet another masked member of the Ancient Order; a member of the boarding party that seized control of the *Mary Rose* airship

- **GARRICK WOOLCOCK,** Royal Mail guard at the Bishop's Bottom mail yard

- **IRVIN YERBY,** another Royal Mail guard at the Bishop's Bottom mail yard

- **ANSON WRIGHTSON,** a beagle (policeman of the Queen's High Constabulary), of the rank of Constable, who secretly serves Assistant Commissioner Drake before Queen and Empire

- **HUMBERT GREGSON,** a beagle (policeman of the Queen's High Constabulary) who holds the rank of Commander, and secretly serves Assistant Commander Drake before Queen and Empire

- **AN ANONYMOUS** (and well on the way to becoming monstrous) Elder of the Ancient Order of Tentacles; a transformed nobleman of unknown identity

THE IRON ASSASSIN

SEPTEMMER 30

He is falling.

It is over. All over.

The game lost, and his life with it.

The soft, tiny glows of a thousand distant gaslamps rise past Langford's gaze as he falls, despair rising bitterly to choke him.

Below, the dark ribbon of the Thames; around it, London sprawling away in all directions into the fog-shrouded night.

The greatest city in all the wide world, seat of the Empire of the Lion, the throne he's been proud to serve. Its once-impenetrable ocean fogs writhing like churning waves, as they always did these last few years, under the billowing plumes of countless smokestacks, the fires that birthed the steam that moved everything. Mills stamped and shuddered, trains squealed, great cogs clattered, driving the Empire on into a brighter, richer tomorrow . . . and with a cruel suddenness, he is leaving it all behind, plunging into death unregarded.

It is all going to go on without him.

Dread Agent of the Tower and Sworn Sword of the Lion he may be—but, in the end, he is utterly unimportant, after all.

The Tentacles assassin clutches at him again, snarling something incoherent, the dagger-tipped fingers of a fanged gauntlet flashing, long and cruel and gleaming.

They clash together in the air, all too close to Langford's throat.

He takes what little satisfaction he can in swinging his cane through them with all the force he can muster, feeling at least one of them snap off, ringing like a bell as it tumbles away through the air. Take that, you foulness . . .

The force of his blow spins Langford into a tumble in the air that, when spent, leaves him facing down to watch his death rushing up to meet him. The dark spires and roofs of Lambeth.

At least the assassin is going to die with him, a last desperate hook of Langford's cane toppling him over the same airship balcony rail the Tentacles man had thrust him over.

Or will his killer live, somehow, saved by some infernal new invention hidden on his person?

There should have been *no* Tentacles agents in the Household Guard—none at all! Is this the only one? Or are there more?

Damn it to the heavens, how far does the taint reach? Into the imperial family itself?

He fights, as the plunge claws the air from his lungs, to get out one last shout.

"For God, the Queen, the Lord Lion, and *England*!"

Does he manage it all, before the heavy crash that brings oblivion?

The assassin is the only being who might know, and, amid the sliding ruin of cracked and broken roof slates, he cannot say— sprawled as he is, mashed into wet red pulp, and too busy trying to shriek as he dies. He fails.

There seems to be a lot of failure about, in London, these days.

OCTEMBER 1

Mister Bleys Hardcastle paused, pipe on its way to his lips but now hanging nigh forgotten in his hand as he stared at the thing that should not have been there.

He took a step back, glancing up and down the dark passage as if several lurking someones were about to catch him in some indiscretion, leaping out with loud jeers to denounce him as a lunatic, a freer of slaves, or one of those wild wits who believes in magic. No, no lurkers. This uppermost hallway at the back of the Lessingham Club was as dimly lit and deserted as he always remembered it being, on his rare glances along it as he hastened across it from the top of the great staircase to the door of the Hargryphon Room.

Hargryphon, that bright-tapestried bower where, until the Lords Temporal had changed the liberties laws, Lessingham's had housed its visiting strumpets for the entertainment of members willing to pay an extra angel or four vintage rose nobles a fortnight. Hardcastle found himself smiling amid fond and vivid memories . . .

Not *now*, b'Jove! Firmly putting reverie aside and returning to the here and now, he cleared his throat as quietly as he knew how and regarded the passage once more.

He'd idly strolled the length of it once, he recalled, and encountered a lost legion of closed and forbidding dark doors, cobwebbed silence—and nothing waiting at the end of it all but a servants' gong on the wall at the head of the narrow and precipitous servants' stair. He could see that gong now, and a choice selection of the doors, too. Nothing had changed, and he was alone in the dim silence, standing before a door bearing a dusty brass nameplate that proclaimed HAVILSTOKE ROOM.

That plate was familiar, but what adorned the upper center of the door was new: a large brass shield from which thrust a flattened but still boldly massive lion's head, eyes closed and jaws clenched around a ring that could have held fast a loaded Thames coal barge.

Surely this knocker hadn't been here before?

Here, on the uppermost floor of a long-established gentlemen's club in Mayfair, five thickly carpeted flights up from the great ground-floor rooms where most members came daily to mutter or snarl over whiskies and cigars.

Beyond the door was a meeting room, all dark-paneled walls hung with dingy paintings—forgettable old masters brought back from the Continent and gifted to the club to pay off whisky debts—a huge round table with chairs, a spittoon or two, and a sideboard with a great stag's head frowning over it. Oh, and a fireplace at one end of the room that would do little to either heat or light the rest of it.

So, why a knocker? Not just a knocker, either; set into the brass shield was a curving row of keyholes to—lock the door shut with multiple bolts?

All this mongery shouldn't be here. Confound it, *hadn't* been here.

Should he use the knocker? Or just throw wide the door and step in?

Hardcastle shifted from foot to foot in indecision.

Then spun, hands clenching in quickening alarm, at the soft scrape of a hurrying stride behind him.

Close behind him.

"Waiting for me, Bleys? How gallant! We can go in fashionably late, and together," a familiar voice rasped, low and breathless.

Jack Straker was almost upon him, and in as much of a lean and hawklike hurry as usual. More properly Lord Tempest, though he never used his title in Lessingham's, and seldom elsewhere.

Straker, or Tempest, the man was perhaps his best—if most exasperating—friend in all the world. A swift-witted man of many endeavors and more secrets, he now clapped one hand on Hardcastle's shoulder as he flung wide the door of the Hargryphon Room with the other.

"Good evening, gentlemen," he said briskly to those inside, practically charging into the room and dragging Hardcastle with him, his fingers suddenly iron-hard talons.

Thankfully, he just as suddenly let go of the shoulder he was nigh crushing in order to bustle on into the room, dusting his hands as he advanced on a tall, substantial wooden box that was leaning, upright, in one corner.

Thankfully, because Hardcastle needed to pause, swallow, and stare.

"Ah, capital!" Straker informed the room. "They've set it the right way up! Splendid, splendid!"

To Hardcastle, Straker's great wooden box looked like a pauper's coffin.

Not that he spared it more than a moment's attention. He was too busy staring at those seated around the table—some of whom were staring back at him.

Others were beyond staring at anyone.

The chairs, table, walls, and old masters were all very much as he'd expected. Facing him across that gleaming acre or so of dark, glossy-polished wood was no less august a personage than Lord Quentin Staunton, founder and sponsor of Lessingham's. Monocle, gently wry smile, lone wavy lock of white hair slicing through his raven comb-back, lace at the wrists of the hands clasped on the jeweled swordstick: the Old Man himself.

At the lord's left elbow sat a hard-glaring man with a nose even more battered than Hardcastle's own, yet it was a beak one barely noticed thanks to the ragged ferocity of the huge mustache beneath it. The man's balding head looked as hard as a knight's helm, and his bowler—complete with bullet holes—sat squarely on the table before him.

As Hardcastle recalled, this man had only three faces: dour and grim, carefully expressionless, and utter fury blazing forth. They'd met twice or thrice before, not in good circumstances, and Hardcastle had hoped to go to his grave—threescore years or more hence—without ever again laying eyes upon him: Chief Inspector Theo Standish, of the Yard.

On the other side of His Lordship sat a fat, large-headed, bespectacled man whose clothes outshone Staunton's in splendor. A man the wider public might not recognize, even with that vast forehead and formidably bushy eyebrows, but all too familiar to anyone who aspired to wealth in the city. A man of Whitehall whose rank was high and whose chief concern was taxes—gentlemen's taxes, ensuring the prompt and full payment of same. Hardcastle had heard his name spat from scores of lips in the rooms downstairs, at races, and in splendid country houses: Halworthy Burton. Burton of Whitehall was not a popular man, and judging by the venomous, self-satisfied expression on his face, took sour de-light in that.

Yet neither the founder nor the poisonous stares of the men seated with him were what so arrested Hardcastle's attention.

It was the rest of the men seated at the table, silent and dust-covered, slumped in the dark frock coats of earlier days, that trans-fixed his attention.

They were so obviously dead, all of them. Long dead. Leaning in their chairs, mummified, dropped jaws yawning and sunken eyes long past seeing anything. One was quite skeletal, and his neigh-bor had collapsed, grisly head having long ago departed decaying shoulders and rolled across the table to a stop—on its side, and thankfully facing away from Hardcastle—nigh the near edge of the vast meeting table.

"Our quieter founders," Lord Staunton explained dryly. "They sel-dom vote these days."

Hardcastle nodded abruptly, trying vainly to think of the right response. He was still struggling when Straker took the need to do so quite away from him.

All lean arms and legs, pantherlike pounce and alert energy, Hardcastle's friend had been unlocking and unlatching like a mad-man.

He now stood back from the coffinlike box with an air of satis-faction, faced the table with a broad smile, and said briskly, "I must apologize for our tardiness, gentlemen. Even this close to midnight, the streets were crowded. London's traffic—as I'm sure you've noticed—grows ever worse."

"Another bid for your elevated steam tramways, Straker?" Bur-ton's voice was flat and sour. "Some of us have heard more than enough of them."

The hawklike young inventor wreathed his reply with an affable smile. "Do you know, Burton? Settled and successful men always prefer matters to be as they were when they rose to prosperity and

rail against the new. Yet the new always comes, however they object and whatever laws they pass to try to prevent it. I'm told your
father railed against the post, saying it would enable malcontents
to more easily send messages to each other from the docks to out-
lying counties and the wilds of Scotland and Wales beyond. Yet no
one would now be without it! Your father and your uncle both opposed establishing colonies across the Atlantic, seeing no benefit at
all in conquering vast and frozen wastes of uninhabited wilderness
called Canada—yet the fur coat you take such pride in came from
that largest of our dominions, and half the steam boilers across
our great empire are now daily stoked with the trees and the coal of
that same frigid wasteland! You yourself were dead set against—"

"*Enough*, Mister Straker," Burton said coldly. "You pursue a
strange way of courting my approval, I must say."

"There's a lot you 'must say,' Burton," Standish said heavily. "Yet
however young and, well, strange this man may be, he's promised
us a weapon against the Tentacles. Let us hear him out—unless
you've something more brilliant to offer."

Burton's head snapped around with the speed of a striking adder.
"Have a care, policeman! You forget your place, by the Lord Lion,
you do! I—"

"Will die of apoplexy some day, Burton, if you don't take things
more calmly," Lord Staunton observed firmly, leaning forward to
fully interpose himself between the mantle of Whitehall and the
swift hand of the Yard. "The Chief Inspector is right. We are here
to entertain Mister Straker's proposal, so . . ." He spread a hand.
"Mister Straker?"

The young inventor bowed. "Thank you, Lord. You are most
kind." He spun around, hand outstretched. "Behold the box."

"We could hardly help but notice it," Staunton replied dryly. "It
contains your new weapon?"

"It does."

"Some sort of blunderbuss?" Standish leaned forward in his

eagerness. "Steam-powered, to hurl out a stream of bullets, as the rumors have been hinting? Silver bullets? I mean to say, the box is rather large . . ."

"It would hardly serve London and its citizens well," Straker replied sharply, "to go about the streets launching streams of bullets at any presumed man of the Tentacles. This is not, after all, *America*."

He drew himself up—and with a conjurer's flourish produced from behind his back one of the fastenings he'd removed from the box earlier.

It was a simple block of wood, from around which he unwound a long wire, to lay bare a folded metal handle. Unfolded, this became a crank, and two of the inventor's impatiently swift steps took the wire to hook about a particular broad-headed metal nail among many such that studded all edges of the box. Straker returned to where he'd been standing and held out his contraption. "Observe."

"It's a block of wood," Burton sneered. "Now, what do I win?"

"Patience, it is to be hoped," Straker told the ceiling briskly. "If England is to go from strength to strength rather than declining in decadence, we need ever-open minds at Whitehall."

"Bolshevik," Burton spat.

"Is that your latest leaning, Master Tax Clerk? If so, your mind is weaker than I'd thought. Bolshevist philosophy employs more than a little rather dodgy reasoning; you'd do better—"

Burton rose abruptly, and caught up his walking stick. "I did not come here to be insulted—"

Lord Staunton's swordcane lashed out, sending Burton's stick spinning across the room to crash against the heavy gilt frame of an unoffending Old Master and clatter to the floor.

"You came here," the lord snapped, in a voice of sudden iron, "because the Lord Lion himself commanded you to. Not only to attend here this day, but to listen, and observe—and use your best judgment in this secret conclave as to what Mister Straker is offering England in one of its all-too-many hours of need. Storm out if you like, but be well aware that if you do so, you will also be walking away from your *position*, Mister Burton. One word from me to the Lord Lion . . ."

"You'd not dare!"

"On the contrary, I was ordered to. By our Dread Sovereign herself."

The swordstick was deftly returned to its former position. "You've made many enemies by your manner, Burton—the glee with which you persecute citizens, seeking more coins here and yet more there. Their complaints wear down even the noblest of queens . . . and Her staunch right arm our Lord Lion is many things, but a font of infinite patience is not one of them."

Lord Staunton added a sigh, then reached up a silver flask from one boot top and held it out. "Now let us set all these hard words aside. Have a drink, and sit back down and listen to young Straker. Madness his weapon may seem to you—but the Tentacle lovers are hardly normal, now, are they? And damn me if I can think of any effective weapon we might use to stop them right now! We must entertain everything!"

"The Lord High Constable's exact words to me, those," Standish said heavily. "We must entertain everything."

"Small wonder," Lord Staunton told him. "The Lord Lion spoke that sentence to me, too—and to Burton, I happen to know. One can hear quite clearly through the peephole in the portrait of Good Queen Alice."

Halworthy Burton had long since gone a sickly yellow-white, but now he turned quite gray. And reached for the proffered flask as he sat heavily back down, looked at the tabletop as his pocket watch gently chimed midnight, and said unwillingly, "I, ah—sorry. I . . . tender my apologies to you all. I've not been myself lately."

"Many of us are in that position, sir," Straker said softly. "Yet we must all remember that, even so, we are the fortunate ones."

Burton drank, gasped at the fiery potency of what he'd swallowed, then growled, "How so?"

"The Ancient Order has not yet come hunting us," Straker explained gently. "So we still have our lives."

The sharp rap at the door was as sudden as it was unexpected. Lord Hawkingbrooke frowned, turning to glare at the two stolid Household Guards flanking the door as if the interruption was their fault. "Who can that be? I left strict orders we were to be undisturbed!"

Before either could reply, the door between them was flung wide. Their halberds came up in swift menace—and were struck aside by a bared and ready sword whose wielder wore a war gauntlet of ancient style, a splendid tabard, and a glower that outdid Hawkingbrooke's own. It was old Throckmorton, the Imperial Herald.

"Away steel!" he snapped. "All be obedient before His Royal Highness Frederick Villiers Hanover, Lord Lion of the Empire, Prince Royal of England and Its Dominions Low and High, Sword of the Seas and Defender of the Two Faiths, and Most Dread Lord of London!"

Throckmorton was a short man; over his gilded shoulders, everyone in the room could see a familiar trim-bearded face behind him, piercing blue eyes outshining the three sapphires in the circlet upon the Prince Royal's brows. They all went to their knees in hasty unison.

"Rise, all of you," the Lord Lion said rather wearily, as he lowered himself into the vacant seat at the head of the long table. "I've seen enough bowed heads this day. Hawkingbrooke, I'm told Langford is dead. Is this true?"

"It is, Majesty," the gray-bearded Lord Guardian said curtly.

"Spattered all over a rooftop in Lambeth. Fallen from the skies. Most likely from the last flight to Calais, yestereve."

"Pushed."

"By someone he dragged with him, yes. A Tentacles agent, by the looks of the gore—and the lack of a body."

"One who got his hands fouled, indeed," Lady Iolanthe Hailsham said in dark satisfaction. "I doubt his stomach was strong enough."

"I'm sure knowing that will comfort Langford's daughters deeply," the scarred man sitting beside her rasped.

"Lord Gaunt," Lady Iolanthe said sharply, "*I* will comfort John Langford's daughters, tonight and henceforth. Before both altars and all men, I'll be their sponsor and their guardian, too, if they'll have me."

The Lord Lion sighed. "It will be years, if ever, before they're ready to serve the Empire as their father did. No trail, I presume?"

"Our best men are searching all Lambeth right now, Majesty," Gaunt said shortly. "Thus far, we've found these."

He pointed down the table at two small and gleaming things that sat on a cloth in front of a gloomy-looking Lord Winter.

"One under what was left of Langford, caught in his clothing," Hawkingbrooke added. "The other in a roof gutter, where it might end up if someone slid—or was dragged—"

"Dripped," Gaunt murmured.

"—over the edge of the roof."

The Lord Lion might have been in the waning days of his thirty-first year, but there was nothing at all yet wrong with either his eyes or his wits.

"Buttons from a Household Guardsman's uniform. So if your best men are searching Lambeth, who's taking a look at all of them?"

"Richmond," the Lord Guardian replied, "and he should be reporting back to us here any moment now. He—"

A commotion arose outside the door. The thunder of boots, rapidly approaching at a run, one man—

The door banged open again, but this time the guards were ready with their halberds. The man they nearly spitted recoiled from them and almost fell, shouting, "Majesty! All of you! Carrington and the Seneschal are both Tentacles men and got away from us, clean! They're—"

His wild gaze fell upon the two guardsmen barring his way, and he sprang back, pointing frantically. "These two I've not yet—"

The halberds swung away from him in a flash of sharp war steel that became a swift and wordless charge across the room.

Right at the Lord Lion's back.

"'Ware, Your Majesty!" Hawkingbrooke roared, hurling himself in front of one halberd—and taking it full in the chest—as the Lord Lion sprang up out of his chair in a frantic dive forward, landing on his stomach on the table and sliding along it.

The gleaming imperial boots kicked at the vacated chair to launch the Lord Lion on his way, knocking it back into the shins of the second charging guardsman—who stumbled, halberd swinging high.

Under it hurtled Lord Gaunt, slamming hard into the face of the charging traitor, fists up and punching.

The two men crashed into the edge of the table together, halberd clanging as it tumbled away and they punched, shoved, and struggled.

A struggle that ended in a sudden spasmodic flailing as the Lady Iolanthe's silver-bladed dagger sank hilt-deep into the guardsman's ear. Two frantic seconds after she'd torn it out of the gore-spurting right eye socket of the other guardsman, who had taken just a moment too long trying to yank his halberd out of the groaning, dying Lord Hawkingbrooke.

Who in turn gave one last choking gurgle—and expired. Sudden silence fell.

Sir Richmond, the Lords Gaunt and Winter, and the Lord Lion all used it to do the same thing.

To stare at Lady Iolanthe Hailsham.

As she wiped her dagger clean on the blood-spattered uniform of one Household Guardsman, then planted one button-booted foot on the seat of a handy chair, calmly hiked her skirts up to her waist to reveal the empty dagger sheath strapped to that leg flanking her garters, and slid her little silver fang back into its home again.

"Lady," the Lord Lion said a little breathlessly, the moment those skirts had safely returned to the vicinity of their wearer's ankles, "you've done us great service."

Steady gray eyes met his.

"Not yet, Majesty," their owner replied, "but I fear I may soon have to." She sighed. "Like Hawkingbrooke here."

She looked from his sprawled dead body to the two just as lifeless Tentacles agents. "How many more serpents are there in our midst, I wonder?"

"We're going to have to do a lot more than wonder," Gaunt growled, nursing a halberd-sliced forearm, "and soon. Or we'll all be dead, and this'll be the Empire of the Tentacles."

OCTEMBER 2

P ray observe," Straker announced, "the box."

He turned the crank on the block of wood he was hold-ing, one slow revolution and then many faster ones, build-ing into a whir. The metal hub of the crank clacked repeatedly with well-oiled, smoothly machined confidence, and occasional sparks spat from various places along the wire linking it to the upright box.

From within which there came a muffled chime.

Straker stopped cranking, set the block of wood down on the floor, and stepped back from it, waving both hands at the box in the "Behold!" flourish of a traveling conjurer.

The box responded with a muffled yet distinct thud, then another.

And then its hinged lid was thrust open from within, and a man lurched unsteadily out, striding with the leaning confidence of a drunkard.

More than one hand in the Havilstoke Room promptly clenched hard around the head of a stick or balled into a fist.

The man was clad in the black, many-straps leathers that knights on horse at imperial weddings and funerals wore under their great, gleaming coat-of-plate ceremonial armor. What could be seen of his body looked dead, his hair-shedding head mere shrunken skin over a skull that still had eyes. His hands and feet were bare, the fingers and toes sheathed in silver-coated iron points.

"Gentlemen," Straker said proudly, "meet Steelforce. Mister Bentley Steelforce. My prototype Iron Assassin. Outside this room, we call him the Silent Man."

Steelforce nodded, slowly and deliberately, lifting his dead lips to bare his teeth in a grotesque smile. Then he started toward the table.

His steps were stiff and slow, and as he came, he turned his head almost mechanically to stare at one seated man and then another. Small wonder, that machinelike quality; over his leathers was fitted a cagelike iron frame, an exoskeleton that glowed with tiny crawling lightnings and gave off sparks whenever its joints bent severely.

"Does . . . does it talk?" Burton of Whitehall blurted out, horror warring openly with revulsion on his face.

"Good . . . *day* . . . Mister Burton," the walking dead man replied coldly.

Then he shuddered, his eyes rolled up in his head, and he froze.

Straker snapped his fingers.

The Silent Man made that ghastly smile again, and his eyes slowly descended to regard the men staring at him.

"Excuse me," he said tonelessly. "I was . . . scenting." He looked at Straker. "There are no Tentacles men near. However, more than one of these men has touched a Tentacles man recently."

Straker nodded. "And so?"

"I follow, watch, and learn. Not attacking. Yet."

Straker nodded again. "Indeed," he said, his voice holding satisfaction.

"Is this man dead?" Lord Staunton asked quietly.

"He is, Lord, yet now lives again, and is content to do so," Straker replied. "In life, he was Bentley Roper, chimney sweep. Killed when he fell off a roof in Hampstead. His wife and children are now provided for, and he is proud to serve the Empire of the Lion."

"I see no steam bellows, no vents," Standish barked. "No boiler or firebox, and unless you've been uncommonly clever, no room to hide 'em. So how does he move?"

"As you've just seen, he moves himself."

"So is he a man," Standish growled, "or a machine?"

Steelforce's head turned in the policeman's direction, and Standish fancied he saw a momentary glow of blue-white current behind those dark, liquid eyes. He fought to repress a shudder.

"He remembers something of his living past, to be sure," Straker murmured. "As to how much . . ." He lifted his shoulders in a gentle shrug. "More when he's warmed up and active, and the current's surging through him, to be sure."

"The current?" Burton snapped. "Like the flow of the Thames?"

"Yes," Straker replied, "and no. This current causes wires to glow and Steelforce to move, to come to life for a time. If too strong, it kills."

He waved at the crank on the floor. "This is merely for demonstration purposes. A velocipede, upended to make it stationary, could be pedaled in harness with this generator I've cobbled together—here, beneath the crank—to generate far more electricity, and do so more quickly and steadily. Not every assassin would have to be accompanied by a man with a crank."

"Assassin," Lord Staunton echoed thoughtfully. "Mister Steelforce kills Tentacles agents?"

"He does. Six so far." Straker pointed. "Observe his fingers and toes. Capped in cold iron coated in silver. With these he burns . . . prey. When he grips them, and unleashes some of his electricity to course through these points, some of the silver—poison to one who's drunk the consecration cup of the Ancient Order—floods through them in an instant, searing them from within. He also has forearm bracers fitted with many blades of cold iron and of silver, for intense fighting."

"A dead man made to walk," Burton muttered. "Lunacy. Your crowning lunacy thus far, Straker."

"Perhaps. Yet have you a better weapon? The Tentacles men grow bolder by the day. How many is it now they've killed, Standish? Six hundred some?"

"Four thousand two hundred and four," the man from the Yard growled. "As of last official reckoning, two mornings ago. The majority of another sixty-three 'possibles' will probably, in time, be added to that."

Straker regarded Burton. "Well?"

"Latest estimates are over six thousand," came the grim reply. "The Ancient Order is not confined to London, gentlemen."

"Good God," Hardcastle gasped, unable to stop himself. "Six *thousand*? And you've not *told* us?"

Burton's glare was stern. "Sir, the figures have been withheld from the press to avoid a general panic. The last time London knew real fear—as you should recall—there were dozens of murders, countless accusations, shops burned, and beatings in the streets. And that was a comparatively tame matter of the infectious crew of just one ship. There is such a thing as social responsibility, young man."

"Not that . . . *you'd* be . . . familiar with it," the dead man said flatly, astonishing them all into silence.

Lord Staunton recovered first. "How does your Iron Assassin work, exactly, Mister Straker?" he said quickly, waving the end of his swordcane in front of Burton warningly to quell an outburst.

Straker clapped his hands together in delight at the proffered opportunity and started to pace like a master in a schoolroom.

"You see, gentlemen, the human brain works by electricity. Little pulses—brain waves, some call them, but in truth they are more like short-lived little bolts of lightning than the waves that crash tirelessly upon our shores day and night—that carry our thoughts, bring back what our eyes see and our ears hear to us, and send back commands from the wits in our skulls, so we move a hand thus or step so rather than flailing about at random—"

"Poppycock," Burton snorted, eyes cold above the gleam of his spectacles. "Piffle."

The Silent Man slowly and deliberately turned his head to regard Straker.

Who gave a swift nod.

Steelforce turned his head again, fixing his gaze on the man from Whitehall. Who sneered back at him, thumbs now hooked into the pockets of his splendid waistcoat, and repeated petulantly, "Piffle, I say."

The dead man started to move. His strides were stiff and lumbering, each step pitching his shoulders from side to side like a man hurrying on stilts, but he went around two chairs as deftly as any dancer, picking up speed as he went.

Around the table in a quickening rush, heading for Burton—whose sneer darkened into a defiant snarl, as he hurriedly plunged his hands inside his waistcoat and drew out a gleaming pistol.

"Have a care!" he said sharply. "Come closer and I'll shoot!"

Not slowing in the slightest, the Silent Man shot out a hand to point accusingly at Halworthy Burton—and from one graying, dead finger leapt a fat blue spark.

It reached the barrel of the shaking gun and raced around it like quicksilver moonlight.

Burton shouted in startled pain and dropped the weapon, his arm jerking wildly. That elbow slammed thunderously down on the table before the gun roared, hurling its death into the ceiling as it cart-wheeled to the floor.

Halworthy Burton was not an easily frightened man. He'd fought Rorcristans in Tuscany and faced down the Mad Monks of Dun Abbey, to say nothing of wrestling more than twoscore departmental budgets through the back offices of Whitehall. Yet he looked up, cursing and clutching his elbow, right into a dead face that loomed above him—and went the yellow-white of old bone, jaw quivering in fear.

"Poppycock," Steelforce said pleasantly, his decaying nose almost touching Burton's. "Piffle."

In the tense moment of silence that followed, he lifted his dead upper lip in that horrible smile again. And turned away.

After one long step back the way he'd come, he bent, plucked up Burton's pistol from the floor, and set it on the table, thrusting it back at its owner with a flick of his fingers.

"So this, gentlemen," Straker said calmly, "is my Iron Assassin. I—"

A deep, thunderous clack-clack interrupted him, from the door. The knocker.

"Enter," Lord Staunton called, and the door was flung open.

The man in the doorway was panting, quite out of breath.

"Richmond!" Straker greeted him with delight. "Doesn't look a bit like Marley, does it?"

"What? Oh, yes, I see," the knight gasped. "Grave news! I've come to—"

His eyes, darting around the room to see who was present, lit upon the Iron Assassin and stopped dead.

"Good God, Straker!" he burst out. "Do you know who your killing man is—or was, I should say, before he—"

Richmond's words ended in an abrupt gurgle. Steelforce had crossed the room like a sudden gale to take hold of his throat.

As everyone in the Havilstoke Room watched, Straker's newest secret weapon tore out Richmond's tongue, then calmly twisted the knight's head around and broke his neck.

He gave one last, horrid wrench as the dying man started to topple, then lurched briskly away with Sir Jasper Richmond's lower jaw dripping in his hand.

B e *damned* to you, sir! Damned to you! I'm well aware of the duty a son owes his father, but this is too much! By all the massed bloody airships of the Empire, this is *too much*!"

A door slammed so loudly that Lady Rose Harminster winced despite herself. She turned hastily away from the open door into the passage and raised the little prayer book she'd taken from her purse, in an all-too-feeble attempt to pretend she'd been lost in devotions and heard nothing of the argument between the younger and elder Seftons that had shaken the very leaded windows around her these last few moments.

Lord Sefton was a hardheaded, gruff, pompous old sea lion, all battered red nose, saber scars, and a walrus mustache that would have choked any walrus Lady Rose had ever seen—and his son, Algernon, had inherited his father's fiery temper but thus far absorbed precious little of his father's deep understanding of the world. As it truly was, behind all the frippery and ballyhoo of the moment and the simplistic statements about the gilded supremacy of the Empire of the Lion that would last forever.

She needn't have bothered with her pretense; Algernon stormed past her open door and on down the passage in a thunder that bespoke his complete insensibility to what was going on around him. She could have set the carpet on fire and danced around it utterly unclad and he wouldn't have noticed.

Distant boomings announced the slamming of the door at the end of the passage and then the one on the far side of the drawing room beyond, and, yes, that squeal would be the orontine doors out onto the terrace being flung open in a greater hurry than their hinges had ever known before.

She sighed, slipped her prayer book away, got to her feet, and hastened out into the passage. She'd have to be quick . . .

As it happened, she needn't have bothered. When she came out onto the terrace fighting for breath—those doors had been *heavy*—the distant figure of Algernon Hartworth could be seen mounting the grassy hill beyond, heading for the folly that crowned it. He was proceeding straight as an arrow, hands clenched into fists and tailcoat streaming out behind him.

Lady Rose Harminster knelt in rather undignified haste to put her skirts up, straightened to crow in several deep breaths, then balled her hands into fists, put her head down, and charged across the terrace and the sward beyond after the furious young heir.

Something had to be said, and right now his father was the last person suitable to say it. Which made it her duty . . .

The younger Lord Sefton was evidently an active man. He certainly had wind and vigor enough to outdistance her, and probably would have done so had she been hampered by no skirts at all. Wherefore he vanished into the folly when she was barely halfway to it.

She slowed her run long enough to draw in a proper breath, then started sprinting up the hill.

Being ladylike was vastly overrated.

Whitehall was not at ease, for Halworthy Burton was simmering. Summoning law clerks and demanding to know exactly what could be done under the law to control the private hobbies of nobles of the realm, sending a messenger to the Commissioner of the Queen's High Constabulary to attend him at once, and sending yet another messenger to the Imperial Herald of the Realm to see if a lord could be stripped of his title for insanity, and, if so, could he begin doing so at once!

The normally staid and hushed halls hummed with activity and echoed with excited whisperings.

If Jack Straker, Lord Tempest, had been there, he'd have found it all highly amusing.

As it was, he was elsewhere, and worrying about more pressing matters than his own neck.

And, from time to time, in snatched moments, amusing himself by imagining the sort of splashings and slowly bubbling descent the likes of Halworthy Burton would make, if tied to a chair, gagged with his own shiny shoes thrust deep into his mouth, and then tossed into the Thames.

Algernon Hartworth turned, face still crimson and furious, drawing in breath for a roaring verbal parry of his father, and took a stride to meet the expected foe.

Which meant the winded Lady Rose Harminster almost fell into his arms as she reeled up the folly's broad stone steps. He cradled her awkwardly, in deep astonishment and sudden embarrassed realization that one of his arms was wrapped around a tightly corseted waist, and the other frankly—if gingerly—cradled a pleasantly rounded bosom.

"L-Lady Harminster! This is, uh, quite a surprise, to be sure! Are you unwell? In need?"

"In need, yes," the woman in his arms gasped, turning to lean into his shoulder with her own. He accepted the adroit rearrangement with relief, for it gave both his hands safer yet pleasant locations to grasp; her hips. "I need to talk to *you*."

"Me? But—that is, I am your servant, and happy to help in any way I can, but my father—"

"Is a stalwart of the Empire, but just now, a rock of stubbornness that irks you greatly," Lady Rose panted. "It is of that I would speak."

His brows drew down. "Forgive me, Lady, but within families—"

"Oh, I don't wish to discuss any specifics of your dealings with your father. That is, as you rightly point out, your own business and not mine. I want to speak to you now as noble to noble, about our common duty."

"Duty?"

Lady Harminster sighed. "Your father has been remiss. He should speak frankly with you more often, as nobleman to nobleman, lord to heir. About the duties we nobles share, among other things. Tell me, what do you know of current Empire politics?"

Algernon Hartworth gaped at her, then shook his head as if to clear it, and said, "Precious little. Not far from nothing at all. Aren't we nobles above all that?"

"Would that it were so. No, Lord. Remember this, if you heed nothing else I say to you today: if one does not do politics, politics will be done to one."

"Heh. Clever, that. All right, duly noted. Now, what's all this about duty and all the things you're going to say to me today?"

The lady who was his near neighbor and, he recalled suddenly, now the head of her house, though she was far younger than his father, opened her mouth to reply . . . and then hesitated.

They studied each other, and Algernon was moved to burst out, "But I forget my manners! Do please forgive me; I was most vexed, and temporarily forgot courtesy. Will you sit?"

He offered her one of the grandly curving but less than comfortable stone seats—copies of cathedral pews, he happened to know—with a flourish.

Gratefully, she sat and thanked him. He nodded in the manner of his father, and sat down on the seat facing her. She had magnificent legs, he could not help but notice; she must have fastened up her skirts to run after him.

Hmph. No woman had run after him since the nannies of his childhood. He discovered he quite liked it.

"You *must* have a basic grasp of the politics of the Empire, my lord," she told him gravely. "So I'll endeavor to provide one, and you must not take offense if you know all of this already. So . . . matters in the Empire are politically delicate, just now. Difficult, if you will. In Parliament, the Crown Anarchists, led by Mister Simon Morrowpyke, vie with the Old Bulls—"

"Led by Lord Basil Cantlemere!" Algernon interrupted triumphantly. "*Our* party!"

"The party of the establishment, yes. The Old Bulls want no change at all and are already locked in bitter battles over innovation and steam-driven this and cog-propelled that, new ways and new machines that cost manual laborers more and more jobs."

"The rash and fool-headed 'down with nobles and the Crown, too' malcontents versus the 'good old England, let it change not' stalwarts; this much I *do* know."

"Then what can you tell me, Lord, of the New and Pleasant Land Party?"

"The what? Nothing; never heard of it!"

"Well, then, be advised that the two old parliamentary foes you're familiar with are now challenged by a third party, led by Mister Darcy Dunslade. The New Landers are pushing for rule not by Queen and Parliament, but by an Electoral College of Esteemed Inventors."

"And what the steam-driven devil is that?"

"A ruling council to which each guild chooses and appoints its representative. So, guild rule."

"What? Ruled by the Rivermen? And the Dungcarters?"

"And the Airship Guild, the Steam Artificers' Guild, the Steamship Guild, the Smelters and Miners' Fellowship . . ."

Algernon groaned. "And the cobblers and scent makers and all! Now *that* is madcap foolery, to be sure! Tradesmen, running the Empire! It'll be an eye-gouging, throat-slitting, up-elbows-all race to see who can snatch the most coins and strip the common cupboard bare!"

Surprisingly, Lady Harminster grinned. It made her look much younger.

"You do politics with commendable fire, sir."

"I'm told I do everything with overmuch fire, these days," he replied dryly. "Yet this is the first I've heard doing so is 'commendable.'"

His visiting neighbor leaned forward, her gaze earnest. "Young men and women are always full of energy and new ideas—and scorn for what their parents believe and hold dear. Always. Your father stormed out of disputes with his father, just as you have now."

Her voice was rising, her eyes were afire. Algernon almost recoiled. Almost.

"But what has endured, what *must* endure, is the Empire itself," she told him fiercely. "The prosperity and stability—even through the fires of constant change—our shared endeavors and experiences earn us. You will hear foolish and complacent folk say the vast and mighty Empire is too big to fail, that it cannot help but go on, perhaps forever, but that isn't so. There have been empires before—the Greeks, the Romans—and there will be empires again. They only last when fought for, and constantly repaired and renewed and improved, and *that* is the work we who hold titles and lands and privilege are suited for. That striving is our duty. Especially in these days, with the Queen ailing and in seclusion, kept alive with—"

"I know, I know," Algernon broke in, a little unsettled by her intensity. Something was rising inside him that made him feel like crying. "Old Crowned Steamheart. Or Ironheart—they call her that, too. Alexandrina Gloriana Hanover, Queen Victoria the Third. The *direct* Third, in a row. An invalid kept alive with steam-driven bellows as lungs and a steam-driven pump for a heart, so the Prince Royal has unofficially but effectively been ruling the Empire for years, now, giving orders to the Sky Admiralty and the

Sea Admiralty, dispensing titles and favors and estates and annuities as if he was King."

"Then you know we nobles are all like the knights of old: *we* are the heart of the Empire, and its strength is in our arms and brains. The Lord Lion is but one man, and a target wherever he goes to the foes of the Empire. He cannot be everywhere—so our vigilance must be."

Lady Harminster ran out of breath then, and they both discovered they were on their feet, staring at each other hard and bright-eyed.

It was almost fashionable among the nobility to decry the call of Empire, to smilingly dismiss any hint of patriotism. Whence had come this sudden flame? They could see it in each other's eyes, stirring, unlooked for . . . almost frightening.

As Rose panted for air, the younger Lord Sefton did not rush to fill the silence. Rather, he stared back at her thoughtfully.

"Tell me, Algernon Hartworth," she ventured softly, "what do you know of the lands beyond the Empire?"

"Little enough. Fancies, tales of rutting and high escapades told by older lords, wildness about massacres and temples full of idols and mountains of gold," he said dismissively. Then took a step toward her and asked urgently, "So what can *you* tell me of them?"

"Well, I've been there no more than you have," she admitted. "A few Paris clubs, some vineyards and shipyards visited with Father when he . . ."

She sighed, waved away happy memories and the fresh grief that overlaid them with a brisk arm, and told him, "Europe is a patchwork quilt of independent vest-pocket duchies and principalities and grand duchies, across which the three great powers glower at each other: our own Empire of the Lion; the rapier-wielding dandies of the slave-taking Empire of Amirondro, who rose from the warring territories of Spain to hold much of the Mediterranean and northern Afrikka; and the Rajahirate Empire, which is every bit as large and wealthy as the Lands of the Lion; the rajahs hold sway over all the jungle lands east and south of the Deserts of the Shahs. Agents of these three powers skulk and murder everywhere, even here."

"Here?"

"Oh, yes. They must do. You've heard of the season wars?"

"Of course. Every summer, there's fighting somewhere. Several somewheres, small and exotic and far away. Savages fight; it's the way of savages. What of them?"

"Tell me, Algernon: why is there never a season war here in England?"

He stared at her. "*Here?* Well, of *course* not! We're civilized, we are! We—"

"Would be at each other's throats in a trice, if agents were not working tirelessly to prevent open strife. Agents like your father."

The Sefton heir gave her a look of amused and utter incredulity. It made him look like a supercilious frog. "My father, some sort of skulking spy? Forgive me, my lady, but don't be *ridiculous*! My father has the skulking subtlety of a rutting *bull*!"

"Oh, I did not mean to say that Lord Sefton is a spy. I have no idea what, in particular, he does to keep the Empire strong and united, and its folk grumbling rather than taking up arms. But he does do something; my Father told me so. And when the passing years take your father to his rest in the yonder crypt, it will be your turn to make a difference, year in and year out."

Algernon Hartworth stared at her, face flushed, eyes glittering, as if he knew what was coming.

"So tell me, Algernon," she asked him softly. "When that time comes, will you be ready?"

He gaped at her—and then exploded in tears, sobbing uncontrollably, rushing forward into her arms to weep against her breast like a small boy blindly seeking comfort from his mother.

Then in the next instant, he tore free of her, stammering apologies and the urgent and pressing need to take his leave of her in confused incoherence, spun about, and pelted down the hill the way he'd come, running as if all the Furies were at his heels.

That should hold him!" the older beagle said with some satisfaction, as the echoes of rattling chain died away at last.

Inside the old but massive cage, the dead-looking head turned to give him a sneering, drooping smile.

"Willum," the younger beagle asked fearfully, "we don't happen to have more locks anywhere about, do we?"

"I'll go look," the older beagle said eagerly.

"And I'll go with you!" the younger one blurted out, backing away from the cage.

The dead-looking man inside the cage gave them both another smile, and with one accord they turned and ran.

Rose watched Algernon Hartworth dwindle and then disappear across the terrace and back inside the great house.

And then she sighed a great sigh, turned away, and trudged almost blindly back to the seat he'd offered her.

She felt suddenly very tired. Drained. She had probably failed, and shamed him, so henceforth he'd avoid her and his duty both, and . . .

She should go.

So much for playing the wise old head of a noble house. *That* had not gone well. No, she should avoid ever doing anything so foolishly forward, ever again. Yet there was this fire in her, that once kindled—

A discreet cough from mere feet away brought her up short. Almost breathless.

"Lady Rose Harminster." A man's voice addressed her, both kindly and grave. "I am honored to make your acquaintance. And even more honored to have heard your address to that fortunate young scion. That was magnificent."

She looked up, appalled. She'd been overheard? Oh, Lord . . .

And by the Lord Chamberlain of the Empire, no less!

Bertram Buckingham was leaning around a corner of the stone folly walls and beaming at her. And, now, extending a courtly arm in her direction.

"Lady," he asked, "will you walk with me?"

Lost for words, Rose nodded and took his arm. Smoothly, he turned, leading her away from the folly, in the direction of the Barnstaple estate.

She couldn't help but notice two stone-faced, burly, impeccably dark-suited men were following at a discreet distance, idly waving walking sticks she recognized as being both firearms and sword-canes. Her father had been presented with one shortly before his death; a Wise & Sollers "Enforcer."

Oh, dear. What *had* her tongue gotten her into?

"You spoke to that young man of duty," the Lord Chamberlain murmured, seeming to address his words to the trees ahead of them. "Forgive me, but I could not help but overhear. How did you learn of Lord Sefton's service to the Crown?"

Rose flushed. "I didn't. I know nothing of it. Yet it's obvious that all lords and ladies who are . . . reliable . . . *must* serve the Crown, or it could not endure."

"I wish it was as obvious to more lords and ladies of the Empire. And that a few more of them were, ah, reliable, as you so aptly put it. The Empire stands now in dire need of such service."

They walked on, arm in arm, climbing the rolling Sefton

meadows and heading for the woods that cloaked the boundary where the Sefton and Barnstaple estates met. Rose did not have to glance back to know that the two men were still behind them. She'd espied others ahead of them, waiting in the trees.

"I begin to anticipate your interest in strolling the landscape with the unmarried head of a minor noble house," Rose dared to murmur.

"Then I'll not insult you with dalliance or euphemisms, Lady Harminster. I am here to recruit you to the service of the Crown, if you'll agree to serve."

"Serve how, exactly?"

"Have you ever heard of the Investigators Royal?"

With their arms linked, she could not conceal the stiffening of her body as excitement leaped within her like an eager flame, or rampant lion. Well, lioness . . .

"Investigator Royal," she murmured. "Dread Agent of the Tower, and Sworn Sword of the Lion."

"All of those, yes." He sounded amused.

"Lord Buckingham, I must confess I am astonished, but also thrilled. I accept!"

He chuckled. "Without knowing the drudgery, the danger, the paltry pay?"

"Without," she told him firmly. "So, how does one go about becoming an Investigator Royal? Is there a vigil? A branding?"

"Good heavens! The young harbor strange notions, indeed, these days! No, I assure you, nothing so . . . medieval."

A few strides later, he added, "Well, there is one medieval skill that will prove useful: the guarding of one's tongue."

"I swear to do so."

"Ah, yes, the oath. We'll get to that."

They came out of a path through the trees into a higher meadow, and he observed dryly, "Should anyone ask you what the two of us were doing together, here, you are to say you've been telling me about your favorite local walking routes."

"Understood, Lord."

In unspoken accord they paused together to enjoy the view. In one direction, across rolling meadows framed and studded with woodlots, they looked down on the village of Bishop's Bottom.

In the other was the Thames. Not all that far off at all, really, and starting just *there,* the filthy, crowded, fast-growing city of London. Smoke-shrouded, its sky filled with airships large and small, buildings beyond counting rising along the banks of the great river in a forest of steel and sooty stone spires, cathedrals mingling with the newer iron latticework mooring masts of the airships.

"The greatest city in the world," the Lord Chamberlain murmured, "and the greatest pit of vipers, too."

"What is most troubling you, Lord?" Rose asked him quietly.

He turned to meet her eyes. His were butter-brown and full of concern. "I must admit that I'm less than comfortable recruiting you. The work is apt to be dangerous."

"Uncomfortable because I'm a woman?" She flared.

He shook his head. "No. Uncomfortable because you're so damned brilliant." He turned his back on London and started to walk again. "I don't know if you should be risked like this. The Empire needs your mind, but just now I'm in desperate need of an agent who can pry where any Sworn Sword already in the ranks whom I send in will be recognized—and so rendered useless—in an instant."

"Pry into what, and where?"

"We'll get to that. After the oath. For now, let me say that we have very good reason to believe that the Prince Royal's life is in grave and immediate danger."

Lady Rose may have been sheltered from some things, but, this close to London's gossip, politics wasn't one of them. She knew the sudden death of the Prince Royal would almost certainly plunge the Empire into bloody civil war.

OCTEMBER 3

The Yard was not that old a building, but it looked like a castle of yesteryear. A frowning fortress of massive stone, it always smelled of damp and stale tobacco smoke, underlaid by sweat and fear. It had been cramped and crowded from the day its doors had opened, and nigh every room and passage was now piled high with stout wooden lockboxes heavy with written case accounts.

This meeting room, for all its grand table and greater size than most chambers in the Yard, was no exception.

The untidy stacks of boxes, labeled haphazardly by divers hands, made an interesting backdrop for the three crisply uniformed officers of the Queen's High Constabulary facing Jack Straker across the lone tobacco-scarred table.

"Lord Tempest," the equally scarred, ginger-haired, and bewhiskered beagle on the left—Commander Albert Hindmarsh, known to all simply as "Old Bert"—said gravely, "We find ourselves in need of your utmost discretion in this matter."

"Of course," Straker replied. "You need hardly issue the caution, sirs. You should know that by now."

The tall lean man in the center of the trio cleared his throat with an embarrassed air and growled through his fiercely drooping mustache, "*Especially* discreet, this one, Lord Jack. *Very* sensitive."

It must be, for the Commissioner of the beagles to even be in this room. Lord Percy Harkness did not like to be seen to personally concern himself with any particular case or concern of the force, though he did like to keep an eye on all dealings the Constabulary had with the nobility. Usually from behind a discreet screen or curtain, so he could later deny having been there and heard anything. There would come a day when a vine or weed tree thriving along one of the fences the Commissioner liked to remain on would have time enough to grow up into a rather tender part of his anatomy, but Straker suspected it would be years hence. Pity. He *did* want to be around to see that.

If Hindmarsh was five ranks below the man beside him, the stolid man on the Commissioner's other side was lowlier still. Chief Inspector Theo Standish was here because he was the beagle who most often had dealings with Tempest. The one who knew best how to find him, if it came to that. They were friends, but the battered-nosed, balding, hard-eyed man was doing his best to conceal that, wearing his expressionless look and keeping the mouth hidden behind his ragged and abundant fall of mustache firmly closed. The florid hue of his nose bespoke recent indulgence in small beer. Much small beer.

"The killing of Richmond has been hushed up," Old Bert growled. "So far."

"I can hear the 'but' in your voice," Straker observed. "What's amiss?"

The three men shifted in their chairs, hemmed, and exchanged glances. Just *what* could they be so reluctant to tell him?

The Commissioner actually elbowed Standish, who sighed heavily, exhaled to blow his mustache out of the way, and announced, "We manacled your—er, the Silent Man—and locked him in an old bear cage we had in the cellars down here."

Straker frowned. "And?"

"Cage, man, and all are gone!"

"Gone *how*?"

Hindmarsh shrugged. "We know not. It's just . . . gone missing! We've searched the building, and the alleyways all around, too, but . . ."

He shrugged again.

Straker sat back, shaking his head. He'd met more competent men than the beagles, but this took some doing, even for—

"We've most of the force out hunting for him right now," the Commissioner said swiftly, leaning forward as if proximity could convince Straker of his zeal, "and set a watch on the man Marlshrike. A slayer of Ancient Order members we dare not bring to trial is one thing, but a killer who can erupt to murder just *anyone* is something *far* different. So if you have any way of curbing your Silent Man, or calling him home, we need you to—"

"Later," Hindmarsh interrupted. "We have bigger fish to fry, just now." He looked around the table grimly. "The Prince Royal is off to hunt foxes again."

Everyone in the room knew those words meant the Lord Lion was going to Bishop's Bottom, to his little mansion in the countryside there. And all of them knew the primary purpose for which Foxden was currently used.

Standish produced a paper and laid it out grimly on the table in front of Straker. "So as you've just heard, we need you to find your Silent Man and bring him to heel, but that must wait. *First* we need you—we need every Sworn Sword who isn't already guarding the Queen—to help us keep guard watch over Foxden. We've guns and men in uniform enough; we need your eyes out beyond our perimeter, in the night. Nor is your duty likely to be mere yawning away the hours up some tree in the countryside. The Crown Anarchists— or someone else!—have again put a threatening warning in several of the papers."

Straker peered down at the poorly printed columns. "'Invest in plantations of ripening tea?' Oh, yes, that's sinister. Very sinister."

"Not *that*, man. Down *here*!" A pointing finger tapped a particular passage impatiently.

Straker read, and frowned. "He who hunts foxes in bed is in danger of losing his uncrowned head." He sat back. "Yes, I see. I quite see."

As an Investigator Royal, he outranked every beagle in the Empire. He was their superior, not their equal, did not have to sit up some tree at their behest. Yet he and the uniformed police shared the same clear before-all-else duty.

Keeping the Prince Royal alive to see the next morning. And the next. And so on.

Norbert Marlshrike was a badly frightened man.

He did not know why one of the highest members of the Ancient Order of the Tentacles had sent for him, but none of the reasons could be good.

And he was bound to the Tentacles for the rest of his life. The mere fact that he knew the man he was going to visit was high in the Order meant they would not allow him to part ways with them and live.

He looked up and down the street seeking anyone paying attention to him before he crossed into the alley, but saw no one looking his way. So he strode across the cobbles with an air of brisk unconcern and went to the rear servants' door he'd been instructed to knock at.

It opened as he raised his stick, and a black-gloved hand shot forth to intercept his stick and wrench it from his hand.

Marlshrike let go of it and found himself face-to-face with a sinister man who'd brought him the words of the Order several times before.

Who beckoned him impassively within, and stepped back into deep gloom to allow him to advance. Expressionless face with eyes the hue of water in a fine crystal glass, sideburns that came to razor-thin points, a gloved hand now holding Marlshrike's walking stick, and an ungloved one that wore a bulky metal gauntlet.

Or rather, as Marlshrike had been told, *was* a gauntlet. A clockwork metal hand that could thrust forth killing blades in a deadly instant.

That hand rose and kept nearest to Marlshrike as the bodyguard silently gestured at him to walk along a passage.

It ended in stairs, so Marlshrike ascended without query, stopping on the landing where they ended.

The bodyguard stepped past him to open the centermost of the three closed doors opening off the landing and murmured sardonically, "Uncle is at home to you."

Marlshrike inclined his head in silent thanks and strode through the doorway. There was a black curtain beyond, and he stepped through it into a cozy parlor dominated by large and splendid models of ships—both nautical and aerial—in glass cases.

Immaculately dusted, Marlshrike noticed. But then, the man *was* a wealthy lord.

"Marlshrike," a bored voice greeted him, from the depths of a high-backed chair.

"Uncle," he replied politely, moving to stand where he could face the masked occupant of the chair.

The bodyguard was already standing behind it, facing him impassively, some sort of weapon Marlshrike did not recognize trained steadily upon him.

"You will have been wondering why I requested this meeting," Uncle began. "You will have felt some small apprehension. You are right to have done so."

Marlshrike merely nodded and waited.

The ghost of a smile seemed to rise to the lips of the masked man in the chair, but was gone again before Marlshrike could be quite sure of it.

"Marlshrike," the lord said flatly, "you're a fool, and your foolishness is becoming a liability."

"How so, Uncle?"

"Your most dangerous foolheadedness is getting romantically entangled with Lady Iolanthe Hailsham. Take a doxy or some farm girl and leave the well-connected nobility well alone. They're all too apt to be spies for the Crown or harbor idiocies of their own. In this case, both. She's poison, man—yours, if you persist in seeing her. Consider this a firm order to have no further contact with her."

"I see. Is that all?"

Uncle shrugged. "For now. It pleases me to see that you can keep a grip on your temper; see if you can similarly govern your . . . urges. Oh, don't deceive yourself that we don't know all about what you're up to, most notably your greedy little sideline of kidnapping street children of London and selling them to experimenters, brothel keepers, and slavers, and keeping a handful for your own experiments. Unsavory and dangerous if you grow careless at it, but we grant that it's financially necessary. The love potions, the poisons . . ." he lifted one many-ring-adorned hand in a dismissive wave.

"Just stay away from Hailsham. Now go."

No doubt he's amusing himself right now dressing down Marlshrike. A waste of breath if ever I heard of one."

"Yes, Lady."

"If you persist in agreeing with me in that supercilious tone, Grimstone, I shall begin to believe that you neither agree with a single word I say nor believe me in the slightest. *Try* to sound sincere; you'll live longer."

"At your pleasure, Lady Roodcannon."

"Indeed, Grimstone, indeed. Now you speak simple truth."

"I strive to be a simple man, my lady."

"And there the deadpan sarcasm returns. Ah, never change, Grimstone. I shall miss your velvet maliciousness."

"I learn from the very best, Lady Roodcannon."

"Base flatterer! You were an expert well before I succeeded my father, as I recall. In many things."

"I find myself in the presence of an exalted flatterer."

"So take yourself hence and get more wine. The chill has quite gone off this."

"It grows warm indeed, my lady."

"Oh, stop it, you!"

The soft chime of the bell confirmed that Norbert Marlshrike had departed the house and the outer doors had been duly closed behind him.

As its delicate din faded, Uncle stirred. He sipped thoughtfully from a wineglass, then turned to the impassive man beside his chair. "Have Lady Hailsham investigated. Use a Whitechapel rat we've no further use for."

His bodyguard wordlessly raised his left hand—the one that had been a clockwork gauntlet for years. Making a fist, he triggered the stud that made wicked blades snick out of it in all directions. Then he lifted his brows in a silent question, face still impassive.

His master replied crisply, "Only if you must. It's cleaner if we do things the usual way. That's *why* it's the usual way, Whipsnade."

His bodyguard nodded and headed for a door at the far end of the room. He was about to reach for it when another bell chimed, unexpectedly.

Both men stiffened, and Whipsnade spun around as if he was a steam tram on well-greased rails and hastened back toward his master's side.

Uncle had set down his glass and caught up a four-barreled firearm from its shelf under his edge of the table, shifting it to where it could fire beneath the table at anyone coming through the door Marlshrike had so recently used.

That portal promptly swung wide, to reveal a breathless underling.

Uncle and Whipsnade relaxed only a trifle. "What is it, Ffloukes?" the master of the house asked sharply.

"Th-three beagles were tailing Marlshrike, sir," Ffloukes gasped. "But they're all dead; I saw to it. Bludgeoned and bodies in the river. No one'll know Marlshrike came here."

Uncle's voice turned even sharper. "So while you stand here spouting, man, who's tailing Marlshrike *now*?"

"Lackland, sir. From the moment he stepped out of this room."

Uncle nodded. "Very good. Start tailing Lackland. If he goes down, take over watching Marlshrike. Clever steamcraefters aren't to be trusted."

———

Lord Tempest," came a voice Straker knew, "a word!"

Straker halted in mid–brisk stride and turned. No one walking the halls of the Yard, beagle or guest, ignored the Commissioner's Hound.

Stout, balding, and massive of shoulders and hands, Assistant Commissioner Alston Drake was all the strong right arm Commissioner Harkness needed to maintain discipline within the force. Not to mention frighten the life and liver out of any member of the public who crossed the beagles and came within the Hound's reach.

Straker put a pleasant smile on his face. "Yes?"

Drake was frowning. "You've heard?"

"Many things. In particular?"

"This Harminster woman. We're . . . less than pleased." The Hound thrust his head forward to peer intently into Straker's face, trying to read the lord's expression.

Straker gave him a shrug. "Early days yet to be enthused or otherwise. Investigator Royals lend the Empire skills possessed by those who by their nature will always stand outside the upstanding strength and discipline of the High Constabulary."

"Yes, yes, man, but a sheltered noblewoman? An Investigator *Royal*? What's the Lord Chamberlain *thinking*?"

Straker shrugged again. "As to that . . . I know not." He knew the cause of Drake's anger; an Investigator Royal was empowered to deal with the Yard and Tower Street as a superior, not an equal. But was it Drake's own temper, or more widely shared? "Yet you're clearly concerned; pray tell me why."

"Well, look here, Straker, the woman's an incompetent meddler!"

"Oh? You've a file on her?"

Drake scowled, planted his feet wide, looked at the ceiling, and recited, "Brilliant, antisocial, fiery-tempered, restless. Chafes at the traditional social roles of women of her class. Has embraced the recent 'airship explorer' movement as a way of breaking out of the restrictions placed on her sex."

Straker spread his hands. "I've known many a man of her age to take up wild and varied interests, seeking to make his own path in the world. Is it not usual, hmm?"

Drake threw up his hands and started to stride along the way Straker had been going. They walked along together. "Oh, I know we must cooperate with her, given her new rank, but . . . dash it, I'm—we're—reluctant, Straker!"

"I confess I'm not personally familiar with the woman. You'd like me to sound her out, or you'd not be talking to me of her at all. So tell me what you're most afraid of."

"Nobles—begging your pardon, Lord; *you* we know—are dilettantes at best. Why, she could harbor any sort of political foolishness in her head!" Drake said grimly. "And this is only his first appointment; is this Lord Chamberlain going to be an utter dunce and a foolheaded danger to us all?"

"That remains to be seen," Straker replied. "As for the lady—if she does, she won't live long. I'll see to that."

OCTEMBER 4

An owl hooted. Again.

And nearer. But was it really an owl, or someone calling out a signal?

Lady Harminster swallowed a sigh and frowned at herself in the growing gloom. The trees of the Bishop's Woods pressed close around the glassless windows of Lord Barnstaple's small stone folly, and evening was coming down swiftly.

She hadn't thought the waiting would be so hard.

And all she was doing was just sitting here and keeping quiet, not doing anything perilous. What had she gotten herself into?

She took her gloves off for the twentieth time and thrust them through the belt of her jacket. She wore breeches, boots, and jacket for riding, deeming that skirts had no place in night forays onto lands other than her own, involving possible danger.

Yes, danger. She felt for the pitchfork she'd found forgotten against a wall outside, felt the reassuring hard heft of its handle, and told herself to relax. Again.

She sat in the innermost room, the only one that was roofed over against the sky, and peered nervously out its windows, moving nothing but her head. For warmth and to avoid making noise, Rose had decided to keep herself pressed into an angle where the stone bench ended and a wall curved out to shelter it, on its way to forming the front wall of the room that was pierced by the archway that was the only dignified way in or out. Close by her shoulder, an open window offered a long drop into the trees; across the room, a larger open window afforded a splendid view over the rolling upper meadows of the Sefton estate—and an even greater fall to the ground.

All the estates about Bishop's Bottom had follies, every one, though she'd visited few of them. Of stone, without exception, though varied architecture, to be sure. The one she'd grown up playing in and around looked like a fragment of a ruined Greek temple, but some were like miniature churches or castles. This one was an uneasy marriage of church and Hellenic temple and had no doubt been chosen for her initial meeting with her unknown contact in the Sworn Swords for its remote location. It stood far from the Barnstaple home, down rolling hills to her left, and was nigh hidden in the forest that sprawled along most of the estates.

Behind Rose, through the trees, was land she knew well; the country seat of her family, the Harminsters. She sat now at one end of the Barnstaple lands, and out the larger window in front of her was the Sefton estate. Beyond it, half-hidden behind a distant line of trees, were the lands of the Rathercoats, and, beyond that, the estate known as Foxden.

So tranquil, all of them, so seemingly far from bustling London, most touched by its nearness not by sounds but by errant odors and

smokes, and by the frequent sight of airships scudding the skies overhead.

It seemed very strange that the foremost sweeping matters of the
Empire should reach out to—should be at play in—Bishop's Bottom.

The Bottom was, after all, a small village. A handful of cottages
around a tiny neat white church with a modest vicarage. Hard by a
rather ramshackle pub, the Bold Royal Fox; a sagging coaching inn
with white-painted galleries, the Old Highwayman; and but one
business, if it could be called that: a Royal Mail way yard and office.

Rose could see its dirigible mast from here, though the mail airship usually moored there was absent. It was a base for shuttle runs
of mail to and from the countryside around, like so many others
across England, and she'd heard it described as smaller and sleep-
ier than most.

Beyond the Bottom's tiny cluster of buildings were only farms
and country places—that is, the half-dozen grand houses and their
grounds. With the River Race, a lazy and meandering trout run that
had ever belied its name, winding through it all. Not a place of bustle, or tinkering, or steam-driven innovation of any sort. Why, the
local farmers grumbled at the steam threshers that—

There was a footfall nearby, and someone suddenly lurched
through the archway.

Rose bit her knuckles to keep from crying out.

It was a man, looming up large over her, all in black but with
tiny lightnings crawling all over him. His face looked like that of a
dead man, his head almost a bare skull, yet his dark eyes regarded
her, alive and interested, out of shrunken sockets. His hands were
bare save for gleaming pointed caps on every finger. As he lurched
forward, she saw that his feet were bare, too, and that he wore some
sort of metal frame over his black, many-straps leathers; the little
bolts of lightning were snarling along its bars and fittings, betimes
spitting sparks from the joints.

His arms spread wide, as if to prevent her escape. Yes, yes, he *was* cornering her where she sat, leaning and reaching to prevent her snatching up the pitchfork.

His hand came down on it and swept it to the far end of the seat with casual ease. He leaned still closer, face jutting toward hers like a snake about to strike.

Then his jaw fell open grotesquely, and Rose bit back a scream.

"*You,*" he said slowly, mouth dry and voice gratingly hoarse. "You are not . . . who I seek."

He turned, flinging his entire body around like a crudely commanded marionette, shoulders rocking, and peered around the bare stone room. Satisfying himself that it was empty of all but the cowering Rose and several old, dried-out birds' nests, he turned away from her and lurched back through the archway.

"You did *not* see me," he commanded severely, glaring at her from the deepening night. Then he was gone, lurching heavily away through the roofless outer rooms and down the steps into the forest.

Rose found herself trembling and panting, more frightened now that the lurching man was gone than she'd been when he was looming over her.

Would he come back? She—she couldn't bear it, she—

Almost sobbing in sudden haste, she pounced on the pitchfork and brandished it in shaking hands, holding it up to menace empty air in front of her as she resumed her place against the wall in the corner of the seat.

Watching two long, rusted, and wickedly curved tines tremble in the dimness, and knowing just how helpless she'd be if he—if anyone—came in and attacked her.

She did not remember dozing, would not have believed she could have fallen asleep in the icy grip of terror, but suddenly someone—a man—was clearing his throat apologetically right in front of her, and she was fumbling to raise the pitchfork with a fresh sob of alarm.

"Good evening," this second apparition greeted her. "I believe you are expecting me." A calm and confident voice, almost drawling. A voice she'd heard before.

This visitor was taller and far more slender than the lurching man. He wore some sort of dark coat, and now took something from an inner pocket of it: a fat round disk about the size of his hand. He unfolded some sort of crank from it—it was hard to see in the deepening night, for the tardy moon had *still* not risen—and wound it vigorously. The disk made a whirring, growling sound.

Then, as abruptly as he'd begun, he left off doing that and flipped the disk open. A coil of wires within it gave off a faint glow, and he held the thing up beside his face so she could see his features. And smiled.

She caught her breath in startled recognition. It was Jack Straker, the flamboyant, debonair Lord Tempest of London's high society.

His smile widened at the sound of her muted gasp. Nodding to her in polite salutation, as if they'd just been introduced in a drawing room somewhere, he said rather dryly, "You can put down the pitchfork. I'm not in the habit of murdering ladies at first sight."

"You are—?"

"The personage you were sent here to meet, yes." Gracefully sidestepping the pitchfork, he sat down on the seat beside her, slipped the disk back into its pocket, and produced a smaller metal object from yet another hiding place in his outer garment. "So, to begin . . . there's an initiation."

"And what might that be, my lord?" she asked quietly, putting the pitchfork down on the floor with a calmness she did not feel but was determined to feign.

"No names," he murmured. He held up the little box between thumb and forefinger. "Nothing more dangerous or energetic than the taking of the snuff."

"A detestable habit," she replied firmly.

"It will only have to be this once." He thumbed open a flap at one end of the box. "Apply your tongue sparingly to the end of one of your fingers, put the finger into this, then put it up your nose and turn it within there—yes, I'm aware that this is both unlady-like and not the usual procedure for taking snuff, but humor me—and we'll be done with the formalities."

Lady Rose Harminster hesitated. What did she really know of this man, after all? Well, at least she knew who it was, and had to admit that under other circumstances she'd have been more than flattered by his attentions. He was among the most dashing of the young and unattached lords of London, and—

She did as he'd commanded, and in a moment was inhaling the strange and unfamiliar scent, and reacting with helpless tears and dismay, thinking wildly she'd been deceived and betrayed, and was about to . . .

Lord Tempest stroked her forearm and then moved his hand to cup her elbow supportively, as tenderly as any kindly aunt.

"Pray forgive me," he murmured, "for I have deceived you. I've given you the Grail."

"The G-g-grail?"

"A truth drug, a secret of the Crown. Let me say merely that it makes everyone's eyes stream, and overwhelms the will. So a trained questioner can briefly get truth out of someone."

Jack Straker did not see the need to inform the lady—who might, after all, not last long in Crown service—that each exposure to the Grail had shorter and shorter effects, so it was used sparingly. The beagles tended to use tiny amounts and ask captives merely "Did you do it?" Only if they got a denial did they ask, "Who did?"

Instead, he asked simply, "Are you a member or sympathizer of the Ancient Order of the Tentacles or the Crown Anarchists po-litical party?"

"No!" she replied indignantly.

Good. Truth, and strongly held at that. He proffered his clean-est handkerchief.

"You'll weep for some minutes, from eyes and nose," he said

comfortingly, "so don't try to speak. I'm just going to walk the outside of the folly to ensure we're still alone, and return straightaway."

The unbroken night song from the forest told him more clearly than his eyes that no one was lurking near. When he returned, the Lady Harminster's face was still wet, but she held out a sopping handkerchief to him as serenely as any duchess returned linen to a maid. He didn't trouble to entirely hide his smile.

"Time to hear my truths," he told her simply, joining her on the seat and keeping his voice very low, so she had to bend close to hear it.

"The Prince Royal has a country retreat very near here. Not a royal palace or hunting lodge, though he has one of each not all that far afield, but a modest mansion with walled grounds, not known to the general public, that he keeps for his assignations. Which are many."

If he'd expected surprise, he got something else. "Foxden," she said. It was not a question.

"How did you learn of it?" he asked sharply.

"I guessed, this very instant," she replied, eyes steady on his. "Go on."

Lord Tempest studied her coolly for a moment, then continued, "The Prince Royal has his casual lovers amongst the nobility, and exotic foreign nobility, too—and a distressing number of those are now residing hereabouts, awaiting their turn."

She nodded. "I have heard the Lord Lion is charming, handsome, and generous."

"He is all of that. Especially generous; he often bestows largess, royal jewels, and even lands and titles on his favorites, since the Queen's . . . indisposition."

Lady Harminster merely nodded. It was hardly a secret amongst the nobility that Alexandrina Gloriana Hanover, the third ruling Queen Victoria in a row to ascend the Lion Throne, had for some years been an invalid, kept alive with steam-driven bellows as lungs and a hissing hydraulic pump for a heart. The Lord Lion had been knighting and ennobling and distributing royal gifts with her full approval from before her time of seclusion.

"However, there remains a disgraceful secret that must at all costs be kept from public notice. It is this: the Prince has a weakness for commoners as his paramours—and, worse than that, prostitutes."

The face so close to his drew back a trifle, still-moist eyes calmly studying his, but he saw no grimace or shudder.

Interesting.

W e've found out who he killed. Sir Jasper Richmond."

"Ah. Interesting. Without warning?"

"Pounced the moment Richmond started to tell the others in the room who he was. Broke the man's neck, then tore his jawbone right out of his head!"

"Eliminating someone who was about to reveal his past."

"Past? Valves and pistons, he's a *chimney sweep!*"

"Indeed. So he was."

"What're you not telling me?"

"Something that could get you killed. If he suspects you know . . ."

"Well, *you* obviously know. Aren't you worried?"

"Of course. Terrified."

"A rather calm sort of terror, I must say."

"I know *so* many things that various persons want to kill me for, and have done so for so many years, that I've grown used to it. Not to mention prepared for it."

"Oh? Prepared how?"

"Knowing that, too, could get you killed, and I'm feeling merciful today. Go badger Marlshrike, and live longer."

I am aware that I raise a topic considered less than delicate," Lord Tempest continued dryly, "but such impudence is my way. Lady Rose, do you happen to know anything at all about prostitutes?"

She felt the heat flooding across her face, and anger at that rose within her, so she lifted her chin, stared straight into his gaze—was the man *smirking*? Well, *damn* him!—and informed him crisply, "Of course I do, Lord Tempest. For a time, when completing my education under tutors in central London, I roomed with two such women, as lodgings in London are so expensive, and at the passing of my parents the family finances were in such chaos, that I thought it best to be prudent. I cooked for these, ah, doves of the evening and handled their correspondence."

He crooked an eyebrow. "A titled lady, slaving in a scullery?"

"Sir," she flared, "I am a woman who does what she must first, and a titled noblewoman second—and a *lady* very much third."

His eyes flashed with—approval? He nodded as he smiled, in a way that banished all derision and conveyed seeming delight.

"So I can tell you of certain douches and other, ah, habitual precautions, and of both bedchamber and public preferred wardrobe."

"Ah. So the currently fashionable public dress of a prostitute would be—?"

"Netting hose—fishnet or chain-net—knee-high riding boots, corsets over abbreviated leather kilts, ascots, greatcoats, and above all, top hats. Many men favor toppers, but a woman doing so is signaling the profession she follows to all."

The lord nodded and asked almost gently, "And do you know more than that?"

"What, sir, are you insinuating?"

"Nothing," Lord Tempest said flatly. "Let me be more specific. Cinammon, in this context, means . . . ?"

"Prostitutes dust their nipples with cinammon, so their clients can enjoy 'sweet afters,' Lord Tempest," she replied readily.

"Preferred scents?"

"Cog oil is 'the' fashionable perfume of the season, but the bawdier sometimes use heavier oils."

"And a cheerful inquiry of a possible client might be?"

"Bit of the old bump-and-plough, me lord?" came the prompt response, in the broad, rough tones of the meaner streets of London.

Silence fell, as Lord Tempest studied her thoughtfully. They regarded each other thus until she asked lightly, "So, do I pass your test?"

By way of reply, Lord Tempest asked, "And if it became necessary for you to pose as such a strumpet, would you?"

Lady Rose knew her face was flaming, but she lifted her chin and looked him in the eye as before. "I swore an oath to Lord Buckingham. I intend to keep it."

They looked into each other's eyes for a long, silent time ere she added, "Is any imminent need for my strumpethood likely to arise?"

Lord Tempest chuckled. "Well played, Lady Harminster! Well played." His face changed. "But I've been indiscreet and made too much noise. Wait here while I walk the night again."

He rose in swift silence but returned soon enough and resumed his seat beside her, continuing as if he'd never left.

"The reason the Prince's coarse tastes must be kept secret for now is that the Crown Anarchist elements in Parliament will seize on it to try to set the Prince Royal aside in favor of the Dowager Duchess—"

"Who aches to regain power," Rose murmured, nodding. Well, the entire interested half of the Empire knew as much. Alice Louisa Hanover, the widow of the German Duke Leopold, who'd been the younger brother of the current Queen Victoria, was a gruff and grasping battle-ax who lived to seize and wield power like a tyrant out of a storybook. For once, the caricature of the popular press mirrored reality almost exactly.

"—and this will plunge the realm into civil war. Once the Prince Royal becomes king, his wenching won't matter, but right now things are . . ."

"Politically very ticklish," Lady Rose supplied helpfully.

He nodded approvingly. "Indeed. What with the Crown Anarchists, the Old Bulls, and the New Landers all engaged in a push of pikes that can only end bloodily . . . the Prince Royal, thankfully, seems immune to the pox and the like and doesn't give gifts to his commoner lovers that might leak his secret in a hurry."

"So what do I have to *do*?" she asked.

"Shortly before noon tomorrow, with a small satchel of whatever you deem necessary for a few days—smallclothes and such—you will be standing in the thicket of trees hard by the Weir Bridge. You need not use any stealth in reaching that spot, but try not to let anyone see you entering the thicket. Stay quiet and close to the road so you can see traffic clearly and emerge without a lot of noise and difficulty. A friend of mine will happen along with a gig, cross the bridge, and stop. Don't come out unless you see no one else in sight. His name is Mister Bleys Hardcastle, and he's a decent sort. More fists than wits, but a true friend in a fray. He knows nothing whatsoever of this little scheme, or of either of us being Sworn Swords—and see that he learns nothing from you."

"And he'll be conveying me where?"

"To Foxden. You do know Foxden?"

"I know *of* it, but have seen only its gates; it's entirely surrounded by tall hedges, and within them a stout stone wall. Very private people."

"Very. The assignations it hosts are many."

"And am I to be one of them?" she asked bluntly.

"Hopefully not," he replied sternly. "The Prince is an . . . avid man, but do remember that the Lord Chamberlain is relying on your discretion. You are to be yourself, but also to pose as a lady doctor, newly appointed by the Queen herself to ensure that anyone who comes into intimate contact with the heir to the throne is . . . clean. Here are your credentials, Royal Seal and all."

"And if I'm called on to examine anyone? I assisted a midwife once, but very much as a pair of obedient 'fetch this, wash that' hands."

"Use what's in this satchel. Swab, place in the waxen envelopes it's stuffed with, say 'hmmm,' and look sternly thoughtful. Arrogant men have been happily collecting fistfuls of gold lions in Wimpole Street for doing far less, for years now."

"My, but we're cynical."

"My, but we've acquired thousands of good reasons to be, and daily collect more. What you're *really* there to do is to get the names and descriptions to go with them—that is, age, sex, height, nose shapes, hair color, and anything out of the ordinary, especially dyed hair or wigs, not to mention any sign of a badge with tentacles on it—of everyone—and I *do* mean everyone—who enters Foxden after you do. Hardcastle will be your messenger; report all of these in confidence to him, but make sure you're not overheard, and always try to look and sound as if you're giving him orders for medicines to be compounded and brought back to you."

"Until?"

"Until he takes you away, or I come for you, or all stream-driven hell breaks loose."

Lady Rose nodded. "I believe I can do that."

"Good," Tempest replied briskly, and rose to depart.

Then he hesitated, cast a look back at her over his shoulder, and asked in quite a different voice, "What *were* you doing with that pitchfork?"

"Preparing—probably in futility—to defend myself. There was a man who came before you. A lurching man, who wore metal braces all over the outside of his body that shot sparks and little bolts of lightning. He said I wasn't the one he sought, and departed."

Lord Tempest looked stern. "And where did he go?" he asked sharply.

"Out there," she replied helplessly, "into the woods. I—I had to wait here, to meet you."

He swore under his breath. "How long ago?"

"Not long before you came. I think. I was frightened, and not thinking clearly, and may have dozed."

The man now pacing impatiently back and forth across the room sighed gustily. "He could be anywhere between Bishop's Bell and Upper Buckden by now."

He strode out of the archway, then turned back to face her just as the lurching man had done. "If you see him again, and he looks like he's coming for you, his name is Bentley Steelforce. Formerly, he was Bentley Roper. Calling him by either of those names *might* startle him into turning aside from harming you. Might, I said. To call out to him from afar with either name would be, I believe, foolish."

He turned away, took a step, swore again, then came back. "Yet it would be foolish and cruel of me not to tell you the *real* foes we face. You've heard of the Ancient Order of the Tentacles?"

"Oh, yes. Several ladies of my acquaintance have dabbled with it. The cult that worships a tentacled god. From what they said, I thought it a rather thin excuse for indiscretions."

"Indiscretions?"

"Orgies."

Straker nodded. "Those who head the Tentacles today were once the secret service of the first Victoria. Officially disbanded long ago—outlawed, for all the murders they did, for queen and country nonetheless—they now serve the Dowager Duchess. The name they use now derives from their former motto; 'We endure through adversity. Sever one tentacle, and two more will take its place. We serve still.' The gullible believe they worship a tentacled god at hidden cellar altars, but the sham cult your acquaintances dallied with has nothing really to do with the Ancient Order of the Tentacles; they merely encourage it to confuse Lion agents with all of its chatter and clandestine meetings and to recruit dupes to serve as fodder in their schemes."

"So they seek to do away with the Queen? And the Prince Royal?"

"Indeed," he said grimly. "Wherefore they are our true foes. Who are much closer to seizing the throne—the entire Empire—than you might think."

He turned and headed out of the folly again.

"Wait!" she called softly. "When shall I see and hear from you again?"

"I'll send word through Hardcastle," he replied, and was gone.

When he opened the door, the room beyond was in pitch darkness.

He knew what that meant and stood right where he was, not crossing the threshold.

"Lady," he told the darkness gravely, "I am here."

"Speak freely," came the expected voice. Low, throaty, calm, and from the bed. Where she was no doubt not alone. Yet she'd said "freely." Which meant her bedmate was either deaf or would soon be dead.

"My lady," he said, "the quarry's been seen. In the Barnstaple stables."

"Alone?"

"Alone. We're watching for any arrivals."

"Send the Silent Man. I don't need the Prince disgraced if I can have him dead. The head is to be brought back to us, mind, with the face intact—or we'll have decades of 'the Lord Lion is alive and in hiding, and in the meantime' shoved down our collective throats."

There'd been a faint but sharp intake of breath from the bed, on the heels of her saying "dead." Her bedmate was more than surprised.

But then, he soon would be, wouldn't he?

He cleared his throat. "Just confirming, ma'am: kill?"

"Kill, Grimstone."

———

Whipsnade stalked on through the darkness of full night, skulking close along rough walls he knew well, a deadly top-hatted and greatcoated shadow wielding a cudgel that could crack a man's skull with ease. And had, many a time.

He was not the only shadow walking the streets, but the other shadows left him alone. As he strode deeper into Whitechapel. Heading for the Raging Lion.

As he turned a corner into Gloucester Street, there came the faintest of scraping sounds from overhead. He took no apparent notice.

At his next step a cobblestone plummeted down from above—and slammed straight into his head.

It crushed his top hat flat and sent him reeling, but Whipsnade's steel skullcap did its job. As a dark and spiderlike figure dropped down behind him on a line, Whipsnade stopped reeling in a grimly satisfied instant and spun around, raising one hand.

The gun up his sleeve roared, and his assailant's face vanished in a spurt of blood and a horrid strangling sob. The dead man toppled to the cobbles, knife clattering away.

Whipsnade unconcernedly reloaded the gun strapped to his arm—ah, but he'd have bruises in the morning—restored his sleeve to its usual trim, and punched his hat back more or less into its proper shape.

Settling it back on his head, he smiled up into the night above from whence others would be watching, then stalked on.

Down Gloucester Street, then into a side alley noisome even by Whitechapel standards. A few squelching steps farther, and he was on the threshold of the Lion.

A scarred face greeted him balefully but melted away upon recognizing him. He stepped into a room so thick with smoke that the publican unshuttered a lantern to illuminate new arrivals.

And very hastily shuttered it again, muttering, "Pardon."

"Accepted," Whipsnade purred, approaching the bar. Sullen men slouched along it shoulder to shoulder, clad in salvaged or stolen motley and nursing drinks and grudges with the silent sag of beaten men.

"Ah," Whipsnade exclaimed in a horrible parody of joviality, as he espied the man he was looking for. "Such a *fair* evening to encounter such a dear friend. Especially as I've pressing need of his services."

The cracksman sunk his filthy-capped head even lower within his ragged collar and tried to turn away.

"Mister Oswald Smedley," Whipsnade purred in his ear, "Uncle needs a little something done. Right now."

Smedley didn't turn his head. "And if'n I'm busy?"

"Uncle will be *most* disappointed. You might say he'll be saddened to death. *Someone's* death."

"I'm terrible hungry," Smedley whispered, "but find myself a coin or two short. If'n I can eat, say, a hot pie, I'll be busy no longer, and right ready to please Uncle, if'n you take my meaning."

"I do indeed," Whipsnade replied, as tenderly as a doting mother, "and so does Long Tom here—*don't* he?"

He spun around to give the publican a bared-teeth smile so suddenly that the man behind the bar, for all his scarred and battered bulk, recoiled back against the wall, setting bottles and decanters to clinking. "Y-yes, sir!" he stammered. "Hot pie right away, sir!"

And vanished back into the kitchen, to reappear almost instantly with a steaming hot pie in his hand.

"I'm thinking a tankard of your best will do Mister Smedley nicely to wash it down," Whipsnade told the ceiling gently, and a full tankard appeared with commendable alacrity.

Whipsnade smiled almost fondly at Long Tom. "Times are changing right fast, these days, and all too much is changing for the worse with them, but it warms the heart to see the Raging Lion is still everything Uncle praises it to be."

The publican stared back at him, half-smiling but with fear clear on his face and rising off him like a slaughterhouse stink.

Whipsnade gave him a nod, turned his back, and said past Smedley's ear, "Uncle came across sixty sovereigns the other day, and told me he thought Mister Smedley might be in need of them about now. Am I right?"

Smedley turned a wince into a reluctant nod. "What do I have to do?"

"You've heard of Lady Hailsham, yes? Has a fine home, she does."

Smedley shuddered. "Yes," he whispered.

"And, just now, she's not in it. She's halfway across fashionable London, attending a ball. Glittering things, balls. Where people drink too much and stay too late. Giving someone plenty of time to pluck up everything she's written on paper—even hidden papers—and bring it neatly outside. That's all."

"I don't know where this particular fine home is," Smedley said sullenly, downing the last of his tankard. Of the pie, mouth-burning hot though it had been, there was nothing left, not even crumbs.

"Of course not," Whipsnade purred, "so I'll take you there. You and your sovereigns." And he handed over a heavy, clinking cloth bag.

Mister Oswald Smedley picked it up, face pale and gray with fear and disbelief, and turned to Whipsnade.

Who led the way, wearing the softest of smiles, through the suddenly silent taproom of the Raging Lion, men parting before them like hurrying curtains, and out into the night.

OCTEMBER 5

Obligingly, the moon chose that moment to come scudding out from behind a dark drift of cloud.

Straker lifted his hat to it in thanks and salute, for he'd just reached a stretch of path—it was really no more than a well-trodden game trail through the woods—where roots were frequent, uneven, and jutted proud. He'd rather not turn an ankle, if it was all the same to the God of the Cross and the newer gods of steam.

And then he stepped around a tree and saw in divers shafts of moonlight the descending arc of path ahead. There was an unmistakable silhouette on it, a dark figure lurching purposefully along with a distinctive and all-too-familiar side-to-side gait.

Bentley Steelforce. His Iron Assassin.

Straker quickened his pace, but his lurching creation was well ahead of him and moving fast.

Over the roots and the uneven ground, even with the helpful moonlight, it was as much as Lord Tempest could manage to keep Steelforce in view.

Out of the woods and down through meadows and past a copse or three and out onto lawns, Lord Barnstaple's mansion standing proud in the moonlight ahead.

The Silent Man lurched around the great house in a wide arc, to and through the rear gate of Lord Barnstaple's stableyard. Tempest put his head down and ran as he'd never run before.

He was stumbling and gasping by the time he reached the gloom of the stables, where one stablehand fled at the sight of Steelforce, lurching purposefully along with arms raised to grapple anyone in his way—but the next stablehand snarled, "Get out, you! Clear off!" and raised a muck shovel threateningly.

The Iron Assassin didn't hesitate, and the shovel clanged off the exoskeleton hard enough to strike sparks—twice, thrice, and then in a frantic tattoo of ringing metal that rose to a fierce crescendo.

And ended abruptly as Steelforce plucked shovel and straining, kicking man off the ground and flung them against a nearby post. A meaty smack heralded a limp, bloody slide down that post— and by then Jack Straker had reached his creation.

He pounced from behind, clawing open the little door in the back of the Iron Assassin's skull, half-hidden under the surviving wisps of hair, and pulling out the control key—even as his creation launched a vicious elbow thrust, that would have done real damage to some-one not expecting it.

The key was actually a small box adorned with a glued-on glass eyeball, to differentiate it from earlier, cruder versions. Yes, his Iron Assassin had an eye in the back of his head.

Even before the little box had been stuffed into Tempest's pocket,

Steelforce had slumped. Straker backed away hastily, but Steelforce had stopped trying to attack him and now started to wander aimlessly along the row of stalls.

Gently, Tempest plucked at his sleeve, snared it, smiled into the slack and unresponsive face, and started to lead his creation back out of the stables.

Steelforce stumbled after him, more dazed than obedient, but they weren't six steps outside the stables when tumult arose from the direction of the Barnstaple mansion: a rabble of servants with bobbing lanterns and wildly waving fowling pieces.

The cracks and flashes of the first hasty shots arose, peppering them both, and it was the sheer mischance of Straker's leading Steelforce that the Iron Assassin was the closest target and got hit several times.

A ball *spanged* off the exoskeleton and burned past Tempest's cheek—and Steelforce went wild, tearing free of his creator's grasp to lay about in all directions with both fists, brawling with the empty air.

A second ragged volley sent the Iron Assassin rushing off into the woods.

As Tempest spun around to follow, he caught a glimpse of two faces staring down at him from an upper gable in the stable roof. One was the Prince Royal, and the other belonged to an unfamiliar and visibly frightened female.

And then, amid more shots, the shouts of the pursuing Barnstaple servants, and the disappearance of the moon and its light behind some useful clouds, he was pelting into the trees after the Iron Assassin.

Who could lurch along through the endless trees and the deep gloom far faster than he could sprint. Straker soon lost track of him.

———

Forgive my boldness, Lord, but did Smedley bring out anything useful?" Whipsnade asked, from the door.

Uncle looked up from his desk. The cracksman had brought quite a bundle of papers from Lady Hailsham's home, and, as he'd suspected, much of it was dross—polite but empty daily correspondence of the "So sorry I missed you" sort—but he'd already set more than a few items aside as promising blackmail material, or fodder that might be spun up into something that could frighten her.

And then he'd spotted the cipher. Sometimes, being the trusted lord he was came in useful . . .

Just two small pages of a code he knew. Notes to herself, rather than a missive or a report meant for other eyes; their very informality made them effective indeed. She suspected him and some others of being Order members and had noted the evidence pointing in that direction.

Damning evidence.

Uncle had just sat back with a sigh as Whipsnade had come to the door. Rather than replying, he held up an imperious forefinger to indicate that Whipsnade was to wait in silence, drew an unused page of notepaper to right in front of him on his blotter, took up his quill, and started writing.

Just a few lines, in his very best, most ornate hand. An invitation to Lady Hailsham to dine at Pitt's, an expensive London club, this evening. "It is most important I see you," was one of the lines.

As he read it over, he felt—he was a trifle surprised to realize—genuine regret for what was to come. Folding it and sealing it with the best wax, for she deserved no less, he held it out to Whipsnade.

"Deliver this to Halworthy Burton at first light, to pass along to Lady Hailsham," he instructed. "Oh, and don't return Smedley to the streets until you're on your way to pick up Lady Hailsham. We don't want him to bolt too far and too fast, if you take my meaning."

"Dyson's not as swift of foot as he once was," Whipsnade agreed.

"We none of us are, Whipsnade," Uncle warned quietly. "It's the curse that steals up to rob us all."

Some folk in Bishop's Bottom, as everywhere else in the English countryside, loved to watch the arrivals and departures of mail airships by night. The silent drift of twinkling lanterns, the swinging lines and grapples, the faint luminescence of light reflected off the bulbous flanks of the great aerial vessels . . . one was coming in to moor at the Royal Mail yard right now.

Small sleepy boys in bedchamber windows and toiling servants alike stopped what they were doing to watch it.

None of them saw a smaller and much-lower-flying black dirigible scudding through the sky nearby.

It was of the oldest, crudest sort, steered by rudders and vanes operated by someone peddling a velocipede built into the front of its underslung cargo gondola, and it was showing no lights at all. As it silently drifted out of the night to pass over Lord Barnstaple's country house.

Some servants saw it then, as clouds parted again and the landscape was bathed once more in bright moonlight. Men were descending from it on rope ladders and lines that had grappled chimneys and shutters and downspouts, men whose faces were hidden behind goggles and leather face masks that covered their heads from chin to eyes, men who wore dark suits overlaid with greatcoats and strapped-on hats and leather gloves with metal-tipped fingers.

They invaded the mansion, kicking in windows and hauling out weapons. They used these to strike viciously at anyone they saw and ransacked room after room in wantonly destructive haste, obviously searching for something. Just as obviously, these murderous agents would stop at nothing to get it.

Then they emerged, climbing the lines and unhooking them, departing as swiftly as they'd come.

Lord Barnstaple's heart had failed him in the midst of a bellowing, barefisted defense of his home, and he'd dropped like a stone. So he'd lain, bloodied, senseless, and presumed dead, with servants fighting to protect his body. The invaders had contented themselves with smiting these loyal wights in passing—and so when they fled, they left behind a lord barely alive, fallen amid many sprawled and dead servants.

Sometimes Jack Straker enjoyed being Lord Tempest, dashing darling of the gossip press, handsome and sought-after lordling. Most of the time, however, he frankly preferred being plain Jack Straker, the untidy tinkerer, the little boy lost in the wonder of what clockwork and salvaged mongery and a little steam could do.

Sitting alone in the moonlight, imagining, examining. Thinking.

He quite liked this little rock outcrop in the woods. Always had. Mainly because the moonlight, unhindered by leaves and boughs, could flood it with cold, clear light. And because no one else seemed to know about it, so he could always find solitude there.

Alone with his thoughts, as he was now. Sitting on a rock in the moonlight, examining the key—the mechanism, that is, freed now from its box. Not just staring, but fondling. Turning it over and over in his hands, gently tugging on this and trying to slide that, seeing if anything . . . moved.

Quite suddenly, something did. It glowed, stroked his palm with the gentlest of vibrations, and opened in his hand like a little metal clam. As he peered into it, fascinated, it moved its contacts by itself. *Click-click.*

"Oho," he breathed. "*That's* how they're doing it!"

He sprang to his feet, thrust the key into his pocket, and told the moon, "I must secure my spares!"

And, as the gutter press put it, rushed off into the night.

He'd always been able to think while running, fighting for breath and slamming along, in this case stumbling over roots and ducking boughs, shredding more than a few leaves in his wake.

Whoever was trying to control the Iron Assassin from afar—almost certainly Marlshrike; no one else really knows how, and *he's* almost undoubtedly working with the Tentacles—must be using etheric telegraphy. *Had* to be. What other invisible waves were all around us in the air? Oh, von Bezold, James Clarke Maxwell, Hughes, and Sir Oliver Lodge might call them by different terms and try to put them to very different uses, but it was all the same thing. At least it was to anyone hereabouts, groping blindly to harness the unseen and half-understood.

His own meddlings had resulted in an unreliable control over the exoskeleton, across a fairly small room at best, and fitful at that. The difficulty was generating the signals; it took an apparatus of three strong men vigorously peddling wired-up bicycles, or a huge steam-driven machine bigger than the boiler of a Thames barge.

Ah, that latter approach would be Marlshrike's way; the man *loved* big, noisy, complex steam piles. That sort of contraption would fill a room and generate the necessary pulse with a spectacular crackling electric arc between exposed poles. And it would have an effective range far greater than his own across-the-room efforts. Greater still when a storm was brewing and the air was alive in its approach . . .

Which meant Marlshrike's machine had to be nearby, hidden in some shed or cellar. Higher would be better, but it would take a stout floor to support the weight. Just how near, only Marlshrike knew. Which meant a certain Lord Tempest would just have to guess at how far afield he must search.

And if Marlshrike succeeded in making his own new key, it would not be just poor Bentley that the Empire would have to worry about. It would be an army of precise and deadly assassins under the control of Norbert Marlshrike.

Straker shivered, despite himself. The thought of anything or anyone being under thin-lipped, thinner-skinned, vindictive Marlshrike's control . . .

It did not bear thinking about. So, panting and ducking his hurried way along a dark but long-familiar path, he returned to thinking of the fastest way to get from here to his workshop.

In his haste and preoccupation, Straker barely noticed a brief but utter darkening of the sky ahead, through the dark cloak of many massed forest leaves in the night—as a small dirigible briefly blotted out the moon.

OCTEMBER 6

The church bell tolled once. Noon.

Lady Rose peered around the trunk of the only tree in the thicket large enough to entirely conceal her. The bridge was empty, with not a soul in sight, but—hark! Hooves, clopping nearer, in the distance.

A lone phaeton, with a bowler-hatted man in an expensive suit sitting in it, the whip stowed upright rather than in use, not hurrying.

Lady Rose nodded approvingly. So this would be Mister Bleys Hardcastle. She peered this way and that, trying to see as far as she could down the road in either direction. Other than her expected conveyance, she could see no one, so she stepped briskly out through the trees, sprang over the ditch in its narrowest place, and presented herself in the road, well ahead of the horse.

Which took no notice of her, plodding along as if well-dressed ladies leaped into its path every few minutes, dumping two satchels against one ankle so as to raise their arms uncertainly in the summons for a hansom cab.

Mister Hardcastle smiled, nodded to her, and lifted his hat, clucking the horse to a halt.

It obliged unhurriedly; Hardcastle sprang eagerly down to offer her a hand with the bluff, open welcome of a man who desires to be friends; Rose tossed her satchels in and followed them briskly, giving the hand she'd spurned a dazzling smile so as not to offend; and in a trice they were clopping along toward Foxden again.

Rose looked back only once, to see no one within sight, but she did so well before a dead-looking man in a metal exoskeleton rose with silent, baleful menace out of the riverside reeds to watch the phaeton dwindle down the lane.

The Foxden gates stood open between the two rather battered stone pillars Rose had passed hundreds of times in her life. She didn't remember ever seeing them open before, though.

Hardcastle directed their aging horse to enter with the easy familiarity of someone coming home. It clopped along a drive of fine oiled gravel that, once inside the gates, immediately swept around in a sharp curve to the right, past a tall and impenetrable yew hedge, then wheeled around the end of that wall of greenery to double back to the left and run along a second hedge even taller and thicker than the first—neatly trimmed, the both of them, but standing like castle walls against all intruders.

At the far end of this second hedge, the drive doubled back again, this time to run only a short distance, up to where a closed and sternly guarded gate—two high, metal-sheathed doors between tall, new-looking stone pillars—awaited.

Unsmiling men who carried hunting rifles and had several pistols each thrust through their belts appeared along the fieldstone wall that flanked the gate. Striding along it from both directions, they converged grimly on the phaeton.

"Your business?" one asked, cocking his gun but keeping it pointing skyward.

Hardcastle nodded calmly to him and announced crisply, "Gone to earth."

The man gave them both a hard look, peered at the satchels behind them—Hardcastle appeared to have no bag or trunk at all—and then stepped back and waved a hand at the gate.

Where someone unseen did something to make the metal doors open outward, admitting passage to Foxden beyond—a pleasant-seeming house of many gables and chimneys flanked by cedars, its broad front doors opening out onto a large graveled turning circle that would have accommodated carriages far larger than their own, drawn by long teams in harness.

As the phaeton crunched to a stop, the front doors opened—more men with guns—and an immaculately dressed man in a tailcoat, white gloves, and the thinnest of lip-line mustaches, his oiled hair arranged just so, stepped out and snapped to attention.

"Well, now," Hardcastle murmured, "the butler of butlers."

Lady Rose hid a smile and accompanied him to the door, catching up her satchels before the row of footmen now marching out of the front door could reach them to offer assistance.

"Welcome to Foxden, doctors." The butler greeted them with cold correctness. "I am Malmerston, and you may rely on me or any of my staff."

For what, he did not say, but turned as smartly as any soldier on the parade square and marched into the house.

There were armed and uniformed soldiers inside the house, firmly ushering them along in the wake of the coldly correct butler, who set a brisk pace.

Once, as he lifted a large ring of keys out of a pocket to unlock a door, Malmerston was heard to mutter disapprovingly under his breath, "A lady doctor; whatever next?"

Lady Rose held her peace, but she doubted very much that this man ever did anything carelessly or absently. That opinion had been voiced to be heard.

The unlocked door led into a pleasant parlor, off which several bedchambers opened; the butler unlocked each of them in turn, then turned to Hardcastle. "I *trust* this will be satisfactory for your needs?"

Hardcastle silently deferred to Lady Rose with a slow, firm gesture.

"Capital, Malmerston, capital," she said briskly.

"And how am I to address you, madam?" the butler inquired glacially, obviously irked at being spoken to by her as if she was a member of the upper class.

"Lady Rose is fine. Lady Harminster if we're being formal," she told him.

The butler's eyes flickered in obvious startlement.

"If your ladyship doesn't mind me saying so," he ventured tentatively, "your ladyship has changed greatly since I saw you last. If you are of the Harminsters who are near neighbors to us here."

"I am," she replied simply, "and I have."

A ghost of a smile rose to her lips. "We all do. Change, I have found, is the one constant in the Empire of the Lion."

Here now," said a voice very close behind Oswald Smedley's ear, "will you look at that?"

The cracksman froze, fear like a sudden leaping fist closing around his heart. He'd been half-expecting this since putting the bundle of writings into Whipsnade's hands in a dark doorway, and had in fact been tramping hurriedly across London, avoiding his usual haunts, in hopes of buying a ticket to a train west and getting himself on it just as fast as he could.

He started to run, but a firm hand had hold of his collar. Its mate was pointing out of the mouth of the alley, at something black, gleamingly new, and wheezingly noisy. A fine steam-driven carriage of the latest make.

"Look you!" the man behind Smedley said insistently. "Isn't that someone you know driving it?"

Indeed it was. Whipsnade, in a finer jacket and hat than Smedley had ever seen on him before, was perched at the tiller.

It swept past with a muted hiss and thunder, its tarred rubber-coated wheels quieter on the cobbles than any hansom, and Smedley knew the chill of fresh fear as he recognized the passenger looking serenely out the nearside window of the carriage: Lady Iolanthe Hailsham. Why, if Whipsnade knew the noblewoman that well . . . Oh, *Lord* . . .

"On the way back from Pitt's, they are," the man chuckled.

And just how did he know *that*?

"Wh-who are you," Smedley managed to husk out, his mouth suddenly as dry as old bone, "and how d'you know they've been to Pitt's?"

"Ah," the man said, dragging Smedley back from the alley mouth with swift ease—steam-driven hell, but he was strong!—and spinning him around to march him deeper into the narrowing gloom of the alley, where the smells grew strong. "As to that, Whipsnade told me. My name's Dyson. They call me Dyson the Knife."

Smedley tried to scream, but all that came out was a sort of muted squeak, because he was shivering so hard and was being run along the alley so fast he was short of breath. That iron-strong grip on his collar became viselike fingers digging into the back of his neck. He kicked out wildly behind him, struck a shin—and was rewarded by being turned and slammed face-first, and hard, against a wall. Teeth chipped and blood spurted, Smedley hoarsely panting for breath around his now-broken nose.

"You've heard of me, I see," Dyson growled, sounding pleased. "Aye, I'm a snuffer, right enough, sent to slit the throats of them as knows too much. Which now, regrettably, mate, includes *you*."

Something flashed, Smedley shrieked as something like ice seared his ear and he clapped his hand to it and discovered his ear was *gone*, and then—

The ice returned, right across his throat, and he was choking too much to care about anything else, ever again . . .

The last thing he heard, faintly and as if from a great distance, was Dyson saying jovially, "And there it is, right enough. Sixty sovereigns, just as Whipsnade promised. Handsome pay for a simple job like this. And it's not as if the meat came by it *honestly*, hey?"

Lord Winter, that was a *superb* meal," Lady Hailsham said happily. "I've never had pheasant so succulent. Yet as I recall you wrote that it was important to see me. On a particular matter, I assume?"

"Ah, yes," her dining companion of the evening said smoothly. "A matter we'll entertain once we're aboard."

"Aboard?"

"My treat, my dear: an airship ride in the moonlight. Aboard my latest. I call her the *Bright New Emperor*."

The lord pointed out the carriage window as Whipsnade turned off the street and through a gate that had just opened on their right, into a moonlight-flooded cobbled yard. Rising above them was a magnificent bowsprit that would have seemed fitting for the grandest admiral's flagship on the seas. It was the front end of the largest gondola Iolanthe Hailsham had ever seen, its proud lines gleamingly new, and above it rose an airship of truly massive size, its mooring lines snaking down all around them as Whipsnade brought the carriage to a smooth halt.

"Come, my dear," Lord Winter said fondly, opening the door and handing her down. A chill breeze brought them the unmistakable and unpleasant reek of the Thames. "The champagne, Whipsnade?"

"Is aboard and ready, milord," came the prompt reply.

The cabin to which Lord Winter conducted his guest was dimly lit by half a dozen lanterns and was dominated by glossy quilted-leather seats and large windows commanding views of the night outside.

The champagne was waiting.

Lord Winter and Lady Hailsham clinked glasses. The airship quivered twice around them as key moorings were let go, and shortly thereafter Whipsnade's head appeared in the companionway, to give his master a nod.

Lord Winter smiled, turned to his guest, and said, "I very much enjoyed our evening together, Iolanthe. A great pity it's your last."

"I *beg* your pardon?" she asked.

"That's one thing, Lady Hailsham, you may not have," he replied calmly, lunging at her like a tiger. Even as she wriggled like an eel, trying to get out from under him and off the seat, his hands closed around her wrists like heavy irons. "You have learned, as they say, far too much for your own good. So now, I fear, it is time for you to go. Farewell . . . forever."

He leaned forward. She tried to head-butt him, but he was ready for that. She tried to knee him in the groin—and discovered, painfully, that he was wearing a hard metal codpiece under his evening-dress trousers.

"Lord *Winter!*" she protested desperately, but he forcibly kissed her—and before she could bite him, drew his head back again and just held her, superior strength against straining effort, overpowering her as they struggled—and Whipsnade almost gently pulled a chloroform-soaked cloth over her mouth from behind, and with his two smallest fingers drove it up her nostrils.

Lady Iolanthe Hailsham shook and fought in one last, brief frenzy, then went limp.

Lord Winter did not hurry about letting go of her. When he did, he caressed her with an air of regret, then rose and told Whipsnade, "Do it properly. Enjoy the champagne."

Then he left the airship without looking back and departed in the carriage.

When the yard was empty, Whipsnade let go the last mooring from the ship end, watching it whip about as it fell. Then he turned to the wheel that controlled the steering vanes, to fly along the Thames.

And take the senseless Lady Hailsham well out to sea, to drop her in the dark and icy brine to drown.

Jack Straker often took different routes to his workshop. Not out of any particular sense of caution, but merely because there was a lot to see amid the warehouses of Limehouse. Some of it even savory.

On this brightly moonlit night he took streets and alleys he'd not seen in some time, and arrived at the familiar nondescript warehouse wherein his workshop was hidden in a back room sooner than he'd expected to. It was near the docks, and always smelled of old mold, dust, rat droppings, and the Thames.

When he unlocked the office door at the far end of the warehouse from his rooms, however, a faint, acrid, and unfamiliar scent overlaid the usual reek. Nothing seemed amiss as he crossed the office, let himself out its rear door, and threaded his way through the dark and silent main storage floor. This was still a working storehouse, but his tenant dealt in season-long layaways, not wares that were needed night and day.

Rats scuttled unseen in the loft, pigeons dozed, and . . . Lord Tempest shot two bolts that were in far better repair than their rusty appearance suggested, swung open a panel soundlessly to reveal a door behind it, unlocked that door, and reached out into the darkness for the oil lamp that he always left ready on the edge of the bench.

Halfway there, his hand met a line in the air that should not have been there—a taut waxed cord, running crosswise.

Tempest flung himself backward and to one side, trying to get around behind the wall and the open panel as he spun on his heels to flee, knowing he'd not have time but also aware that every foot farther away was—

Behind him, the darkness exploded with a roar that he felt more than heard, a hammer blow that smote his ears an instant before the foremost wave of the blast shoved at his back, snatching Tempest off his feet and flinging him back across the storage floor like the proverbial rag doll, to rebound off the flimsy office wall and the sacks of grain thankfully piled there.

His workshop was ablaze, an inferno of blazing beams, exploding vials, and . . . his keys!

His ears were ringing and his legs weak, but the dump door and its chain was a mere three strides yonder.

He flung his weight against the lever and had the trap up. It took but a moment to catch hold of the chain and swing, until it dropped into the sewer below with a splash. He slid down it, immersing himself entirely, then clambered back up and sprinted right at the flames.

His spare keys were in a false bottom of the right-hand drawer of a salvaged old desk pedestal clear across the room. All he had to do was haul the whole drawer free and carry it back out.

Cogs and boilers, but it was hot! He slipped on something, tripped on something else, was vaguely aware of a blazing post toppling on his left as part of the loft overhead sagged in the raging flames, and . . .

Had it! The drawer was heavy with spanners and awls and the pieces of a disassembled old knurl cutter, but . . .

Back out onto the floor, Straker, panting in pain, flung the smoldering drawer toward the office and rolled after it, trying to put out the worst of the flames licking up from his clothing. He should get out of here.

His roll brought him to a stop just shy of the drawer. He overturned it with a blow of his fist, heedless of the tools, clawed the bottom off, and—

Nothing. His older, cruder keys to command the Iron Assassin were gone.

Stolen.

The Tentacles—or Marlshrike—or someone else now had enough keys to give five such assassins simple orders. Once they managed to duplicate the mechanisms, they'd be able to create an army of lurching slayers, and—

The world behind him erupted in a rolling maelstrom of shrieking, tumbling timbers and flames, flames everywhere, racing out into the night.

Lord Tempest went tumbling helplessly with them, sounds and lights his dwindling shroud, down into darkness.

OCTEMBER 7

The signal flashes sent from here to the Yard had been clear enough: "urgent" and "94," which was him. Over and over again.

So Chief Inspector Theo Standish lost no time, once the beagle flitter caught and latched onto the Tower Street beagle station moorings, in flinging wide the door and hastening down the iron steps from the mooring mast.

They'd only *just* beaten the storm. Behind him, rain was falling like a swiftly advancing curtain along the Thames, lightning stabbing down here and there to strike various airship masts across London. Gusts were hurling airships across the sky. This would mean aerial-traffic shutdown, probably until morning; right now, extra mooring cables to tether against high winds were being hastily fastened all over London.

Lighting cracked blindingly nearby, and Standish fell down the last few steps with more haste than dignity, banging through the door in none too good a humor.

Into a room crowded with a generous handful of the glowering refuse of London's streets, muttering foul words or mumbling incoherently in the narrow "standing cells" that lined the room. It smelled strongly of them, and of spew and urine and even emptied bowels. His bowler started to slip as he stalked along, and his temper wasn't helped by the titter that arose behind him as he caught at it, straightened it, and fetched up at a littered desk where a sad-eyed sergeant was checking over arrest reports and getting several surly constables to supply what they'd missed writing down the first time around.

"Well?" Standish growled.

"Well, *what*? Wait yer turn, wait yer tur—oh. *Sorry*, sir!"

Standish waved the apology away. "Urgent. Ninety-four. I'm here."

The sergeant half-rose to point down the rest of the room, at a distant door. "In there. Blakeslee will tell you all, sir."

"*Thank* you," Standish said, adjusting his bowler again and stalking on.

Shortly he found himself in a back room lit only by two dim lamps above a countertop where several men were standing conferring, their backs to him. There was no light at all over a bare table in the center of the room that someone had been laid out on. Someone wearing good boots, who'd been in a fire.

Tempest.

"Chief Inspector Standish?" This must be Blakeslee. Clipboard in hand, mustache that looked as if the rats had got at it, standing with a young constable with ears that stuck out like tankard handles.

Standish nodded, already bent over the body. Jack Straker was alive and bandaged here and there. Bruised and burned all over, and twitching as if dreaming of moments of violent action. A mess.

"Where was he found?" he asked.

"In a burning warehouse near the docks, in Limehouse. A fire that was set. Kegs of black powder and lamp oil and probably a few more modern propellants, joined by fuses snaking everywhere. We found what was left of Dyson the Knife there, too; little more than a skeleton, but someone had broken his neck for him. After breaking his elbows and wrists. The sergeant first on the scene dragged Lord Tempest out and fell over more than a dozen trip wires doing so. Said he'd never seen so many outside the pages of a wild-headed magazine serial."

"Any tentacles drawn anywhere? Anything that looked like a squid or octopus?"

Blakeslee gaped. "Why, *yes*. There was a squid chalked on one of the warehouse doors."

Standish nodded impatiently and straightened up, letting his fury show.

Blakeslee misinterpreted, and said hastily, "He's been doctored by the best we could find—Cramner *and* Guildenstern—and he's been muttering and murmuring, off and on, but hasn't woken up yet. I—"

"Have someone stationed here to write down everything coherent he says, yes," Standish said heavily. "I appreciate what you've—"

The door he'd come in by opened again and a grim-faced sergeant came into the room. It was a man Standish knew, a veteran and a good one. Blunt, that was his name.

Sergeant Blunt came up close and muttered, "The floating dead have been brought in, sir. There's something you should see. Ah, that is to say, some*one*, rather."

Standish sighed. What *now*? He'd nigh forgotten that since the Blackwall beagle station had burned down a few months back, Tower

Street had been where bodies that wash up or were found floating in the Thames east of Tower Street were brought. So, a suicide? More likely, a murder sent into the river in hopes of the body never being found.

He followed Blunt wearily into another room, even gloomier than Blakeslee's lair, where half a dozen sodden corpses lay dripping on stained and battered tables. A light had been positioned over just one of them.

The only female. Whose clothing had been disarranged here and there to show a trifle more of her than would be polite, even at an intimate party. He knew the face at a glance, and froze.

Blunt was watching him.

"Lady Iolanthe Hailsham," he said, as gently as any comforting vicar.

"Where was she found?" Standish asked.

"Off Sheerness. Floating."

"Murdered," they agreed grimly.

Standish let out a long sigh, looked at the ceiling for a moment, then said grimly, "Have her moved into the room with Tempest. I want him to have a proper look at her when he wakes up. He has the knack of seeing things we miss—or miss the meaning of, I should say. And have someone heat up a pie for me."

"Hungry, sir?"

"I will be. I'm not leaving that room until Tempest and I are done with the lady."

"And then?"

"And then," Chief Inspector Standish informed Blunt quietly, "someone shall pay. In full."

He turned away and made for the door, but not before Blunt saw that the Chief Inspector's hands had become fists, and that they were shaking.

Foxden was . . . large. Low of ceiling and intimate for the most part, all warm wood furniture and stucco and exposed beams like a country cottage, but it went on and on, room giving into room and unexpected passages opening out around corners. Bright morning sun was flooding through many windows.

Rose explored cautiously, strolling with an idle air and trying not to appear to peer at anything closely, under the eyes of the silent guards who stood like footmen beside many of the doors. They were still and silent, their scrutiny an ever-present watchful weight in the near-total silence. It seemed as if she was the only thing moving in Foxden.

She found an arched door very much like those of the sacristy and vestry in the Bishop's Bottom church, except that the uprights of its wooden frame were narrow bookshelves holding an untidy array of mismatched books. Reading shelves, rather than formal storage. Intrigued, she opened that door and beheld a small library, with a central reading table equipped with several sloped tabletop lecterns. A thin, earnest-looking young man with large, round-framed glasses was seated at one, bent over a book of heraldry.

He looked up, in momentary irritation that became embarrassed but eager greeting.

"Oh! Hello! I'm Gerald Prycewood. Ah, Herald Pursuivant to the Empire. And you are—?"

"Lady Rose Harminster. I'm a doctor. I'm sorry—I didn't mean to disturb you."

"Oh, not at all, not at all. The library is for everyone, I've been told, but, ah, few seem inclined to use it."

He lowered his head, as if he'd said more than he was wont to, and looked back at his book. Rose smiled, bade him farewell, and went out. So that was the quiet and respectful understudy to severe old Throckmorton. Well, at least this wasn't a house entirely filled with guards and doxies.

A few rooms later, she found herself in a hall that seemed a trifle familiar. After a few moments, she decided the double doors yonder must be the front doors she'd come through on her arrival. The guards had been here then, but had this strange concealed object against the wall across from those doors?

It stood taller and bulkier than most furniture—an armoire, perhaps?—a large and ovoid shape covered by several overlapped sheets.

Rose eyed the still and silent guards, then strode boldly to the thing, plucked up the edge of the sheeting, and started to peek under it.

"Here! Come away from that!" the nearest guard said sharply.

Rose dropped the sheet and backed away. "But—but what is it?"

"Something secret," he replied tersely, striding swiftly to place himself between her and the large covered object.

Rose sighed. "Very well, then, but as a doctor, I demand to know if it's anything that can do harm—so I know what injuries I may in future have to deal with."

"It's a weapon," he told her stolidly, "and that's about all you need to know."

Someone glided smoothly to a stop at Rose's elbow. It was Malmerston, the butler.

"If you'll step this way, ma'am . . ."

Seething inwardly—had he been shadowing her, all the time she'd been exploring?—Rose did so. Malmerston led her through a door, closed it carefully behind her, then stepped across the room to unnecessarily rearrange some flowers.

As he did so, he murmured sidelong. "The soldiers have their orders, but I am allowed a little more leeway. It's some sort of gun, invented by the Lord Tempest, that forcibly projects—fires?—lengths of chain. The idea being to bludgeon and entangle someone. It's in some sort of round housing and aimed at our front doors. None of us knows precisely how it works, so it's best left alone."

"I . . . thank you," Rose said in astonishment.

"Glad to be of service, ma'am." The butler bowed his head, held the door open for her, and once she'd stepped out of the room, glided on his way.

So Foxden's defenses ran to more than stiff-lipped men with guns. Well, that was a good thing, of course. And Malmerston liked, or at least respected her. Even better.

She continued on her wanderings in a better humor, passing Tempest's mysterious weapon and turning down a passage running toward the back of the house. Into another wing than that of her own room, perhaps?

The guards were more frequent here, standing at one meeting of ways as thickly as trees—but they neither moved to obstruct her nor spoke to her, so she strolled past them, trying to pretend they were statues and not men watching her every move.

Taking a passage that led to her left at random, Rose passed through an open archway and found herself suddenly in territory where there were no guards at all. Ahead, some doors stood open, light and the sounds of movement and quiet converse spilling out.

The first open door showed her a pleasantly furnished sitting room with a spinet and a writing desk in its far corners.

The second was a bedchamber dominated by a palatial bed—and in front of it, a partially clad couple stood side-on to her, locked in an intimate embrace.

Rose hastily turned away, but not before they both broke off a kiss to look in her direction.

The lushly beautiful woman she didn't know, but the man was the Lord Lion—the Prince Royal!

Rose fled back the way she'd come, but a voice—the woman—hailed her saucily, and when she hesitated, its source overtook her, strolled unconcernedly past her and turned to bar her way, clad only in a garter and a smile, and said, "One meets the *nicest* class of people here in Foxden! I'm Lil—a working woman, just to be candid—and you must be the lady doctor!"

"I, uh, yes. Yes, I am. Rose Harminster. Uh, Lady Harminster."

Lil took her hand, smiling broadly, and said, "Now don't be shy. The Prince wants you to join us."

"Join?"

"You know—the three of us, abed."

Rose could feel heat flooding her face as she protested, "I'm a doctor, not . . ."

"No?" Lil leered. "It's by way of being a royal command, don't you know!"

Rose snatched her hand away and started to flee down the passage.

And then stopped, drew in a deep breath, squared her shoulders, turned—and then, fists clenched, spun around and reached for Lil's hand again.

"Lead on," she said firmly.

Simon Morrowpyke strode through Knightsbridge like a conquering hero, waving his walking stick airily and nodding and smiling in response to the various hails and lifted hats. The Crown Anarchists were more popular than they'd ever been, and rising daily in public acclaim; it would only be a matter of time before he was the Prime Minister of the Empire. And no wonder. Old Cantlemere was a stodgy fool whose sneerings and refusals to budge a fingerbreadth on divers issues had made him many enemies down the years. Morrowpyke counted himself proud to be among them.

Yet he was determined not to be the sort of party leader who sniped but offered no alternatives. With a bit of cultivation before votes, he just might get major changes forced through Parliament before becoming Prime Minister—or use the battle over them to bring down the government and seize his chance to sweep the Old Bulls aside.

Which was why he was strolling through fashionable Knightsbridge at this time of day. On his way to call on Lord Tempest, one of the younger and more handsome of the stylish young nobility, a man other younglings looked to. If he could convince Tempest to support the Abolition Act . . .

He was proud of it. The newest bill of the Crown Anarchists, and largely his own work. Legislation sure to goad Cantlemere into one of his spitting fits. An act to set aside the royal family in favor of a ruling Parliament that would see to sanitation, road and bridge building, defense, banking, and hospitals—and leave all else to private citizens. As matters should be.

Green fanlight, twin stone lions serving as railings to the front steps—ah! There it was! "Seven fourteen," right enough. Tempest had the topmost floor . . .

The door was open, and the place seemed deserted. He ascended steps that creaked only a little and found himself facing a single door flanked by a polished copper plate bearing the simple legend JACK STRAKER/LORD TEMPEST.

The door stood a little ajar, and at his knock moved inward a trifle. Enough for him to see disarray. Furniture overturned, papers strewn on a carpeted floor.

"Hello?" he called. "Anyone there?"

Silence. He listened for a long time, and then frowned and used the end of his walking stick to propel the door inward, open wide.

"Good *God*!"

A scene of utter devastation met Morrowpyke's gaze. The airy, pleasantly lit room before him had been ransacked. Empty bookcases leaned precariously forward, torn away from the walls after every single volume they'd held had been plucked from the shelves, rifled through, and flung at far walls. They were now leaning on the desks, wingback chairs, and side tables they'd fallen against. Broken decanters lay here and there, their splashed and spilled contents still wet.

Was that—? No, just coats, still hooked on a stand that had been toppled. Not a body.

The windows were closed, there was still no sound from the rooms beyond, the one open doorway he could see through showed more signs of damage, and—

Heavy feet ascended the stairs behind him. Lots of them.

Morrowpyke turned hastily. It would not do to be found—

Beagles. Almost a dozen of them. Burly, hard-faced men in bowlers and dark suits. The hands of the foremost pair could break him in an instant. He fell back, stammering, "Hi! Have a care! I—I—I just arrived here, and found this! I'm—I'm Simon Morrowpyke, head of the Crown Anarchist Party, and I—"

That first fearsome pair had rushed past him without a word, and so had the second. The third pair of beagles stopped in front of Morrowpyke and advanced on him, glaring. He gave way before them until he fetched up against an unseen wall and stumbled to a halt.

"Ransacked, all of them, but no sign of Tempest," one of the beagles called, from the depths of the rooms.

The oldest beagle, who seemed to hold some sort of rank senior to his fellows, though Morrowpyke was admittedly no expert on such things, strode forward until his nose was almost touching the politician's.

Morrowpyke felt moved to hastily protest that he had, "Nothing to do with this, nothing at all!"

The senior beagle gave him a look of contempt. "Of course not, sir. Whoever did this was bold, thorough, and cunning. You're none of those three."

"Here, now!" Morrowpyke protested. "You don't even know me!"

"No, sir, but I've heard you speak in Parliament and read the bills you've drafted. That's quite sufficient to reach the conclusions I hold." The beagle leaned forward, crowding into Morrowpyke's face, his cigar-scented breath warm on Morrowpyke's chin.

"Yet seeing as you're here, standing amid criminal disarray

wrought by others, suppose you tell me just why you *were* here. Just to avoid misunderstandings, sir. I'm sure you, being the leader of the Empire you are, understand that we want to avoid those."

And Morrowpyke found himself gabbling like a frightened schoolgirl. He hated himself for it—but staring into the hard, steady gazes that the tall and burly beagles looming all around him were giving him, he found he couldn't stop.

Lady Rose stood stiffly beside the royal bed, trying not to look at Lil entwining herself around the man—the man whose face she knew from dozens of portraits and a few fleeting glimpses across crowded rooms full of finery—who was, just now, wearing only a smile.

"You sent for me, Your Royal Highness?"

"I did indeed, Lady Harminster." The Prince Royal flashed her a winning smile—God, but his eyes were blue! And he had a nice smile, a smile she liked very much—as he gently disengaged Lil's hand from what it had burrowed under the bedclothes to find.

"Leave us, Lil," he said gently, in what was unmistakably a command. "Delcoats has the bath warm by now, I believe."

Lil pouted visibly but obeyed, rising silently and deftly and padding swiftly to a door in the far wall. It closed behind her as softly as a sigh.

The Lord Lion of England and the Empire then rose from the bed right in front of Rose, careless of his nakedness. She could not help but stare, though she could feel warmth rising on her cheeks. He was a handsome figure of a man, with only the slightest beginnings of a paunch.

Giving her another friendly—brotherly? not ardent or flirtatious, at least—smile, the man who was almost King and Emperor unhurriedly took up a silken robe that was draped over a side table. It was of the deepest, most exquisite royal blue and embroidered with the royal arms on the breast. He donned it, and only as he tied up the sash did Rose see what had been lying on the polished tabletop beneath it.

A wickedly long-barreled pistol.

The Prince took up the pistol and dropped it into one of the robe's deep front pockets, kept his hand in there with it, slid his feet into leather slippers, and said, "Walk with me, Lady. I wanted to meet you."

"Of course, sir," Lady Rose replied.

The Prince led the way through another door, along a passage and through yet another door that he unlocked by thrusting his fingers into the correct few of a cross-shaped pattern of many holes.

It gave into a private courtyard, open to the sky in the heart of Foxden, where flowers and small trees overhung a massive stone bench by a tiny pool. He indicated wordlessly that she should sit on the bench. When she did so, he sat down beside her.

Not like a suitor, or a gossip, but like an old friend reclining at ease on a bench somewhere in the rolling countryside.

"We've met before, you know," the Lord Lion said softly, gazing into the pool. "You were a little thing then, of course, and so was I. Forgive me if my . . . paramours offend or unsettle you. Despite what Lil implied, it is not my intention to seduce you. I have plenty of that when I . . . desire it, and find myself more in need of loyal people I can trust. You came armed, of course?"

"No, sir, nor do I—"

The Prince took the pistol from his pocket and clapped it into her hand. "Royal gift, and it comes with a royal command: have it with you at all times, and keep it loaded. If Buckingham hasn't arranged for shooting practice for you, I'll see that he does. Hope you'll never need it, but I'm afraid we both know the world better than to consider such hopes as anything more than forlorn."

He reached under the bench, felt to the right until his reaching arm was almost under her, then pulled back, dragging a plain, dark, and evidently heavy metal box out into view. It opened with the flip of a simple clasp to reveal several pistols and bullets for them. Selecting the smallest, the Prince Royal loaded it with the swift ease of a hunter handling a familiar weapon and put it into the same pocket that had held the gun he'd just given her.

Then he turned to face Rose, looked her straight in the eye, and asked, "So, what do you think of me?"

"Sir," Rose replied quietly, aware she was blushing again, "I hardly know you. I've heard rather more truth about the Lord Lion than, say, the press offers, or widows gossiping in Wapping, yet even so, I know the lord regnant, not the man."

The Prince waved her words aside with a casual hand. "Of course. Forgive my politeness. Let me speak more bluntly. Does what you've been told of my behavior disgust you?"

"No," Rose told him steadily, "not at all. I cannot be a bold champion of women being allowed to be their own masters and to live their own choice and style of life as much as circumstances and money allow yet deny that same freedom to one who is supposed to enjoy the most mastery within our Empire—yet carries such a burden of demands, expectations, and time-taking practicalities as to have all too little real freedom."

The Prince nodded, and there was approval in his eyes. "Well said. And yet?"

"No, sir, there is no 'yet.' Truly. You of all men have every right to do as you please, with whom you please, as often as you please. I do not judge."

She smiled, for a fleeting instant, and saw her pleasure reflected in the Prince's face. He wore the same expression that her father had done from time to time, and she had never forgotten what he'd said the first time she'd exclaimed at it—that he found himself wishing he could see her smile longer and more often, for her smile lit up her face.

"So long," she added dryly to the Lord Lion, "as my father used to say, you frighten not the horses."

"Ah, yes, your father. I remember him very favorably. You miss him."

"Of course. The passing of my parents forced me to become what they had been, even with my aunts and my brothers as my elders. None of us are carefree younglings any longer."

The Prince nodded. "A common affliction," he agreed, in tones as dry as hers. "Buckingham will have briefed you, or had someone brief you—but not enough. Never enough. Not a woman; they always believe there are some things better left unsaid. You are aware that I have more than my share of enemies, even within the Empire."

It was not a question; Rose nodded.

"Have you been told anything of Lady Roodcannon?"

"No, sir. I know the Lady Constance Roodcannon to be beautiful, and can call her face to mind readily, for I have seen her at many exhibitions of art. Bold, bright-edge-of-the-moment art. Which she sponsors and invests in, I'm given to understand."

"Indeed. That she does. You will also have heard that she and I were lovers for more than a decade."

"Yes, sir. All the Empire knows."

"And does all the Empire know the danger she poses to the Lion Throne now?"

Rose shook her head, genuinely puzzled. "No."

"It did not end well between us, and she went to the Continent."

Again, a flat statement.

Rose inclined her head. "That much, I do know, and I believe most of the Empire heard."

"This is not to be bruited about, but—Roo has become my deadliest foe. Although I knew it not at the time, she departed England then for a remote Austrian castle, bearing my child within her."

Rose winced. She did not need the import of *that* spelled out for her, but the Prince Royal quietly and calmly did so.

"Her year was spent in hiding effective enough that she gave birth to my son without anyone in England knowing. She has reared and controls the child, who is thus far my only progeny. So if I should die—a demise she seeks to hasten—she will no doubt emerge as my 'secret bride,' produce my Lionel as the royal heir, and rule as Regent. With the backing of certain lords whose identities Buckingham is very busily trying to uncover. Thus far without much success."

"Your Royal Highness, why are you telling me this?"

"I *hate* secrets, Rose Harminster. They may be the grease and oil that enable the gears and pistons of the Empire to turn daily, but they are poison between persons. I want no secrets between us, or any I consider trustworthy and loyal. And I very much want to trust you and rely on your loyalty."

"Sir," Rose almost whispered, "you have it."

The Prince tilted his head and gave her an arch look. "Careful, Lady Rose. Don't say that next line."

"Might they be the words, 'Take me, O my Prince'?" she asked, with an impish grin.

The Prince Royal threw back his head and guffawed, then thrust out his hand to clasp hers and shake it heartily, as if she were a man.

"Buckingham," he said happily, "has chosen well."

Jack Straker ran and ran toward the light, but it seemed to recede around him, leaving only darkness, a flickering gloom as hot and sulphurous as hell, complete with sparks. And now flames, too, raging up around him as he raced desperately on, though the light he sought was ever farther away, and he was—he was—

Gasping and springing up from a hard surface beneath his

shoulders, panting into bright lights above him that were shining down into his eyes except where a burly shoulder blocked them. The solid dark shoulder of . . . Theo Standish.

The man from the Yard was bending over him. Straker peered up and managed to husk, "You missed me that much? My, my."

"Lord Tempest," the beagle said grimly, "you shouldn't be alone for this."

"For what?" Straker asked. Standish just shook his head. His cheeks were wet.

Standish *crying*?

Tempest fought to sit up. He hurt all over, and his arms didn't seem to obey him; he was shaking like an unbalanced steam engine by the time he managed it, and it took him a moment or three to clear his head and focus.

Corpses. Corpses on tables just like his, ranged down the room, and right beside him—

Iolanthe?

No. No. But it was. Part of him wanted to scream *Nooooo!* even as his eyes told him, yes, yes.

He looked at Standish, Standish looked back, and as if from a great distance Lord Tempest heard himself mutter, "Oh, *hell*. Boiler-bursting, steam-sparking hell."

And then he started to cry.

Somewhere in the torrent of helpless weeping, Standish silently came and clasped his shoulder.

Jack tried to turn to his friend, tried to form words, but . . . they wouldn't come. His old friend lifted him up into a sitting position and wrapped strong arms around him.

They sobbed together.

OCTEMBER 8

Norbert Marlshrike was getting a mite weary of presenting himself like a naughty schoolboy before the various leaders of the Ancient Order, but if doing so was the price of funding his experiments . . .

The footman escorting him opened the towering, magnificently carved wooden door before him with a white-gloved hand, stepped back, and indicated that his charge should enter with a silent, understated flourish.

Marlshrike gave him a polite nod and did so, striding forward on the crimson carpet with as strong and unconcerned an air of confidence as he could, coming to the inevitable stop at the spot where he was forced to by the arrangement of furniture in the room.

He was in a private chapel, and the gap where his carpeted route passed between the two sides of the altar rail had been blocked by filling it with a prie-dieu. That prayer desk didn't match the rest of the furniture, so it must have been hastily brought from elsewhere.

Ahead, the carpet ascended two steps to the former apse, which had been cleared of altar, font, and pulpit to accommodate a huge, spire-topped, carved wooden throne facing squarely down the carpet at him. Seated at it, framed by a magnificent round stained-glass window behind her in the Garandin style of "airships and smokestacks conquering the stars," sat the Lady Constance Roodcannon, at ease, her long legs crossed over each other. Standing silently behind the left end of the throne was her watchful armed bodyguard Grimstone, all in black leather, his eyes cold as they measured Marlshrike. In one hand he held a steam-propelled dart gun pointed at the ceiling and emitting lazy curls of steam as the unseen piston that maintained its pressure slowly rose and fell; in the other, in just as ostentatious a display of menace, he hefted a glass globe that contained a hungry, angry viper, ready to hurl.

Lady Roodcannon was as beautiful as ever, from her lush mouth to her deliciously rounded bosom, which the leather stomacher—or whatever women called them these days; Norbert Marlshrike paid little attention to feminine fashion—she wore supported, uplifted, and displayed. Her leather gown was slit high, so all could see that her unblemished and curvaceous legs were as ivory white as her shoulders and bosom; her jewelry was tiny and exquisite; her raven-black hair lustrous, straight, and seemed almost impossibly long—and her large, liquid black eyes were as cold and lizardlike as ever.

She was stunningly beautiful, but to gaze into those eyes was to shiver, or have to suppress doing so.

"Report, creature," she murmured, as if teasingly encouraging a lover.

Marlshrike stiffened from the effort of quelling a shudder, managed a polite smile and a briefly bent head, such as a butler might give the lady he served and respected, and said, "I enjoy *some* progress with the five keys. However, the Iron Assassin continues to wander the countryside. Completely uncontrolled, so far as I have been able to establish. The junior members of the Order you so graciously assigned to me have been most helpful in searching for Straker's creation and reporting back to me as I experiment. Their observations confirm that no matter what I do to any of the mechanisms—short of dismantling or destroying any of them, of course—the Assassin is entirely unaffected and shows no signs of knowing control attempts have been made."

"So the keys might in future prove useful to us, if you alter someone—five someones—so as to be controlled by them."

"Indeed. There is a possibility of modifying at least one of the five keys to try to control the Silent Man, and I believe I now know how to go about doing this. It will take some time, and further experimentation—but far less of both than procuring and preparing five new assassins."

"Then do so," she ordered. "With all speed. Grimstone will show you out."

Well, "all speed" obviously meant "waste not a second longer" in courtesies.

That had been close to the shortest meeting of his life.

He must take care that it did not also turn out to be one of the last meetings of his life.

H e fell back onto the table, eyes and throat raw. Cried out. For now.

"Standish," he husked. "There's something I must tell you."

"Not now, Jack," the Yard man said gently. "Let it fade. Once said, it can't be—"

"Beagle work, damn it," Straker croaked. "That fire was set to kill me and make sure I couldn't quickly make more keys, and to hide the fact that my early mechanisms were gone. Stolen. Someone, probably the Ancient Order, has the control keys to compel five assassins."

"*Five?*" Standish swore.

"But not the Iron Assassin; *I* still have that key. My most advanced control mechanism." He fished in his pocket and held it up triumphantly.

A blackened fragment fell from its midst.

And then another.

"Oh, *hell*," Jack Straker snarled weakly.

He settled the mask into place, gave his mirror a smirk and a mocking salute, and passed out of the bedchamber through his office, the lush maroon carpet soft and nigh silent underfoot, into the first of the three large galleries of paintings.

Its floor and pillars were of polished marble, the gleaming burl-oak-paneled walls hung with painted scenes of exquisite beauty, many of them larger than many barn doors, there were two even larger rooms, similarly adorned, beyond this one—and it was his, all his.

Oh, this stately pile was inherited, of course, but although he'd spent lavishly, he'd made far more, and his wealth was increasing month to month. Much of it ill-gotten, but what of that? Neither a king nor pontiff could claim that every coin was gained justly and ethically—not if they had any acquaintance with honesty at all.

That thought took him through the last gallery and down a back stair of polished marble and windows as tall as four men to a grand and gilded ballroom that stood empty and almost dark, with only one of the new electric chandeliers lit.

He crossed it, his gilt-heeled boots echoing down its deserted length, passed through a retiring room beyond, flung open a door himself because his servants had all been forbidden to come near this part of the house until noon tomorrow, and stepped into a back hall where eight people stood waiting.

They were murmuring together, but the talk died in an instant at his appearance. Gratifying.

They were all masked—one woman and seven men—and were garbed as finely and expensively as he was. Small wonder, for they were all fellow nobility and fellow senior members of the Ancient Order.

"Uncle," one of the eldest men greeted him politely.

He inclined his head in silent reply, then announced to them all, "I've decided to put our plans on hold for the nonce. Marlshrike is experimenting with a means of controlling the Iron Assassin that should meet with success, and in time give us the ability to send out our own compelled assassins—half a dozen or so. That is so valuable a goal that I don't want to get in his way. Moreover, Auntie has earned the right to try her scheme first."

"Roodcannon, always Roodcannon," one of the masked men— "Cousin Alfred," though that was very far from being his real name— complained. "She's barely one of us! Doesn't even ride to the hounds!"

"She's spoken to me of villainy and opposing the Prince Royal as some sort of *game*," said another scornfully. "To be pursued for entertainment's sake, not for the greater good."

"Nevertheless," Uncle told them sternly, "she *has* made the best progress so far and deserves the right to proceed." He shrugged. "Should she fall at the next fence, well, she'll have weakened the royal forces substantially, making all of our strivings much easier. So we sit back, and watch, and *wait*—is this quite clear?"

Reluctantly and raggedly, under his watchful eye, they all muttered "yes."

The last of them to do so—the woman known here only as "Blushing Niece"—had just given her acceptance, in a thin-lipped, far-less-than-pleased manner, when a bell set high on the wall chimed suddenly, once.

Taken aback, the eight stared up at it, but Uncle strolled unhurriedly to uncap a speaking tube in the wall beneath it and ask, "Yes?"

"Our eyes in Tower Street, sir, say two bodies have been brought in and laid out on a table in the station. Lady Hailsham and Lord Tempest. Both dead."

The eight broke into startled applause, but Uncle frowned.

"*Tempest* dead! Are you sure?"

"So our source says, sir. She drowned, and he blown up when a bomb went off in his London rooms."

"Auntie's doing?" Cousin Alfred asked skeptically. "*This* subtlety is what you want us to let unfold?"

Uncle ignored that, instead saying into the speaking tube, "Get there *now* and make very certain as to who is alive and who is dead, Whipsnade, and report back just as soon as you can—but don't let yourself be recognized."

"Yes, sir."

Uncle covered the speaking tube.

"If Straker's dead," he told the gathered Order members grimly, "that leaves Marlshrike as the only man in the world who knows how to control iron assassins. And if he blows himself up experimenting . . ."

"So what do we do?"

"Steal Marlshrike from Auntie and procure some more expendable experimenters for her to 'find' as his replacement," Uncle replied promptly.

"I don't know . . ." one of the men said uneasily.

"Of *course* you don't—and, yes, of course it's a gamble for us all," Uncle snapped. "Bids for power are never easy and are always fraught with daring chances, worry, and setbacks. If they weren't, we'd all be trampled underfoot in the thunderous rush of every sooty-faced, horn-handed factory jack out there to mount their own bid for power."

He strode for the door he'd come in by but turned to add over his shoulder, "Remember that, and think on it when your nights are sleepless, as I do. Because one day—and I pray it be long after we are all dead, gone to graves gently after rich, long, and full lives—they will. Rise up, every last one of them, admitting no betters, and try to snatch the gold rings and high houses for their own. And God save the Empire then!"

Rose sighed, not for the first time, and stared out the window again. At what little could be seen in the first hint of dawn of what she knew to be a pleasant little slice of garden, sheltered between this wing of Foxden and the next, which hadn't yet in her admittedly short experience of Foxden seemed to be populated by anything more than the occasional butterfly. It was sharing a cool breeze with the room, but it wasn't a vista that changed much. She quelled a second, welling sigh.

"Once more into the waiting arms of incipient boredom," Hardcastle remarked with a smile, looking up from trimming his nails with a pocket knife. He was reclining on a couch displaying every evidence of contentment at being idle, whereas Rose itched to be up and *doing*.

She let out her sigh, and said as much.

Hardcastle shrugged. "I long ago lost track of how much of my life has been wasted just sitting around and waiting. Yet, believe me, I *do* know how you feel. It used to eat at me, too."

"So tell me: how did you come to accept it? the waiting?"

Hardcastle shrugged. "Had an employer once who told me if I couldn't manage sitting silently thinking, he'd set me to work digging my way down to Hades, shovelful by shovelful, and I could pass all waiting times that way. Well, my back soon told me that sitting quiet was preferable."

"So tell me," Rose bade gently, genuinely curious, "how you came to work with Ja—with Lord Tempest."

Hardcastle blinked. "Long story." When her glance told him she seemed silently ready to hear every word of it, he stared at the ceiling for a moment, then said, "Like many another less than brilliant but moneyed men of my generation, I've always invested in more than a few of the constant stream of steam-driven innovations of the Empire. Whatever caught my eye, y'know."

He put away his knife unhurriedly. Rose practiced mute acceptance of waiting.

"I can't remember just now how Straker and I first got thrown together, but we found soon enough that we liked each other. Trust. That's what it is, above all; we trust each other. We once got around to talking investments of an evening, and we were in my rooms at the time, so of course I hauled out all my share certificates and notes of hand and receipts—no doubt you've seen plenty, and know how grand they look, all printed up with blazons and engraved scenes of towers soaring to the stars and fleets of airships crowding the sky and suchlike."

He chuckled. "Straker sorted through them in a trice, told me I had three worthwhile investments out of the lot and two more that might break even—and that all the rest were dross. He heaped them up, swept them aside, and told me I should consider that money lost to me but keep them in the faint, faint hope that we could both be pleasantly surprised by a ship coming in or a dead nag somehow finishing first. He told me that what I was buying was hope, and some of those selling it were out-and-out swindlers and liars, and others were deluded by their own hopes. My good bets, he said, were just that: good bets. My bad ones were . . . foolish wagers."

"Good heavens," Rose said faintly. "I inherited cases and cases of grand-looking shares from Father. I've looked through them, but . . ."

"Well, if I were you, I'd let our mutual friend Lord Tempest look them over. You see, I took him up on a wager that night: we'd haul them all out again in a year and see if he'd been right. If he was wrong, he'd pay me double the amount he was out by, in gold bars—

don't ask me where he intended to come by them—but if he was right, I'd take his guidance eight times out of ten in my investments thereafter. Well, he was right on every count, of course, and just between you and me, I've been guided by him every time I've laid out money since—and I've done quite well."

"So far," Rose cautioned.

"Indeed, but 'so far' has been seventeen years now, and I've made the proverbial pots of money. Particularly in the mass steam-cooking of meals, hams, sides of beef—and the steam-cleaning of rugs, linens, and clothes as a byproduct of factory-machinery steam emissions." He sat up and added proudly, "Doing the clothes was actually my notion, so Jack invested in me—and rode the men we hired hard when they tried to do sideline work on our coins and hand us the costs, too. He's not just a toff; he can let fly with his fists in alleys with the best—ah, against the worst—of them."

Rose studied Hardcastle with increasing interest. "And are you more comfortable with the toffs, or in the alleys?"

"Left to myself, the toffs, every time. It's what I was reared to, you see. Clubs and hunting, riding, and shooting. But standing at the elbow of Jack Straker has shown me alleyways enough to see, well, the bones of the Empire, what all the rest stands on. Lord Tempest is Jack Straker, and Jack Straker isn't all that far from a dockworker or a miner—except for his brilliant brain and how he uses it. He *cares*."

"You admire him."

"How could I not? He's . . . beyond envy. I just watch the fire and fun, and feel honored to know him. We've been as thick as thieves for a long time, now. Every man needs a confidant, even those sworn to secrecy, and we've been that for each other. Though he kept every hint of his work on this Iron Assassin hidden from me until he demonstrated it at Lessingham's, he did!"

"Well . . . perhaps he thought it might all come to nothing, and so was better kept secret until it, ah, flourished."

"Perhaps," Hardcastle replied, sounding unconvinced. Then he leaned forward to peer sharply at Rose, and asked, "So, now, you tell me: what d'you think about this business here and now, with seemingly half the sinister sorts in the Empire thinking up deviltry against the Lord Lion?"

Rose shrugged. "Those born to wealth can be as spiteful as anyone else, and too many of them measure their worth in small and petty victories over those they wish to tear down. Unlike those whose hours are filled with work, they have time enough to indulge their . . . unpleasantness to others. I've heard the gossip, and have come to suspect that the Dowager Duchess is probably behind all of these machinations against the Prince Royal."

Hardcastle smiled wryly. "Well, she's spiteful enough, I'll give you that. But I've met her, and I'd peg her as small-minded and lazy, too. Incapable of subtle organization or sustained drive. Moreover, I've overheard both Tempest and Harkness—he's the top beagle; forgive my presumption if you already know that—say they believe Lady Roodcannon and—or perhaps it's 'or,' but they're both leaning towards 'and'—the heads of the Ancient Order of Tentacles are manipulating the Duchess."

Rose's eyebrows rose. Her escort was more than a good-natured and gallant thickhead, for all his simple-soul manner. Being a Sworn Sword certainly meant you encountered interesting people. Increasingly interesting . . .

Through the window came the sudden crunch of carriage wheels—and hooves—on gravel. Rose hastily got up and went into the other room to peer through the sheers covering its bay window.

A window that afforded a view of the graveled turning circle before the front doors of Foxden. Seeing all arrivals was, after all, part of her job. The lamps flanking the doors were lit, and in their glow she beheld a closed coach, drawn by horses. Two women who looked on the saucy side, and also familiar with Foxden, alighted.

"Time for me to play at being lady doctor," Rose murmured, and started for the door.

"'Play'?" Hardcastle asked gently.

Rose froze, abruptly aware that she'd given the game away and remembering Tempest's warning that his friend Hardcastle didn't know either of them were Sworn Swords—and mustn't learn as much from her.

"Lady Rose?"

"I—I must go," she said hurriedly, and rushed off down the passage. Only to hear his swift footfalls behind her.

She stopped and turned, and Mister Bleys Hardcastle came to a hasty halt mere inches from slamming into her.

They stood nose to nose for a moment, looking into each other's eyes.

"It's all right," he murmured, as if he was soothing an upset younger sister. "So you're one of them, too. A Sword. Like Jack. Be at ease, Lady; I've known all about that for years. I don't let on, because it's easier for us both. For the three of us, now. Worry not; your secret is safe with me."

"I . . . thank you," Rose told him, and meant it. "Thank you. Yet I *must* go."

"Of course," he agreed, bowing his head and waving her off down the passage like a flamboyant butler. "Scream if you need me."

I've about decided," Jack Straker told his old friend wearily, "that I've seen enough of the peeling paint up there. Somewhere above us, the roof of Tower Street Station *leaks*."

He rolled onto one hip with a groan of pain, stepped down off the table—and promptly crashed headlong to the floor.

Standish rushed to him and hauled him upright. Straker groaned again.

"You've been burned and hurled a good distance by an explosion," the beagle reminded him grimly. "Flesh and blood, not steam-driven pistons and clockwork, remember?"

"I create things," Straker panted, standing only by virtue of the arm he had around Standish's shoulders, "and discover things. Just now, I've discovered—the hard way—that I'm too badly hurt to even *walk* without assistance. Damn it."

"Chair," Standish replied curtly, pointing across the room, and started helping him in that direction.

Behind them, the door banged open, and a young beagle who was panting in his haste burst into the room.

"Chief Inspector, sir! Doings in Knightsbridge! The Lord Tempest's rooms have been ransacked! I—*oh*." The beagle had just seen the face of the man crumpling gratefully into the chair, and recognized the very peer he'd just mentioned.

He looked to Standish uncertainly for orders.

Standish looked at Tempest. "Was there anything there the Order—or anyone else—shouldn't get to see?"

"Yes," Tempest snapped, and tried to struggle to his feet. Only to sag back with a groan of pain.

"Get word to Hardcastle," he gasped. "Tell him I need the blue steamer trunk. The metal one with the three big brass bull's-eye locks. He doesn't know it, but he has custody of my prototype exoskeleton, the first one I fashioned for the Silent Man project. I made it to fit me, so I could try things out and tinker with it. Now, it's going to help me walk."

Lady Rose Harminster reached the front doors of Foxden just as four armed guards—dressed in livery, to seem footmen—opened it to admit the two arrivals. Who promptly screamed as someone loomed up out of the night, rushing for the door with frightening speed. Someone familiar—the dead-faced man who lurched, and whose limbs were encaged in metal!

Even as fear rose crawlingly within her, the coachman and the guards all fired at the lurching man, blazing away repeatedly—as more guards came pounding down several passages, converging on the hall inside the front doors.

At the head of one group of guards ran Malmerston the butler, lugging some sort of weapon. Or rather, he held the aiming part of it, which looked like a long fire nozzle or a shiny silver blunderbuss, and guards right behind him cradled a hose running from it to a large tank with massive projecting handles that six guards were hefting along.

As the Iron Assassin staggered up to the threshold, one arm up to shield his face as if all the bullets and balls striking him were so much slanting rain, Malmerston did something to what he was holding—and it belched out a long jet of flame!

It alone gave the Iron Assassin pause. He backed away, batting clumsily at the flames with both arms, then turned slowly and lurched away into the night.

The coachman stepped into his path, to try to stop him—and got smashed to the ground like a rag doll, his skull crushed with one mighty roundhouse swing that left his brains spattered on the gravel.

The two women who'd come in the coach shrieked wildly.

Malmerston gave Lady Rose a curious look, and she realized she'd drawn the gun the Prince Royal had given her and was holding it up and ready, pointed at the ceiling, in case of immediate need.

"*In*, ladies," she and the butler said in unison, then exchanged half-amused looks.

"You, Lady Harminster," Malmerston murmured, "have been deceiving me. You're rather more than a lady doctor, and even more than the simple spy I took you for. You're a Sworn Sword."

"*Mister* Malmerston!" she protested, with a wink. "You took me for a simple spy? Whatever next?"

That startled a smile out of him.

OCTEMBER 9

The fast carriage was experimental—and *very* noisy—but the jets of scalding steam it emitted almost constantly not only cleared the streets of anyone afoot who might be reluctant to get out of the way of a speeding beagle carriage but also softened the jolting of rushing wheels on cobbles.

For which Lord Tempest, still feeling his burns and bruises, had been heartily thankful. Word of his need had been taken to Foxden, Hardcastle had brought his original exoskeleton to Tower Street, and now the carriage had just jolted to a hissing halt and they were all—that is, the pair of them, Standish, and a brace of beagles he'd ordered along—alighting outside his ransacked Knightsbridge rooms.

It was almost comical, the way they hesitated and hawed over helping an injured lord up the stairs. Perhaps they were wary of the exoskeleton he now wore, and what it might do. They did, after all, taste more danger from dangerously faulty new inventions and deliberately deadly steam-driven weapons, traps, and gewgaws than most citizens of the Empire, to be sure . . .

So Lord Tempest led the way into his own rooms, the exoskeleton he now wore attracting some curious looks from the beagles who'd been left to guard his door, and was soon pleased to discover that whoever had turned his digs upside down had found nothing critical.

"They did a thorough job," Standish commented, peering at what was strewn on the floor.

"Very," Straker replied dryly. "However, what they were sent to find eluded them."

"You're certain of that?"

"Very," Straker repeated, "for it's all here." He went to the doorway into the bedroom, reached up and tugged at the top of the doorframe—and that polished piece of molding came away in his hands. He put it into the grasp of the nearest startled beagle, took hold of the two uprights of the doorframe, and lifted them away from the walls—to reveal a tall, narrow, dark recess on either side of the threshold.

"The top piece acts as a wedge, and the side plates sit in recesses in the threshold, and so can't budge at the bottom."

He drew forth two thin books—which proved not to be books at all but book covers glued to thin wooden frames that held "some of my Investigator Royal stuff; evidence awaiting future use" and "what they were after: some of the tools I fashioned while animating and controlling the Iron Assassin." Sliding the two book frames between his feet to free his hands, Tempest reassembled the doorframe and said, "Board the place up in case they decide to start another fire and let's go."

"Go?"

"Back to examine what's left of Iolanthe," Tempest explained, a little wearily.

"Before she starts to smell," Standish muttered.

Tempest shrugged. "So many stenches have arisen regarding this affair before her unfortunate demise, and now crowd close, that one more reek hardly makes a difference."

Standish nodded sadly, turned, and told the beagles who'd been standing guard to, "Secure that door, so it'll take men with tools some time and a lot of noise to get it open again." Then he said to three of the six beagles who'd come with them from Tower Street, "Back to your regularly assigned duties, lads. Street patrol, yes? By all means stop for a pint on your ways back to your beats."

The beagles nodded and clattered back down the stairs. Wilkins and Summers were young and new to Tower Street, so they didn't think it unusual that the third man, Oldtree, turned left when they were out in the street outside, rather than turning right and walking with them. Not that there was much leisure for thought amid the noise and confusion of the waiting beagle carriage steam cleaning the stretch of cobbles it was standing on and a second and more conventional fast-piston beagle houndcar screeching to a halt behind it and disgorging Sergeant Blunt, who rushed past them and entered the building they'd just left in haste.

"Blunt!" Standish greeted him on the stairs, as the remainder of the group who'd come from Tower Street descended. "What news?"

Blunt peered at Lord Tempest and Mister Hardcastle for only a doubtful instant before reporting, "The man Miles Whipsnade was seen by one of us on duty outside Pitt's last night to have been driving Lord Winter's carriage—in which he took Lord Winter and Lady Hailsham away."

Standish frowned. "So you've detained him for questioning?"

"No, sir. That I did not. He has a guest in his rooms, sir, and they've been drinking."

"So?"

"The guest is Sir Fulton Birtwhistle."

"The magistrate?"

"The magistrate. Sir."

Standish uttered something unprintable, then snapped, "We'll go and question him anyway. With all due civility, of course. Get a houndcar."

"One brought me, sir." And so it was that in short order Tempest, Hardcastle, Standish, and Blunt rushed off to Whipsnade's lodgings, while the other beagles took the experimental carriage more sedately back to Tower Street.

L ady Rose Harminster stood watching from a doorway, bemused. It seemed Lil and one of the new arrivals, Bess, were *very* close friends.

She'd gone to their rooms to make her examination of the two new arrivals in accordance with the role she was playing—only to find herself watching Lil and Bess, now clad in spectacular clockwork gowns of burnished copper, embracing and kissing.

And then, rather more than embracing.

As they gasped and moaned, lips locked together, the cogs on the bodices of their gowns meshed, whirring together and causing clamps to close on their nipples, then tug rhythmically to stretch those points of flesh for mutual pleasure, as their fingers grew busy below . . .

"Good heavens!" Rose whispered to herself, blinking.

"Oh, I doubt goodness has all that much to do with it, ma'am," Malmerston murmured in her ear, sounding amused, as he glided past her into the room, to set down two large goblets of strong drink handy on a table beside the amorous pair.

W e're looking into the disappearance of the Lady Iolanthe Hailsham," Chief Inspector Standish explained gravely, "and it seems that you, sir, were among the last persons seen in her presence last night."

"Seen by whom, Inspector?" Sir Fulton Birtwhistle snapped.

"By a member of the Queen's High Constabulary, on duty," Standish said calmly, as if continuing his query to Whipsnade rather than answering the eminent magistrate. "So I was hoping you could confirm for us in what capacity you were in the company of Lady Hailsham and the circumstances—and precise whereabouts—in which you saw her last."

"Disappeared, has she?" Whipsnade asked. "Do the beagles really keep this close a watch over all nobles? One slips out to a bed not their own overnight, and the beagles come around asking after them before the sun is fully up?"

"Mister Whipsnade is commenting in an abstract, hypothetical sense," Birtwhistle interjected smoothly, "rather than making any specific inference as to Lady Hailsham's behavior, last night or in general."

"Is he, now?" Sergeant Blunt asked, looking up from his notebook.

"Is this a formal interrogation?" Birtwhistle snapped. "I haven't heard you caution my—" He stopped, abruptly, and shut his mouth like a trap.

"Was 'client' the word you were heading for?" Standish asked mildly. "It seems only right, if we're being so careful about the niceties, Sir Birtwhistle, for you to tell us if you and Mister Whipsnade have discussed Lady Hailsham between, say, yesterday morning, last night, and right now? Or Mister Whipsnade's whereabouts and doings last night?"

"I resent the inference of any conspiracy between my *friend* and myself," Birtwhistle snapped, "or that I have any involvement at all in . . ."

He stopped himself again.

"In what, sir?" Standish asked quietly. "You were going to say?"

Whipsnade grinned, cast a swift look at Birtwhistle—and then recoiled at something across the room. Standish and Hardcastle both looked to see what Whipsnade had shied away from and was now firmly averting his gaze from.

Lord Tempest was standing as still as a statue, ignoring everyone in the room but Whipsnade. His face was calm and at rest, but his eyes were riveted on Whipsnade, and despite his silence fairly shouted cold malice.

"I-in whatever you're investigating," Sir Fulton Birtwhistle said hastily.

"Your concern is noted," Blunt told him, with the thinnest hint of contempt. Just enough to be unmistakable, but not enough to be seized upon and complained about; Blunt was a veteran of the force.

"So, Mister Whipsnade?" Standish pressed.

"What?"

"I am still hoping you can confirm for us in what capacity you were in the company of Lady Hailsham and tell us all about where you saw her last and what you were doing at that time and what you observed her to be doing."

Whipsnade drained his glass, turned his back on the Inspector, and strolled away—not to his decanter, but in the vague direction of the nearest window. He did not speak.

"If the surroundings and company are distracting you, we could take your statement down at the Yard," Standish murmured. "In a nice, quiet room."

"Chief Inspector Standish," the magistrate snapped, "you would do well to remember that the Queen's High Constabulary are charged—in the very act that created the organization, and gives it the authority it enjoys—to treat innocent citizens *as* innocent citizens, and politely, too!"

"I was unaware that I had been anything less than polite. I believe this lord and this gentleman with me, and the written record the sergeant is maintaining, will attest to the courtesy with which I have treated Mister Whipsnade thus far. I was merely making a helpful suggestion as to how he could most easily assist us in our inquiries, and so more swiftly return to his own doings, unhampered by our presence and interest."

With that, Standish strolled past Birtwhistle, to where Whipsnade would have to face him when he turned around. "Mister Whipsnade?"

"As you are no doubt already aware," Whipsnade told the window, not turning, "I am employed as coachman to Lord Winter. In that capacity, I called on Lady Hailsham and took her to Pitt's, to dine with my employer, and after their meal—which was not a hurried affair, and was concluded late at night, or rather early this morning—I drove her and Lord Winter, in Lord Winter's carriage, back to her London home. She was, if I may venture a boldness, rather sleepy at that time, possibly thanks to the rich food and her enjoyment of my lord's selection of wine, but seemed in perfect health and control of herself when I opened her gate for her, and she passed through it and onwards. Polite good nights were exchanged—without any physical contact between us, I might add—and I closed the gate again and took my lord home. He can confirm all of this, as no doubt Lady Hailsham will do when she reappears from wherever she's gone and you have the opportunity to question her."

He turned around and managed a smile—but everyone in the room noticed he did not look directly at the motionless and silent Lord Tempest.

"So how late, or early, was it, when you closed Lady Hailsham's gate? What was the weather, at that time?"

"Dark," Whipsnade replied. "It's a condition frequently associated with nighttime."

"Not the best of time for a jest," Blunt told his notebook. Birtwhistle stirred, as if to make complaint at that, but caught the eye of Standish and lapsed back into silence.

Standish took another slow and deliberate step forward, and Whipsnade gave way a half step and added hastily, "As to the precise time, I really can't say, Inspector. When you're standing in the damp and cold, with the horses, and others are inside in the warm and you can hear laughter and see lamplight and know the toffs are having a good time, it *seems* forever. The meal was longish, but as to how long exactly, I really can't say." He fell silent, then added, "I do hope you find her."

"Thank you, Mister Whipsnade," Standish told him gravely. "It seems likely we'll have further questions for you in future, as we confirm details from others. For now, good day." ·

He turned, gave Tempest a "come now, and no trouble" look, and made for the door. Blunt closed his book, Birtwhistle relaxed visibly, Hardcastle started to follow Standish—and Tempest stood like a stone.

A glaring stone.

Birtwhistle noticed and stirred again, but Hardcastle gave him a warning look, put a firm arm around his friend, and led him out.

T hough the sky was clear but for some wisps of cloud in the distance and the airship above their gondola was scudding gently over green fields, leafy woodlots, and the occasional church spire of the English countryside, the breeze whistling past was flirting with icy.

The three lords facing each other across a hamper of champagne and chilled lobster were masked for this meeting for other reasons than the cold. Lady Roodcannon had good reason to believe the beagles—and others—were training spyglasses on her vessel during daylight flits in these latter months.

"Do *not* make the mistake of underestimating the Lord Chamberlain," she told her two guests sharply. "I, for one, regret the death of Hawkingbrooke. He was a formidable foe, yes, but this mild-mannered, mutton-chopped, fat and blinking seeming buffoon is anything but. Bertram Buckingham is far more capable than the Old Hawk ever was. He watches over the Prince Royal like a hawk indeed—and if we don't arrange an accident for him soon, he'll be well on his way to forever balancing the reputation, safety, and schooling of the heir against the need to keep the ailing Queen supreme in authority and the public's regard and her rule safe from the malcontents who want her gone."

"Your estimation of Buckingham I don't dispute," one lord replied. "Yet I doubt just now is the best time to eliminate him. If we move so heavily and so soon after Hawkingbrooke's demise, we give the Prince Royal the excuse he needs to unleash all his hounds. He'll come for us, evidence be damned, and they'll have instructions to shoot as many of us in the fighting as they can—as traitors trying to escape justice. No, we must be rather more subtle in our timing."

"*Really*, Uncle!" laughed the other lord. "The beagles? You're frightened of the *beagles*? Most of whom can't hit a stable door at ten paces?"

"They're fodder," Uncle replied curtly. "Brave beef, and for the most part plodding, I'll admit. Yet I wasn't referring to them. I meant the other hounds the Prince Royal commands."

"The Sworn Swords?"

"The Sworn Swords. Few and eccentric they may be, but—"

"But *nothing*. Buckingham's so desperate he just named a young *noblewoman* to their ranks. Bringing them to a fighting strength of— what? *Eight*?"

"Dismissing foes too lightly has long been the besetting weakness of the Empire," Lady Roodcannon said quietly. "It saddens me to see the same weakness within our circle. My lords, I thought we were *better* than that."

"We are," Uncle said dryly, lifting a lid and wielding silver tongs. "Lobster tails, anyone?"

Hardcastle assisted Tempest out of the houndcar and kept hold of his friend's arm, steadying him with one hand as he closed the steam carriage's door with the other.

The driver heard the thud and let the conveyance start to move again. Standish watched Blunt peering out the window back at the two men they'd just dropped. When they were out of view and Blunt turned back to him, Standish remarked quietly, "Someone has no doubt at all as to Whipsnade's guilt."

"Five someones, I'd say," Blunt grunted. "You and me, sir, Birtwhistle and Whipsnade himself, and, yes, Lord Tempest."

"Without more evidence, we've no case against Whipsnade at all."

"We need evidence, but I doubt Tempest will wait long for it." Standish smiled mirthlessly. "So we're agreed?"

"That Tempest will get him? That we are, sir. That we are."

No need for men at all," Lil informed Lady Rose proudly. "Not for pleasure, at least. Now, *I* like a man to talk over the shining future of the Empire, *if* he knows what's what, or across the board from me for a good game of chess, or—"

"You play chess?" Rose interrupted, too surprised and delighted to mind full courtesy.

Lil grinned, displaying bad teeth. "Enough to be feared in Macammon's *and* banned in the Ivory Rooms. After I beat all the masters there one afternoon that lasted the evening long. One after another, every last one. They made me a member on the spot—so they could throw me out."

Lady Rose didn't try to hide her openmouthed astonishment. The foremost chess masters in the Empire frequented the Ivory Rooms.

"Fancy a match?" she asked, when she could find the words.

Lil smiled like a lazily hungry cat.

"Of course. I know what I want if I win," she purred, looking Rose up and down, "but what do *you* want? If, perchance, you should best me?"

Rose smiled. "To borrow something for a short time. Just to use here, in Foxden. Set up your board."

"I'll fetch a good Rhenish, some Red Leicester and the blue Cheshire," Malmerston murmured, from the middle distance. "Will you want cigars, ladies?"

It's very late, my lord," Whipsnade commented, bringing the decanter to refill his lordship's glass.

"So it is, Whipsnade, and yet for all the long hours of this evening, you've neglected to tell me about the visitors you entertained in your lodgings this morning."

"I judged it not worth bothering you about." The wine gurgled into the depths of the glass, poured in a hand as steady as always. "You sent around Birtwhistle, his presence made all the difference, I delivered the agreed-upon tale and said nothing more, and the beagles left warning me they'd be back for more. All as you anticipated."

Uncle smiled. "You neglected to mention the presence of Lord Tempest and his toady Hardcastle."

"Ah. Yes, that is an oversight on my part—and I want to assure you, Lord, that I do *not* make a habit of neglecting to tell you things."

"Well?"

"Tempest knows. He gave me the eyes of death all the time they were there. Said not a word, did nothing but stare at me. I've seen that look in men's eyes before. He'll be coming, right enough; we must be ready."

Uncle nodded. "Of course." He raised his glass. "My thanks, Whipsnade. This will be the last of my needs tonight, as it happens."

Whipsnade bowed and withdrew. Headed for the kitchens and the good roast beef dinner that was waiting for him. A routine Uncle had established long ago so that when he at last had need to silence his most useful of servants, the vehicle for the poison would be ready, waiting, and hopefully beyond suspicion.

Alone at last, the man who preferred "Uncle" to his name or title sipped his wine and regarded the dying fire.

He realized he wasn't afraid in the slightest at the prospect of Tempest coming for him.

Rather, he was excited.

OCTEMBER 10

Another bright morning, and another ride in the phaeton out to Foxden. Hardcastle quite enjoyed the trips, with the birds calling and flitting and the grime and steam-driven noise of London falling away in their wake, though admittedly thus far he'd not had to make the journey in the driving rain. Beside him, Lord Tempest seemed in better spirits than he'd been since Lady Hailsham's death.

It was high time to inform Lady Harminster of what they'd learned and to tell her they'd consulted with the Lord Chamberlain yestereve and now, in light of Tempest's injuries, needed her to take a more active role.

The guards tensed at first sight of the exoskeleton, but Straker shook his head and rather ruefully waved them away.

They went in, leaving the phaeton for the guards, and hastened to the rooms Hardcastle and Lady Rose had been given.

Rose's bedchamber door was closed.

Tempest strode straight to it.

"Lady Harminster?" Hardcastle called hastily.

His friend shot him a withering look over one shoulder, flung the door wide, and strode in.

Hardcastle took two swift strides after him and came to an abrupt halt, aghast.

"Good *God*!"

Tempest hadn't stopped but had slowed, once inside the room, to circle the Lady Harminster. An approving smile was rising onto his face.

She was facing away from them but turned unashamedly to greet them. Hardcastle frankly stared.

She wore an extraordinary thing. A gown of copper mail covered with elaborate clockwork, the hips and front overlaid with an intricate labyrinth of interlaced gears, push rods, and mounts that framed an open bodice, where a mere wisp of lace entirely failed to conceal rouged curves. Hardcastle hastily looked elsewhere and saw that gaudily heavy makeup covered her face, too.

Rose's eyes were twinkling with dark challenge.

She turned, one hand on a shapely hip. "*Yes*, sirs? *Is* there something?"

"Lady Harminster!" Hardcastle burst out, unable to conceal his shock. "What—whatever's got into you?"

Almost bare, creamy shoulders lifted in a shrug. "I . . . don't know. But I find I rather like it."

She pirouetted languidly. "You, I take it, do not."

"I . . . I have not said as much, madam. Yet I cannot help but observe that there is no pressing need to look like a cut-rate trol-lop," Hardcastle informed her, desperately seeking some sem-blance of dignity.

"And how, sir, would you know what a cut-rate trollop looks like?" Lady Rose inquired, arching one flashing, gem-adorned eyebrow at him. "Casually interested minds would like to know!"

Tempest's grin had already grown wide; at that, he guffawed.

"Where *did* you get that, ah, rig?" he asked. "Or rather, from one of the Prince's play-pretties, of course, but, ah, why?"

"Having seen one in action, so to speak," she replied—and both men were interested to see that when Lady Harminster blushed, her color flooded from the roots of her hair right down the shapely length of her body to the tips of her delicate toes—"I wanted to try one out. So I borrowed one from Bess Lalbrooke. Purely in the inter-ests of experimentation and innovation, of course."

"Of course," Tempest agreed dryly. "And what—pray tell—did you discover?"

"It looks like a corset mechanically mated to a gown," Hardcas-tle said doubtfully.

"That it is—and more," she purred. "Observe the clockworks here, where my waist is flattest, and how they ascend, gear by gear and rod by rod, to my, ah, breastworks. For lone and private pleasure, to be sure—"

Coy fingers gave the two staring men a momentary glimpse of a demure rose-pink nipple clasped between two copper calipers that stretched and pinched that bud of flesh to make it jut forth in red-dened and presumably painful splendor. Calipers crowned the end of an intricate array of tiny gears descending into the greater link-ages of the corset. Rose did something with her other hand, and with the softest whispering whir, they saw the nipple teased far-ther, then tugged rhymically.

"—but also for the shared delight of a companion."

Her slender fingers did something else to the lowest of a row of small levers above her nearest hip, and two of the gears at the upper front of the corset spun outward on lengthening shafts and extended small claws. Hardcastle could see that their inner ends were directly linked to the movements of the nipple calipers.

"A partner, similarly clad . . ." she murmured, gesturing to indicate imaginary breasts in the air in front of her, equipped alike with claws that could mesh with hers. By way of concluding her sentence, she smiled a catlike smile.

Tempest chuckled and turned to his friend. "A trifle warm in here, isn't it?"

Hardcastle seized his cue with a surge of relief, hastening to reply brightly, "Indubitably! I had indeed noticed as much and attributed it to the sudden rise in the price of potatoes, word of which was all over the streets this morning—such excitement stimulates the blood of every man and woman in all the Empire, and inevitably a general feeling of warmth suffuses . . ."

"You two," Lady Rose told them fondly, "are idiots. *Likable* idiots, mind."

Tempest bowed low, the exoskeleton clanking. "At your service, ma'am."

Then his voice changed, and from the depths of his bent posture he said sharply, "Hardcastle, help me. This damned contraption has jammed. Again."

It was a rare thing indeed, Uncle reflected dryly, to have a uniformed beagle standing in this room.

Yet here one was, as large as life and looking more like a sweating walrus, with that untamed mustache, than a hound of justice. Even a bloodhound of justice.

". . . So you see, Lord, that he had it all hidden in the walls, behind his clever removable doorframe," Oldtree was saying.

"That's all that was in there, those two cases with the contents he described to the inspector?"

"That's all I could see, sir. When they were out, the 'tween walls looked like empty darkness to me. But you never know."

"Indeed. With Tempest, you never know." Uncle smiled softly. "At least the man affords us all endless entertainment. A pity he'll eventually become expendable enough to be eliminated. I shall miss him."

"Miss him? But your aim is getting better," the beagle joked.

He chuckled, but his mirth faltered as Uncle stared at him coldly. Long, stretching, and chill moments passed.

Then, abruptly, Uncle shouted his sudden laughter.

Algernon, this is *delightful*."
    Algernon Hartworth felt himself flushing, but minded not a whit. He felt like he was strolling amid the clouds, a bright and sunlit hero striding along twelve feet tall.

He was with Heliotrope at last, and they were walking hand in hand through the sun-dappled Sefton woods. *His* woods, someday.

The picnic hamper in his hand was heavy with wine and delightful foodstuffs yet felt light as a feather. Every time he saw Heliotrope, she was prettier than their previous meeting, and this afternoon she was positively stunning.

Not to mention willing. She'd kissed him twice now, the first time in full view of his father's favorite window, and the second time she'd pressed herself against him long and ardently enough that he'd felt the full thrusts of her shockingly firm bosom. And once they were in the woods, she'd turned to him and *winked*.

Pistons and boilers, it was enough to make a man ache! He was aching now, but his heart was flying. He laughed aloud at the thought, and threw back his head to give the sky overhead a broad smile.

A mail airship promptly scudded past overhead. Fluffy clouds were drifting lazily across the sky, and the late afternoon sun was golden. It was going to be a glorious sunset, and a warm evening. And just ahead was the little dell, where the brook tumbled past and there was a mossy bank in the shade and a sunny sward where the sun lanced through. Already Heliotrope was exclaiming in delight—

And then Algernon's world turned dark in an instant. There were men in the distance, on the path ahead—masked and gloved men in dark suits, some of them with pistols in their hands. They were looking his way. *Heading* his way.

Trespassers! In *his* woods! Eight of them, no, eleven—twelve!

"Heliotrope," he said warningly, but she had already gasped in alarm, and her hand had tightened around his.

Algernon swung her around as if she'd been a prize pony, and said, "*Run!*"

And they ran, hands still clasped, leaping like frightened rabbits, hearts pounding, stumbling in their panting haste. Sneering laughter rose behind them but seemed at least to stay well behind them.

They kept on running, past the folly and down the hill, until they were back at the great house, where they came to a panting halt and looked back.

To see no pursuit at all. Not a single masked man. The Sefton lands, rising up green and rolling, looked peaceful and deserted under the warm sun.

"Heliotrope," Algernon said urgently, "go inside and right up to the parlor where we met. Take this. Tell the servants that there are intruders on our land, and they are to close and bar the doors and tell my father. Take this; you'll be hungry once you're settled."

She clung to him, eyes large and frightened. "But—but *Algy*! You can't be thinking of going back!"

He met her eyes, feeling more heroic than ever, and said grimly, "I must. This is my land, and they're up to no good; the beagles must be told what they're up to, and my father warned. He'll want details, to know how best to respond; my duty is clear."

"Oh, Algernon!" she breathed, eyes bright with admiration.

"We'll have our time together, no fear," he murmured, giving her a kiss that left her gasping and blushing crimson. Then he whirled away from her with a wave and started running back up the hill.

And as he went, all his gallantry left him, and his fear, too, and all that remained was a rising anger.

An anger so deep he wanted to cry. Gone were his disputes with his father, his insecurity, his self-loathing at being a headstrong ignoramus. He was a Hartworth, a Sefton, the youngest lord of a long line of gruff, fierce lords who'd fought for what they had and fought against those who crossed them. He'd see these blackguards taught a lesson that would warm their backsides and make them quail at the thought of ever setting foot on Sefton land again.

Oh, he'd not do battle this day. Not one against a dozen, and some or all of them armed against his bare and empty hands. No, once past the folly he'd stop running and do off his tweeds, then put on the old beekeeping darks and turn spy.

He wanted to see what this lot were up to, here on his land. He'd go creeping like a fox, and peer and listen, and find out.

Hopefully discovering something that would see them all hanged and win him the approval of Father, and . . .

Bah! Time for daydreaming later. They had *guns*; he could be dead soon, if luck or the gods weren't with him.

Yes, there was the hut, and the key was still hidden where it always was, in the little buried-to-its-brim clay pot by the old stump, and he was out of tweeds and the white silk shirt beneath and into the old black—long since sun-faded and dirt-smirched to mottled brown—beekeeper's overalls and hood. He caught up the gloves, too, and traded his brogues for the old boots, then closed up the hut again, put the key back, and started creeping.

He'd done this for hours in play, not really all that many years ago, but this time it was for deadly real, and he must be the Horned Hunter so well and so silently that they wouldn't see him.

There was a game trail that climbed to the right of the path he'd been walking along with Heliotrope, and he took it, crawling on hands and knees, moving purposefully but not hurrying. If he got too hasty . . .

He must assume they'd posted sentinels, or he'd be seen before he saw them. And it would only take one shot . . .

There! There they were, all dozen of them. Down on the path he and Heliotrope had taken. So they hadn't come after him. No, they were clustered around someth—digging! They were digging . . . but digging what?

Cautiously, he worked his way closer, from tree to tree, keeping low and making no sudden movements. It was confoundedly hot in the hood, and the sweat was running down his face so fast and hard it was dripping from his chin in an almost-constant stream. His favorite silk shirt would have been ruined.

The masked men were finishing their work now, letting down short ropes to help each other clamber out of their creation. It looked to be nothing more than a big pit—right in the middle of the path. A pit they were now covering with those same ropes, crisscrossed. Dirt and leafy boughs were being tossed on the ropes, and then a large mat with vines and old branches sewn to it was being laid out over the ropes, to completely cover the pit. Handfuls of dirt were being enthusiastically scattered over it.

Algernon peered hard at the trees around the pit, trying to fix what they looked like in his mind so he'd know exactly where the pit was, for later. The masked men had chosen a spot where the path was overlooked by several old trees that had been pollarded years ago but then left to grow on their own since, so they sprouted a great number of large boughs, in all directions, fairly low down. Great climbing trees, if he'd still been six summers old. Or a masked man—because they were all climbing up into those trees now, leaving the path suddenly deserted, the pit hidden.

Algernon sat down behind his own current tree, not knowing what to do but deciding for now to do as the masked men: wait in hiding. For whatever they were waiting for. It *looked* like they were hoping to capture a person or beast coming unawares along the path, but who would come—*he* would! He, himself, with Heliotrope.

Was this some sort of crazed scheme to get a ransom? Or kidnap nobles into slavery? It sounded like something out of a cheap book of derring-do, but—

There came a loud but distant crashing then, from another part of the woods, and the men up in the trees jumped down and went racing away along the path toward the disturbance. Which, if he'd placed it right, was farther along the path, which curved in that direction . . .

Hardly thinking, Algernon Hartworth was on his feet and racing after them. Keeping back in the trees, but within good sight of the path and the mob of running men.

Some of whom suddenly let out shouts and vanished!

They'd—yes, they'd fallen down *another* pit trap in the path! Obviously they'd misjudged its precise location. The rest of the men kept right on running, leaving behind those in the pit, and, amid all their crashings of footfalls and yelling, Algernon abandoned all stealth and sprinted to catch up with them.

He soon came to their destination and hastily swung himself behind two close-grown trees, panting, to watch.

They were manhandling a struggling man up out of yet another pit. Their captive was wrapped up in what looked to be the borrowed shrouds from a ship. Yes, the mesh of thick, knotted ropes from a ship's rigging.

As Algernon stared, flabbergasted—what, by all that was holy, was going *on?*—the captured person fought. Whoever it was seemed to be terrifically strong, landing punches that knocked masked men cold, or dashed them over backward like rag dolls, but there were so many masked men—well over a dozen, even without those lost back in the other pit, that they soon buried it under their sheer numbers, several of them clinging to each limb.

Three of them were struggling near its head, now, snatching the mesh of ropes back to bare it. Algernon peered. That revealed head looked like a skull, or like a river eel, lunging and biting energetically, snapping its teeth as it tried to stop the men.

Who *opened a little door* in the back of that skull-like head and clapped something inside!

Then slammed it and fell hastily back.

Free of their grasp at last, the captive shuddered violently, then stood up very tall, shedding the netting. There were still loops of rope around its chest and shoulders that became slanting lines like the ropes that held tents and fete awnings up, held taut by masked men crouching at the other ends of those lines, as far away from their prisoner as they could get.

The skull-headed man—or was it some sort of grotesque automaton?—stood looking down at the masked men contemptuously, and for the first time Algernon saw that the captive's arms and legs were clad not just in dark clothing but in some sort of sturdy metal frame or cage fitted closely to each limb.

Suddenly it twisted around, thrusting its arms out wide, sawing at the ropes now bent over the bars of the metal cages on its arms.

Then it turned the other way, the ropes it had pulled tight sagging suddenly slack, some of the tensed masked men falling and rolling in the sudden release of tension—while the ropes on the captive's other side thrummed and went tight, the masked men there straining to hold.

The captive twisted back the other way with a savage jerk,

tumbling still more men, then turned again. Masked men were cursing and falling all around it now—as it jumped forward, pulling them all toward it, then flung itself over on its back, pulling hard with both arms as it did so.

Masked men were flung bodily through the air, some thudding helplessly face-first into the trunks of trees, and the captive snatched the ropes—no longer at tension and holding him between them, but now mere loose loops around its torso—over its head and sprinted out of their midst.

Then it turned, reached down with one hand and caught up a masked man by the throat, broke that neck with apparent ease, flung the limp body down, and reached for the next man.

At that, masked men fled in all directions, three of them right toward Algernon—who dropped behind the trees and lay still, peering hard between the trunks so as not to miss one moment of the goings-on.

The three masked men stopped and turned to watch, too, as their fellows closer to the skull-headed thing hauled out their pistols and formed a hasty, frightened line.

Their former captive lurched fearlessly up to them and towered over them, as Algernon shook his head in disbelief—if this *thing* came down to the house, how could it be stopped? Even if all the beagles in London and his father's shooting companions were all massed there to fight it, like an army . . .

The skull-headed thing reached for the nearest man, staggering a little under the hail of point-blank bullets that erupted then.

Only to stop, hand extended, and stiffen.

Silence fell as the masked men stopped firing. Then Skullhead stood tall again . . . and turned, its movements abrupt, in the direction of Bishop's Bottom.

It swayed for a moment, as if undecided or bewildered, then adjusted the way it was facing slightly and lurched purposefully off through the trees, in a straight line, departing the path immediately to crash through bushes and old dried underbrush.

The trio of masked men nearest to Algernon relaxed visibly, sighing in relief.

"He's sent it to kill the Prince Royal," one said in satisfaction, loudly enough for a horrified Algernon Hartworth to overhear.

A splendid repast," Lord Tempest commented in satisfaction, leaning back in his chair.

"You *were* hungry," Hardcastle grunted, returning their plates to the tray. He peered out the window. "Gorgeous sunset, but look at those clouds; it'll be dark soon."

"That late? Hmm; it appears the lady will miss out on food that no one should miss," Tempest observed, looking at the silver dome of the one steam hood that remained undisturbed on the tray.

"You're not *still* hungry, surely!" Hardcastle chuckled, heading for the sideboard and a decanter of Old Islay he'd spotted earlier. "You're like a hunting hound that gulps down everything in sight—you'll be sick!"

"It *is* worth gulping down, if you've a mind to," Lady Rose agreed merrily, as she slipped through the door. Her borrowed clockwork gown was gone, returned to Lil, and she now wore her own favorite riding breeches and jacket, which were of the style usually worn by men. "I had two heaping plates, I must admit. *So*, my lord . . ."

She plucked off the dome and offered the plate meant for her to Tempest, who took it with a hungry eagerness entirely devoid of shame.

"I thank you," he said, digging into the still-warm quail stew heartily. "It's *so* nice to encounter the work of a cook who isn't afraid to use a bottle or three of wine in the kitchen!"

"Eat up," Rose told him, accepting a half-filled glass from Hard-castle with a smiling nod, "and tell me how I can help."

Tempest nodded gravely, then shot Hardcastle a mock-severe glance and said, "I am informed, by the Lord Chamberlain no less, that you are aware of rather more about my, er, status than you let on knowing—and that you have been in the know for some sea-sons now!"

Hardcastle shrugged, smiled, and handed his old friend his own half-filled glass of Islay. "We all have our secrets. No harm done, what?"

"So we can speak freely," Rose concluded, and waved her hand in a grand gesture that indicated Tempest should, accordingly, do so. She performed it with a flourish that would have done credit to a duchess.

Jack Straker grinned at that. Then he set aside his plate a trifle regretfully. "Well, I'll be some time healing, even whilst taking all of this excellent food aboard, so . . . as you can see, I'm wearing an exoskeleton. It was my prototype—I experimented on myself be-fore attempting to work on Steelforce—and is a trifle crude. Prone to what we might term 'locking up,' I fear. So I'm somewhat less than my usual agile, dashing self. Which in turn means that, lady-like reputation to maintain or spurn, you'll have to help Hardcastle with the usual running around posthaste, and the pratfalls, too."

"You make it sound *so* inviting," she replied, amused.

"Indeed. We invite danger into our parlors daily, we do. And all too often find ourselves practicing ever-wilder, more flamboyant, and ridiculous pratfalls."

"You make light of matters, Lord Tempest, but it seems to me that the Ancient Order of Tentacles is both a formidable foe and very much 'up to something,' as my father liked to say."

"They are. Right now those who lead the Order are thankfully embroiled in something of an internal dispute over ways, means, and priorities. So their full, concerted might is not being hurled at

anyone. We cannot trust that this state of affairs will continue—
and their feuding and their pursuit of various personal pigeons hasn't
stopped them employing another means of deviltry that may do their
bidding at one remove, and so provide them both the fruits they
seek and sufficient distance for them to escape all punishment for
what befalls."

"You speak of this Silent Man, this Iron Assassin?"

"I do indeed. *My* creation, so they can deny all involvement in
whatever Steelforce does. Just now, it is quite likely under the control of a rival of mine, the unscrupulous tinkerer Norbert Marlshrike.
He is almost certainly working for the Order now, in part because
he's chronically short of coin and they can both pay him and fund
his work. His own greed and the history of thefts he's developed as
a result make it very easy for the Order to deny they've given him
any support at all, if ever it came to exposure and hard questions in
Parliament or from the Crown. Moreover, it's quite clear that they've
hired Marlshrike, who is the only other man in the world I know
of aside from myself who can do such things, to achieve control over
my Assassin and to devise new ones to serve entirely at their bidding. Sent to kill targets of their choosing—notably, right now, the
Prince Royal."

"Right now," Rose echoed.

"Indeed. So Steelforce will be coming *here*," Tempest warned,
"and probably soon."

Hardcastle cleared his throat and said hesitantly, "Suppose you
clear something up for me. I know your Silent Man is controlled
by means of what you call a key, that the key that was in his head
is damaged—likely beyond repair—and that Marlshrike probably
has your old keys. Yet tell me *how* he controls this Steelforce. Does
he dictate and somehow record commands, so they're stored in the
key and compel the man? Or can he send orders from afar, and
change those orders without ever coming into contact with Steelforce?"

Lord Tempest sipped Islay, sighed as its pleasant burn started down his throat, and asked, "The 'from afar,' not a recorded compulsion, though when I started out, it was the other way around. Have either of you ever heard of etheric telegraphy?"

"I know of the telegraph," Rose said without hesitation, "and 'etheric' implies the ether, the air around us, which in turn would mean, I would think, a telegraph that needs no wires but can send its signals through air."

"*That* explanation was ease itself," Tempest observed triumphantly. "Imagine orders sent as electrical impulses into the brain—our brains work with their own electricity, you know—from afar, perhaps a mile or more. You see, there are waves we cannot see, hear, or feel that wash through the air constantly, and certain impulses and sounds can ride those waves. If you follow any of what the popular press sometimes calls 'the fancies of so-called science,' you might have heard the names Wilhelm von Bezold, James Clarke Maxwell, David Edward Hughes, or Sir Oliver Lodge . . . no? Well, let us just say by harnessing these invisible waves, Marlshrike can, across some distance, 'turn on' and compel my Iron Assassin."

"Yes," Hardcastle said, "but *how*?"

"It takes power," Tempest replied grimly. "*Lots* of power. A steam engine larger than a coach—more the size of a small cottage—to generate the electricity needed to send influencing orders far enough on the waves."

"So Marlshrike must have such a machine, and it must be nearby," Hardcastle mused. "So we must find it and smash it."

"As always, my friend, you demonstrate an effortless grasp of the essentials."

"Simplicity itself," Lady Rose agreed with gentle sarcasm. "All we have to do is find this hidden and undoubtedly guarded machine and smash it."

Tempest chuckled. "Indeed. Only Marlshrike knows the effective range of the machine, so I don't know how far afield we must search. And if we give him time enough to build more machines, he can send forth that many more assassins."

Hardcastle shook his head, looking grim. "You know what you've loosed on the Empire?"

"I do," Tempest replied curtly. "And I suspect all too soon I'll know the price of my atonement, too."

As if his words had been a cue, a loud disturbance burst upon their ears—gunshots, men shouting, then a terrific crash of splintering wood and breaking glass.

Hardcastle sprang up and reached out a long arm to haul Tempest to his feet. The Lady Harminster was already out the door and running down the passage like the wind, her unbound hair streaming out behind her.

Guards were pounding down the passages, too, converging from all directions on the front hall, where the front doors stood open.

Rose didn't need to see who stood outside to know what was happening. The Iron Assassin was trying to break into Foxden.

Guards were blazing away at the lone, lurching intruder with all manner of guns, including something Rose had heard of but never seen before: steam-powered air rifles that fired darts.

The Iron Assassin was being hit repeatedly and was obviously injured, staggering and groaning in pain, clawing at the air as if to wave away all the projectiles, and his pain with them.

Yet he was lurching doggedly forward. And the time came when there were no more guards arriving at a run and the forty or fifty guards gathered in the hall—the room seemed full to Rose—had no more ammunition left.

Yet the riddled Silent Man outside the doors was still on his feet.

And advancing. Grim orders were given, and the guards ran, however reluctantly, to meet the intruder.

Defender after defender of Foxden hurled himself bodily against the Iron Assassin, slowing and staggering him, but paying the price by being maimed or knocked cold.

By then, Tempest and Hardcastle had not only arrived, Tempest had taken a long and careful look at his creation.

"Help me," he told Hardcastle now, "and the moment I drive him back from the doors, you slip out and try to get the key out of him. But keep to one side, mind, or the chains will kill you!"

Together, Tempest and Hardcastle plucked the sheets and then the two halves of the oval housing off the shrouded device that stood aimed out through the front doors.

"Down and aside, everyone!" Tempest shouted—and everyone in the hall except Hardcastle and the Lady Harminster obeyed. Rose caught a glimpse of Malmerston calmingly going to his knees amid all the guards.

At the sight of Tempest, the Iron Assassin let out a roar of fury and charged, but his creator caught hold of the chain-gun's handles, stamped down on its lock lever, and fired it.

At the proverbial point-blank range.

Lengths of chain spewed out of the thing with a harsh rattling roar, and the Iron Assassin momentarily vanished behind a hail of whipping chain. When Tempest let go of the grips that both aimed and fired it, and the chain-gun fell silent, Bentley Steelforce had been driven well out into the graveled turning circle and looked to be wrapped in chain, his arms pinned to his sides. He jerked and shook, apparently helpless, sparks and rippling lightning playing about his chains.

"Now!" Tempest called, and Hardcastle sprinted out through the open doors.

Lady Rose Harminster was right on his heels, running hard.

Tempest started to shout something more, then bit it back. If she was smart enough to keep out of his line of fire . . .

She was. Hardcastle circled around to come at the Iron Assassin from one direction, and she ran at him from the other, shrieking like a harpy.

Steelforce had sent a glare at Hardcastle and started to back away, but at her screams he turned his head to stare at her.

And Hardcastle raked the back of his head, clawing open the little door and—wrenching out the control key.

The Iron Assassin screamed, shrill and much, much louder than Rose. He staggered wildly back and away, shedding chain in a frenzy.

Hardcastle sprinted for the doors, heading back into Foxden.

Right behind him, Steelforce charged again, racing fast enough to make Rose gasp in disbelief. He was going to catch Hardcastle before—

Tempest stared vainly at them all, unable to fire at the Iron Assassin—who was clutching his opened head and roaring in pain as he ran—without killing Hardcastle.

Who somehow burst through the doors *just* before the not-so-silent man caught up to him.

And then spun around, lowered his head, and rammed right into Steelforce's gut, as hard as he could.

He might just as well have run headlong into a solid stone wall.

He reeled back, dazed, and the Iron Assassin caught hold of his shoulder in one large hand and flung him aside with casual ease, dashing him against the nearest wall.

Hardcastle tumbled senseless to the floor, the control key falling from his grasp and clattering to a stop.

The Iron Assassin lurched toward it.

Rose burst through the doors, making a desperate dash for the key.

One of Steelforce's legs came down to bar her way. She'd just launched herself into a dive, arms extended—and slammed into his shin, coming to an abrupt halt.

Her shoulder felt . . . broken. Rose rolled over on her back with a gasp of pain, saw a massive fist descending to shatter her head—and then heard the Iron Assassin blurt, "Pretty!"

That massive fist halted in midair.

Abruptly, Steelforce turned away and brought both fists down on the control key. Tiny pieces of it flew up into the air, and he stomped on it with his feet, one after the other, for good measure.

By then, guards were slamming into him from all directions.

He ignored them, as a bear ignores stinging flies, turning in dogged triumph to lurch off into the falling night, casually shedding guards in all directions.

From somewhere, Malmerston flung a small round bomb at the back of the Assassin's head. Its fuse was unlit, and it thudded off Steelforce's skull, its only apparent effect being to slam the little door that had covered the key shut again.

The Silent Man, now silent again, didn't even bother to turn his head. He just lurched off into the darkening distance.

Leaving everyone in his wake collapsed or at least slumped, exhausted or in pain, or some combination thereof. The splintered front doors of Foxden stood open.

Through them, a few long and groan-filled minutes later, burst a breathless arrival, staggering out of the night.

It was Algernon Hartworth, making his way past a guard wobbling to his feet in challenge, to pant, "Is the Lady Rose Harminster here?"

"I'm here," Rose managed to reply, from the floor.

"Thank heavens! You're the only one I could think of to warn! There were masked men in the forest, digging pits, and they caught a man with a head like a skull who was wearing metal cages all over his arms and legs. They said they sent him to kill the Prince Royal! That horrible killing man is coming here—you must be ready!"

His words were met with bitter and then hysterical laughter from the men strewn all over the hall. He stared around at them in utter disbelief, really noticing them for the first time. Amid their groans, he received a polite "thank you, Lord" from the Lady Rose Harminster, who was somewhere on the floor amid them.

OCTEMBER 11

Feckless *and* fickle," a severe-faced housekeeper told the teapot, setting down the morning newspaper beside it with a snap that would have done credit to an officer on parade. "Can you really afford to continue this relationship?"

"Miss Peabody," the man with three sets of spectacles perched on the bridge of his long, sharply pointed nose said coldly, looking up at her darkly over all of them, "I don't care to discuss this further. The manner and timing of my revenges are my own affair."

"I merely point out that your likelihood of remuneration from Finsbury and Sons has just sharply declined," came the tart rejoinder, as the housekeeper's bony forefinger tapped one of the lesser headlines, "and that the stack of billings I already have insufficient funds to pay is both thick and growing daily."

"That will *do*, Peabody," Norbert Marlshrike snapped. "Pay the fishmonger so the cat won't starve and ignore the rest. I'll see that you have ample to pay them, very soon—and your own wages, too, of course."

The housekeeper nodded rather grimly and departed, leaving him to lift the domed lid of his breakfast platter and discover a thin mass of cold pickled oysters, whelks, and periwinkles, spread on soggy, still-warm toast.

Hmmm. Money *must* be tight.

Marlshrike thrust it all into his mouth, almost choking, rinsed it down his throat with the last of his tea, and hastened to his laboratory.

If he didn't get his own animated dead man up and killing to order soon, he might have to begin going out on the streets by night with a sharp knife himself.

W ell, who *is* it, Jenkins?" Lady Amelia Rathercoats looked up from her tea and her torrid book with some irritation. "One comes to the countryside to get away from all the London callers. I'll grant that we can almost see our city home from here, but all the congestion at the bridges, and their relative paucity and therefore the lengthy journeys entailed, *should* free one from the interminable interruptions of society. It's not as if we're in *trade* here, or up to our eyebrows in steam-driven innovations!" The deepest Rathercoats scorn always seemed to include immersion to the eyebrows.

"No, ma'am," the butler agreed patiently. "It's not a society caller. It's . . ." He hesitated, then said, "A man from your past. Or so he claims."

Lady Rathercoats favored him with a look that would have frozen the heart of a lesser man but merely snapped, "And has he a name?"

"He said to say he was once Bentley Roper."

Lady Rathercoats stiffened, then said slowly, "Well, well. Show him in, Jenkins, then close all doors and see that we are not disturbed. You may listen at a keyhole—so long as you have your long barrel loaded and ready."

"Very good, ma'am," the butler replied expressionlessly, bowed, and went out.

Leaving Lady Rathercoats alone to frown and murmur aloud, "'Was once'? So what is he now, I wonder?"

Her question was answered almost immediately. She tried not to stare, but the looming figure lurching toward her was . . . frightening. Yes, frightening.

Conscious of Jenkins watching her, she straightened her back, lifted her chin, forced a smile onto her face, and said, "Mister Roper! Such a surprise! Will you sit and take tea and talk with a neglected old woman for a while?"

His eyes were different, yet the same. They regarded her with more than a hint of malice, but a certain sneering humor.

"Oh?" he replied. "You have a neglected old woman here? Where are you hiding her?"

She barked startled laughter, and as her mirth ran down gave Jenkins a look. Obediently, he glided back out through the door and closed it.

Leaving her alone with . . . with what the man she'd known so long ago had become. Bentley Roper loomed up over her, taller than she remembered. His face looked almost corpselike, his head was a bare skull but for a few stray wisps of hair, and his sunken eyes, fixed on her, were dark and terrible.

He was clad all in black leather, a suit of many straps and buckles that was covered with a jointed metal frame like a series of intricate open cages fashioned to fit him closely, metal bars that were a-crawl with constant tiny bolts of crackling lightning that often spat sparks. He walked with a lurch, stiffly, and his hands and feet were bare—or, no, his fingertips were capped with gleaming metal.

He was staring at her with something that looked horribly like hunger.

"Please," she said hastily, her rising alarm sharpening her words into a near command, "sit *down*."

She almost sighed aloud when he did so, taking the chair opposite hers.

Those dark eyes never leaving hers for an instant.

His hands were like shovels, the fingers hard and massive. He could probably tear her apart with ease . . .

"We are alone now," Lady Rathercoats murmured, pushing the dish of chocolate-dipped ginger biscuits in his direction with her fingertips, "so tell me: Why have you come? And whatever has *happened* to you?"

"I . . . died," her unexpected visitor told her flatly. The man who had once been a young chimney sweep who'd made love to a much younger her on the very roofs of this grand house. While her husband snored unsuspectingly several rooms below. "Came because . . . lonely. Cannot go back to my Nell like *this*. Have needs. Needs *you* understand, Amelia."

"*Mister* Roper! Surely you can't—"

"Roper no longer. *Steelforce* now. Since I . . . came back."

"And—and how did that happen, exactly? The manner of your coming back, I mean," she asked hurriedly. She was frightened of this brute, with his burning eyes and his lurching manner. And yet . . . and yet . . . on the roof, in the moonlight. The first man who'd ever loved her, fierce and yet tender. And so endowed that—that—

That the handful of men she'd known since then had been but poor echoes.

She swallowed at the memory, and knew sadness. It had been so long since she'd known intimacy, and that last time—an admiral, whose entire dumpy, hairy body had reeked of cigars—had been a decided mistake.

A mistake she ached to rectify.

Yet . . . and yet . . .

His hand was moving across her tabletop. Walking on its fingertips like a purposeful spider. She shivered, despite herself.

Toward her, but not directly. Past the toast rack, past the jams and jellies in their fluted glass bowls cupped in silver . . . and stopping at the honey. To tap it, meaningfully. "Get you ready," the dead man across the table said.

Good *God*!

She sat back, unable to disguise her dismay. And unable to quell a certain stirring within her, a rising excitement . . .

She shot up out of her chair, discarding her book with a slam, and announced, "This is all so *sudden*. I am *not* in the habit—"

"Ah," her visitor rumbled, "but you were."

Lady Amelia Rathercoats opened her mouth to say something severe, and noticed the door open a trifle. Enough to show her a questioning eye—and the gleaming maw of the long barrel just beneath it. She shook her head, then lifted her chin sharply to order Jenkins to withdraw.

Her mess, so hers to clean up.

The door closed again.

"I am afraid, sir," she announced, with a calmness she didn't feel, "that 'were' is the word of most capital importance. My affections were for Mister Roper, and a long while ago. A Mister Steelforce, striding unexpectedly into my today, is a different kettle of fish entirely. A new suitor, who must woo me and hope to win me, the dance between us giving us both time to foster a deepening affection for each other—or not. And I tell you plainly, sir, without that affection, no amount of force—nor all the honey in the world—shall win you willing intimacy. You may overbear and possess, but you shall not receive warmth or a welcome."

Steelforce stood stiffly, the chair clattering to the floor behind him. "Then let my wooing begin."

Lady Rathercoats backed hastily away, out from the table and all of its expensive glass and silver, out into the open sweep of the room where only fine Persian carpets were at risk.

And her person.

"I have never stopped thinking of you," her visitor said. And took a step forward.

"Even in my grave, I thought of you."

That fascinated her. In his grave?

Cold, dark, the mold . . . rats? Thinking of her?

"Your gentleness," Steelforce growled. "Even when you bit me. Your . . . hunger."

Lady Rathercoats reeled, remembering.

"Your *teats*," the man rumbled. Opening his arms, almost beseechingly.

She backed away, but found herself adjusting an errant lock of hair.

Behind them, the door opened a crack again. Faithful Jenkins.

"I have missed you so," Steelforce grated.

Hunh. One of the lines the writer of her current torrid book was overfond of and had his characters utter every twenty pages or so.

You'll have to do better than that, dead man.

Or will you?

Would every bullet the long barrel could fire stop a dead man? Or . . . ?

"Your nipples," the tall dark man hissed, taking one long stride toward her, "await me."

"*Mister* Steelforce!" Lady Rathercoats exclaimed, scandalized. "I cannot *believe* what I just heard you say! And in my own home, too! How *dare* you?"

Bentley Steelforce paused for a moment, regarding her in flat-eyed silence. "Pray pardon," he said slowly. "No offense is meant."

After another moment, he added, "You mention our location. Hmm. It is evident that my offer is unwelcome, or my timing at fault. Perhaps both."

He fell silent again, standing as still as a sentry.

Lady Amelia Rathercoats regarded him doubtfully for a moment. His gaze, now directed past her shoulder, was as unchanging—unblinking—as the eyes of the nursery dolls of her youth. Sudden fear rose in her, and she plucked up her skirts and hurried away, daring to look back only once, as she passed out through the still-open door.

Steelforce was still standing just where he'd stopped, as immobile as the great casement clock behind him.

W hipsnade scraped the last of the wax away with infinite care and added it to the softened blob. A little more of the candle flame, a deft lift of the combined wax on the point of the knife that never left this room, drop it back onto the message *just* so, and apply the signet ring no one knew he had. And small wonder; he'd robbed a royal tomb to get it. Done. He held the resealed message up in the best light and studied it critically. Yes, done. Uncle would never know.

He turned, set the message carefully on the velvet-covered pedestal, then moved like a hurrying wind. Extinguishing the candle, hiding away signet and the copy he'd made of the message behind the moldings only he knew how to remove, and setting all else to rights. Snuff the lamp, undo the six bolts and three locks, pluck up the message, and out and relock, then away and none the wiser.

Uncle was expecting this report, a brief coded missive from an Order member working with that rarest of treasures: a double agent among the Investigators Royal. It had taken Whipsnade considerable time to figure out the code, but he'd mastered it last fall, and so now knew what the Lady Rose Harminster was up to at Foxden and that Tempest was alive but injured and was now working closely with her. Tempest was aware of what Marlshrike was attempting—and was keeping the Prince Royal fully informed, too.

There was an art to keeping royalty and the nobility fully informed. That is, so they felt they knew everything and never suspected how much you were keeping from them.

After all, if what they knew wasn't carefully controlled, how could they make the right decisions?

Norbert Marlshrike was sitting in his littered office, thinking hard. Pondering, the older generation would have called it.

By which they meant "thinking about possibilities, unlikely wishes, and fancies." Marlshrike liked pondering such things. Making some of them real was what he lived for, was the only truly *exciting* thing in life.

Unfortunately, all too much of his time was spent pondering what he needed to live *on*, not for. Everything was so expensive, and bills crowded upon bills until one was soon drowning in them, if one didn't do something drastic.

The tinkerer flipped open one of the little brass-bound boxes that was serving as a paperweight on his desk, atop an untidy stack of—yes—bills. Out sprang a severed human hand, small-fingered and soft, the hand of a young child. It scampered nimbly across the top of his desk like a scuttling spider bent on escape and made for the floor, so Marlshrike leaned over and opened a second, larger box.

"Catch," he ordered the larger, hairy-backed hand that rose slowly out of this second container, and he pointed at the first hand. Obediently the second hand set off after the first, bounding like a small dog.

"Luckily," Marlshrike murmured, watching them chase each other around the room and idly wondering if he should release more of his growing collection of animated hands to join in the fun, "I am growing increasingly experienced—accomplished, if I may be so bold—at doing something drastic."

This current business of controlling assassins *was* exciting. So much power might be his, if he could keep one assassin ahead of what the Order knew he had at any given time. And for the dullest jobs, a controlled man could finally solve for him the inability of being in two places at once.

Yet even this most important matter was sidelining his pet projects. Using etheric telegraphy to operate switches from afar and detonate bombs, learning to read reflected etheric waves to locate sunken ships and other undersea features and eventually concentrations of metallic ore underground—and perhaps even figuring out how to use etheric transmissions to make a specific person's blood boil or heart burst from afar while leaving others standing with him entirely unharmed.

He set aside all of these interests for the moment to once again take up his perennially most pressing need: to get more money, to pay his bills.

He needed to find someone wealthy but paranoid enough to keep most of their coins at home—then murder that person and take them.

Preferably tonight.

A handbell clanged with more cacophony than pleasant musicality.

"Bread's here, ma'am!" came the cheerful call, ere the bell was rung again.

Lady Roodcannon let a pained expression cross her face for just the instant it took to stride to the window and throw it up.

"The back door is open," she called down flatly, then closed the window again and returned to her chair, her book, and her goblet. A lamp shone over both of her shoulders, illuminating beautiful curtains that covered the wall behind them: cloth of gold and crimson leaping lions, woven in the farthest eastern reaches of the Rajahirate Empire.

A few minutes passed before she heard him coming up the stairs. Deliberately making more noise than necessary, as agreed upon. Then he rapped enthusiastically on her study door.

"Enter!" she commanded, cocking the oversize pistol that rested in a cradle on the table before her and sighting along it to make sure it was still aimed at the door.

It was the first thing Whipsnade saw as he let himself in and doffed the flat cap. He winced. "Terrible mess that might make, if it went off."

"I am not unused to making terrible messes," Lady Roodcannon observed darkly. Then she looked him up and down and frowned. "What a perfectly *frightful* disguise!"

Whipsnade shrugged.

"I'm quite serious," she said sharply. "Arriving at my London abode as a baker's assistant, delivering fresh bread and rolls in the baker's cart? What precautions did you take, to ensure you weren't followed?"

Whipsnade carefully refrained from sighing and replied, "The real baker's assistant overcome where there'll be no witnesses, then strangled and tossed in the Thames. The cart is soon to follow—after the harness is worn through with files rather than being cut, and the still-harnessed horses set free."

"This must be important, for you to go to such trouble," Lady Roodcannon said dryly. "So . . . what is it?"

He stepped forward and laid the copy he'd made of the report to Uncle on the table beside her cradled gun, then swiftly stepped back to stand by the door—just to one side of the pistol's line of fire.

Lady Roodcannon half-smiled at that. When she took up the report and glanced at it, her smile went away but she bent forward in keen interest.

She looked up from it and said crisply, "You have done me a great service. Please speedily pass on to me anything else of this nature that may come within your reach."

"Of course," Whipsnade agreed, without the slightest hesitation.

"I'll see your loyalty properly rewarded. Now go, swiftly; it wouldn't do to let anyone notice their bread is getting cold."

"Indeed," Whipsnade agreed, and they gave each other real smiles, in the instant before the door closed behind him again.

He went down the stairs as noisily as he'd come up and slammed the outside door. Grimstone promptly emerged from behind the lion-adorned curtains, waiting, a loaded gun in his hand, and went to the window to make sure Whipsnade had departed.

"Merton will have been watching to make sure he left nothing behind, took nothing, and did us no deviltry, on his way up or down," he said, "but . . . I don't trust that man."

"Grimstone," Lady Roodcannon said quietly from her chair, "only fools trust anyone. *I* don't even trust *myself.*"

Something in her tone made Grimstone turn around, frowning— only to find the lady he served was on her feet and rushing toward him.

She flung herself upon him, tearing at his clothing and kissing him fervently.

"As you can see," she gasped into his ear, before nipping it with her teeth and proceeding with her clawing off of his clothes.

Recovering from utter astonishment, Grimstone started to respond in kind.

OCTEMBER 12

Rose winced as the loud hammering arose again, loud and insistent. It was *very* early in the morning. A rain-drenched morning, at that.

Chief Inspector Standish, Assistant Commissioner Drake, and a host of beagles had descended on Foxden in the wake of the attack and spent the night patrolling as if they were zealous sentries of an army encamped in enemy territory. Now, with dawn barely upon this misty corner of England, the front doors were being repaired.

Last night Straker—she'd best get used to everyone calling him Lord Tempest, she decided—and the Prince Royal had both been unyielding stones that the blustering fury of the Assistant Com-

missioner had crashed and broken upon repeatedly yet hadn't managed to mar or move. Both had dismissed all criticisms of the defense
of Foxden and refused to hear of the Lord Lion being moved to one
of the larger castles and, there, defended by rings upon rings of
airships, big guns, and soldiery.

"If we decide to behave as if we're at war," the Prince pointed out,
"then suspicions rise everywhere, every citizen looks at every pass-
erby differently, and there will inevitably be blunders, honest mistakes that will leave someone hurt or shot dead, someone else
detained and plunged into fear and with their day's work lost . . ."
He shook his head, as if seeing calamities, and added, "Every decision we make affects the citizenry, high and low. We owe it to them
to make the right decision, as often as we can."

"But the Ancient Order of Tentacles—"

"Wants me dead, yes. *They* don't care what their deeds do to citizens, but I do. I must, or I am no better than they are, and no more
worthy to have my hand on the tiller of the Empire."

Drake coughed. "Uh, Your Highness, that tiller is under your
hand because you're the royal heir, born to helm the Empire."

"Yes, and I've been raised and trained to *think* as I steer, to have
a care for all, highborn and low. I cannot stop doing that now—
and I can't hope to do it well if I hide behind castle walls and never
even see any citizens who aren't wearing uniforms and serving me
directly. What kind of a leader does that?"

"The usual kind," Tempest muttered under his breath, but he took
care to say it quietly enough that no one but Rose heard it—and
his words only reached her ears because she was leaning past his
head, trying to peer around him to see the positions of the pieces
on the chessboard in front of the Prince, as she wondered whether
the Lord Lion was white or Lil was playing that side.

"Come," Tempest told her then, leading the way through a door
Rose hadn't been through before and into . . . a map room. Hardcastle hastened to catch up with them.

Ignoring a gorgeous map laid out on a central table and a vast open rack that wouldn't have been out of place in a wine cellar but that held not bottles but leather cylinders that undoubtedly contained rolled-up maps or nautical charts, Tempest went straight to a small corner shelf, reached down a rolled map obviously familiar to him, and passed on through yet another door.

It took them into a splendidly furnished but deserted parlor, dominated by emerald green walls and matching carpet. Tempest strode straight across it, plucking a silver bowl full of the newly fashionable sugar cubes from its central table as he went.

On through another door, into a crimson-walled study dominated by huge wingbacked leather chairs. The lord collapsed into one and told Hardcastle, "Drag that table over here, and two more chairs. We need to try to find Marlshrike's infernal machine."

No sooner was the table in front of him than Tempest unrolled the map, pinned one of its far corners down with the purloined sugar bowl, and waved at Rose to find objects—an ashtray here, a silver-mounted rack of quill pens there—to anchor the other corners.

"Behold Foxden," he announced, placing a long forefinger on a small cluster of buildings. Hardcastle and Rose bent over the map with the same eager delight; it was magnificent. "One of the Prince's best maps of Foxden and the vicinity," the nobleman added. It was one of the very expensive "verified by airship" maps, like the two on public display at Greenwich.

Tempest bent over it and scooped up a generous handful of sugar cubes. He put one down on Foxden and another on the Barnstaple family folly. "Let us try to mark every sighting of the Assassin we know of on this map, a cube on each one as precisely as we can place it, to see if this gives us any indication as to the most likely whereabouts of Marlshrike's etheric telegraph machine."

"Here," Hardcastle said immediately, putting a finger down on the map. "And here."

Cubes were placed, and Tempest frowned and added a third far more slowly and tentatively.

"I miss Iolanthe," Tempest muttered as they peered at the maps. "She could *smell* when a peer was hiding something or was more worried than his wont. Or her wont."

"The wheels turn, and the days pass . . ." Hardcastle murmured.

"And the Empire endures," Rose added the next line of that lyric.

Tempest gave her a twisted grin. "Well," he said, "with a bit of help, perhaps."

T he scuttling hands were all back in their boxes, for Norbert Marlshrike craved peaceful quiet in which to think.

If one must finalize the details of murder, why not enjoy doing so?

Lacking the public profile and immediate full weight of beagle response enjoyed by the banks, the "twisters"—as the lower orders called them—were an obvious target. They, the banks, the very-well-guarded vaults of the largest underwriters, and the even-better-guarded mint buildings were almost the only locales in southern England where lots of coin could be had in one place.

Moreover, the twisters were decidedly unloved. If they suffered losses, they were by and large on their own, with no one's hand raised with overmuch enthusiasm to their aid. The citizens of the Empire generally saw them for what they were: fat, filthy rich moneylenders who backed ventures too risky for the banks to touch—and who guarded themselves against ruin by such savory activities as opium-running, slave trading, arms-dealing (often using weapons stolen from Her Majesty's armories), and embezzling from the banks when they could, too.

So it had really come down to which particular twister to plunder, leaving Marlshrike pondering a choice between the three he knew and six others he'd have to learn a lot more about to dare moving against—learning that would require time he didn't have to spare. So, the three: Aunders, Micklethwaite, and Pauncefoot.

From the first, he'd leaned toward Pauncefoot, and after considering all the good reasons he could concoct for choosing someone else, he returned to the selection his instincts had made from the first: Montague Pauncefoot.

A grotesquely fat man who spent his days sitting in an ornate chair in Demaeleon Hall, his London mansion, devouring the finest meals a succession of short-hire fine chefs could prepare—auditions for his sponsoring of their restaurants, for a copper saved is a copper earned—and guzzling the very best wine and whisky.

Pauncefoot had lots of sinister hired guards, all of them huge beefy thugs well armed with revolvers, metal smash gauntlets (Marlshrike had helped refine these; they were brass knuckles that covered the entire hand and forearm, reinforcing wrists against strain), and frying rods (electrical batons charged by flywheels attached to sewing-machine treadles, then carried about in shielded leg scabbards; they worked by end touch only, and, whereas beagle batons merely stunned, Marlshrike had made quite lethal ones for many clients, Pauncefoot included). So, having equipped Pauncefoot's guards, Marlshrike had a fairly good idea of how many guards the man had under hire.

Knowing that and what he did of Demaeleon Hall, he considered himself ready. The moment, that is, he returned from the back pantry with an empty box of sufficient size.

T his entire area is the most likely," Tempest concluded, tracing a kidney-shaped and all-too-large area in the air above the sugar-cube-studded map, "but we really don't know enough yet to eliminate here and *here*, I'm afraid . . ."

The door behind them opened. They all looked up—into the eyes of an unfamiliar beagle, who said, "We've received a report from the butler at Rathercoats Manor—one Jenkins, by name. The Iron Assassin is there right now. Inside and remaining, I'm given to understand. Sirs and madam."

"Thank you," Tempest snapped, and struggled to his feet. Hardcastle sprang to assist him, and they hastened after the retreating beagle.

Lady Rose hurried with them, announcing crisply, "I'm *not* staying behind. The Prince has a houseful of big strong beagles with guns; he doesn't need me to protect him."

At that, Tempest looked thoughtful. "The beagles," he said. "We don't think enough about the possible danger from *them*. That is to say, from traitors within them."

Hardcastle spread his hands helplessly. "When we get back?" he offered.

Tempest nodded, and they started hurrying again.

The ride was both deafening and jolting, not to mention noisome, but wouldn't be a long one.

Marlshrike hung from his ice tongs, breathing the stench of the filthy tarpaulin covering him, and tried to stay still, his toes hooked under the lowest grab iron of the ladder that led up the back of the coach to its top. He knew by the echoes when they passed through the arch in the Demaeleon walls but kept motionless until he heard the drover cluck to the horses and their clopping hooves begin to slow. Then he unhooked his toes, let go of the tongs, leaving them still closed around the topmost grab iron, and dropped out from under the tarp, striding briskly away the moment his feet touched the ground, the large box under his arm.

As with many illicit entries, one could go far and achieve much by acting as if one belonged in a place, and was unconcernedly going about one's business.

The moment he was far enough away from the wagon for its crew to assume he belonged to Pauncefoot's men, he headed for the open back door into the pantries, which the foremost grocer had just propped open so he and his lads could form the usual line, shuttling the foodstuffs they'd brought in to place on the tables under the watchful eye of the cook.

Whom Marlshrike ignored, striding past with his box held up carefully level in front of him. As he'd expected, the cook assumed he was one of Pauncefoot's contacts, bringing something precious and probably illicit for the master's eyes only, and said not a word as Marlshrike walked on into the depths of Demaeleon.

In truth, the box was full of Marlshrike's scuttling hands. He couldn't really control them, not beyond simple orders to slay anything living except him, so he released them in a dark and deserted alcove to go and do just that, while he sought Pauncefoot's library.

It proved to be as dusty and disused as he'd expected, so he closed the door and went to relax in an armchair he doubted Pauncefoot could fit into these days, to calmly dip into a handful of the most interesting volumes he could find in a brief inspection of the shelves.

He read with idle disinterest, more to kill time than to educate himself. He was, after all, waiting for his hands to kill everyone else in the large house. He'd give them four hours or so, then go looking for tea as he called them back to himself.

Through the closed door came the muffled sounds of gunshots. Norbert Marlshrike smiled and went on reading.

The fields were drenched with heavy dew, but Straker was heading for a destination adjoining Foxden, so it was faster to walk across country than to have a carriage readied and go by the roads.

As they neared Rathercoats Manor, an airship passed overhead.

Straker glanced up at its dark, silently scudding bulk, then over at the great clock gleaming wetly atop Westminster Towers.

He favored it with a frown. "The transoceanic mail is late," he said disgustedly. "Again."

"This is news?" Hardcastle asked dryly.

"To assume the institutions of the Empire fail daily is not an act of loyalty," came the reply, in the mellifluously dignified tones of an elder lord of the Empire.

"No, it's the act of a realist," Hardcastle retorted. "Of whom the Empire stands in increasingly short supply."

Rose chuckled. "A hit, a palpable hit!"

Tempest chuckled, too, and asked her, "How well do you know Lady Rathercoats?"

"Not well," she replied. "She did not foresee success for our family, with Father having but one heir, of what she deemed the 'wrong' sex, and said so. I was thought to be too young to care, but I did—and considered it churlish of her to blame me for my gender, seeing as how I had no say in the matter. So we've had very little to do with one another."

"This," Hardcastle observed, "bids fair to be interesting."

Jenkins greeted them in grateful silence and led them to the upper rooms used by Lady Rathercoats. Tempest led the way, lurching stiffly in his exoskeleton in a way that reminded Rose—she shivered, despite herself—of the Iron Assassin.

Who proved to be sitting with the last of the Rathercoats on her bedroom balcony. Lady Amelia Rathercoats was old and wrinkled and looked rather grotesque in the somewhat racy and decidedly diaphanous lingerie she'd donned. It seemed likely to Tempest that she'd dressed this way to dissuade her ardent suitor—but had then felt the chill and thus put on a fur coat over her silks and was now sipping strong cordial after strong cordial to gain warmth and a measure of courage from that source.

The Iron Assassin was sitting across a small circular white table from her, stirring a pot of honey with his finger and regarding Lady Rathercoats rather sadly.

Tempest struggled out onto the balcony, bowed low to the lady, and almost fell headlong in doing so, then turned and confronted his creation.

"Steelforce," he said, "you're a hard man to keep up with!"

The Iron Assassin shot to his feet, glaring. "*You*," he said, and plucked up the table and flung it over the railing with casual ease to give himself room to stalk forward. "You."

Rose and Hardcastle gently but swiftly lifted Lady Rathercoats to her feet and rushed her back inside.

"Get her well away, to where he won't easily find her, and leave Jenkins guarding her," Hardcastle hissed, "then hurry back."

Rushing to do so with the feeble self-recriminations of Lady Rathercoats quavering in her ears, Rose found herself treasuring those last three words of his.

The Iron Assassin towered over his creator. Who hadn't retreated an inch and showed no signs of doing so.

"I . . . *hate* you," the skull-headed man told Lord Tempest.

"As well you might," Jack Straker replied, meeting his glare with a look of remorse. "For I perceive I have wronged you. Yet I did what I did with the best of intentions."

"*Intentions*," the Silent Man snarled, taking another step forward and flexing his hands. "I'll give you . . . intentions."

"I had the good of the Empire foremost in mind," the tinkerer noble told him, neither retreating nor flinching. "And submitted myself to the experience first." He held up his hands, open and empty, palms up.

The Iron Assassin lurched to a halt, peering at them, appearing to notice the exoskeleton Tempest wore for the first time.

"I sought someone who needed a second chance. Someone who was dying, who would be lost if I did nothing. So I did something."

Tempest took a step forward, closer to his creation.

"I did it for the Empire, yes, but I also did it for you. I insisted, as my price, and the Lord Lion agreed. So your wife and children are well provided for: good food and lodgings, good educations, Whitehall employment awaiting—not many sons of chimney sweeps rise *that* far, and for your wife and daughters there will be positions in the royal household when they're ready, if *they* want them; the obligation is the Crown's, not theirs."

"Bentley Roper will be a name folk fear," the Assassin said bitterly. "I never wanted that."

"Bentley *Steelforce* is the man they'll fear," Tempest told him gently. "You see, I know what it is to besmirch one's name and live with the consequences. I'm the crazed lord, remember?"

The Silent Man regarded him thoughtfully, a frown playing about his brows as he wrestled inwardly. Then, slowly, he nodded, his gaze falling again to Tempest's exoskeleton.

Which chose that moment, as if it had a mind of its own, to spit some sparks, leaving its wearer wincing in pain.

"I walk the walk," Tempest said, from between clenched teeth, "rather than just glibly sending others to do dirty-handed work while I play the clever lord. Sometimes, I feel not so clever. At all."

"Not so clever," the Iron Assassin echoed, and sat down again. Then he looked around in bewilderment for the table, which seemed to have gone missing.

After a moment, he peered over the balcony railing, sighed heavily, and slumped in his chair.

"Not so clever," he repeated mournfully.

Norbert Marlshrike consulted his pocket watch, nodded contentedly, and unhurriedly returned the books he'd been reading to their places on the shelves.

Then he ventured out of the library into a still and silent Demaeleon Hall.

The dimly lit passages were roamed by oversized scuttling spiders, his animated hands, now drenched in fresh blood, running along on their fingertips.

Here and there lay the evidence of their, er, handiwork. Gouged-out eyeballs lying glistening, mostly, but as he proceeded deeper into the great house, Marlshrike came across the sprawled and strangled corpses of Pauncefoot's thugs and servants.

He wended his way slowly but methodically, checking inside every room and listening intently for sounds that might mean someone was lurking nearby, as opposed to his aroused hands prowling.

When he came to the kitchens, he came across a still-warm teapot and helped himself to its contents. He took his tea black and couldn't abide sugar in it or dribblings of milk. This was good tea.

Marlshrike sipped and enjoyed it, taking his time and deciding not to think of what had probably befallen the cook.

Eventually, he went on his way refreshed, having checked the readiness of his pistol and the knife on its ankle sheath inside his sock, adjusted the armor he wore under his clothes slightly because one edge of his chest plate was digging into his hip at each step, and borrowed a duster pole from a maid's cupboard.

Death was everywhere in Demaeleon Hall, though he found no sign of Pauncefoot or his riches. That didn't mean his quarry wasn't at home; it almost certainly meant Pauncefoot was in his office, the room Marlshrike had deliberately left for last.

He did not enter it by its usual door. Rather, he made use of the secret passage he'd learned of years before, whose door into the room was concealed by a bookshelf. He thought a twister was less likely to put traps on his preferred escape route than on the door his clients—potential future enemies, all—would be conducted through.

The bookshelf door squealed, which surprised him not in the slightest. Twisters only grew more paranoid as the years passed; if they failed to do so, very soon years forever ceased to pass for them.

As it opened, he hung back, in case Pauncefoot was ready with artillery or perhaps a glass canister of some noxious gas—easy access to plentiful steam allowed just about twisted anybody to play slaying scientist these days.

The opening door afforded him a rear view of the moneylender sitting alone in his chair. The smashed remnants of many hands he'd bludgeoned to immobility lay scattered all around him. A heavy cane and a walking stick lay ready on the desk in front of Pauncefoot, who was even fatter than Marlshrike remembered. His smartly clad but drooping flesh overlapped the seat of his grand chair on all sides; perhaps he couldn't rise from it without assistance these days.

Or perhaps he could. Well, at least there was no servant lurking in the kneehole of the desk with a brace of pistols, or anything of that sort . . .

Warily, Marlshrike pushed the door all the way open with the duster pole, peering this way and that for any sign of a servant waiting along the wall on either side of the passage door with weapon ready and murderous intent.

Nothing and no one.

Nothing but silence, broken at last by Pauncefoot's wheezing, which rose to become a bitter snarl. "Oh, come *in*, man. You're letting in a draft."

Marlshrike set the pole where it would prevent the door from closing behind him, sidled cautiously into the room, and hastily sidestepped along the wall, peering everywhere for any sign of traps, other doors into the room, or anyone in hiding. None of any of those things was immediately apparent, so he came cautiously around to regard the moneylender, keeping well back from the desk.

It was a massive and magnificent piece of furniture, with rounded carved-oak legs thicker than many men Marlshrike knew and a top that was bare of papers and inkstands. In fact, it displayed nothing at all but a huge and unblemished blotter and the cane and walking stick lying parallel across it.

Above them, Mister Montague Pauncefoot was glowering.

He was bleeding down one cheek and from his chin, from fresh, shallow gashes made by the nails of the hands that had leaped at him. With his sad, baggy eyes and drooping skin, he looked like a bloodhound. An extremely *annoyed* bloodhound.

From under bristling eyebrows, he glared at Marlshrike.

"I thought so," he growled. "Such a gift, and you use it for *this*?"

Marlshrike shrugged. "I find myself unashamed."

"No doubt. You think this will profit you?"

"I believe it to be a swifter form of piracy than yours and find myself in pressing need. No particular ill will, man—though your greed is not to be commended—but rather hard necessity. You are . . . *convenient*."

"'Convenient.' Hmph. Hardly a stirring epitaph, is it?"

"I always prefer to avoid drama. Flamboyance. The overly grand gesture. Besetting faults, in my opinion. Wastes of time, energy, and enthusiasm that would be better put to advances, large and small, for the benefit of all."

"Yourself first, of course."

"Of course. Why, Pauncefoot, did you think yourself the only one who understands the way the weary world works? Make yourself too annoying, too inconvenient, too great a drain . . . and you make it worth someone's while to remove you rather than continuing to endure you. The error of overreaching, I fear."

"Speaking of overreaching . . ." Pauncefoot growled, and tried to lever himself up out of the chair.

Only to fall back with a growl.

Again—and this time, to descend in defeat with a groan.

By the third time, Marlshrike was drifting closer to watch and smirk—and this time Pauncefoot sprang to his feet with no effort at all, snatched up the walking stick, pointed it at Marlshrike's face, and did something to its handle.

The room rocked as the stick fired, with the crash of a heavy gun rather than the "crack" of a light piece.

Yet Marlshrike hadn't been idle. Throwing up one arm to shield his face, he'd flung himself back and away. Pauncefoot, anticipating such evasion, moved the walking stick as he fired, to follow the moving target.

In the wake of the crash, amid the drifting smoke, Marlshrike reeled, sobbing for breath. He'd been driven back across the room, half-deafened, and he hurt—*God*, he hurt; his collarbone must be broken and perhaps a rib or two, and his chest would be a mass of yellow-brown bruises—but he was alive. Thanks to the now-dented chest plate beneath his clothes.

He gave Pauncefoot a smile that fell almost immediately into a sneer. "A single-shot weapon, I perceive. How unfortunate for you."

"Someday, Marlshrike, your luck will run out," the twister spat.

"Perhaps. Yet I work hard to make my own luck, in the main. Unlike, say, a moneylender."

Marlshrike took out his pistol; took a careful step closer to the desk, wincing at the pain that flared with that movement; and told Pauncefoot pleasantly, "You're going to tell me where, in this house, you're hiding all your money."

"You," the twister replied, in similarly mock-friendly tones, "can go to hell."

"Undoubtedly," Marlshrike smiled. "In the meantime, if you would be so kind?"

"I don't think so," Pauncefoot murmured.

Marlshrike fired.

He'd spent quite some time practicing, in good light and bad, and was gratified to observe that he hit what he was aiming at; Pauncefoot shrieked.

And wrung a hand that was now spurting blood and had one less finger.

"No?" Marlshrike inquired politely, and after waiting for what he deemed was long enough, fired again.

Pauncefoot roared in agony and fell heavily back into his chair, crying like a child. Yet when Marlshrike asked again, he shook his head violently—so Marlshrike let him have another bullet. Three fingers gone.

Pauncefoot's sobs died down somewhat, and Marlshrike became aware of a scratching at the front, official door of the room. He put a swift bullet in each of Pauncefoot's shoulders so the moneylender couldn't lift his arms, then approached the door cautiously, looking for traps and peering back at the desk several times to make sure the twister wasn't trying to trigger anything.

The scratching was patient, insistent, and down at floor level. Marlshrike opened the door with infinite caution, peered out and down—and found himself staring at two of his animated hands. The mismatched pair trundled forward on their fingertips, and as he ushered them into the room, a third appeared, following them in.

Marlshrike sent them to the desk to climb the twister's body and strangle him. By the time he was done reloading, it was done. He set them to clambering up the shelves of the room and plucking books off, in case any were false or a safe or other hiding place was hidden behind them.

While he sought out more likely hiding places. The desk drawers and any secret drawers behind them—nothing, and he was good at finding even the cleverest secret doors. A cigar box held a handful of everyday coins and a cigar cutter, but the desk was otherwise empty. Its legs were certainly large enough to encompass large cavities, but try as he might, he could find no indication that they were anything other than solid . . .

By then, an impressive heap of books had built up on the floor, and he hastened to check under the room's large and ornate carpet while he still could. He was rewarded with a stone trapdoor that dropped down into a sewer far below. The underside of the beveled stone block that formed the trap had a sliding slate plate. It proved to close off a cavity that held dies for the stamping of gold sovereigns . . . but not a coin or any gold.

It wasn't until he tried to shift the desk that he realized it shouldn't be *that* heavy; it was as unmoving as stone. Taking out his knife, he scratched one edge of the thick slab that formed its top—and saw the glint of gold. Under the blotter, the sheen of woodgrain was *painted on* so skillfully—a cathedral painter, no doubt, and quite likely violently dead for his troubles—that he couldn't tell it was false even with his nose touching it.

The entire top of the desk was a single poured slab of gold.

Soft, unwieldy, and damnably *heavy*. With a sigh, Marlshrike headed for Pauncefoot's stables. It had been years since he'd harnessed his own horses to a coach, but no doubt he could manage it.

If, that is, his obediently murderous hands hadn't been at the horses . . .

T he hour is late," Uncle observed, decanter in hand. "Something to drink?"

"Oh, *hell*, yes," one of his three visitors—the ginger-whiskered lord known in the Order as "Old Horsley"—snarled. "You still have some of that superb Austrian?"

"Horse piss," another of the trio muttered, causing the third lord to snort in amusement.

The first of the three Ancient Order leaders turned and observed coldly, "Quentin, some folk lack any taste at all. It's breeding as does it—or lack of same."

"My lord, pray remember that here and now I am 'Cousin Quillan' and compose yourself. Or, rather, save your seething for she who so richly deserves it."

"Ah," Uncle observed, pouring and passing out glasses. "So this is about Lady Roodcannon. I confess myself less than surprised."

"The woman's a *menace*! As bad as the Dowager Duchess!"

"Worse," the third lord, Redhaired Nephew, said grimly. "She's full of energy, she's doing things and seeing things and still able to think past her prejudices—and she's *here*."

"Her most recent deeds," Cousin Quillan announced, as if speaking in Parliament, "are dangerous. Among many smaller things, the egregious blowing up of Tempest and the keeping of Marlshrike to herself. My lords, they warn us of her true tyranny; by such bold actions, *she* controls matters, and not the Order. Not only is she being too forward, acting in a manner that demands responses from the beagles and the agents of the Crown and increasingly making us untrustworthy villains in the eyes of the rabble, but she's behaving as if she is Empress and we are but lackeys. When has our approval been sought? Where has our part been in this decision making? I hear talk of Tempest's Silent Man being sent to slay targets of her choosing—how soon will it be ere such a target is one of *us*?"

"Eloquently put," Uncle commented. "I find I cannot disagree." He waved them all to chairs and sipped unhurriedly from his own glass. "And so, my lords? You've crossed half London on a wet night to sample my decanters, and . . . ?"

"Get your support for what *we've* decided," Old Horsley growled. "We're recommending she be eliminated."

Uncle assumed his best pained expression. If he didn't act reluctant, they would smell a proverbial large rat, and very swiftly. Inwardly, of course, he was delighted. This saved him the time and trouble of delicately approaching each of them to settle on these very same views. He must "allow" himself to be convinced.

He sat down in his favorite chair, shaking his head. "Serious dispute—as opposed to reasoned debate—among us is the true peril, the evil I promised myself long ago that I would fight against whenever and wherever I detected the slightest whiff of it. It remains our greatest danger, the one weakness that could destroy the Order. And yet . . . and yet I find myself in vigorous and firm accord with Cousin Quillan's conclusions. The lady *is* deciding things as if she were Queen, or Empress, not one vote among a dozen. Her deeds are making we of the Tentacles more prominent and therefore a more pressing problem for the authorities, who will therefore feel justified in taking more drastic actions, when for years they have bumbled along largely doing nothing and ignoring us, in hopes we'll go away. Or do exactly what she threatens to plunge us into: destroying ourselves from within. And the lady is neither stupid nor unaware of consequences. She has been warned. This *is* clear defiance on her part, sirs."

He looked from one man to the next.

"And yet," he sighed, "and yet . . ."

"And yet *what*, Uncle?" Old Horsley growled. "Now you're playing the very beagles you sneer at, turtling and hoping the problem will go away so you needn't take a stand and *do* anything. While that woman goes on 'doing' day in and day out, making things worse for us all. The Order, the beagles, the Crown, those in Parliament working to make small and necessary changes . . . we all suffer."

Uncle nodded and sat watching his own fingertips as they traced the carved pattern in the arm of his chair. "You are very convincing, Horsley."

He sighed, then sat forward and spoke more briskly. "So," he asked, "what shall we do about this matter? One foot wrong, and it will mean disaster. The Order will be torn apart by any protracted war between Lady Roodcannon and the rest of us."

The three eyed him doubtfully.

"Well," began Redhaired Nephew, "that's why we came to you, instead of just . . ."

"Doing something behind my back?" Uncle asked quietly. Then he shrugged. "Go on."

"We thought you'd plan something better than we could," said Cousin Quillan.

Uncle half smiled. "Perhaps. Let me think . . ."

He leaned back in his chair and pretended to ponder.

In truth, all he was really doing was deciding how much of his long-refined plans to tell them at this point, so none of them would think it prudent to start entertaining notions too . . . independent.

OCTEMBER 13

The masked, top-hatted figure on the far side of the beaded curtain was waiting for her answer. His patience would not be infinite. As if to remind her of that, he shifted slightly, and the row of diamonds that ran down the front of his top hat caught the light, winking and sparkling for an instant. Then he was a dark, motionless greatcoated bulk once more. Waiting.

"It's not yet the right time to strike against the Prince Royal," Lady Constance Roodcannon told him smoothly, watching his eyes follow her movements. The elegant gown she wore left her smooth, ivory-hued shoulders and arms bare and flirted with showing the world a little more. He was trying to enjoy her display.

Lady Roodcannon reminded herself that her visitor's vertical column of large diamonds set in diamond-shaped silver settings weren't mere adornment, they were trophies. Each one marked a rich and important lord slain.

"Right now," she added lightly, "the others who lead the Ancient Order are deciding they've had enough of me, and having my child without me will suit them just fine, so it's time to move against me."

"Your child is elsewhere and safe, of course."

"Of course. The children they'll find—the first, and several more beyond that first one—are there for anyone too inquisitive to find. They look like my son, and each of them has been reared to believe they *are* my son, but . . ."

She shrugged and smiled.

"Life is so regrettably full of deceit," the figure beyond the curtain murmured, sounding amused.

"Indeed. So for the time being, if you see to the safety of Marlshrike, I'll take care of those who believe they command the Tentacles."

"And Lord Tempest? What of him?"

"We need just one of the two tinkerers to survive, and none of us can keep *him* safe. Not the way he behaves."

"I am inclined to agree with you," the masked man said dryly. "I shall endeavor to safeguard Marlshrike."

"Let him gain the resources he needs to field his army of assassins but think he's done it himself, and he'll keep to his den cackling gleefully and working himself to exhaustion—as safe as anyone can make him."

"And what of our safety—and that of everyone else in London— with his assassins on the prowl?"

"As to that, we at least should be able to guard ourselves adequately, if we intercept his assassins just long enough to introduce these into their footwear. Grimstone, the box."

Grimstone stepped forward from behind her, holding forth a box. He swung its lid up to display its contents: a dozen small metal gewgaws. They looked like jewelry that's been trodden on and made dirty by the streets.

"And these are?"

"You might call them 'echo reflectors.' The same etheric telegraphy by which Marlshrike controls the Iron Assassin from afar can be used to send out signals—like the tolling of a church bell—that can bounce back from these."

"So we can track the movements of anyone who has one of these in his boots."

"We can." Lady Roodcannon gave the man beyond the curtain a wide smile and said pleasantly, "And anyone who does business with me would do well to remember that I have far more surprises than these up my sleeves."

"I've never doubted that," her masked visitor replied in like tones, "and my memory is, I'm told, very good."

He tipped his diamond-studded hat to her and departed.

Grimstone hurriedly closed the box, set it down on the floor, and vanished swiftly through a side door.

Lady Roodcannon stood as still as a statue and enjoyed the solitude. It was rare enough, these days, and it gave her the opportunity to really think.

She was almost lost in her thoughts some minutes later, when Grimstone reappeared to report, "He went straight out to the street, doing nothing suspicious that I could see, and tarrying nowhere. I've locked and secured the house."

Lady Roodcannon threw back her head and laughed delightedly, the full-throated gusto that so few women permitted themselves. "Ah, but I'm enjoying this."

She spread her arms, shook out her hair, and purred, "Get me a sherry, Grimstone. The bottle with the rubies in it. And pour yourself a glass; I feel in a celebratory mood."

He did so, and as he handed her a full glass, ran his fingertips up one bared arm in a caress.

With lightning speed she stepped back and drew a tiny derringer-like pistol from its holster low down in her décolletage.

"Dare that again," she told him coldly, "and I'll blow your brains out. *I* decide and I initiate. Every time. Any man who neglects to respect that doesn't continue to live."

"I—I—I'm sorry, Lady Roodcannon," Grimstone apologized hastily, going to his knees. "Truly. I shouldn't have presumed . . ."

"Indeed. Yet seeing as you have . . ."

She drained her glass in one long pull, set it down on the nearest sidetable, undid her gown—it was a simple matter of flipping the row of metal clasps that ran all up one hip and the flank above—and stepped forward, letting its folds fall away as she towered over the man on his knees. "You may pleasure me. From down there."

A peacock shrieked suddenly outside, and the Dowager Duchess sighed and went to slam the window. Oh yes, this was the one with the peacocks.

She had several castles in this country, and a handful more scattered across the Continent, and all of them had balconies and windows overlooking extensive gardens. Only this one had gardens where peacocks screamed.

The birds had *no* sense of occasion. *Such* an important message, and it needed her full attention.

She read it over again to make sure there'd been no mistakes made when decoding it. There had not. The encoding meant missives could be sent as everyday letters, reaching her by mail carried on a regular airship run across the Channel. Venetta had done the decoding, writing out the true message in her small, neat hand under the swashbuckling scrawl of Blücker's bold quill. Her maid might be entirely too independent-minded and snippy, but the girl *was* capable.

And the message rang true; this was certainly Blücker's writing. Of events in London that were far more dramatic than she'd grown used to reading about in these latter months. The Ancient Order of Tentacles had seized control of the Iron Assassin, but the automaton had been driven off in its first attempt to kill the Prince Royal, and there was now disagreement and dispute within the Order over the uses to which the Iron Assassin has been put.

She rang for Venetta. It was time for a little raging.

The ring of the bell was always imperious, but sometimes it was more imperious than most. Venetta knew what was coming. So she scratched the itch on her nose, yawned and stretched, and prepared herself for her expected role as she hastened up the stairs.

Well, as prepared as one could be without earplugs and infinite patience.

The Duchess let her get to the center of the room and standing primly to attention before starting to screech.

"Vat is *wrong* viss these people?" The old noblewoman marched across the room, clawing the air in frustration. "*Allvays* the same! Yu giff them a leetle power, und they think themselves *gods*! It iss the curse of zis modern age, I tell yu! Jumped-up farmers und hod carriers empowered viss clockvurk this und steam-dreeven that, und suddenly zay are all leetle emperors!"

She reached the wall and the grand furniture lined up along it and spun about, leveling one bony finger at Venetta. "Yu vill go to Eeengland undt find every Order member and speak viss them privately. Yu vill tell them all I haff married the Markgraf Hereszen, und—"

"But—but he's dead!"

"I *know* zat, yu stupid girl! Who do yu think poisoned him, hey?

But zo long as he lies undiscovered in our crypt here, the vurld thinks him alive! Now, heed me! Yu vill tell them all I haff married the Markgraf Hereszen, und tell them zay are to tell *no one* this, no one at all!"

"Very good, your grace."

"*I am not finished yet,* yu! Yu vill tell them all this, und then yu vill listen and vatch, to see who tells who, and yu will take careful note uff whose tongue wags this spurious secret—und yu vill bring back that list to me, quickly. They vill be the first I haff killed. Now go get a coat, my traveling writing box, vhatever monies yu need, und *go.*"

"But, your grace! Your tea! And your supper!"

"I am not such a useless old cow, despite what yu no doubt think, that I cannot find things in a kitchen! And if I cannot, vell, there are cooks enough down there that I can haff vipped! *Go!*"

She would, too, Venetta reflected, rising from her deep curtsy to hasten out of the room and down the hall. Have people whipped, that is. As petty, spiteful, and lazy as ever, Alice Louisa Hanover, *the* Dowager Duchess of the Empire, loved to "haff people vipped" almost as much as she enjoyed tirades—and these days, any excuse would do.

Venetta unlaced her stays as she strode down the passage, and the moment she was inside her own room, off her maid's wear came, to be flung into the bottom of the first wardrobe as she wrenched open the door of the second one.

And stopped to wince at the pain that movement brought her. The scars across her shoulders and back from her own most recent whipping were still fresh and raw.

Yet she'd endure far worse to get back to England. Where they were somewhat slower in indulging any zeal to "haff people vipped."

The beagle carriage rattled teeth-shakingly over some bad cobbles. Chief Inspector Standish flung up an arm to guard his head from slamming against its insides and indulged himself in a gusty specimen of the sigh of a man who's seen entirely too much of what he was going to look at. And knew he would see plenty more.

A beagle had brought urgent word that Chief Inspector Standish must "come see something," and he suspected he knew all too well what that meant. So he'd taken one of the faster steam-driven carriages to the worst of London's slums, Old Nichol. With the shutters down over the windows to protect them—and him—from the worst of what would be hurled at it from the shadows. The carriage rattled again, even more loudly, then started to slow.

Standish peered ahead, over the driver's shoulder. They were coming to a stop in a back alley, where a cluster of heavily armed beagles were standing over a sprawled corpse. There was a lot of spreading blood at one end of him. Head bashed in.

Standish clambered out, almost absently raising a riot shield, out of long habit, to intercept a bucket's worth of chamber-pot emptyings that came hurtling down from a window at his head.

The dead man had dropped a box he'd been carrying. A wooden box that had spilled some of its contents. Bottles.

Standish nodded at the gathered beagles, then peered down at labels. "Oil of earthworms, everlasting pills . . . pharmacist's runner, then?"

"Perhaps, sir, but what I called you for was to see *this*." The beagle pointed at what someone had drawn on the cobbles in the dead man's blood.

A circle with wavy tentacles protruding from it in all directions. "And this."

The beagle had already pulled off the dead man's left boot; he now turned the foot so Standish could see a toe ring, then turned the ring itself, on the toe, until its device came uppermost.

An oval etched with tentacles.

"Ah," Standish said grimly. "You did right to call me. So it's begun. Those of the Order are killing each other now."

The tea Jenkins had brought was the best Rose had ever tasted. And that was a good thing, for she was sipping it in uneasy company. Jack—Lord Tempest—to her left, Hardcastle on her right, and Bentley Steelforce, the Iron Assassin himself, directly across the table from her.

And it was a small round table of the sort best suited to two conspiratorial ladies. They were sitting and taking tea, trying to befriend the Iron Assassin, put him at his ease, and find out—without being overly pushy in their questioning—what he wanted and needed. Not to mention what he intended to do.

Surprisingly, he was countering with questions of his own. "First," he rasped, "I'd like to know what *you* do."

"Well," Tempest said smoothly, "Lady Harminster is a doctor, Hardcastle here is—"

"No," Steelforce interrupted flatly. "What do you *Sworn Swords* do that Marlshrike and those he works with want all of you dead so fervently?"

"Ah. Well." Tempest seemed unperturbed. "As the Empire flowers, new inventions building upon new inventions, it is a time of great opportunities, advances, and excitement—but some of that excitement is anger at being bested or at changes that shatter long-cherished livelihoods and customs. We battle those clever enough to bottle their anger, control it, and use it wisely. The beagles, the soldiery, the navies all across the Empire—they deal with all the angry men who can't take it anymore and erupt."

"I should remind you," Rose heard herself saying softly, "that there's something more savage smoldering in the Empire than angry men. Something unleashed only at great peril."

"And that would be?"

"Angry *women*, gentlemen. Angry women. They have been bottling ire for far longer and under the goads of more cause—and when *they* erupt, God help anyone who gets in the way."

The Iron Assassin's eyes flickered. "I believe," he announced grimly, "I know how they feel."

OCTEMBER 14

A splendid morning, sir," Whipsnade announced, setting the neatly folded newspapers down beside his master's tankard of steaming broth.

Uncle looked up in some amusement. "You managed to convey an unmistakable and even resounding 'but' in those three words, Whipsnade," he observed. "Pray elucidate."

"My lord, Hollander just came to the pantry door to report that the maid who serves as eyes for the Dowager Duchess has just arrived in London. She came on the fastest, most expensive airship from Hamburg, too."

"Ah," Uncle said delightedly, "so the old crow's grown impatient, has she? Good. This will serve our ends admirably. Let her learn of the perfidy of Lady Constance Roodcannon—and we'll watch her react accordingly."

H ow can you know where he's going?" Hardcastle asked curiously. "He refused to tell us one word on the matter!"

"And thereby told us all we need to know, old friend. My Iron Assassin has set out to find his wife and children. I'll wager he doesn't intend to reveal himself to them, but rather wants to see for himself that they're safe and well—and precisely where they are and how they're being treated."

"Understandable," Rose put in.

"Indeed. He must know their location and situation so as to ascertain what will be involved in hastily snatching them away to somewhere else. For if he must, ah, cross the authorities in future—and he will—he anticipates someone thinking to use them as a means of influencing or outright controlling him."

Hardcastle frowned. "Yet when first we spoke of this, you said it all 'hardly mattered.' Why?"

"Marlshrike still has the use of the Order's merry band of dirigible-riding masked men. They'll pounce on him before he gets far. That's why I took care to tell him we'd be leaving for Foxden, directly."

"But—but then we'll have to stop him all over again! Why didn't you stop him going out that door?"

"Bleys, sometimes . . . d'you recall disobeying your pater, when you were young? And how you came a cropper, just as he'd said you would, and you learned from that, and didn't do whatever it was again?"

"Yes. Oh. *Oh.*"

"Indeed. Besides, this way we shall see more of Marlshrike's intentions. He's the greatest potential threat, you know. Get him out from under the shadow of Lady Roodcannon and his helpless lust for her, and you'll see a foe too brilliant to read and too subtle to be easily influenced."

"Like you," Rose observed dryly.

Tempest looked at her. "Oh, I'm not out from under my own controlling shadow yet." He held up a hand to forestall the obvious question and said, "Hand me the spyglass, will you? I believe this is our sinister dirigible already. Cads; they *might* have let him at least get past the duck pond."

The first masked man lunged like a flamboyant swordsman on an East End stage, thrusting a glowing-tipped rod at the Iron Assassin.

Steelforce slapped it aside and landed a blow to the side of the man's head that sent the Order agent sprawling, brains spewing from his mouth—but the second man from the dirigible held a glowing rod, and the third and fourth, too.

As he caught hold of one rod, the other two rapped his exoskeleton—and the surge of searing pain that rocked him back on his heels coincided with his exoskeleton's going rigid, the joints smoking in a fit of spitting sparks worse than he'd ever experienced before. He toppled helplessly to the turf, and ungentle hands rolled him over on his face in a trice.

He felt the door in the back of his head tugged open and something put inside, settling into the square niche and—

His world went gray again.

"Sir? We've installed it successfully, sir!" The slam of the door seemed almost an afterthought.

"*Good, good,*" purred the satisfied voice in his head—and spilling out of his head, thinner and fainter but clear enough. "*Let go of him and stand back, and I'll test this. Oh, did you use the rods on him?*"

"Yes, sir. Worked a dream, they did."

"Then work his joints for me. Two of you to his shoulders, two to his elbows, and two to his wrists. Just back and forth, gently but firmly, the way you would a real person. Then the same for his legs."

A real person, hey?

Steelforce seethed, silently and helplessly. Marlshrike's orders were carried out, albeit with several gasps and groans from his masked molesters, as more sparks spat and snapped. The exoskeleton responded as the charge that had left it tinglingly rigid ebbed.

"Well done! Now get back, all of you. Well back. The Iron Assassin is again under my command and is about to undertake his most important mission: the killing of Jack Straker, Lord Tempest. His creator. And when he is done, the Ancient Order shall be triumphant—and I, Mister *Norbert Marlshrike, will be the only master of assassins in all the world!"*

Bentley Steelforce felt himself rolling over and clambering clumsily upright. Masked men cowered warily back from him as he lurched around to face Foxden.

Gleeful gloating, he decided, sounded no better when coming out of your own head.

They saw each other only at the last instant, but they were both agile men.

So Whipsnade and Grimstone didn't *quite* crash into each other.

They twisted, striking shoulders in a glancing manner and snatching out weapons . . . and ended up each facing back the way he'd come—and facing each other—on a game track in the woods outside Foxden.

The branches they'd disturbed swayed and danced around them. Both men looked each other up and down, each ascertaining the other was armed to the proverbial teeth.

Whipsnade managed to grin first, and Grimstone to speak first.

"I believe it most prudent," he said, "to ask you what you're doing here. I promise to tender a reply as complete and truthful as I receive."

"I accept your terms. I've come here on my own, to try to kill the Prince Royal."

"As have I. I cannot help but notice, however, that you said nothing whatsoever as to why you've undertaken this . . . endeavor."

"So long as we're being brutally honest . . . to either head off the infighting in the Ancient Order I can clearly see coming—or to establish myself as a credible candidate to head the Order, in the event that said infighting takes down the current leaders."

"Blunt candor, indeed. In the same spirit, I freely admit to precisely the same reasoning. My alternative, in the event that the Prince is beyond reach, is to capture Lord Tempest. Thereby furnishing the Order with an alternative to Marlshrike and so weakening the influence of the Lady Roodcannon."

"That scheme was my fallback, too," Whipsnade agreed. "So, then, does it strike you as prudent to work togeth—"

He broke off abruptly at a distant sound in the underbrush. The two men stared at each other, listening hard and hearing smaller noises of disturbance grow steadily nearer, then with one accord ducked off the trail, to crouch behind several shrubs and saplings whose foliage afforded a little cover.

A lone man came through the trees, lurching along in as straight a line as the forest would permit, skull-headed and all too familiar in his exoskeleton. It took only a few seconds to see that the Iron Assassin was headed for Foxden.

"Off to kill the Prince Royal," Grimstone whispered.

"Again," Whipsnade whispered back.

As still as two crouching stone lions, they watched the grotesque animated man dwindle into the distance. It was only after he had gone from view over a rise that Grimstone spoke again.

"Well?"

"Why don't we follow? To work around the edges, so to speak?

While they're all battling the Iron Assassin, we can take advantage of matters to try to accomplish the Prince's death, Tempest's capture, and the killing of as many important beagles, Investigators Royal, and courtiers as we can."

Grimstone's smile came slowly, but it was wide and genuine. "We *do* think alike. Lead on, loyal Tentacle of the Order."

Full night had fallen. Grimstone lowered his spyglass regretfully. "If the Lord Lion is anywhere near a window," he announced, "*I* can't see him."

"He won't be," Whipsnade replied, not bothering to get out his own spyglass. "They're not unacquainted with firearms, you know. As it happens, I know exactly what he's doing, though which particular inner room he'll be doing it in . . ." He shrugged.

"Oh?" Grimstone asked, a little resentfully. "I suppose you know her name, too?"

"You misunderstand me. Right now, the Prince Royal is *not* entertaining any of his minxes. Rather, he'll be reviewing the latest cost estimates for bridges designed by Mister Isambard Kingdom Brunel and giving his approval to invest Royal Treasury funds in their building, to lower the cost if Parliament balks at the price tags."

Grimstone blinked. "Uncle?"

"Uncle."

Grimstone nodded. "I wonder where Tempest's assassin has gotten to? Or were we wrong about who he's after? He was certainly headed here."

"Marlshrike was up to something—in his tinkering, I mean. Aiming to have Steelforce on a tighter leash, to be more biddable than a hound set loose. I'd not be surprised if he's been testing him. Fetch this, move that from there to there . . . that sort of thing. Waiting until the time is right. And being as Steelforce is not indestructible, and Marlshrike's control key even less so, I strongly suspect he won't come right up to the front doors this time and try to wade through all the defenders and everything they can fire at him. That's why I led the way around here, to overlook this side of the house. I think we'll see him try for yon windows."

"Up those creepers? They'll never hold him."

"Something he'll no doubt discover the hard way. I—there he is. Look."

Grimstone looked. The Iron Assassin had come striding out of the darkness, up to the back doors of Foxden this time.

The kitchen and pantry doors, on either side of the walled kitchen garden. They were locked, of course.

Steelforce stepped back and stood for a moment in thought, then went to the wall where the creepers clung most heavily and started to climb, heading for a shuttered window above.

Shots cracked out of the night; beagles, stationed downslope from Whipsnade and Grimstone, closer to the house.

The gunshots attracted attention; more beagles could be seen now, moving inside the walled garden and along the outside walls of Foxden, converging on the climbing man.

Whipsnade and Grimstone exchanged glances and nods, leaned over, took careful aim, and shot down the beagles below them.

The shutters of the window Steelforce was climbing toward swung open, and those of an adjacent window, too. Beagles leaned out to peer down—so Whipsnade and Grimstone shot them, too. Beagles collapsed limply over the sills, and one toppled out to crash heavily to the ground, his own fellows shooting at him as he fell.

Grimstone took down a beagle in the walled garden, and Whipsnade picked off the nearest one creeping along the walls of Foxden toward the assassin.

More shots told them that the surviving beagles were getting nervous, but none of them seemed to hit the Iron Assassin—who'd slipped twice as creepers tore off the wall but had evidently found a trellis that could support his weight, and was now . . . yes, over the sill and through that upper window.

Whipsnade and Grimstone reloaded and looked at each other.

"So?" Grimstone asked.

"Every beagle down helps the Order," Whipsnade replied. "Let's sew a little mayhem."

They shot at every beagle they could still see and then rushed the house, to rifle all of their fallen victims for weapons.

Vastly reinforced, they tossed a statuette over the garden wall, then scaled the wall on the other side of the walled garden and gunned down the beagles who'd rushed to the distraction. Which left just one constable they knew of, still making his cautious way around the outside of the house.

They waited for him lying flat on the ground, and when he came around the last corner fired as one, their bullets lifting the man off his feet to crash onto his back and lie still.

Dead, they found, as they relieved him of his pistol. Then they set off around the house on a tour of their own, shooting in through every ground-floor window they encountered, to provide the Iron Assassin with a distraction and to kill as many of the Prince's defenders as possible.

"Every beagle down helps the Order," Grimstone said, grinning, as they fired a volley into their most recent window and heard an answering cry of pain from inside Foxden.

Above them, voices rose in panic, the last sentence ringing out clearly. "Well, *do* it, man!"

As they flattened themselves against Foxden's outside wall, well to one side of that upper window, a panicked beagle inside shot a firework up into the night.

"Distress signal," Whipsnade murmured.

"Reinforcements urgently needed," Grimstone muttered back. The firework burst overhead, lighting up the night in a bright conflagration that briefly put the stars to shame, and its last dying sparks had barely faded before the bells of the Bishop's Bottom church started to toll.

"My, my," Whipsnade murmured. "Let's go back to the height again for a bit, while we see what sort of reinforcements come. If any."

"Oh, there'll be some," Grimstone replied, setting back off up the slope. "This is the Crown, remember?"

As he spoke, lanterns kindled at the Royal Mail yard, reflecting palely off the curved white underbelly of a mail airship moored there for the night. By the time they regained their vantage point and crawled in under bushes that might cloak them from anyone peering down from an arriving airship, the still-tolling bell had lured the mail sorters out into the night, to peer curiously in the direction of Foxden.

Inside which, if one could go by the gunfire, a battle royal was now raging.

"We may be mere tentacles," Grimstone murmured, smiling up into the moonlight, "but if you anger us enough . . ."

The din made Rose wince more than once. The Iron Assassin had come down from the upper floor into the far wing of Foxden and was now trudging through beagle after beagle, still on his feet despite being shot dozens of times. According to the constable who'd just come running up to his on-duty superiors, white-faced and breathless, Steelforce was splintering down locked doors, breaking necks, and crashing through improvised furniture barricades. Seemingly unstoppable.

Those senior beagles looked at each other, then turned with one accord to Tempest and the others.

"That settles it!" said Commander Adams, the highest-ranking member of the Constabulary at Foxden since the departure of Assistant Commissioner Drake. "We get the Prince out of this house while we still can!"

Hardcastle and Malmerston both nodded, but Jack Straker shook his head violently.

"*No.* To do so now would be rank treason—you'd be committing regicide!"

The commander frowned. "How so, man?"

"Steelforce is no marksman. Nor can he be in two places at once. All that firing into the house from outside proves that more killers—or kidnappers—are waiting out there in the night for any attempt to escape. Unless you have secret tunnels up your sleeve that I've never heard of, waiting here for reinforcements is safer than stepping outside into a firing squad."

"Hear, hear!" Lil and Rose piped up, together.

The commander gave them a dismissive "And what do women know of warfare?" look, but Malmerston and Hardcastle were nodding in support of Tempest now.

"If we play for time," the butler ventured, "and those reinforcements get here . . ."

"The lurkers outside will butcher them!" one of the senior beagles snapped.

Tempest pounced on this. "Ah, but what price the royal neck? That's always the hard choice, isn't it? How many commoners does one sacrifice to keep alive the prince who's running the Empire? And whose death will almost certainly touch off dozens of skirmishes, perhaps even a dozen wars? How many graves will have to be dug *then*?"

Another beagle cursed, under his breath.

The commander looked at Tempest. "Can't you turn your killer off? Stop him in his tracks? I don't pretend to know how Steelforce, ah, *works,* but surely, man, you built in something that gave you overriding command?"

"I did, but he's someone else's killer now. That's the problem, at the sharp and ever-advancing steam-driven edge of things. You do something, and someone *improves* on it, and you watch it race ahead, out of your control."

"Like an empire," Rose murmured.

They all turned to look at her. It was Malmerston who nodded first.

"Like an empire, Lady Harminster," he agreed quietly. "Very well put."

The silence that followed was broken by a distant, splintering crash.

It wasn't nearly as far away as the previous ones had been.

Tempest turned to Lil. "Bedchamber!"

The rouged prostitute nodded, turned, put her head down, and ran.

"What's 'bedchamber'?" Commander Adams snapped, frowning.

"The room you and your men have to keep the Iron Assassin from reaching," Tempest told him crisply, "at all costs."

Then he sprinted after Lil, Hardcastle at his heels. Malmerston and Lady Rose ran after them.

The beagle commander clenched his fists, stared at the ceiling, and cursed loud and long.

"Why," he implored the painted roses on the plaster above him, "are the lawful constabulary of this Empire always the *last* to be told things? *Why?*"

W ith all the beagles and soldiers and staff inside Foxden, the stables were deserted, so Whipsnade and Grimstone could move freely. Wherefore it took them no more than a few minutes to use straw and ladders from the stables to build a fire against the front doors of Foxden.

The church bell was still tolling, but reinforcements, if any were coming, were still on the way. Well back among the topiary, Grimstone and Whipsnade watched the front doors burn.

"You didn't think to bring any chestnuts?" Whipsnade joked in a whisper, just before the first shouts arose from inside the house.

The two Tentacles men drifted closer, the better to listen, taking care to keep well to one side of the graveled turning circle.

They could hear faint coughing and choking from inside Foxden now, coming through the shutters. With so many of the windows shot out, sound traveled more than adequately.

One of the three windows above the doors burst open, but Whipsnade had been waiting for that. He let the beagle with the bucket lean out to try to pour accurately into the flames and shot the man through the head.

For a moment, it seemed as if the dying man would plunge down into the flames, but there was someone behind him who hauled him back and reached out to haul the shutters closed; Grimstone did the honors, this time, and the man fell back with a gurgle, leaving the shutters swinging open.

There was more choking—"More *enthusiastic* choking," as Whipsnade put it fondly—coming from the hall inside the front doors. The defenders of Foxden obviously feared the house would burn down if they didn't fight the growing conflagration, for they suddenly thrust open the doors as far as the carefully entangled burning ladders would allow. Sparks swirled, and Whipsnade and Grimstone stepped out of concealment side by side and fired carefully, felling beagle after beagle after soldier, until everyone was down or had fled, leaving the doors ajar and the disarranged fire dying.

The two men of the Order exchanged glances. Aside from a few single-shot derringers both had hidden on their persons and hadn't preferred to reveal to each other yet, they were both almost out of ammunition. However, some of the men at the door had been holding pistols, and presumably all had been armed.

They slipped along the front wall to where they could plunder the fallen and eventually found themselves the new owners of no less than seven loaded pistols. They left the truncheons and knives on the bodies, except for one billy that Whipsnade tossed into the house.

There was no reaction from within. The two exchanged glances, shrugged, and slipped through the open doors, keeping low.

The front hall was deserted.

Though they had no idea just which bedroom the Prince Royal might be using, or where His Highness was just now, both men knew as much of the layout of Foxden as builders' plans revealed. They chose the most likely passage and set off along it, darting along with pistols ready.

It took them quite some time to kill their way to the Prince's bedroom, and by then the crashings and shooting had ended—was the Iron Assassin down, or had he succeeded and departed?—and their pistols were no more than clubs.

Fireplace pokers served better, and Whipsnade and Grimstone went back from room to room until they each had a good hefty one in hand.

Being out of bullets seemed to be a common affliction; the servants and beagles standing desperate guard in front of the doors of this last room didn't aim or fire anything at the two advancing men of the Order, just clutched pistols like clubs, and in one case raised a pitchfork that looked like it had come from the stables quite recently.

Grimstone chose a beagle at one end of the row and took a hearty swing. The man shouted in pain as the poker shattered his thumb and sent his empty pistol flying; when the man beside him rushed to his aid, Whipsnade met that second beagle with a vicious swing of his poker, splitting the man's head. Blood and brains splattered, men screamed and spewed, and the two Order men murderously battered the first beagle, caught between them, to the floor.

That still left three frightened men and a lad in front of the doors, wavering uncertainly. Whipsnade gave them a cheerful grin as he stalked forward, and the boy let out a moan and bolted. Or, no, took two steps and fell to the floor in a dead faint. Whipsnade promptly kicked the body into the ankles of the men behind it, toppling them forward to where he and Grimstone could smash in their skulls, swinging their pokers freely.

They had a little fun with the last man, stabbing him with their pokers as if they were fencing masters, while he was busily, desperately holding up his pitchfork to defend his head. He stared at them in disbelief as he went down, fighting to breathe and spitting blood with every wheeze, so they silenced him with blows to the head, then served the senseless lad the same way.

"Now," Whipsnade told Grimstone, "let's see if royal blood really does flow blue."

Grimstone stood cautiously to one side of the door, tried it, discovered it was locked, and said with a sigh, "They *do* make things as difficult as they can, don't they?"

I *refuse*," the Lord Lion of the Empire said obstinately, "to cower inside this room while others face death on my behalf. I must insist you open that door."

Pistol in one hand and drawn sword in the other, he gave Tempest a stern look and added, "That, my lord, is a royal command! *Open that door!*"

"Yes, Your Highness," Lord Tempest said wearily and set aside the fireplace poker he'd taken up to head for the door.

Just as Malmerston whirled around and landed a magnificent roundhouse swing to the point of the royal jaw.

Tempest spun around and rushed—and was just in time to help lower the senseless Prince Royal onto the edge of the bed.

"There's an old priest's hole," the butler panted. "Help me—"

Tempest and Rose helped hold the Lord Lion in place, draped along the edge of the bed. Lil was busy on the far side of the bed, or rather in an open closet there, struggling with something huge and metallic and trailing a steam hose, dragging it out into the bedchamber.

Malmerston did something to a carving in the polished wooden moldings that sheathed the wall behind the head of the bed, and a secret door swung open. There was just room enough around the headboard—which proved to be backed by thick new metal plates—for he and Tempest to lift the limp and unconscious Lord Lion and bundle him into the darkness beyond.

They more or less fell through the secret door together, kicking it closed—just as two doors into the room crashed open.

Rose shrieked and ducked under the bed—just as the Iron Assassin lurched in through one door, and Whipsnade and Grimstone burst into the bedroom from the other.

All three then came to a sudden halt to gape at what they saw on the canopied four-poster bed.

There was no Prince Royal in the room. No men at all, in fact.

However, there *was* a woman.

Lying on the bed, from which arose the insistent wheezing of a steam piston. She was lushly beautiful, her magnificent bosom was bared, and there was a wanton smile on her rouged face. She beckoned them, writhing on the silks.

"My, my," said Whipsnade. Just as Lil chose her target, rolled off the large steam mitrailleuse she'd dragged out of the closet and hidden under herself, and emptied the volley gun into the Iron Assassin, opening up visible holes in his torso and hammering him back through the door he'd come in by, right out of the room.

She tried to horse the gun around, but its head of steam was dying, and Whipsnade and Grimstone pounced on her before she could even put her hand on the crank.

Even as she bit his hand, Whipsnade snarled to Grimstone, pointing with his other hand, "There's a secret door behind the head of the bed, yonder! They were all gathered to guard it; *he* must be in there! The Prince is ours!"

OCTEMBER 15

Whipsnade's pointing shout became an agonized *"eeeep!"* as Lil drove a very hard knee into his most tender of places.

"Count not your unhatched chickens," she gasped in his ear in the instant before she bit it—hard. He shrieked like a young lass.

Grimstone abandoned him to his fate and turned, slipping on the silks, to dive off the bed and head for the secret door.

Just as the closet door on the other side of the headboard banged open—and Whipsnade, Grimstone, and the struggling Lil beneath them were buried under the sudden fist-swinging onslaught of Hardcastle, Standish, and four brawny beagles.

A lesser bed would have collapsed under the weight of so many punching, clawing bodies, but the royal four-poster had been built by the same shipwrights who'd crafted ships of the line in the era of sail, and it could have supported ten times as many combatants. Even its canopy was as sturdy as a deck—which was a very good thing for Rose, who slipped out from under the ominously creaking bed during the fray, amid the grunts and snarls and smacks of fists on flesh, and tried to get through the secret door.

No matter what she did, it wouldn't open, so she turned and, in desperation, climbed one of the bedposts—unnoticed by the brawlers—and disappeared up onto the canopy. Which proved to have its own floor, low brass rails all around, and a collection of lingerie, whips, and leather paraphernalia that she would have found intriguing indeed at another time.

Down below, one of the beagles bellowed in pain as he rolled over the hard volley gun and the jutting handle of its crank, under the onslaught of some hard knees. Another growled like a bear for a moment, then fell abruptly silent as Grimstone's hard kick to the side of his jaw slammed his head hard into a very solid bedpost.

Whipsnade had bitten Hardcastle's knuckles, causing Bleys pain enough that he'd forgotten all decency for an instant and was now trying his damnedest to punch Whipsnade's throat into a flattened ruin of flesh and bone—attacks that would have been fatal if Whipsnade hadn't been wearing a metal gorget against this very peril.

Grimstone found himself pinned under Chief Inspector Standish and two decidedly heavy beagles, all of whom seemed to be masters of the solid punch to the kidneys, and he, too, might have expired had he not managed to slide back the sheath on his finger ring, which had tiny metal fangs tipped with potent paralytic snake venom. Something he'd repeatedly dosed himself with so as to gain partial immunity to its effects—effects that the beagles, by their swift descents into limp immobility, were enjoying to the proverbial hilt.

He rolled himself out from under them, slapping Lil across the face with his ring for good measure and enjoying her startled look of openmouthed horror as she toppled back onto the silks, and retrieved his poker.

Which he promptly swung viciously at the back of Hardcastle's head, felling the man right out of the bed on a chute of helplessly slithering silks.

Whipsnade drove his fist into the throat of the last beagle atop him, and Grimstone served the reeling constable a generous helping of fireplace poker, then shoved the senseless man aside so Whipsnade could get up.

"Nice fight," he commented with an unlovely grin, retrieving his own poker. He and Grimstone looked around the room—bodies, bodies everywhere, and no foe standing—and then approached the secret door.

"Batter or pry?"

"Pry first. The more we damage it, the harder it'll be to pry with success."

So they thrust the tips of their pokers under the top corner of the door and set about prying. Metal shrieked, then groaned, and then tried shrieking again.

And the no-longer-secret door started to give way.

I t had been a long time since Bentley Steelforce had been anything akin to a "silent man." He wasn't being anything close to silent right now. He might no longer need to breathe or eat, but he could still feel pain.

God, he could still feel pain!

The stream of bullets that had slammed him had shot holes right through him, grisly gaps from his belt to halfway up his shattered ribs. Every step was agony, and when he made the mistake of *twisting* . . .

He just wanted to get *away*. Stumbling along the passage the bullets had driven him down, putting more and more distance between himself and that terrible weapon, he . . . he was done with this.

You will turn around, creature! Marlshrike's voice, in his head, was rising in fury and fear. *You will go back and fight through every obstacle until you reach Tempest and kill him! Tear him apart, so that there can be no doubt that he is dead! Bring me back his head as proof—yes, tear it from his body! NOW!*

Steelforce smote his own head with a fist, trying to silence that railing. He started to run, sickening pain jolting him at every footfall, as he got farther and blessedly farther away . . .

Bodies underfoot. Door. Smash open, out into the night, cooler and darker and . . . trees, run into the trees . . .

You will turn around! Turn around now! I command it!

Lights—headlamps, and the roar of hurrying steam carriages. Men shouting and pointing, the crack of shots.

Through the panting, the sobbing, the groans, he managed to say, "I—"

Beagles and soldiers, carriage after carriage, roaring and screeching. More gunfire.

Turn around, Steelforce, or I'll—

He tried again, more loudly. "I am—"

Into the trees, footfalls crashing on gravel behind him, men bellowing at him to stop. On into the trees, not slowing, bashing head into branches to see if he could make the voice in his—

"I am *the Iron Assassin*!" That shout echoed through the forest.

Trees and darkness and running, running, running; the voice in his head braying unheeded; the pain his shield against his commands . . .

Darkness deepening, the pain a waiting pit.

Bentley Steelforce flung himself into it and fell forever.

That's got it," said Whipsnade, with some satisfaction. "Back behind it, now, and we'll haul together . . ."

Back beyond the hinges of the door where gunfire shouldn't reach them, Whipsnade and Grimstone hauled hard with their pokers, peeling back the steel door. It was rather like opening one of the new tins of sardines. So, would the Prince Royal weep and cower or burst forth like the lion all the stirring tales from the Palace made him out to be?

"Let's see the real color of your blood," Grimstone murmured, as the door folded back with a last protesting creak.

Leaving them staring at a tall, narrow doorway into darkness.

A silent, waiting darkness.

"Come out, you coward!" Whipsnade called, expecting no answer and receiving none.

He looked at Grimstone. "No echo, so not a tunnel. It *should* be just a little room. So unless this whole thing has been a ruse, with all of these fools fighting like tigers to protect nothing at all, with His Royal Nibs elsewhere all along . . ."

"Toss in a lit oil lamp," Grimstone replied calmly, "and, one way or another, we'll see."

"Derringer?" Whipsnade suggested, as he stepped back to look around for an oil lamp.

"Derringer," Grimstone agreed, reaching into his sleeve.

It was at that moment that Lord Tempest burst through the narrow door and charged right into him. Head down and trying just for speed, ramming the Tentacles man right in his gut like a bull and keeping right on going, rushing the staggering and winded Grimstone across the room.

Whipsnade raced after him with poker raised—or tried to. It was hard to race anywhere with a woman's garter around your neck and wrapped around your poker, and with a woman dropping to the floor right behind you, putting her full weight into strangling you.

He arched over backward, sobbing for breath and trying to get one hand under what was cutting so cruelly into his throat, while he tried to tear the poker free with the other.

"Excuse me," said a cultured voice, "but I *don't* think so."

Whipsnade had a brief glimpse of the butler—the *butler?*—striding past him from the priest hole, an ancient but recently shortened halberd in his hands. That comment had been directed at him, and Malmerston reinforced it by deftly slashing a few fingers off Whipsnade's poker-wielding hand.

Whipsnade tried to scream but lacked the air. Lady Rose had her knees up against his back and was pulling with all her might; if the garter didn't break, there would be no more screaming for Miles Whipsnade, or anything else . . .

The garter broke.

By then, Malmerston had run the business end of his halberd through Grimstone's leg, and Lady Roodcannon's faithful aide was doing enough screaming for both agents of the Order.

Sobbing for breath, Whipsnade fell forward. He kicked out viciously behind him as he did so and sent his unseen assailant tumbling.

Snatching out his derringer, he fired—at Malmerston's face, but the halberd got in the way. The result was a clang, sparks, and Malmerston's wringing a bleeding hand as the halberd cartwheeled to the floor, its shaft striking Tempest across the forehead and leaving him dazed.

It was at this juncture that the two men of the Ancient Order decided they'd had enough and staggered for the bedroom door.

"Victory!" Grimstone gasped, limping and bleeding copiously as they hastened down the passage outside.

"Survival!" Whipsnade husked in reply, clutching his throat with both hands.

Had even one of the Foxden house cats barred their way, the pair might have gone down to defeat, but the felines, being sensible creatures, had hidden under beds upon the Iron Assassin's violent arrival, so the way was clear.

A shouting army of reinforcements were cautiously approaching the front doors of Foxden, with more guns and lights than Whipsnade had ever seen gathered in one place before, so the two men of the Order turned and made for the kitchen door, and the waiting night outside.

Where it was dark, and the foremost soldiers sent to form a ring around the house were still stumbling and cursing their way through unfamiliar terrain, firing bullets through offending topiary that loomed up out of the night like silently waiting men.

The two battered Tentacles agents raced past the soldiery and into the forest, which seemed to be alive with bellowings and crashings.

"I am the Iron Assassin!" echoed one shout, nearer than the rest.

"That's—" Whipsnade panted.

"Certainly *sounds* like him," Grimstone panted back.

They stopped to listen, clinging to each other and a handy tree for support. It very soon became clear that the Assassin was off *that* way, and most of the crashings were coming from persons pursuing him.

"So if we merely keep him between us and his pursuers, it matters little what noise we make," Grimstone concluded.

"Find the path," Whipsnade croaked, "and things will go more quietly, anyway. Back to London."

"Back to London," Grimstone agreed. "Good innings, what?"

"Good innings," Whipsnade agreed, and stumbled after his fellow Tentacle, rubbing his aching throat. He couldn't *stop* rubbing it.

He'd never been desperately garroted before, and he hadn't expected it to *itch* so much.

Lord Tempest?" Malmerston inquired imperturbably. "Are you . . . functional?"

The man on his knees groaned, explored his left temple with tentative fingers, and replied, "That's been a . . . matter of debate for . . . some years."

"Ah. I was hoping you might assist me with a small matter of bandaging."

Jack Straker staggered to his feet, finding his knees more than a trifle rubbery. His head hurt like blazes—especially the head on the left. "Er—ah?"

The butler held out a hand from which blood dripped steadily from the fingertips. "If you would be so good as to wrap this bandage tightly around this gash, here . . ."

"That gash, Malmerston, is a bullet hole."

"Be that as it may, sir . . ."

"Of course, of course; here, let me—there. Tight enough?"

"I believe so. Tie it so the ends . . . yes. Quite so, sir. I thank you."

"You're welcome, Malmerston. So, did we win?"

"They got away, sir. I believe the Lady Harminster is only bruised and winded, sir; I have assisted her to a chair. The others—Mister Hardcastle, the Chief Inspector, and the rest—appear to have suffered the effects of something causing paralysis, but it is already passing off."

"Yes, but the Prince, man! Is he—?"

There was a thump from the secret doorway, and the Lord Lion of the Empire staggered out of the priest hole into the bedchamber, asking aggrievedly, "Who hit me?"

OCTEMBER 16

It was the custom of Mister Halworthy Burton, Lord Staunton, the Lord Chamberlain, and the Commissioner of the Queen's High Constabulary to meet at dawn in Burton's innermost office in Whitehall at least once a fortnight—and in these latter months, more often once a week—to discuss threats to the Empire.

They were meeting now, over steaming cups of the blackest coffee, amid the reek of the thinnest and most fashionable new black cigars. Outside the windows, the fog hadn't yet lifted off the Thames, but it was busily doing so.

Which meant matters were coming to a seeming boil on both sides of the windows.

With a relatively new Lord Chamberlain at the table, some old arguments had become new ones. Bertram Buckingham, like Lord Staunton, was apt to be more accepting of progress and innovation than either Burton (for whom "the new" always meant more headaches—new laws and regulations, new dodges, new unforeseen bad consequences) or Lord Percy Harkness, who had to enforce laws and regulations and liked to know where he—and for that matter, the Empire—stood. Hopefully on solid ground that shifted little or not at all.

"Burton," the Lord Chamberlain sighed now, "why can't you *ever* see the larger picture? The longer view?"

Lord Staunton rolled his eyes, anticipating one of Burton's potted speeches. He was not disappointed; Halworthy Burton wheeled an all-too-familiar verbal cannon into position and let fly.

"There are those who say we should concern ourselves with grand plans and bold schemes and that only the small-minded concern themselves with the characters and doings of mere individuals. Yet in *my* experience, people who hold such views are the very same souls who are most apt to ride roughshod over anyone who holds views that don't accord with their own—or just anyone it pleases them to play the charging bull against."

"Ah. I see matters rather differently. I see someone who begins our every debate with either 'That won't work, and I'll tell you why' or 'We must not under any circumstances allow that, because.' Which may well be the right way to avoid all work but rather a poor way to run an empire—where change will be thrust upon us no matter how energetically we forbid and deny. I would rather steer change than be booted up the behind by it, time and again."

"Lord *Chamberlain*," said Burton heavily, exasperation clear in every syllable, "you seem willfully unaware that we of the Crown do, in fact, daily manipulate which steam innovations succeed most swiftly by either supporting or frustrating inventors."

"'Frustrating' as in—?"

"As in," Harkness growled, "setting fires in workshops, perpetrating strategic thefts and vandalism, and—oh, yes, as very much a last resort, it seems, 'hiring aside' certain inventors into other work." The lawlessness was obviously a sore point for the Commissioner.

"We've had this out before, Harkness," Burton snapped. "The ends *far* outweigh the means. Why—"

"There speaks the archconservative," Buckingham interrupted. "Just because a matter has been debated before does *not* mean it has been settled until the end of time and can never be raised again. Governance consists of continual revisiting and reevaluation, or we'd still have slavery and serfdom, and—"

"Ah, but that's just it, Buckingham," put in Lord Staunton dryly. *"We still do."*

"If we could return to the point," Burton said fussily.

"Which is always whatever point *you* wish to pursue," Harkness said flatly, "rather than whatever we're getting around to discussing that you don't want discussed."

"Yes," Buckingham pounced. "I, for one, would very much like to discuss just *why* ends always justify means. Isn't that the position of every tyrant? Every warmonger? Every—"

"Oh, *do* leave off *speechifying,* man! You're not in Parliament right now, you know!"

"If you want me to stop making speeches, Burton, suppose you return to specifics. Name me some of these tinkerers we're encouraging and some of those we're working to stop. If I like your choices, you just might find that my resistance on this issue vanishes like river mist in the noonday sun."

Burton blinked across the table, then said slowly, "Well, that's reasonable enough, I suppose. We're encouraging Halvingham of Surrey, who's working on small steam-pump vacuum effects under glass domes, for domestic uses—tube systems to whisk small items around a house or shop and to remove air under a dome to make food get stale or spoil more slowly. Our aid consists of lowering his taxes for a year and seeing that he has unfettered access to suppliers—the best glassblowers, the rubber importers. We're helping Blustard of Liverpool the same way; he's trying to make large rubber roundels for carriage wheels that he calls 'tyres.' Imagine the rumbling of carts by night being a sort of whishing sound or the din in some factories losing all the thunder of wheels and just retaining the hissing and piston noises of the steam."

"Both of those seem worthy of encouragement. So, one you're trying to stop?"

"Tyndale and his lightning gun," Harkness put in. "Zaps anyone and everything within half a mile—more when a storm's coming and the air is heavy. He's killed sixteen people we know of, so far, just with his prototype—grandmothers, young lads and lasses—oh, and any number of birds, family pets, and livestock. Cooks chickens but leaves them raw."

The Lord Chamberlain shuddered. "That, too, I have no quarrel with."

"The real danger," Halworthy Burton told him, leaning forward across the table, "is the maverick, the gifted amateur—Tempest, for instance."

"So he is," the Lord Chamberlain agreed, "but your maverick is also the source of most of the great advances, the ones that don't come by increments and painstaking refinement but are truly new. Innovative."

"*Dangerous,*" Harkness and Burton growled together.

"Enough of this," Lord Staunton said firmly. "We have some truly pressing concerns before us, and we can revisit these particular battlegrounds whenever we have the leisure and inclination to do so. I believe we are all agreed that the Ancient Order is raising steam for something?"

"It certainly seems that way."

"Yes, but it *always* seems that way," Burton growled. "They achieve importance by the controversy they court, by being outrageous. They never stop."

"Thereby wearying you, so you won't react fast and hard enough when they make their *real* move," Harkness told him. "I'd say they're counting on that."

"Well, then, impress me. Convince me that this is a 'real' threat and not the usual 'each agent tries to make a name for himself by seeing how much he can accomplish' alarums."

Harkness looked up. "Buckingham, you can put it more clearly and quickly than I can, and we've wasted enough time. Go to it."

"Well, I'll try." The Lord Chamberlain cleared his throat, pushed aside the ashtray in which the Commissioner's row of three lit cigars were smoldering, and said, "The most worrying signal is the arrival of Venetta Deleon, maid to the Dowager Duchess, and her visits to seemingly *all* who carry weight within the Ancient Order of Tentacles. The woman is wearing out shoes; those we have following her certainly are. And being as some of those she's going to see include high-ups in some guilds and all of the important political parties, this looks to be really big; the future of the Empire may well be at stake."

"Speechifying again," Burton muttered.

"Perhaps, but I *cannot* overemphasize the gravity of this. The Dowager Duchess is trying to talk to everyone of consequence in the Ancient Order in a matter of days."

"A call to war?" Staunton asked quietly.

"Looks like," Harkness agreed.

"Well, then," Burton said, "the question before us is: What do we *do* about it? Stop her?"

"No," Buckingham replied. "We'll only delay whatever's about to happen and drive the Duchess to using other agents."

"No," Staunton agreed, "because this Deleon woman may yet reveal to us the identities of some new and hidden Order members in her travels."

"I, too, vote for not stopping her," Harkness agreed, "but I must caution that watching and following everyone she's visiting is going to strain the resources of the Constabulary to the limit. We're hard-pressed to keep patrols on the streets right now, and rushing out to Foxden every night for a few more of my men to get shot dead or sent to hospital with major injuries isn't helping matters."

"So strip the counties," Burton suggested. "Bring your most competent men in from the countryside."

"All three of them," Harkness grunted.

"Strip York, Manchester, Liverpool, and the Tyneside nearly bare," Staunton put in, "sacrificing their safety—as quietly as possible, of course—to ride herd on everything in London. And arm every last beagle watcher and follower, and damn the consequences. If innocents get killed, so be it, if greater disaster is averted. We need sufficient armed might to move fast, win battles, and clamp down if need be."

They all looked at Buckingham, who sighed, nodded, and said reluctantly, "In this case the end *does* seem to justify the means. Do what you must."

"Well, then," Burton said, reaching for his cigar, "it seems to me that we need to commandeer the royal airships, too."

The Lord Chamberlain frowned. "The—?"

"Both the huge sky yacht *Britannia* and the little *Swift* that shuttles the Lord Lion to and from his, ah, more private engagements. We need to be able to follow Order members who have their own airships—such as the Lady Roodcannon, who's been known to ferry entire shooting parties to stately homes all over the countryside and, we suspect, arranged that some of those shooting parties were really sniper training."

Buckingham winced. "I've no objection."

Burton looked around the table. "Anyone? No? Decided then."

Buckingham rubbed his upper lip with a thoughtful forefinger. It was amazing how Burton went from being the embattled odd man out to deciding and dominating. Perhaps it was because it was his office and his table . . .

Harkness took a small hammer of the sort used for cracking sheets of hard sweets and a small bell hanging from a hook like a drooping bluebell and struck the one with the other. The room echoed with a piercing ring, an astonishingly loud sound from such a small bell.

It brought Assistant Commissioner Alston Drake into the room in a rush. Burton had already finished scribbling something on a paper, which he folded and handed to Harkness, who put it in Drake's hands and ordered, "Take this to the Prince Royal at Foxden and get his approval. Don't tarry."

Drake hurried out, and the door had barely closed behind him when a distant explosion rattled the windows, smiting at their ears like a blow.

All four men rushed to see what had happened out on the river.

They had to crane and peer for quite some time and wait for more fog to lift, but it became apparent that two ships—or rather, a steamship and a row of barges—had collided. The Thames filled up with small boats full of shouting men trying to help, as the barges sank beneath the waters and the steamship started to list, giving off a huge plume of black smoke. It looked to be an accident, rather than deviltry or a deliberate ramming among rivals.

"Third one this week," Harkness commented. "*More* work for my lads."

"There's going to be more and more of that—and in the air, too— if we don't keep a firm hand on the tiller, gentle sirs," Burton said crisply. "We need strict and clear laws, and plenty of them, and soon. Things are moving too fast."

"Things are *already* moving too fast," the Lord Chamberlain retorted. "Just as laws always lag behind the troubles they seek to redress or curb. It's never an excuse for running roughshod over liberties."

Burton gave him a look of open dislike. "So what would you have us do, my lord Liberty for All? Loose the hounds and have no one whipping them or calling them off?"

Lord Staunton shook his head. "No. That's not working."

Burton turned to give the nobleman an incredulous look. "What?"

Lord Staunton met it with a smile and said mildly around his cigar, "Oh, yes, we're trying that right now, Burton. Haven't you noticed?"

Uncle looked up from his steamed frogs and kedgeree. "You were missed at breakfast, Whipsnade," he observed. "Suppose you tell me why."

"Foxden, sir," Whipsnade husked. "Didn't manage to bag the Prince, but there are a lot of beagles and soldiers—and so-called royal servants who're really the Prince's bodyguards—who'll never see another sunset."

"I see. I don't recall ordering you into the vicinity of Foxden." Uncle's voice was mild, but Whipsnade knew that glint in his master's eye.

"You commented regarding the arrival from the Continent of the maid, sir. Said her arrival couldn't help but create a stir and force us to see to things we'd been neglecting."

"Such as the murder of the Prince Royal? Small matters of that sort, that I might have overlooked?"

Whipsnade winced.

"Suppose you tell me about it. Omit nothing. Who struck whom, who hit back, all that sort of thing. Mind you don't leave out a detailed description of whoever tried to garrote you."

"Yes, sir," Whipsnade replied, and did as he was ordered.

As his narrative unfolded, Uncle's anger gave way to amusement, and before he was done, his master looked eager, almost delighted.

"I trust you've learned a lesson regarding frolicking with noble-women," Uncle commented, then sat back, put down his cutlery, and smiled.

He stared through the far wall, thinking, and his smile broadened. Whipsnade waited.

Then his master stirred. "I shall be most interested to see what unfolds as a result of this," he announced, and pointed at his plate. "Take this away, Whipsnade. The frog is entirely too froggy this morning; I'll have none of it. Bring me some fried snake, instead."

The room was shrouded in black taffeta, walls and ceiling. It had no windows and was dominated by a mirror taller and broader than even a strikingly large person. That plain but beautifully silvered mirror was flanked by two gaslamps that protruded from the taffeta on long, upcurving brass arms. It was Lady Roodcannon's most private chamber, the refuge she sought out when she needed to talk to herself.

She was talking to herself—in the mirror—right now.

Lady Constance Roodcannon was by no means as icily or breezily self-confident as she liked the Empire to think she was. Yet a woman who showed the slightest weakness got savaged, swiftly, by the human sharks who cruised tirelessly, watching.

It had been a very long time since she'd been savaged, and she fully intended that it would never, ever, happen again.

Just now, she was troubled, and she hated that, had worked hard these last twenty years to ensure that very few things troubled her. Every matter that did was, after all, a weakness.

The maid Venetta had just departed. The messenger from the Dowager Duchess, who'd called on her in accordance with detailed instructions from the Duchess. The call to arms she'd delivered had so obviously been a bid for absolute control over the Ancient Order.

Not to mention a warning to anyone who presumed to act with any measure of independence at all, noble ladies more than others, and noblewomen named Lady Constance Roodcannon in particular.

So.

Before coming to this room, she'd gone and reassured herself that the love letters from the Prince Royal she'd kept for so long and the physician's letter stating that the Prince was the father of her son—who was a dead ringer for the Prince, anyway—were still safe. They were, and their defenses were now redoubled.

She'd known this challenge would come and heralded a battle that would come soon. Why, then, was she so filled with sudden misgivings, her heart *thudding* so?

Grimstone. It was Grimstone. Where had he gone? Oh, he often vanished of nights to do her bidding or to see to any of the scores of minor matters that kept her household running smoothly, and she trusted him to do so. Thus far without any hint, no matter what spies she sent after him, that her trust was misplaced. Yet he usually reappeared long before this time of day; what could have happened to him?

She *was* fond of him—she could admit it now. And it would be *so* tiresome to find and train a proper replacement.

And if—horrors!—he'd betrayed her and thrown in with a rival, it would be utter disaster—but, no, she couldn't bear to dwell on such possibilities. Not until they became probabilities and had to be faced.

"So," she told her mirror, "the Duchess has married a German noble. And one of the most thick-necked brutes among them, too. Why, I wonder? For his money? Or in his dabblings in the slave trade has he built himself a band of thugs strong enough to be useful when she sails into our midst to conquer the Ancient Order of Tentacles?"

The image in the mirror gave her no answers, staring back at her with a solemnity that bordered on sadness.

Staring into her own somber eyes, she came to a sudden decision.

Stripping off her clothes—everything, every last piece of jewelry—she donned the leather trousers and jacket of an airship pilot, headpiece and goggles and all.

Throwing a dark inverness over them, she turned off the gaslamps that flanked her mirror, making the pilot in the mirror vanish in an instant, and hastened out.

Grimstone was heartily sick of limping and staggering. Almost sick enough to be glad to see Clarence Sarkbottle.

Officially, Sarkbottle was a doctor no more. The courts were rather unforgiving of doctors who did some of the things he'd done. Nor was he a handsome man, or wealthy, or well-connected.

Wherefore he could now be found here, in this ramshackle shed and yard that stank of dead dogs, in a part of London not safe for a lone wounded, limping man. Grimstone had been forcibly reminded of that several times during his journey, and although he had prevailed, his temper had suffered.

The door opened before Grimstone could pull the rusty chain that rang the bell, and Grimstone found himself regarding one of Sarkbottle's thugs. He had to look up to meet the man's childlike face, marred by the grotesque hole left behind by a missing nose. Sliced off years ago. Sarkbottle had stitched on any number of replacements, but a man looks even worse with someone else's rotting, dead nose dangling from his face.

"Urrr?" the man inquired, in unfriendly tones.

"Sarkbottle," Grimstone replied. "I need to get stitched up."

The thug's eyes flickered, and he stepped back and slammed the door.

Grimstone waited, leaning on the stick he'd liberated from the clutches of a timid old man some thirty streets back.

Sarkbottle appeared at the door, as sour and chinless as ever, his thick glasses even more smudged and ill repaired, and greeted his visitor without enthusiasm.

"Halberd through my leg," Grimstone explained tersely. "Want to be able to walk."

Sarkbottle peered down at a leg that was by now black with dried blood and soaked dark red with the more recent bleeding of Grimstone's adventuresome journey. "The price will be high."

"I'll pay it, or I wouldn't be here."

"In," Sarkbottle replied, retreating from the threshold so Grimstone could do so.

What followed was bloody and excruciatingly painful, and the price was high, but whatever Sarkbottle injected into him numbed the pain entirely—for now. Grimstone retained the walking stick, for later, and went to get the doctor's payment.

Sarkbottle ensured his clients paid by sending two burly thugs with them, two unlovely and unshaven mountains Grimstone privately thought of as Noseless and Fang. Noseless was the lout who'd opened the door, and Fang was an older man with just one tooth left—a canine that protruded down over his lower lip and gave him the look of an old and crotchety crocodile.

Grimstone led them across London to one of the older city cemeteries, where he went to a grand but overgrown family crypt that did not bear the name Grimstone.

"Here," Fang snarled, "what're you playing at?"

Grimstone went up the worn stone steps, unlocked the ornate black door, and said, "Wait here."

Noseless did just that, standing like a patient fence post, but Fang shifted from foot to foot for a short time, lost patience, and went up the steps and through that dark door.

Where he found himself looking down the barrel of a large pistol—and feeling the hard, round maw of another in his gut.

"I told you," Grimstone said very quietly, "to wait outside."

Fang blinked, backed away, and found himself being herded back down the steps. The inevitable ravens flapped past, to land atop the headstones of the lesser dead, cock their heads, and watch with interest. Professional interest. You never did know where your next meal was coming from.

Grimstone returned to the crypt briefly, then emerged again and relocked the door. "Don't try to rummage in there later on," he warned. "The traps will kill you. Painfully. And you'll never find them all."

Fang was taller than Grimstone and so had caught a glimpse of what was in the casket Grimstone had opened. A moldering, reeking corpse alive with gnawing worms, that seemed afloat in a sea of gold coins, and of course more pistols. Aside, that is, from the two he had menaced Fang with and was undoubtedly carrying now.

"What is all this, then?" Fang demanded, waving at the crypt.

Grimstone regarded them both for a moment, considering. Then decided telling them the truth was the best way to frighten them into leaving his hideaway alone.

"I," he announced, "am a bone thief."

They paled and shifted their feet, backing away from him a little, so he knew they grasped at least a little of what that meant.

"On the side," Grimstone added pleasantly. Noseless just looked blank, but Fang started to frown in puzzlement. It promptly started to rain. Cold and hard.

So Grimstone explained, "Sometimes, I'm ordered to kill people, and their bodies are left to be found, as warnings. Other times, the body isn't to be found; they're just supposed to vanish. Yes?"

Fang nodded. Noseless looked at Fang, then started nodding, too.

"So when I have to make them vanish, I go to one of the older boneyards, break open a crypt, and put the body in one of the coffins that's in there. I have to take the bones that're already there out, to make room—so I sell them to rag-and-bone men or, better, to the likes of Doctor Sarkbottle, who'll pay more, because he can re-sell them to tinkerers and cultists and the like. That's why he agreed to doctor me at all—because he'd promised."

"We keep promises," Noseless intoned, obviously repeating what Sarkbottle had told him.

"Indeed. Which is why you're going to promise me now to leave this crypt alone. Never come near it, never open its door, never tell anyone else what's inside. Even Doctor Sarkbottle."

"Why?" Fang asked bluntly.

"Because you'll live longer, that's why—and you won't die slowly, screaming in agony."

"Oh," Fang replied, and looked at Noseless.

Who smiled brightly, and said proudly, "Never come back. Under*stand*."

He led the way out of the cemetery, and Grimstone successfully repressed a shudder as they headed for the yard full of dead dogs.

There were times when he *really* appreciated having Lady Rood-cannon as an employer, for all her faults.

His manhood started to itch then, as if reminding him. But of a fault, or a benefit?

Foxden resounded with many hammerings, sawings, and fre-quent clatters of boards and posts being dropped atop more boards and posts. Why were carpenters always so abominably *noisy*?

And this lot were making this infernal din despite the fact that they were being watched over by a coldly suspicious army of defenders!

Still, perhaps royal household carpenters were used to such scrutiny—and to repairing the aftermath of wild gun battles, too.

Beside her, the bruised and bandaged Mister Hardcastle fumbled with his teacup and almost dropped it. Rose stopped reflecting about carpenters, noisy or otherwise, and rescued it *just* before Hardcastle slopped it all down her leg. And a good thing, too; her wardrobe was *not* infinite.

He mumbled a mingled thanks and apology, and the two of them returned their attention to Jack Straker, across the table. Lord Tempest, still in his exoskeleton, was more battered and bandaged than the two of them combined yet was talking as excitedly and energetically as if he'd never been in any fights, suffered the slightest discomfort, or missed any sleep, either.

Rose stifled a yawn, shook her head ruefully, and made a mental note to just *stop* thinking of such things.

"We *must* remove this new control key from the Iron Assassin to get him uncontrolled again, but I'm afraid—what with this damned exoskeleton of mine getting damaged in the fighting—I now lack the mobility to do it."

He looked across the table. "So, as much as I hate to ask this of you, my dear . . ."

"You don't have to ask," Rose told him. "I regard it as my duty."

"Ah, capital, capital! That means Bleys here won't have to tackle Steelforce alone. I'm thinking he can do the distraction and fisticuffs, whilst a certain Lady Harminster flips open the access door from behind."

The wounded Hardcastle winced. "I ache just thinking about it," he said, reaching for his tea again. "Mane of the Lion, but I hurt!"

"We are a trio of wounded old soldiers, aren't we?" Rose murmured ruefully.

"Indeed," Tempest agreed, pouring more tea for them all. "This isn't like a magazine serial or one of those fanciful tales about consulting detectives, where people conveniently confess and everything gets wound up tidily at the bottom of a page. Real life is almost never so clear-cut, so definite, so clean. It's all messy and dirty and disorganized loose ends." He flashed a grin. "That's what I love about it."

"Excuse me," Malmerston interrupted smoothly, bending over their table to address Tempest. Behind him, half a dozen burly soldiers were sweating under the weight of some crates of rather unusual dimensions. "There is an immediate and pressing need, my lord, to know where you want all this clobber. Sir."

"In the room you gave me. It's large, but not so large that it can't share space with my bed. If I feel the need to waltz with someone, I'll borrow another room."

Rose leaned forward. "Is *what* large, if I may ask?"

"My machine that can trace etheric waves, so we can have a go at tracing Marlshrike," Tempest replied—just as Malmerston was shouldered aside by Drake of the Yard.

"This is your doing, isn't it?" he snapped furiously at Tempest.

"Drake, you seem perturbed," the lord observed calmly. "Have some tea."

The Assistant Commissioner of the beagles ignored that suggestion in favor of bellowing, "I am *furious*! Furious at anyone trying to bring a potentially *lethal* device, whose purpose isn't understood by us and for which we must trust a—a maverick inventor!—"

Tempest nodded and smiled.

"—so close to the most precious man in the Empire: the Lord Lion we all serve!"

"*I* trust him," said a voice from behind Drake.

The Prince Royal's utterance brought utter stillness to the room.

During which Drake dropped his face into his hands, shook his head, then spread his hands wide in an eloquent "I give up" gesture.

S arkbottle had been paid, and, thus far, Grimstone's leg was holding up. It ached, mind you, but his limp was gone and he was no longer bleeding with each step and feeling that the leg might collapse under him at any time.

So that left him with business to attend to, alone. Those two thugs had too much bone between their ears to ever be thoroughly terrified—or to refrain from talking about what they'd seen, somewhere and somehow.

Which meant, if he wanted to see the rest of his coins ever again, not to mention some quite useful pistols, he had to get right back to the cemetery in a hurry and shift his valuables from the now-known crypt to another one a row over.

The crypt the two thugs had accompanied him to was locked and undisturbed, but a surprise was waiting for Grimstone when he trudged into that second row, his first sack of valuables in hand, and up to the crypt he'd pillaged there a few months back.

Someone familiar was just stepping out of *another* crypt, three doors down.

Miles Whipsnade.

Who was carrying a sack of his own. Its shape told Grimstone its contents without having to ask: bones.

"Well, well," Whipsnade said with a lopsided smile. "We meet again."

"We do indeed," Grimstone agreed sardonically. "Two upright gentlemen with, it seems, the same sideline profession."

"Oh?"

"Bone thief."

"Ah. *Such* a harsh term. I prefer 'remains relocater' myself."

"Indeed. Such a coincidence that we chose the same cemetery."

"Among others."

"Among others, of course. Crypts are ideal for such pursuits, don't you think?"

"I am gathering the impression," Whipsnade observed carefully, "that we are both using crypts for more than just 'bones out, and valuables in.' I sense . . . kindred needs. As if I am not the only faithful servant in London who sees the prudent need to slowly and *very* carefully assemble certain evidence against my master that might someday prove useful if I must attempt to save my own skin. If, for example, I am ever collared by the beagles on a charge of . . . murder."

"Kindred needs, indeed," Grimstone replied, meeting the other man's eyes. "When we're done here, perhaps a pint together, at—"

There was a loud thud from nearby—from back the way he'd come.

From his first crypt, as it turned out. He and Whipsnade hastened there together and found one of Sarkbottle's two thugs lying dead on the crypt threshold, his head crushed by a falling-block trap.

It was Fang, by his boots. There wasn't a lot of his head left to get a proper look at his face.

"That didn't take long," Grimstone observed calmly. "Help me drag him inside so we can reset the block fall. With any luck, we'll bag the other one."

"You first," Whipsnade replied. "Being as I'm sure you have other traps in there."

Grimstone showed his teeth in what was almost a smile. "But of course."

The gates of the Tower of London had always been forbidding. Iron spikes, painted black, thick and so close together that only a thin man's arm could thrust through them beyond the elbow. Sir Fulton Birtwhistle had just discovered that he did not possess a sufficiently emaciated arm.

The discovery did not hearten him. Neither did the reception he was getting from the guards inside the gates, who were steadfastly refusing him entry.

Well, at least it had stopped raining. For now.

Not that the cessation of the downpour had done anything to improve Sir Fulton's temper. He had a *client* in there and was being denied access to the man! Prisoner in the Tower or prisoner in a village lockup, it made no difference! No citizen of the Empire could be denied their clear right to counsel!

So this is what "utterly furious" felt like. *Well.*

"You have no right to deny me, sir!" he bellowed, rapping his walking stick upon the bars. "Citizens of England have clearly established legal rights that you, sir, are flouting! I demand to see—"

"Demand all you like," the Yeoman Warder he'd been dealing with said coldly, drawing the fattest pistol Birtwhistle had ever seen from a leg holster and cocking it meaningfully. "He's not here."

"*What*? Well, what have you done with him?"

"Not at liberty to say. Sir. Go away, sir."

"I—I will not, so long as you deny me access to my client! Tell me where he is, or I'll assume you're *lying,* and that he is indeed insi—"

"Birtwhistle," an exasperated voice said from behind the Warder, "he's telling you the truth. There's been a gas leak, and although no one's hurt, we've moved *every* prisoner out of the Tower for the time being. He's in lockup at Cannon Street; take yourself there."

It was Halworthy Burton. Sir Fulton stared at him, eyes narrowing. Burton's every third sentence was a lie, if his own experience was anything to go by, and he detested the man. Moreover, the man detested *him*. It was hardly a relationship likely to foster trust, and here he was, being expected to trust—

A steam-powered coach rumbled up out of the night and stopped before the closed gates. Out climbed the Lord Chancellor of the Empire, who gave Birtwhistle a quizzical look. As he was doing so, a second coach wheezed up out of the night—and it disgorged old Throckmorton, the Imperial Herald, followed by the junior herald, Prycewood.

Sir Fulton's eyebrows rose, then lowered into a real frown. He turned to Burton. "Highly placed gas fitters you call, indeed!"

"Get gone," the Yeoman Warder said grimly, "or I'll—"

"Or you'll *what*? Shoot me down in cold blood?"

"Or my finger will slip on this heavy, awkward trigger, and this just *might* go off."

Whatever reply Sir Fulton might have made to *that* was lost forever in the steaming din of a third coach arriving.

Men sprang out of it, a lot of them, and commenced to advance threateningly on Birtwhistle. Uniformed, every last man—beagles and members of the Royal Household Guard.

Sir Fulton Birtwhistle backed hastily away, shaking his head.

Their presence could mean only one thing. Still in that third coach was the Queen herself.

Gas leak, indeed.

U ncle was eating a late-evening repast of snake with fried mushrooms. Whipsnade stood at ease at his master's shoulder, ready with the decanters.

"Something seems to be afoot, sir," he reported. "Assistant Commissioner Drake of the beagles pushed two houndcars into breakdown, one after the other, to get from Foxden back into London in great haste—and he's just been sighted leading a small force of heavily armed beagles from somewhere they were hiding—in Hackney, of all places—to the Tower of London. Fast."

His master gave him a look of real surprise. "Has a prisoner escaped?"

Whipsnade smiled like a cat. "That's the thing, sir. It seems all of the prisoners were removed from the Tower earlier today, *very* quietly. And the Lord Chancellor, the Imperial Herald, and the gray-haired half of Whitehall are already there."

Uncle's eyebrows shot up. "Cordon, yes? So we can't contact our spy inside the Tower?"

"Cordon."

"*Well*, now. I think you'd better pay a visit to Lady Rood—"

"Her private airship was seen departing London earlier today, sir. Heading south."

"South? Good heavens, as they say. Well, then, collar Smythe and Hulbread and Riverbree, and the thugs they lead, and head for the Tower. See what can be seen, learn as much as you can—and everybody armed, so anyone who gets a good look at you dies. After all, any dead beagle—"

"—is a good beagle! Sir!" Whipsnade nodded and hurried out.

I s it working?"

Tempest looked up from needles dancing wildly across dials. "Of *course* it's working, Drake. That's what my machines *do*."

"Well?"

"Well, *what*?"

Drake waved impatiently at the array of dials. "Haven't you found him yet? That's what your machine does, doesn't it?"

Tempest favored the senior beagle with a rather scathing look. "Haven't you got murders to solve? Go do something about that, Drake, or have a drink or something! Night's only just fallen, so all the noise the sun puts out is fading, but this device of mine traces etheric transmissions—any and all transmissions, *not* signals emanating from Norbert Marlshrike and no one else. There's quite a bit of sorting out in my immediate future. Perhaps a night or two of sorting; who knows?"

"Bah!" The Assistant Commissioner strode angrily away. "Music-hall flummery! Conjurer's tricks!"

Hardcastle uncoiled himself from where he'd been leaning against the wall, gave Tempest a grin, and asked, in nigh-perfect mimicry of the belligerent beagle, "So, is it working?"

His old friend chuckled, then tapped one of the dials. "I'm pretty certain *that's* Marlshrike. But only pretty certain."

"Ah. 'Pretty certain' being better than 'somewhat certain'?"

"Much. Yet *look*!"

"At?"

"The needles, man! Look how they're dancing! It's almost as if he's *talking*!"

"Well, what if he is? Talking on the ether, I mean?"

"*If* he is, and if I can rig something up, we might just be able to hear him—for a moment or two, that is, not listen in; the signals are leaping all over the place."

"But if that moment or two is long enough for us to identify him—"

"*Precisely*," Tempest said delightedly. "Here, help me with this. We'll power down—disconnect the steam pump, thus—and then, if you'll help me with these rods . . ."

"Jack," Hardcastle said quietly, "these are *lightning* rods."

"Yes?"

"Well, ah . . . how *safe* is this?"

"My dear fellow, tinkering is *never* safe. That's why only crazed men like you and me—"

"I accept the compliment," Hardcastle said heavily. "So what must I do?"

For some minutes, to the flow of Tempest's excited instructions, they worked feverishly, aligning rods and propping them in place with untidy stacks of books hastily scooped off the Prince's shelves, coiling bare wires around the ends of the rods, and . . .

Tempest sat back with a sigh. "No," he said at last. "No, we can't hear the man, if it's him. Not with what I've got here. If I had the time . . . but I don't. We'll just have to settle for tracing this signal I *think* is Marlshrike."

"Ignoring all others?"

"For now. Only this one seems to originate close to here. If it proves to be something else—after all, Marlshrike isn't the only tinkerer in southern England, and quite a host of men seem to grasp the potential of etheric telegraphy—then we'll concern ourselves with the weaker and less likely."

"I follow your thinking," Hardcastle agreed, "but I'm not the tinkerer here. I understand the dangers of steam and lightning better than how we harness them."

"Which, Bleys, puts you head and shoulders ahead of the general populace. So let go of that rod, O heeder of danger, and we'll have another stab at tracing."

That stab took only moments before Tempest sprang to his feet, rushed to the map on the table, laid several rods across it, frowned at them and then rushed back to his dials, returned to the map and made minute adjustments to the rods, then pointed.

"*Here.* Where there's a disused mill, I believe. Not all that far to the west of Bishop's Bottom, as it happens." He looked up at Hardcastle. "Go and tell Drake   "

"I heard," the Assistant Commissioner interrupted from the doorway. "So you've found him. Have my thanks. And sit tight here, both of you. This is now a job for the Constabulary, not you or any other handful of dabblers blundering about the landscape with—"

"Beards grown long and gray waiting for your lot to draw up plans and contingencies, train everyone, *re*train everyone, and—"

"Lord Tempest," Drake growled, "your wildly misplaced personal opinions of the force have no place in—"

"*I,*" declared Lady Rose Harminster firmly, from the doorway behind him the beagle commander, "am ready to go. If Assistant Commissioner Drake is not, woe betide the Empire, and small wonder so many murderers go unapprehended. Bleys?"

Hardcastle caught up his hat and walking stick. "I'm ready."

"What're you—? Really, this is *most* irregular. And unwise. I cannot allow—" Drake sputtered.

"It is the role of the Queen's High Constabulary to apply the laws of the land," Tempest snapped, rising to confront the Assistant Commissioner nose to nose. "It is not their role to take it upon themselves to, outside the laws, 'allow' or 'disallow' anything. We have the courts for that, and Parliament, and the Crown. God knows the three of them are large and powerful enough to manage that between them. May I remind you, Drake, that Sworn Swords and Dread Agents of the Tower outrank you and for that matter Harkness? *We* give orders, and *you* follow them, not the other way around."

"But-but—*he's* not a Sworn Sword!" Drake growled, pointing one large and shaking finger at Hardcastle.

"Oh? And how is it, exactly, that you know that? Since when is an Assistant Commissioner privy to the membership rolls of the Dread Agents of the Tower? Or familiar beyond all doubt with the *unwritten* roster of the Sworn Swords?"

"I-I—oh, hang it," Drake sputtered. "Go. Go and gallivant. Just don't come crying to me when . . ."

Tempest peered at him closely. "When what?"

The Assistant Commissioner waved a dismissive hand. "Figure of speech," he said curtly. "The Constabulary remains ready—as always—to haul your carcass out of whatever trouble you get yourself into, Lord Tempest. Ready and willing."

Rose had seldom heard the word "willing" uttered in more unwilling tones, but forbore from commentary. *Someone* in this room had to display a little prudence.

"As it happens," she said crisply, "Lord Tempest's carcass is too valuable—and too battered at the moment—to risk any gallivanting. I and Mister Hardcastle shall be, ah, sallying forth."

Drake looked her up and down. Knee-high leather boots, riding breeches, airship-crew leather jacket, cap, gloves, and night goggles . . . well, at least she wasn't foolheaded enough to try marching out into the forest by night in a gown, petticoats, silk stockings, and fashionable heels.

"Far be it from me to presume to give a peer of the Empire orders," he said heavily, "but as a friend and as one all too experienced in tramping about the countryside by night, may I strongly *suggest* you just locate this Marlshrike's whereabouts and *not* attack the place, try to capture the man, or even reveal your presence to whoever's there?"

"Assistant Commissioner," Rose said politely, "your suggestion has been entertained, but—"

"But I *can* give you orders," Tempest interrupted her, "and in this, I agree with Drake. Not that I think you'll obey. Hardcastle, when things get rough, get her and yourself out of there as quickly as possible. No heroics."

Hardcastle gave him a mocking bow. "Of course."

Rose gave him a look. "So now you're my keeper? Who's the Sworn Sword here, if I may ask?"

Hardcastle took a step back—and winked. Then he mumbled, "You are, m'lady, but you're also new to this, and I thought . . ."

"Oh you did, did you? Well, as it happens, I, too, share Commissioner Drake's misgivings, so I agree fully with his suggestions."

"Oh," blurted out Drake. Then he added hesitantly, "Actually, Lady Harminster, it's *Assistant* Commiss—"

"Ah, well, for now, perhaps," she said sunnily, giving him a sparkling smile that left him blushing and standing taller.

Then she whirled around and strode from the room, slapping her thigh with her gloves as if they were a riding crop. "Come, Mister Hardcastle. We have a mad and evil tinkerer to find, and the night grows steadily older!"

Hardcastle looked at the other two men, rolled his eyes, adjusted his hat, and hastened after her.

Leaving Tempest and Drake to look at each other.

The Assistant Commissioner coughed. "Uh, having women, uh, mixed up in things certainly livens matters up," he offered.

"Indeed," Lord Tempest agreed, eyes twinkling. "You should try it on the force."

Drake choked and backed away, red-faced and aghast. Then, eyeing the lord seated behind his dials, decided Tempest was joking. Scowling, he emitted an exasperated sigh and stormed out of the room.

Tempest's explosion of laughter was as quiet as he could make it, but his bid for silent mirth was not entirely successful.

I t's a nasty choice," Hardcastle whispered, as they crouched down in the lee of an oak tree that had probably been young when the first castles were being built in what would become England, well downriver. "Keep to the paths, where they can't help but see us and probably have traps *and* ambushes ready—or blunder through the forest and sound like a wild herd of large and drunken somethings trying to creep closer."

Rose suppressed a giggle. "You put things so eloquently, Mister Hardcastle."

"Call me Bleys," he whispered back. "It's shorter."

She rolled her eyes at that, rose, stepped back onto the path— and promptly fell over on top of him in some haste, as a bullet came whining out of the night, along the path, far too close for comfort.

Hardcastle wrapped his arms around her and rolled over in a frenzy of disturbed leaves, and then lay still. Silence slowly returned to the dark forest . . . and then the small night sounds, the hootings and rustlings, began again.

"*Mister* Hardcastle," Rose whispered, into the face so close above hers, "what do you think you're doing?"

"Shielding you against the next shot," he replied, as if explaining matters to an idiot.

Well, at least he wasn't one of these greasy Lotharios, smilingly seizing on any opportunity.

"I appreciate your gallantry," she whispered, "even if it is entirely misplaced. However, I can't help but observe that it's going to be very hard for me to get closer to this mill and attempt to locate Marlshrike with you pinning me to the ground and holding my arms. So unless you'd like to feel a rather sharp knee where it's unlikely to do you any good . . ."

"Umm," Hardcastle replied, hastily rolling off her. "Delicately put."

"Your point about the nasty choice, however, stands," she hissed. "Have you any solutions in mind, or—?"

The rest of her words were lost as she gasped to a halt. The woods in the direction they'd been heading had suddenly erupted into what sounded like open warfare. Guns blazed away, at least a dozen men jumped or fell heavily out of trees and started running, crashing very noisily through leaves and underbrush, and someone screamed.

"What the devil?" Hardcastle exclaimed, trying to peer around a tree and keep his chin low to the ground.

"Drake's doing, do you think?" Rose asked.

"The beagles, without lanterns and a lot of 'stand and surrender in the name of the law' shouting? Doubtful," he muttered.

The battle seemed to be heating up, not subsiding, although there were fewer noisy descents from trees nearby.

"All those men were waiting for us," Rose gasped, realizing how close they'd come to being killed.

"There may be more," he replied. "If Drake's not going to shift until daylight, why shouldn't we wait a bit, and see if they kill each other off?"

"I'd be more sanguine about such a tactic if I had the slightest idea who 'they' were—either side," Rose told him.

"*Look!*" Hardcastle hissed, pointing. Flame had kindled, off to the west, in the direction they'd been heading. Flaring up vivid and sudden, shining through the trees so brightly that—

"It's the dirigible!" Rose gasped. "That the Order's masked men have been riding about in!"

The blaze *was* higher than the trees—just—and lit up the wood as it drifted away; they could clearly see men in masks and dark suits and gloves rushing through the trees, gleaming pistols in hand. A few had walking sticks in their fists, and one or two wore long coats. They were all hurrying west, to where more firing was breaking out. Rose and Hardcastle could see muzzle flashes and men staggering and falling.

Suddenly, Hardcastle started chuckling.

"What," Rose asked him, "is so funny?"

"You realize," he replied, "that Drake is going to think *we* started all this. No matter what we do or say, he's going to believe we defied him and deliberately—"

The dirigible exploded, so loudly that their ears rang, and so violently that entire *trees* came cartwheeling through the forest, crashing enthusiastically along in a splintering, shredding chaos that clawed deep gashes through the forest, roads to nowhere opening up in a few terrifying moments.

"You know," Rose murmured a little dazedly, "that I once considered studying to become an arborist?"

"Lady Harminster," Hardcastle replied formally, "I did not. Yet I find myself entirely unsurprised. Your—*someone's coming.*"

He plucked at and caught her hand, hauled Rose to her feet as if she was a nigh-weightless child, and rushed her back along the path, so swiftly that she stumbled but had no time to fall in his suddenly iron grasp.

"*Mister Hardcastle!*" she gasped, "unhand me at *once!*"

He kept right on running, and now she was running beside him, as fast as she could, to relieve the strain on her trapped arm and speak to him face-to-face.

"How," she panted, "am I to be a Sworn Sword if I'm *running away* from everything? Answer me *that*, sir!"

"We're not running away," he snapped, "we're returning to cover."

And as abruptly as he'd snatched her, he turned off the path onto another, smaller one that Rose vaguely remembered seeing earlier, as they'd passed it.

"Returning to cover? What does *that* mean?"

"This," he replied tersely, and swung her down and into a dark hole so abruptly that she had to stifle an instinctive shriek.

Where he put an arm around her and bore her to the ground—which was hard-packed dirt, studded with the occasional small but very hard stone. They lay there together, side by side and breathing hard, and before Rose could think of how to phrase her protest, Hardcastle turned and whispered directly into her ear, the dampness of his breath tickling the inside of her head, "You will please oblige me, Lady Rose, by keeping *very* quiet for a time; no whispering at *all*. Very shortly, I suspect we're going to have visitors."

Rose decided she quite liked the sound of "Lady Rose." Why—

Her thoughts were interrupted by another, even quieter whisper. "To soothe your curiosity, this is what's left of an old gamekeeper's hut. It's on one of Jack's maps."

She tapped him twice with a forefinger by way of reply, and then they lay as still and as silent as they could, their breathing gradually slowing. The ground was cold and hard, and Rose was just beginning to grow restive when they heard the unmistakable rustling of at least two people striding through dead leaves, very close by and getting closer.

"Ah, here it is," a man's voice said in satisfaction, low and quiet and very, very close.

"Here's what?" a second voice asked irritably.

"The hut. It's supposed to be our rallying point. Orders."

"No one tells me *nothing*," the second voice said gloomily.

"Be glad of that. It means no one can ever scrag you for making the wrong decision—because they're not letting you make any decisions."

"Huh. That's where you're wrong. You're thinking they'll be fair and reasonable. Tell me, would *you* call Old Horsley reasonable?"

"I'm not going to be foolish enough to venture an opinion. Now shut it. We sit here and smoke and wait."

"Why are we *doing* this, anyway? All this to burn their little flitter-blimp?"

"We're doing this to get Marlshrike and take him away from here. Away from the clutches of Lady Roodcannon."

"Why? Isn't she one of us?"

"She *says* she is, but she's been pleasing herself and ignoring what the others in the top circle—and the Elders, too!—have decided, for the better part of a fortnight now. I think they lost patience with it and confronted her, and she defied them, so now they know she's trying to run her own affair. And you don't *do* that to the Ancient Order."

"For we have Tentacles beyond Tentacles, and one of them'll get you." Those words were said in sour mockery.

"And so we will, Mase. And so we will."

"And don't you forget it." The mockery was even stronger this time.

"Here, now, enough of that."

"All right, all right . . . just tell me this: I unnerstand this Marlshrike's a brainy one, a tinkerer, and worth a lot to us, but why risk shooting him, like we're doing, just to get him away from her? Why not just take away what he makes, whenever he makes it, and let *her* go on feeding him and paying for all his knobs and tubes and fiddly bits?"

"Because he's the only real prize she's got, and if we take him, she'll be forced to send the Tentacles loyal to her out to try to find and recover him. Then we'll know for sure who they are, and they'll be sticking their necks in whatever noose we prepare where we're holding him, and we can pick them off."

"Right. Got it. So what's this hut like, anyway?"

"*Don't* be going down in there! That's where they've been stashing the special acid Marlshrike needs. You break anything, and it won't be just your clothes that start dissolving!"

Rose froze, hardly daring to breathe.

"Glencannon? Mason?" a new voice called, low and harsh.

"Here," Glencannon replied quickly.

"Come on! New orders! Apparently this tinkerer has a metal box or some such he can hide in and scurries inside it whenever he hears gunfire . . . so we can shoot up the mill as much as we please. Let him hide in his box; we're to kill everyone defending the mill, every last one of them, now that they can't all fly away on their jaunty little flitter."

"Right," Glencannon responded, and Rose and Hardcastle heard the thumps of the two men landing as they came down off the roof of the hut and then the rustling of them trudging back out onto the path. Followed by a lot more thudding, of many booted feet passing by. Heading for the mill.

From which direction, fresh gunfire began. And built into an almost-deafening ongoing din.

"Acid," Rose murmured, "that dissolves *clothes*. You certainly know how to entertain a lady, Mister Hardcastle!"

"We strive to give satisfaction," he replied sardonically, helping her up. They staggered out of the hut in a crouch and peered cautiously around.

To discover that a bright moon had arisen in a cloudless sky and that the forest was now bathed in long strips of cold moonlight— wherever the dirigible explosion had caused gaps in the canopy of foliage.

Something abruptly blotted out much of that moonlight, and—as distant church clocks struck midnight—they looked up together.

And beheld a large airship passing overhead. Low and slow. So low that they both recognized the ornate bowsprit of its oversized gondola.

It was Lady Roodcannon's airship. All of its lights were out, in defiance of the law. Like a smuggler.

It was heading for the Tower of London.

OCTEMBER 17

S o we know where Marlshrike is—or was," Hardcastle muttered, looking at Rose.

Who looked back at him and said, "And we certainly can't capture him in the face of an army. Still less, *two* armies, with both of them firing at each other."

They nodded in unison, and Hardcastle gestured that Rose should speak next, so it was she who voiced what they were both thinking. "Telling Tempest, the Lord Lion, and the others that Lady Roodcannon's airship is headed for the Tower is far more important than Marlshrike."

"Agreed," Hardcastle replied, and they hurried back along the path together, heading for Foxden.

"Roodcannon or Old Horsley?" a voice snapped at them, out of the night.

"Old Horsley!" Hardcastle barked back, not slowing.

"So why are you running?"

"Reporting back, as ordered!" Hardcastle shot back, and they kept right on running—though Rose felt an itch between her shoulder blades, not to mention a little chill of fear, and ran along half-expecting a bullet to come out of the night to bite through her there.

Nothing came.

They were challenged again, and this time it began with a warning shot.

Hardcastle answered that with a blistering string of oaths and a demand that such a "traitor to the Tentacles" explain himself.

The voice that replied was female, cold and unfriendly, and advised him to state his precise reasons for "fleeing like a schoolboy." Hardcastle invoked Old Horsley's name and orders to report back something to him in all haste. The voice then demanded to know what that something was, and why she'd not been told agents of the Order would be running through her guard post. Whereupon Hardcastle turned cold and menacing himself and inquired if she was familiar with the concept of secret orders and checks and balances and the right of the leaders of the Order to determine levels of secrecy. A little silence followed, and then the female voice sullenly suggested they "be on about their errand, then."

So they continued along the path, running again, and once again Rose's shoulder blades awaited ventilation that thankfully did not come.

Their next encounter involved no bullets, but no questioning, either. There were just suddenly fists hammering on them out of the night, bushes crackling and rustling in loud chaos as assailants erupted from behind trees on this narrow part of the path.

Hardcastle was a competent, sturdy fighter, and had at some point decided that the figurative gloves were off and it was permissible to use the brass knuckles he'd brought along on both of his hands. Yet it was Rose who surprised herself—and her foes—with her agility, fearlessness, and a certain viciousness born of her rising anger. She kicked and raked at eyes and drove hard knees into yielding guts and crushed hats down over faces and ran stumbling men face-first into trees.

After they'd run on, leaving groaning masked men in their wake, one of them snarled, "Orders or no orders, I'm putting a bullet through that bitch. After all, who'll know?"

He fumbled inside his coat for his weapon—and was just dragging it out, with an air of grim satisfaction, when a skull-headed man whose limbs were encased in battered metal cages loomed out of the night, broke his neck in an instant, then tore the pistol out of his hands and apart.

The other Tentacles men gaped as the murderous apparition stalked on down the path, in the wake of the running pair. Lurching along nigh silently, his face grim in the moonlight.

The docks of London never sleep—neither those lapped by the water, nor the newer masts that soar above them, where airships hang moored in the night, aloft.

The Limehouse masts were always busy, both the cluster of five and the one off by itself made for larger vessels.

The *Mary Rose* was moored to the large-vessel mast right now. Out of Portsmouth, it was a large, ruggedly built freighter, broad and fat and with a gondola thrice the width and six times the length of any passenger liner. Its crew was rather wearily watching the cranes of the dock lower the last pallets of its load of raw tin down to the waiting wagons below. There'd be the usual cursory inspection, and then its next cargo would start coming up, to be shoved and then lashed into place. Finished woolens, for somewhere on the

Continent the crew didn't much care about at this particular moment. Not that those wagons had arrived yet. Meaning they'd have to wait. As usual.

"We're certainly earning our cuppa tonight," one hand grumbled. It was the last thing he ever said.

A hired flitter passing by suddenly did something forbidden under Port of London rules. It turned in a steep climb—and passed over the moored freighter.

Letting down a dozen lines at once as it did so, with men on the end of them. Masked men, bearing knives that were busy almost before their boot heels struck the deck of the *Mary Rose*. One of those knives slit the throat of the grumbling hand as he turned his head to see what the noise was, behind him, that shouldn't be there.

His killer obeyed orders, catching hold of the blood-spurting, choking man and lowering him to the deck to die, rather than letting him topple and thud.

By then, however, stealth no longer mattered. The deck was swarming with masked agents, and all the crew were down with their throats open and bleeding. Their killers stepped over them without another glance and either went below to turn any still-alive crew into corpses or took over the crane lines, to begin busily loading cargo up and aboard.

Not the waiting crates of woolens but the contents of wagons that were just creaking to a stop beneath the mooring mast. Smaller crates that were stamped with the warning DANGER—EXPLOSIVES.

S ir Fulton Birtwhistle seldom drank this heavily, but he was still angry—damn it, what *was* the Empire coming to, when a lawyer could be prevented from seeing a client at the Crown's whim? How far was that, really, from, "Off with his head! Why? I don't like the color of his nose. That's why!"? And the sherry was very good.

Winthrop's happened to be open all night, and moreover happened to be near the Tower, so although it wasn't Sir Fulton's favorite of the dozen or so gentlemen's clubs he belonged to, it would do. A haven in troubled times, as the old saying put it.

So he'd been lurking in Winthrop's ever since his unceremonious departure from the gates of the Tower, knocking back very dry sherries.

Without really noticing, he'd accumulated an impressive row of empty glasses, outlasted several conversational partners who were bound for home and bed—or mistress and bed—and was now verbally fencing with old Lord Dunster, whom he'd just informed snippily, "I like to feast, yes, but *not* upon the latest gossip."

Only to have the lord come back at him sourly. "You make the cardinal mistake of the newly empowered, sir. That of believing that the bright future of the Empire is only realized if unfolding events enrich *you* and follow the interests you happen to hold dear. In short, you see yourself as the lion tamer, rather than one opportunistically following in the prowling lion's wake, scooping up the scraps it lets fall. I fear you need better spectacles."

Sir Fulton leaned forward, enraged anew and warming to the opportunity to cuttingly put someone in his place who was deluded or mad or a dissembling liar and in any case very much in the wrong, and—

Froze with his mouth open and his lungs puffed up full, ready to do battle, as someone tapped his shoulder firmly from behind and asked almost reverently, "Sir Birtwhistle? Magistrate Birtwhistle?"

He turned and found himself staring into the face of a middle-aged beagle with tired eyes and an impressive brush of a graying mustache, who was busy being professionally expressionless—and doing a good job of it, too.

"Yes?" he demanded, very much aware of Lord Dunster watching with amused interest, obviously believing Birtwhistle was about to be arrested or at any rate receive a well-deserved comeuppance.

"I can get you inside the Tower right now, sir, if you want to come. There's something unfolding inside you should see, sir."

"'I should see'? I—but—well, how would you know? You don't even *know* me!"

"The judgment isn't mine, sir. It belongs to someone highly placed whose name I'm not at liberty to divulge, sir."

Sir Fulton stared at the constable, gazing into sad eyes of infinite patience that belonged to a man now waiting without caring if the offer he brought was accepted or rejected. Well, now. Was someone appreciating him at last? Or counting on his obstinacy, his opposition to all who bent laws or trundled nonchalantly around them?

Well, there was but one way to find out.

He shrugged and rose to the bait, draining his last sherry and telling Lord Dunster more airily than severely, "I find events have robbed me of the time it would take me merely to elucidate the number of ways you are wrong, my lord, let alone enlighten you as to the errors of your judgments. Another time, perhaps. It seems the Empire calls."

And with those grand words Sir Fulton took his leave, striding briskly along beside the beagle, an important man on his way to be a part of important events, rather than a prisoner being taken in charge.

Out into the night again, to find it had turned noticeably colder. His breath curled briefly in front of him in the damp air as the pace quickened once more. He was led to a steam-driven armored hound-car, one of the rugged new models. It was running, steam curling up steadily around its rear, but its headlamps weren't lit. It promptly pulled out of the alley mouth in which it had been waiting and joined a line of identical vehicles—also showing no lights, none of them— all heading for the Tower.

"You're rounding up all the magistrates in England?" Sir Fulton jokingly asked the beagle who'd fetched him and was now sitting beside him on a bench seat. It was one of five such seats in the hound-car, the others all full of uniformed beagles.

"No, sir," the beagle replied patiently. "Just you. The units before and behind are all carrying heavily armed members of the Constabulary. And before you ask, I can't tell you why. Yet you'll see for yourself soon enough."

The line of houndcars entered the Tower at a crawl, unchallenged, and through a dark, lightless gate, driving only a short distance before stopping in the same line they'd come in by. Everyone got out—quietly, every door left open rather than being slammed shut.

"Come, sir," the beagle murmured, and led the way up a dank and gloomy stone stair, moving at a steady pace now rather than hurrying. Sir Fulton followed, climbing steps worn down in the center with age, then along a passage that ran for a long way and was lit only by storm lanterns swinging in the hands of every tenth beagle or so.

The passage finally opened out into what were probably extensive stone cellars, though Sir Fulton couldn't see their size in the gloom. He could hear beagles dispersing in all directions, though—just the rasp and shuffle of their boots, for not a word was spoken. Some climbed unseen steps to a higher level; most turned off and walked away along other passages hidden in the darkness . . . and Sir Fulton's faithful beagle led him between a lot of barrels and then racks of what were probably halberds to another flight of ascending steps and up into a narrow room where light was coming in through holes in the wall. Spyholes.

The beagle swung around and put an upright finger across his own lips, frowning severely at Sir Fulton past it.

Sir Fulton nodded to show he'd understood. Keep silent.

The beagle then pointed to one of the holes and went to the other beside it and peered through. Sir Fulton heeded that message, too.

And found himself looking out into a large square stone room that was probably the ground floor, or near it, of the White Tower.

It was a large chamber, with many doors and stairs half-visible in its gloomy far reaches. Close to the spyholes was a massive plain table that looked as if it had been used for centuries for dining, crude surgery, and armor smithing—judging by the scars and burn marks covering it. A plain wooden wheel of candles with drip shields hung over it on a chain, eight chairs were round it, and four of those chairs were occupied.

The men sitting in them were the Lord Chamberlain of the Empire, the Imperial Herald, the Constable of the Tower, and the Commissioner of the Queen's High Constabulary.

"I don't *like* it," Sir Percy Harkness was growling, as Sir Fulton reached his spyhole.

"Nor do I," old Throckmorton agreed.

"Well, what better place can you suggest?" Buckingham asked, a trifle wearily. "The royal apartments are the only area in this fortress suitable for the Queen. Not only is she the crowned head of the Empire, and a woman used to cleanliness and *some* comforts— she's neither young nor well, and this confounded damp won't do her any good at all!"

"That's just it," Harkness snapped. "She's the *head* of the Empire! And the topmost floor is vulnerable to bombs dropped from airships! Move her down! Not just to here, but to the undercroft below us!"

"In with the polearms and the pickles." The Constable sighed. "I'm sure she'll be *very* pleased."

"I shouldn't have to remind *you*," Throckmorton said sourly, "that the undercroft connects to more tunnels than I have fingers that she can be taken through, to more-secure deep chambers elsewhere in this fortress."

"Might I remind you gentle sirs that the Queen is our sovereign and has a mind of her own? *She* will decide where she gets 'taken,' if she agrees to be taken anywhere at all." Buckingham's patience seemed to be at an end. "We obey her, not the other way around. We are all here because of a command she gave. I doubt she'll want to hide from Lady Roodcannon or meet with her in a dungeon somewhere."

"Well," Harkness said dryly, "it will spare Roodcannon a long walk to whichever cell is going to be hers, henceforth."

"Spoken like a true beagle who decides guilt before anyone is called to court," Throckmorton observed. "I happen to agree with you, Percy, but, before God, you might want to think about such jests before uttering them."

"*Before* you gentle sirs get to trading insults," the Constable said quickly, "I would like to know what all of you seem acquainted with already: *Why* does the Queen wish to, ah, entertain—or at least meet with—the Lady Roodcannon here? And now?"

"Prudent enough, Fairweather, prudent enough," the Lord Chancellor agreed. "Let me think on where to begin. Well . . . you are no doubt aware that the Lady Roodcannon is the owner of a rather large and well-appointed airship?"

"I am now," the Constable replied dryly. "I was raised by Fairweathers who told me to ignore the doings of nobles as much as possible, because their world of feuds and fads and endless intrigues was fantasy, whereas the daily running of the Empire was decidedly real—so ignoring its details and specifics could get one killed."

"You were raised by wise people," the Lord Chancellor observed, with an approving smile. "Well, the Queen has come to the Tower because Lady Roodcannon recently broke the law, in that she piloted her airship so as to pass over Whitehall—"

"Which is forbidden," Harkness supplied helpfully.

"—so she could drop a written message there, announcing her intention to present the 'rightful heir to the throne' to the Queen herself at the Tower 'before the sun rises again.'"

"And the Queen rose to the bait," said the Constable.

"She did. And has been issuing royal commands ever since. Which boil down to ordering us—everyone within reach, actually—to get her here."

"Well, now that I know the reasons for her arrival here, I find myself in agreement with the Imperial Herald and the Commissioner. I don't care what pretext or pretense or cozening we resort to, I want the Queen moved down to where she's safer. It is my professional opinion that we cannot protect her while she's up in the royal apartments; not even if we invaded them with every last Yeoman Warder and Crown lackey within the walls of the Tower. They'd simply die with her if an airship sailing overhead—as this Rood-cannon woman seems to do with impunity, escaping all consequences—dropped an explosive of sufficient strength."

Bertram Buckingham threw up his hands. "Then I bow to you three and the weight of your professional judgments, gentle sirs. We move the Queen."

"*Now*," Throckmorton added. "If there's more to jaw about, let us do it when the Queen is safely shifted to—"

"*Oh*, no, you don't!" said a new voice. A voice Sir Fulton Birtwhistle had heard before. Assistant Commissioner Alston Drake.

Sir Fulton shifted hastily to look through his spyhole in another direction—as did all the beagles at all the spyholes on either side of him.

Drake stood inside a door he'd just burst through, with a gun in his hand. He was surrounded by beagles wielding what looked like four-barreled shotguns, tipped with wicked-looking bayonets.

"Who the hell—?" Harkness barked.

"My personal constabulary," Drake informed his superior smugly. "As in, personally loyal to me. Oh, yes, I should inform you all that *I* will be giving the orders here!"

"Are you *mad*, Drake?" the Lord Chancellor shouted. "High Commiss—"

Drake smiled and shot Buckingham through the head. The Lord

Chancellor's body was still toppling, head half gone, when he shot the Constable of the Tower down.

Fairweather's body, struck in the act of springing up from his chair, crashed back down into it, arms and head flopping.

"Drake! Down arms and surrender!" Harkness barked. "That's an *order*!"

Drake didn't bother to reply. Instead, he snapped an order of his own to the men around him. "In the name of the Dowager Duchess," he said grandly, *"kill them all!"*

Bullets flew.

Amid the deafening crashings of all the firing, Birtwhistle watched in disbelieving horror as beagles, courtiers, and agents in the room in front of him were gunned down.

Around him, beagles were cursing and snatching out their own guns and firing through the spyholes. Some were bursting through doors, firing.

"Sir," said the beagle who'd brought Sir Fulton to the Tower, as he crashed into the magistrate's chest and slammed him to the floor, "I must ask you to stay down and crawl in that direction. It's all too easy to die in a wild shootout."

"N-no doubt," Sir Fulton replied shakily, obeying with alacrity. The beagle was right behind him, crawling back out of the gallery and down the steps chin first, as the cavernous room of the Tower behind them echoed to the cracks of pistols, the booming of larger firearms, and the whine of many bullets.

"This way, sir." The beagle slapped at Sir Fulton's right calf and then led the way through the gloom, the din of battle fading somewhat as they moved away from the gallery and got behind solid walls where they could stand in relative safety. Stray ricochets still spanged and rattled around them, but the firing was dying down as the combatants either died or ran out of bullets. The beagle wrenched open a plain, slightly rusty metal door and hissed, "Hurry, sir. Drake knows this route, so his men will be coming this way soon."

The magistrate hurried after his guide, up old and worn spiral stairs ascending the inside of an ancient stone cylinder. "Where are we?"

"Climbing the northwest turret stairs, sir. Getting up to the royal apartments by the back way. Drake's foremost men will be fighting their way up the main stairs right now."

The sounds of shooting grew steadily louder as they ascended.

"They're inside the receiving room already," the beagle hissed, his manner strongly suggesting that this was *not* good. Sir Fulton Birtwhistle sighed, then shrugged. Oh, well; he'd been raging like a proverbial lion to try to get inside the Tower earlier and had managed it, so he couldn't really kick at any perils he found or faced here now. At least he hadn't been hit yet, which was more than a lot of the poor beagles could say . . . if they were still alive to voice or hold any opinion at all.

The stairs opened onto a small landing that held only heavy metal torch sconces on the walls and two closed doors. The beagle opened the right-hand door warily, waving Sir Fulton to the wall, to be behind the door and out of the line of fire—and it was well that he did so, for two bullets promptly sped through the opening gap and cracked down the staircase behind them.

"What's behind the *other* door?" he whispered to the beagle.

"The royal bedchamber, sir. Which is why we're going through this one, to the receiving room."

Where the fighting was obviously raging. The beagle went to his knees and then to all fours, waving at Sir Fulton to do the same, and then shoved the door wide.

The room was full of drifting smoke, steam, and plaster dust, for the shooting had been thunderously heavy—and although it had fallen to sporadic just now, the sounds of hasty reloading could be heard all over the room.

There were bodies everywhere. Hard to the left, where the front wall of the royal bedchamber turned off, a small band of people struggled furiously to get the chamber doors open; Sir Fulton caught the briefest glimpse of the Queen herself among them, but all the men with her—Commissioner Harkness and the aging Imperial Herald among them—were shielding her with their bodies, and doing a good job of it.

Across the room, beagles wrestled to reload their four-barreled guns. The weapons had to be broken open like shotguns, and the dangling barrels were clanking and clashing with those of adjacent beagles.

"Leave that for later, fools!" Drake roared, from somewhere behind them. "Lock your bayonets and *charge*!"

And they did. The beagle escorting Sir Fulton shot out one knee of the foremost charger, spilling him into an ungainly fall that demolished a no-doubt priceless side table and caused other charging beagles behind him to trip over him in a satisfyingly widespread crash of flailing arms and legs and flying, bouncing shotguns.

It was still going on when those of Drake's men who'd managed to reload let fly at the Queen and Sir Fulton's escort.

Commissioner Harkness let out a roar of pain and staggered to one side as he sagged, trying to clutch both one arm and his gut at the same time. The crawling beagle in front of Sir Fulton fell on his face, shuddered once, and lay still, blood spreading out from his face or throat in rather impatiently lengthening fingers.

Sir Fulton Birtwhistle shuddered, too. He was unhurt, thus far, but . . .

The bedchamber door banged open, and the knot of men protecting the Queen surged through it. More of Drake's men fired at them or charged, but the door banged shut again.

Still on his hands and knees, Sir Fulton spun around to flee— then remembered the door. Whirling around again, he crawled faster than he'd ever crawled before, clambering over the body of the beagle who'd brought him here to catch hold of the door, low down, and drag it back shut.

He only *just* managed it, slamming it right in the faces of on-rushing beagle traitors.

It had latch cradles and a metal bar on a swivel joint hanging down its frame beside its hinges—but, thank the steam, it was well-oiled and came up in a trice when he hauled on it.

And latched it into place, a bare breath before heavy bodies slammed into the other side of the door, then—amid much profanity—tried to haul it back open.

Knowing what would be coming next, Sir Fulton had already dashed to the other door—the rear door of the royal bedchambers—and was trying to claw it open.

He flattened himself against it when the expected volley of firing came, some of the bullets bursting through the door lock to *spang* and sing around the landing and down the stairs. At some point in the heart of that thunderous din, the door gave way, and he fell into the royal bedchamber, rising to look right into the dark mouths of half a dozen cocked and ready pistols.

"I'm for the Queen!" he gasped. "Loyal to the Empire! Don't shoot!"

"Down arms," growled Commissioner Harkness. Who then spat blood and toppled forward. Several of his men caught him and eased him to the floor, where he groaned twice or thrice as they settled him on his back between two floral-print adorned highback chairs, somewhat out of the way.

Sir Fulton looked up. Beyond the shockingly small handful of armed men stood a terrified maid, wringing her hands. Beside her was the Queen—who looked surprisingly calm, more irritated than anything else—and behind them both could be seen the legs of a second maid, who'd presumably fainted, protruding off the edge of the soaringly magnificent gilded royal four-poster. Old Throckmorton had caught up a poker from the fireplace and was hefting it with a fierce awkwardness.

"Lock that door," he ordered.

"And we'll then be locked in," the Queen observed sharply. "Now would be an excellent time for someone to come up with a brilliant plan, gentlemen. Or even a workable one."

"Bring up the blaster and blow the door in!" Drake bellowed faintly, from beyond the bedchamber main door.

"Well, there's one traitor who has little skill at subterfuge," Queen Victoria observed. "I seem to recall an endless succession of devices that blast; which particular one is he referring to, I wonder?"

No one answered her, so it was Sir Fulton Birtwhistle who ventured hesitantly, "A-almost certainly he's referring to the, ah, steam-pressure apparatus used by the bea—by the Constabulary to destroy locked and barred doors. Warps frames, bursts wood, bends metal. It tends to scald everyone near the held side of a barrier."

"Behind me, my Queen!" Throckmorton said instantly, striding to stand between Queen Victoria and the main bedchamber door.

"Throck, Throck! None of that, now, my dear," the Queen murmured, patting his cheek. The old and gruff Imperial Herald was seen to blush like a schoolgirl, in the instant before heavy metallic *clangs* from outside the door announced the arrival of the steam blaster, its plates being dropped into place and dogged down in their positions. Then the hissing began.

"We're *all* going to get scalded," Throckmorton warned. "Pryce-wood, Birtwhistle, and all you constables—we need a barricade. Not against the door, but back from it about *here*. A wall of furniture solid enough to stop their first shots, mind. Use everything; if bullets reach our Queen, she won't be needing this splendid bed, now will she?"

They all stared at him for a moment, then sprang to obey, even before the Queen ordered, "Well, *come* on! A barricade! Drag my wardrobes, you and you, and do the Imperial Herald's bidding! Hurry!"

Just the other side of the door, the hissing was growing louder.

Sir Fulton found himself puffing under the weight of a well-stuffed high-backed chair that was much heavier than it looked. Wedging it thankfully atop a tangle of lesser chairs that the beagles had assembled in mere seconds, he gasped, "How much time do we have, before the, er, thing on the far side of the door—?"

His question was promptly answered for him. No more time at all, as it happened. The door exploded off its hinges, the frame shattering into fragments that flew across the room in a wild and tumbling cloud, impaling one unfortunate constable and gashing the face of another.

Right behind the shards, scalding mists billowed.

"Close your eyes!" Harkness bellowed weakly, from the floor. *"Close your eyes!"*

The still-awake maid shrieked first, but her scream was drowned out by shouts of pain from the men in the room as they got scalded.

"The Queen!" Sir Fulton cried, under the arm he'd flung up across his eyes. "Protect the Queen!"

"Done!" the Imperial Herald called back. "I'll lay down my life for my Queen gladly! Both an honor and a duty, that I*iiiiiiii-iaaaaAAARGHH*!"

Abruptly, old Throckmorton fell silent, and from beneath him could be heard the Queen groaning hoarsely, "Oh, Throck, why do you always have to play the hero? You're getting too old . . . God defend me, but you're heavy! Get *off* me; I can scarce breathe! Get . . ."

Beagles dragged the lobster-red, staring old herald off Queen Victoria.

"Is he—?" she and Sir Fulton asked, in untidy unison.

When one of the constables nodded grimly, the Queen of the Empire started to sob.

"How very touching," came the voice of the traitor Drake, from the far side of the barricade. "A replacement royal lover would seem to be required. Men, shoot dead anyone who tries to get out from behind the furniture—except the Queen. We need her alive, for now, to lure the Lord Lion. Shoot her ankles, if you must, to stop her fleeing, but otherwise leave her be. I'll be back with some globes soon enough."

"Globes?" Sir Fulton hissed, to the nearest beagle.

"Knockout gas," came the answering whisper. "Throw globe, it breaks, out comes gas that puts you to sleep. We have plenty here, in two of the Tower armories."

"I'm dying," the Queen announced tremulously. "Get word to my son. I need him."

"Your Majesty," one of the beagles kneeling over her asked uncertainly, "is that wise? To bring him into the reach of these traitors?"

"I've done many unwise things in my life," came the royal reply, "but doing what is needful and proper for the succession isn't one of them. Traitors be damned. Deliver a royal summons to my son. I want him by my side just as soon as he can be here."

A beagle peered around the edge of the barricade, and four pistols barked as one. His body was propelled backward, suddenly and messily faceless, to bounce on the floor. It twitched once or twice, and then lay still.

The junior herald, Prycewood, took a stand over the cooked body of his predecessor, snatching up the poker Throckmorton had dropped when shielding the Queen.

"Take the turret stairs down," he told the beagles fiercely, "and get out of here. Drake *can't* have men enough to block them all. And whatever happens, you find him, and you see that he hangs for this. Because if he somehow gets off, I'll hunt him, and I'll find him—and then nothing, but *nothing* will save him. With these two hands I'll break his neck, I will. And stab him through the heart, burn what's left, and dance on the bloody ashes."

Sir Fulton felt tears welling up. "You, sir," he declared, "are full of what is good about England, and the Empire."

"Save the speeches. Just get *word*," the Queen gasped, faintly, "to my son."

"I'll do it," Sir Fulton promised. Then he turned to the beagle who'd told him about the knockout gas and murmured, "*Is* she dying?"

The constable muttered, "She believes she is, and, after all, it's *her* body. Look at her; obviously a lot of pain. Who knows?" He shrugged. "Yet a royal command is—"

"A royal command," Sir Fulton joined in. "So I'll go. Is there any armor here that can stop bullets?"

"Armor doesn't stop bullets," another beagle informed him grimly. "Not direct shots, from pistols like they're using. And armor helps steam cook you and will slow you down, as you're not used to it. Just run."

"And get shot down like a bunny munching prized flowers in a garden," Harkness rasped, from the floor. "A diversion, men!"

"Rush them and die, you mean?"

"Three of you. The rest, form a ring around Birtwhistle—and you, Pritchard—and get them both out the back way. Pritchard, get to the signals and send to our West Hill tower. The summons, but warn the Prince he's heading into a trap."

"Signals? West Hill?" Sir Fulton asked, a little overwhelmed.

"We have a signal tower here at the Tower. Uses colored lanterns hung in patterns. The West Hill tower is in Wandsworth; messengers can hurry from there to Foxden. In case something happens to you."

"Then why . . ."

"Risk you at all? You have a better chance than Pritchard, sir, if Drake's men hold as much of the Tower as I think they do. There's no cover for a lot of the way he'll have to go."

Sir Fulton Birtwhistle sighed. "Right," he said. "Let's do it."

Helmeted beagle heads nodded all around him, men started to rush—and bullets started to fly.

The first two men who rushed around the end of the barricades were shot down before they got more than a few running strides toward Drake's waiting men—who shouted as they saw, over the heaped furniture, the top edge of the bedchamber back door move as it swung open.

"They're making a break for it! The Queen's getting away!"

Thank heavens for that latter assumption, Pritchard thought, pelting down the turret stairs just behind the already winded and puffing magistrate. *It just might keep us all from being blown up, or gunned down in a no-holds-barred barrage.*

Sparing me the irony of being killed by our side.

Outside the White Tower itself, Drake's force was spread thinly indeed, just to hold all the vital points in the maze of buildings, tunnels, and fortress walls that made up the Tower. So the ring of rushing beagles around Birtwhistle stood a pretty good chance—if they didn't blunder and take the wrong route—of getting out and away.

While he himself, one of Drake's secret conspirators and therefore knowing exactly where his fellow traitors had orders to be and to fight to hold, had a clear, safe run to the signals.

He would send the signal to Foxden, though it would just be the urgent "the Queen is dying" summons and include no mention of a trap.

But first . . .

Pritchard reached the signals out of breath but was recognized by the two fellow conspirators standing guard there. They waved him to the lanterns.

Where he caught his breath, smiled, and set about sending his first and most important message—to the *Mary Rose.*

The airship should have been seized by now at its mooring in Limehouse. Which meant receipt of his signal would make its new crew of fanatics with parachutes commence to sail the airship to the Tower, loaded with ready explosives.

There. Done. Sent twice.

There came an answering flash from Limehouse.

Good. Pritchard turned the signaler around to face distant West Hill.

He was just starting to unhook lanterns when he saw a small, fast "flitter" airship in Westminster livery rise into the air, banking with an alacrity seldom seen in court voyages, to race off toward Foxden.

Well, well. It seemed even pompous, troublesome magistrates could really run when they felt the need.

R ose and Hardcastle burst into the room rather breathlessly.

Tempest looked up from something small and metallic he was tinkering with, which was clamped between metal frames at a littered table, and he gave them a smile.

"*There* you are! I shut down the machine, as I believe I now know *exactly* where Marlshrike's apparatus is. We can—"

"Lady Roodcannon's airship is headed straight for the Tower!" Rose interrupted excitedly.

"With its running lights all out," Hardcastle added, "which means—"

"She's up to no good," Tempest finished for him. "Well, now!" He sprang up, strode to the wall, and tugged heartily on a bell-pull.

"Is that *food*?" Rose asked, peering at the litter on the table and suddenly realizing how famished she was.

"Oh, yes," the tinkerer noble replied, looking around in some surprise. "I never got around to the kippers. Too busy testing this new control key for the Assassin. Help yourself, m'dear."

"I, too, am starving," Hardcastle observed, with some dignity, following Rose to the plate.

Behind them, the door they'd come in through burst open, and a beagle peered in. "Sir?"

"Go tell the Lord Lion that an airship, its lights out, has been sighted heading for the Tower. Lady *Roodcannon's* airship, mind. The first of your fellow constables you see on your way to the Prince, tell him to get up to the hill with a spyglass and look for signals from the Tower—oh, and from the West Hill Constabulary post. The second constable you see, send to the kitchens; we need something fast, simple, and filling for two tired agents to eat, in very short order. Then go make sure everyone's awake, dressed for battle, armed, and ready."

"Sir?"

"And anyone who disagrees with you—or you, if you don't want to take orders from me—know this: Commissioner Harkness and I discussed such situations (well, all but the protocol for feeding tired agents, that is), and these orders he gave to me to pass on. So you might say they come from the Commissioner himself."

"Yes, sir," the beagle replied dryly. "You might say." But one corner of his mouth was lifting in a grin as he hurried out of the room.

"For a kipper," Rose said appreciatively, "*this* is a darned good sausage."

"Oh, did I miss one of the sausages? Well, my loss and your gain, m'dear. Now, let me just do one thing more . . ."

Tempest touched two wires to either end of the control key in its clamps and pumped a foot treadle. There was a hiss of steam, and then a spark snapped blue-white and angry as it leaped from wire to key and then to the other wire, and the key briefly glowed with the same hue.

"Good. It will work," he announced, satisfied. Tossing the wires in opposite directions, he undid the clamps, plucked out the control key—like all the others, a little box, akin to a square snuffbox, though this one lacked any glued-on glass eyeball or other adornment—and handed it to Rose.

"If you would do me the great service of carrying this on your person, Lady Harminster, my mind would be greatly eased. I would consider the key safe."

"Oh?" Meeting his eyes, Rose slipped the key down her bodice and into the soft leather bag she wore under her bosom when she had occasion to carry valuables along the streets of London. She was carrying a small vial of pepper there now, for dashing into the eyes of assailants—though in the woods full of wildly firing masked agents, she'd found no prudent targets for such an intimate-quarters weapon. "Safe enough?"

Tempest grinned. "And is there a safe answer to that question? I wonder. For now, let it suffice to say—"

The door behind them banged open again, and his face changed.

Rose didn't waste time turning around to see what the peril was. Not when doing so was quite likely to bring her nose to nose with whatever it was—and she had her suspicions about that—without any time to dodge or defend. Instead, she sprang past Jack Straker and his littered worktable to fetch up against a wall before she looked back.

In time to see Bleys Hardcastle grappling with an all-too-familiar lurching adversary.

Even as he landed a solid punch to the Iron Assassin's jaw, Bentley Steelforce caught hold of the front of his jacket, lifted Hardcastle off his feet as though he weighed no more than a child's doll, and flung him away.

He landed with a tinkling crash atop Tempest's machine. Sparks spat, metal tubes spun and clanged away, steam hissed—and Bleys Hardcastle shouted in pain and bounced to the ground, spasming as tiny bolts of lightning raced down his limbs and snarled out from his fingertips to fade away.

He was still groaning and moving—feebly—so he wasn't dead, but . . .

The Iron Assassin stalked toward Tempest. Who coolly stepped forward to wrest a length of pipe out of the midst of his damaged machine. Hefting it, he faced his creation calmly.

Steelforce loomed up over the nobleman, moving with slow, silent menace, spreading his arms wide as if he expected Tempest to try to dart away.

The tinkerer stood his ground, launching no attack on the Assassin. Rather, he held the pipe up in front of himself, in both hands, vertically as if it was the shaft of an umbrella.

Steelforce raised his spread arms—and then brought them down to grasp and rend. *Yes, yes,* came a tinny, gloating voice from the back of his head. *Slay Tempest, my creature! Tear him limb from limb!*

Jack Straker smiled bitterly at that, as he spun the pipe into a horizontal position and sank down, so those descending arms couldn't come together and their owner had to bend over and over to reach him at all.

Then the tinkerer struck, shoving the pipe up to knock against Steelforce's hands as he touched one of the wires to it and kicked at the steam treadle again.

Fat blue sparks spat, the Iron Assassin threw back his head and howled—and Tempest dashed him across the chin with the pipe, let go of it, and fled.

Under the table and past his machine.

The Assassin turned and lurched after him, flinging the table aside with a casual ease that made Rose shriek. It was splintering against the far wall of the room when Steelforce made his next grab for Tempest.

Who ducked low, sidestepped, turned the movement into a spin worthy of any music-hall dancer—and sprang up and over his own machine.

He *almost* made it, but his heels caught in a tangle of hoses and wires that sent him crashing headfirst to the ground, quite a few pieces of his rapidly dismantling apparatus tumbling and clanging in his wake.

The Iron Assassin didn't bother with any leaping nonsense. He simply trudged forward into the heart of the machine and started smashing his way through it.

And Tempest, with a tight and triumphant smile, spun around on his shoulders and kicked hard at the nearest legs of his machine.

Having come from a folding sewing machine, they did what they were designed to do. They promptly buckled and folded up, dragging the machine sideways into a toppling fall—that dragged Steelforce off his feet with it.

No! The voice shouted faintly, out of the Assassin's head. *Don't let him—stop! Don't—*

Tempest was up and rushing around his creation in a trice, avoiding Steelforce's wild grab and leaning in to flip open the door in the back of the Assassin's head and claw out the control key.

Marlshrike's control key. That was crackling faintly now, the violence of its distantly shouting creator silenced with its removal.

Steelforce made a sound that might have been a sob or might have been a pleading growl and flung himself around to face Tempest in a titanic effort that dragged half of the disintegrating machine around with him in his slow and staggering turn. He promptly made another straining, reaching grab for the key.

His fingers came up just short.

Jack Straker looked at the man he'd brought back from the grave, and the man who had been Bentley Roper looked back at Straker . . . and the tinkerer stepped forward and gently put the control key into the Iron Assassin's hand.

That hand tightened into a fist, quivered with a force and fury neither Tempest nor Hardcastle could ever match, and then opened again.

Shards of metal and winking dust spilled out between the spreading fingers, to clink and sigh onto the floor.

Rose and Tempest stared at the Iron Assassin, and he stared

back at them. As Hardcastle's faint groans faded and a tense silence fell.

And stretched.

The sound of shattering glass had never been more satisfying. Alston Drake smiled and cocked his head to listen.

Silence.

There were gasproof masks in the Tower, but they were all under his control, not in the royal bedchamber. From which came only silence. Which meant the Queen and her handful of defenders were now asleep.

"Sir," one of the beagles asked, "your orders?"

"Move the explosives I listed earlier up from the Tower armories. I want four chests just there, then break down that door and put two more in *there,* and then find Alworthy and have him wire them up. Oh, and address me henceforth as 'my lord.'"

"Uh . . . very good. My lord."

Drake smiled. "See? That wasn't so hard now, was it?" Then he gave the man his best scowl and roared, "Hop *to it*! *Now!* As fast as if all steam-driven hell was after you! Move, man, *move!*"

The beagle moved, and so did all the others within earshot, scrambling as if their very lives depended on it.

Drake's smiled widened as he hefted his pistol. Perceptive fellows. Their lives did.

Once the explosives were set, he sent them down in small groups to rearm, then positioned them in a well-hidden cordon in the towers that ringed the White Tower.

"Yes," he murmured to himself, feeling more satisfied than he had in years. "We'll let the Prince get in, all right. Yet whether the lady's plan works out or not, neither Queen nor heir shall get out alive."

———

Captain!" one of the beagles shouted. "Behind us! Coming up *fast*!"

The captain of the flitter whirled around so quickly he almost knocked Sir Fulton Birtwhistle over. Grabbing for railings, the two men stared up at what was looming out of the night.

Black as ink, showing no running lamps and blotting out the stars and city lights with its ever-larger bulk, was an airship—an airship with a distinctive, ornate bowsprit carved to look like four entwined and very affectionate gilded mermaids were climbing hand over hand along a central harpoon.

Both the magistrate and the side-whiskered old flitter captain knew it at a glance. The ship bearing down on them was Lady Roodcannon's personal vessel, *The Steel Kiss*.

"She's going to ram us," the captain snarled, and spun around again to haul hard on the flitter's helm. Catching hold of the king spoke, he wrenched it down to his right, slewing the flitter around so sharply that men shouted in alarm from one end of the ship to the other as they started to tumble or lost hold of items that promptly began to plummet down on sleeping London below.

The wheel spun in the old man's hands as he fell into a kneeling position, his knees on the treadles that would tilt vanes to send the flitter soaring. They were too low over the rooftops to try diving under their huge pursuer.

Clinging to a railing with both hands and all the strength he could muster, Sir Fulton Birtwhistle caught a brief glimpse of the Thames glimmering below, waters reflecting lamplight from dockside warehouses, and then the flitter's sharp turn became a sharp climb, and all he could see was the dark emptiness of the night sky, a handful of stars twinkling serene reassurance at him as—

The bowsprit of Lady Roodcannon's airship slammed into the left rear of the flitter like a giant's fist, numbing every man aboard the flitter in a breath-snatching instant. Sir Fulton saw the mermaids thrusting *through* the flitter deck, men and lines being flung up in all directions—as *The Steel Kiss* sheared shriekingly right through the back of the flitter, slicing away rudder, steering cables, hull, and all.

Ballast stones tumbled, the portside flotation bladder exploded with a fierceness that flung the flitter through the sky head over heels over head again—and then they had stopped tumbling and were falling . . . plunging down through the darkness in a sudden, sickening quiet in which they could hear a woman's low-pitched but gleeful laughter fading behind them.

Lady Roodcannon, it seemed, was amused.

"That's her at the wheel," Sir Fulton snapped, catching a glimpse of long hair streaming out behind shapely shoulders. "She rammed us, she did!"

He turned to the flitter captain for the old man's reply and found himself alone on the open wheel deck. There was blood on the spokes of the unmanned, freely turning wheel—and, far below, the captain's limp body was falling through the night.

Sir Fulton turned and looked wildly around the flitter decks. "Is there anyone who can fly this ship?" he shouted. "Anyone?"

Beagles looked his way, but no one answered. He saw some of the constables were uncoiling mooring lines from the deck capstans, wrapping the ends around their waists and thighs in loose and untidy belays, and jumping over the side.

What were they *doing*?

As Sir Fulton swarmed along the railings, not daring to let go for an instant as the flitter deck tilted alarmingly again, he saw something else.

The sky above and ahead was very dark, blotted out by the huge bulk of Lady Roodcannon's airship. It was coming around in a great sweeping curve to head for them again.

He could feel the flitter under him sinking fast—and shuddering, too, reacting to dozens of sharp little tugs in this direction and that. What—?

Oh. The beagles, on their lines. Sir Fulton peered gingerly over an edge of the deck and saw that all the beagles were kicking and waving their arms, trying to—nay, succeeding—make their lines swing back and forth, back and forth, in ever longer arcs.

The flitter's wandering fall had taken it a long way west, crossing the serpentine Thames several times, out beyond the city to the heaths, woodlots, and straggling villages. They were barely above treetop level now, and as Sir Fulton watched, he saw one of the beagles brush some tree branches with his boots, his swing noticeably faltering—and then, on the return swing, that same constable let go and flung himself at another treetop, arms spread to try to grasp.

Branches shattered as the man plunged through them, starting to tumble, and then the flitter started to tilt the other way and hid the man's fate from view.

Sir Fulton Birtwhistle started to look for an unused mooring line of his own. Flitters had a lot of them, so they could be tied in tandem with others of their kind in tight quarters around—

Gunfire blazed out of the night, bullets humming like angry hornets across the flitter deck and stitching holes across the cabin roofs in brief dins of splinterings and the *tanging* sounds of metallic ricochets.

Those guns—five, no, six of them—were fitted to Lady Roodcannon's airship, and the gunners were sweeping the decks of the flitter . . . and now dipping below.

Sir Fulton's wild scramble to the only capstan he could see that still had cable wrapped around it ended in a bruising meeting with his destination, as the flitter yawed suddenly and side-slipped across the sky.

A dark line of trees—no, more than that, a wood of considerable size—rushed up darkly to meet the starboard side of the deck. Luckily, his capstan was on the port side. He clung to it, clawing at the mooring line, trying to start its uncoiling as Lady Roodcannon's guns spat. Beagles on the lines in midair jerked as bullets tore into them or lost their grips and fell, some screaming and some limply silent.

The airship passed over him, vast and terrible and no more than twice his height above his head, its guns falling silent. For now.

Sir Fulton stared up at its stern as it scudded away. At its helm, her long hair stirring in the wind of her ship's passage, Lady Roodcannon looked back at him over her shoulder. Back and down, and . . . was that a sneer?

The mooring line moved at last under his hands, and thankfully he set about uncoiling, uncomfortably aware of how close the ground was and how swiftly it now seemed to be rushing up to meet the stricken flitter. Whose decks were already a mass of splinters and wrack that could thrust through him as keenly as any sword or pike, if—

The Steel Kiss was banking in the air, turning with slow, menacing majesty. Coming back to strafe everyone on or hanging from the flitter again.

Which meant he probably didn't have long to live, at all.

Sir Fulton Birtwhistle said a word that would not have been appreciated in court, softly but deliberately, wound the end of his mooring line thrice around his chest, undid a lot more of it by walking around the capstan, made sure he had firm hold of the end of the line by wrapping it around his fist, and jumped over the edge, kicking off as the flitter dipped and trying to get as far away from the edge of the falling ship as he could.

The moment he was off the deck, he became aware of two things: just how fast its dive was, as he was far behind it in an instant and being towed along, hard, and that something behind them all was flashing wildly in the distance.

Signal lamps, from atop the Tower of London. Winking on and off as they were unhooded, being rushed into different patterns with an urgency he'd not seen for a long time.

Not that he knew how to read them. For him, as for most Londoners, the lamps were just *there*, every night, part of the unsleeping arm of government and the mails and the Crown alone knew what else.

Someone aboard *The Steel Kiss* did, though.

The great dark airship's nose lifted, and it came out of its tight turn and the descent that would have brought it just astern of the flitter to riddle the last of the flitter's crew with its guns, to head toward those urgently flashing signals.

Deliverance for him, but probably doom for the Queen and Prycewood and the rest he'd left behind in the Tower.

Abruptly, a branch raked Sir Fulton. He was being towed through the edges of a row of trees. He looked ahead, managed to kick air enough to turn himself until he was being pulled through the air boots first, then waited for the large oak he was now sweeping down to meet.

And as it rushed up to meet him, he spared an instant or two to wonder gloomily about the sort of England he'd find himself in, if he lived through this night.

And whether it would still have an Empire or would be plunged into endless wide-ranging war in which everything was lost, the world was changed, and many dreams drowned in blood.

Then the oak put a sudden and painful stop to such thoughts.

"Dashed inconsiderate of it," Sir Fulton thought aloud, as he crashed through branch after branch, scratched and bedraggled and tumbling helplessly—and lost his grip on the mooring line.

It spun him around like a top as it let him go, snatching his breath away in a few frantic blurred instants, and then dumped him on the ground with a solid but surprisingly gentle thud.

Leaving one of England's foremost magistrates bruised and of torn wardrobe, but surprisingly intact, to wobble dazedly to his feet and witness the rending *keerrraaahsh* of the flitter into the trees a mile or so distant. Its boiler burst with a deafening hiss of steam jetting in a dozen directions, and . . .

Around him in the night, bedraggled beagles were staggering nearer, converging grimly in what seemed to be a field of lavender—lavender?—and looking to him for guidance.

"Orders, sir?"

Sir Fulton Birtwhistle opened his mouth, without a thought in his head as to what he'd say.

"Foxden, sir?"

"Foxden," he heard himself agreeing firmly. "We have to get to Foxden, as fast as possible."

"The road's yonder," one constable said, pointing at the dark line of trees that bounded one edge of the field and then waving his pointing arm along it. "And it'll be that way."

"Then let's go there," Sir Fulton announced, and started trampling lavender in that direction.

It was hard to say who was more surprised, some minutes later, when the battered group of beagles was almost run over by a trap being driven at speed along the road. Algernon Hartworth was more than a little startled to find constables blocking the road, and the amorous and decidedly tipsy young lady he was taking home from a house party was both dumbfounded and scared.

It all turned to excitement, however, when Sir Fulton Birtwhistle and the senior beagle clambered aboard and crisply commandeered the trap, retaining Algernon as their driver and his ladylove as a willing but unable navigator, and hastened for Foxden.

The other beagles, trudging along far behind the speeding conveyance, ran to rather darker emotions than excitement.

Behind the Iron Assassin, the door crashed open again.

"Good heavens!" exclaimed the Prince Royal. "Tempest, did you lose your temper? We heard you smashing your machine, and—"

He and the beagles and soldiers with him froze as Steelforce turned, and they realized that what they had thought was the man-high surviving central core of the tinkerer's apparatus was the Iron Assassin himself, draped in cords and pipes and other fragments of the machine.

The Lord Lion stared into the eyes of the man from the grave who'd been sent to kill him more than once, and the Iron Assassin stared silently back.

Then the man in the exoskeleton took a lurching step sideways. Every pistol in the room came up, but he ignored them, taking another step, and then another.

Out of the ruin of the machine he went, away from the Prince and Tempest and the rest, to thread his stiff and unsteady way through the armed soldiers to the door.

The Prince lifted a hand to quell any firing, and in deepening silence they watched the Iron Assassin shoulder his way through the door and then start to run, loping lopsidedly away.

"No one," the Prince Royal commanded, "is to fire."

And no one did.

Most of the men firing at us in the woods were fellow members of the Order!" the larger masked man snapped angrily. "Treachery among the Tentacles, as we've feared for so long!"

"Obviously," Marlshrike said soothingly, "we were right about those fears. Yet you said 'most,' by which I take it that there were Crown agents lurking about? Sworn Swords?"

"There were," the smaller masked men said grimly. "And so far as we can tell, they got away."

"After accomplishing *what?*" Marlshrike asked sharply. "Did any of them get close to here? Do you think they know I'm here?"

The larger masked man shrugged. "They were searching for

something. We don't think they managed much searching or found out anything much."

"But they *were* looking in these woods?"

"They were."

Marlshrike sighed heavily, shook his head to try to quell his surge of anger, and snapped, "My thanks. Now go away; you've given me much to ponder, and I need to get to thinking about it. Alone."

Without waiting for a reply, he mounted the stairs that led, floor by floor and flight by flight, to the top of the old mill. He did think best alone, and up here he knew he'd find solitude. The stairs all creaked, and so did most of the floors; he'd soon know if anyone was up here.

It was almost dawn, and the first birds were awakening. Their squawks contrasted with the silence all around him, whenever he stopped his climb.

Which he did in the upper hoist room, at the very top of the mill. Yes, he was alone.

He went to the topmost window, his favorite view. It looked toward London, and he liked to gaze out of it, safely hidden here in these woods, up above the rabble, and contemplate his rise.

He didn't want to rule or to have any political presence at all. That meant endless time wasted talking to people, and he detested most people. Nasty, grasping, small-minded rats—or, worse, dim-witted sheep whose uninformed prejudices always stood in the way of progress, always . . .

Bah! He'd been through such thoughts a thousand times upon a thousand more! His plans were advancing at last, and that meant real danger—and excitement, too. Yet just now he *had* to get his hands on ever more money. He might be a far wealthier Norbert Marlshrike than he'd been a month ago, but he was now caught in this ticklish stage he'd foreseen where he was still essentially alone, and so too weak to defy the Ancient Order, yet he had to show these same Tentacles—ruthless cretins who could butcher him in any angry moment—genuine results in order to keep their support. And real progress in any hurry meant buying what he needed, and when it came to his sort of work that meant money. Lots of money. And Pauncefoot's gold was running out so, so fast . . .

He sighed and thrust that thought aside for a moment. He liked to look out of this window best by night, when instead of distant airships, plumes of smoke, and tiny smudges on the horizon that might be church spires or might be mooring masts, London showed him its lights.

Twinkling, glittering, splendid, and on rare occasions even mysterious, they were the lights of progress. The lights of dreams, dreams energetically made reality, the sort of energy he could subvert and harness and ride on into riches and eventually glory, a time when Norbert Marlshrike would be a name uttered with reverence, when he would be recognized as *the* preeminent tinkerer of all time, when men would turn to him for advice and solicit his skills for handsome fees to guide teams of welders and foundry casters, wire makers and riggers and all the rest . . .

He loved watching the lights. They were an exciting comfort, if such a contradic—

What by the dancing imp of steam was *that*?

He peered at the flashing cluster of lights. Flashes that shifted slightly from blink to blink, in a tight and repeating pattern—signal lights of the Constabulary. From their Wandsworth tower, but sent in this direction, out into the countryside.

He snatched out his ever-present spyglass, focused it on the lights to make absolutely certain of their message, and read the repeating message with great care.

Alone in the silent upper hoist room of the mill, he murmured the message aloud like a schoolboy, twice through, then lowered his spyglass and thought hard.

So it had come at last. The Ancient Order of the Tentacles was trying for the Lion Throne.

And if they failed, but only just, the result would be war. If they succeeded, one Tentacle would turn upon the next, and again: war.

Strife right across the Empire, a nasty, endless, bloody skirmish in which tinkerers would become pawns.

Which meant he should get away from here and into hiding just as fast as he could. Pack only what was most vital and get *gone,* right now.

He was rarely awake at dawn—a chilly time when he was usually deep in his slumbers, thanks to being late abed and chronically short of sleep—but when he was, he liked to watch it break slowly over England.

Not today. He turned away and started hurrying down the way he'd come, to assemble the few things he couldn't do without.

Behind him, dawn came, unregarded.

O h, it can be rebuilt," Tempest assured the Prince Royal. "When we need it again. Right now, I rather fear we have—"

There was a stir at the door, beagles speaking sharp challenges and being snapped at in reply. Out of that knot of stern armed men burst a breathless Sir Fulton Birtwhistle, crying, "The Prince Royal is summoned!"

"Sirrah!" Chief Inspector Theo Standish rebuked the flushed-faced magistrate sharply. "*No one* 'summons' the Prince Royal."

"The Queen does," Sir Fulton shot back. Then caught sight of the Lord Lion, squared his shoulders, and addressed royalty directly.

"Your Highness, sir, the Queen desires your presence at her side immediately. She says to tell you she is dying and to use all speed, for she would see you again ere—"

"Thank you," the Prince cried, rushing past him to the door.

"Gilreth!" he bellowed, before he was all the way through it. "Your fastest horse!"

Aboard the *Mary Rose,* one masked figure rushed up to another who stood at the helm.

"Explosives all wired." The report was given tersely.

"The boats?"

"Last two being lashed down right now."

From the helm, they could see the cranes swinging away from those last two getaway boats. Crude glider gigs that had steering rudders operated by crew members pedaling as if they were riding penny-farthings. At the last moment, they'd slice those lashings with the sharp knives every man carried, kick off hard to get clear of the decks, and hope.

Most of them would probably get caught in the blast, but—

The men at the helm looked at each other and shrugged. They planned to depart a little earlier, and every endeavor has its price.

Sever a Tentacle, and six more rise to take its place . . .

There was a shout and a brief signal flash from the deck. Last boat tied down.

The men at the helm called their own orders, and the *Mary Rose* lifted off its moorings into the chill dawn. After a moment of drifting, it gathered sudden speed as steam jets fired, almost leaping through the air.

It seemed in a hurry to head to its own immolation.

Jack Straker shook his head. "I don't like this," he snapped. "I smell treachery."

"Treason at the Tower?" Rose murmured. "It's a fitting place— *the* fitting place."

"Indeed. We *must* get there, and faster than the Prince!"

"Impossible!" Hardcastle protested, flinging his arms wide to express impossibility.

"Not with an airship." His friend smiled. Attacking his ruined machine, he tore open a compartment in its depths, snatched out some small, heavy cloth bags, and hurried for the door with them. "Come on! Grab pistols, but not if you have to rummage or turn aside to do so!"

Chief Inspector Standish silently handed the tinkerer his own gun.

"And just where are you going to get an airship?" Hardcastle demanded, reaching out imploringly to the nearest soldier for a firearm—and receiving one.

Tempest turned in the doorway to give him a wider smile. "The mail run."

Standish gawped at the tinkerer noble. "Now hold hard, there, sir! There are laws about interfering with Her Majesty's mail—"

He found himself talking to empty air. The Lady Harminster had passed him like a rushing wind—a hastening gale that blew Hardcastle and Tempest, ahead of her, through the door. The three of them hurried to get out of Foxden, Tempest thrusting the cloth bags into Hardcastle's hands as they went.

The senior beagle stared after them, listening to the dwindling sounds of their headlong departure.

Then he shrugged, shook his head with a wry smile, and started barking orders. The soldiers could do as they pleased, but every constable here at Foxden was going to get to the Tower as fast as possible, in a proper armed force, to support the Prince.

Lady Constance Roodcannon finished the plate of Stilton and pears, sipped her favorite cordial, its ruby fire sliding warmly down her throat—ahh, *most* welcome in the chill air of dawn—and sent the servant away with a nod.

She wanted to be alone as she brought *The Steel Kiss* around in another sweeping turn, its sleek and mighty bulk cleaving the chill dawn air over London, to gloat not in front of servants, but to herself.

This would be *her* victory, her triumph. Hers alone.

She'd been circling London for some time now, waiting for the tardy Prince to rise from his bed of doxies and hurry into her trap.

And now, with the sun rising to shortly light the city of so many stacks and mooring masts and plumes of smoke beneath her, he was on his way at last. This was it at last. The opportunity she'd waited so long for, the small but necessary achievement finally brought about by her manipulations.

At long last, despite the stern security precautions and the coolness between severe and ailing mother and young, wayward son, the Queen and the Prince Royal would be together, in one spot.

Whereupon her fireship would swoop down . . .

By now, the *Mary Rose* was an aerial bomb, in the air and crossing London. If anything flew to intercept it, she herself would deal with them.

At her signal—once royal mother and son were both in the Tower—the explosives-laden ship, set afire at the last moment, would dive down into the explosives-stuffed Tower of London and crash into it.

Eliminating a tiresome queen and the heir to the throne and leaving her own child the sole legitimate surviving heir to the Empire of the Lion.

The new wine was here at hand, chilled and ready.

She uncorked it with a practiced slice of the very sharp knife she always carried these days, poured herself a glass, and murmured, "To the New Lion."

Then she downed it. It was magnificent.

She poured herself another glass, brought the great airship under her smoothly out of its turn, sat down again in her high-backed captain's throne with glass in hand, and settled back to watch the fun.

T hose gates look more than a little sturdy," Rose murmured, gazing up at welded iron bars that rose in a small-windowed lattice three times the height of her head, bars thicker than her wrist that bore very little rust indeed and ended in uprights topped by sharp arrowhead-like points the size of spears. "Just how are you going to get in?"

Nor was the Bishop's Bottom Royal Mail yard unguarded. Not far away on the other side of the large lock plate they were approaching, a bored-looking uniformed mail guard was beginning to look less bored and more concerned and was heading their way with a frown.

"I'm a tinkerer, remember?" Lord Tempest produced a worn-looking leather pouch from within his waistcoat, undid a catch and flipped it open, and bent to peer into the keyhole and straightened again all in one smooth movement. Selecting one slim metal instrument from a row of similar gleaming tools, he thrust it into the keyhole and probed delicately. Only to withdraw it almost immediately, replace it in the pouch array, select another, and explore the keyhole with bold confidence.

"Hoy, there!" the mail guard snapped, "what're you up to?"

The tinkerer noble made no reply but probed more deeply, acquiring a frown of his own. He looked exactly like a surgeon Rose had once watched, who'd been puzzled by what he found in a wound.

Then he spun around, thrust his open pouch into Rose's hands, murmured, "Hold it open, please," and, the moment she had hold of it, used his freed hand to slip out another lockpick, slide it into the keyhole alongside the first he was still holding deeply inside, and turn it. Then he arched an eyebrow, withdrew it a trifle, and turned it in the opposite direction—and nodded in satisfaction.

The lock gave forth a loud *click*.

"Here, now," the guard snarled, trying to reach his hands through the bars and grab Tempest's arm. "I'll have the law on you, I will!"

Tempest removed both picks, turned and replaced them in the pouch, clapped it closed, then breezily turned and stuffed his pouch down Lady Rose's bodice.

The guard gaped at her in astonishment, then transferred his stare with obvious effort to Jack Straker.

Who gave him a broad smile, thrust the unlocked gate open with a firm hand, in the process ramming it into the man's face, and strode purposefully through it with Bleys Hardcastle right behind him. Hardcastle was putting his shoulder against the bars and leaning with each step, bracing himself to prevent the man from shoving the gate closed again.

As it happened, that strongman tactic wasn't necessary; the man fell back and grabbed for a whistle swinging from a fine chain around his neck.

The foremost of the three intruders snatched it out of the air with his fist and announced, "We *are* the law. Lax, my man, lax; you really should keep gates like this locked, you know!"

"B-but—"

"Surprise mail inspection," the smiling man whose fist was still closed around his whistle informed him. "I am Jack Straker, Lord Tempest, and these are my associates, who hold such lofty Crown ranks that I shan't bore you with them at this time of night. Suffice it to say that we dine and jest and play at cards with the Prince Royal himself. Now, if you'll just tell me what *this* is, down here . . ."

A long, patrician, and imperious finger indicated one of the rusty dog-spikes set into the ground to prevent the opened gate from swinging too far and crashing into a lamppost beyond.

"You've never seen a *dog*-spike before?" the guard managed to ask, battling through incredulity as far as audibility.

"No, no," Tempest said rather testily. "Not the spike, sirrah, but this mark on it, here!"

The guard bent obediently to peer, the chain for the whistle was whipped up from around his neck in an ear-numbing instant, and he found himself sprawling on his face in the dust of the yard under the prodding of a firm shove on his shoulder.

"Follow me," his ungentle questioner murmured over one shoulder, and set off at a brisk pace across the well-lit yard to the foot of the mooring-mast stairs. The man's two associates followed.

The guard wallowed, scrambled up, drew breath for an angry shout of alarm—and found himself sneezing helplessly.

"Dust!" Tempest bellowed happily back at the man, from most of the way up the first flight of steps. "If you kept things clean, man, this wouldn't happen!"

The mail yard was by no means asleep or deserted at this hour. The sorting sheds were a hastening hive of activity, the tied and labeled sacks being transported in open hoppers up covered chute ways by strong men working winches in pairs to a platform under a rain roof, where sweating men were loading the deck bins of the *Woolwich Windolphin,* an unlovely but sturdy mail airship typical of her "cutter" type. The bags had to be securely tied in clusters by destination to a common harness of air balloons secured across the boards by swiveling deck hooks. Thus, they could be easily freed in midflight, weights hung on them according to local winds, and dropped into fenced mail paddocks en route.

Tempest climbed briskly past several mail guards and aboard the *Windolphin.*

"About done, then?" he asked the guards overseeing the deck crews jovially. The decks did look to be almost covered.

"Near as—hey, and who the deuce might you be?" the nearest guard replied.

"New Crown mail inspector," Tempest replied promptly, smiling as he turned to Hardcastle, extended open hands, and murmured, "Two of my bags, please."

"What?" the guard asked disbelievingly. "Mail inspector? Since when did they start appointing inspectors young enough to not yet be in their dotage? Old Alf could be your great grandfather! So who are you, *really?*"

Tempest, pistol out, saw the man behind the guard reaching for a gun and thus accepted the two bags from Hardcastle, adding a nod of encouragement upon seeing Hardcastle hefting the remaining pair of bags, and then turned back to the guard and dashed the pistol from his hand with one bag, letting him have it with the second bag across the chin.

The man stumbled back into his fellow guard before that worthy could raise his gun, and Tempest sprang after him, introducing each of his bags to a face.

Hardcastle was right behind him, and before Rose could step around them all to deal with the last guard, men were going down and their guns clattering to the decks. Leaving just one guard to flee after the deck crews.

Someone sounded an alarm, a steam horn that wailed like a mournful ox in pain. Tempest winced at the sound but, through its din, turned to Rose and asked, "Get to the helm and hold the wheel steady, will you?"

She nodded and ran for the helm. As Hardcastle and Tempest sprang to untie mooring lines, the alarm rose in pitch and volume, and men scurried in a dozen directions in the yard below, some shouting threats and orders, and others calling to each other in fearful bewilderment.

They were still at it when the *Windolphin* lifted unsteadily, Tempest slashing the last line with a knife.

In their haste, none of them noticed the few guards on the platforms below who'd found rifles: they had all been flung aside like rag dolls without managing to get off a shot. Their assailant was a lone, skull-headed, lurching man who moved like a ruthless and vengeful wind—and he sprang aboard at the last possible instant to lie still among all the mail sacks and balloons as Tempest hurried to the helm.

The Lady Harminster had never steered an airship before, still less dealt with a gusty rising crosswind, and the ship was tilted alarmingly thanks to that persistent last mooring line, and unevenly loaded besides.

Yet she managed to turn the *Windolphin* in the right direction, even before Tempest got to the wheel.

"Where has *this* been all my life?" she laughed to the wind—an instant before her hair came unbound and swirled almost blindingly around her face.

The river mists were racing along the Thames like fleeing ghosts as the horses clattered up to the Tower of London at full gallop.

And were greeted by withering gunfire that swiftly emptied saddles all round the Prince Royal, who rode at their head, face afire with anger.

Drake's men had strict orders not to shoot the Lord Lion, but if the heir to the Empire rode into the Tower of London alone, that would be just fine.

He almost did. No more than a handful of men were still with him, horses shrieking and falling all around them as Drake's men opened up in a last-moment attempt to eliminate everyone but the Prince, whose party got in through the gate that had been left open for them, stormed through doors that should have been guarded but weren't, and descended to the tunnels that would take them into the White Tower itself.

Down in dimly lit stone passages and hurrying, they never saw the *Mary Rose* show up in the sky.

———

A wind had arisen, and the *Windolphin* was riding it like a skittish pony, dancing along on the gusts almost playfully—and slipping sideways with each one. When Tempest took the helm, Rose relinquished it gratefully.

"Whereabouts will we land?" she asked. "I don't recall any masts near the Tower, and there certainly isn't open space anywhere to . . ."

"We won't be landing," Tempest told her grimly, pointing into the brightening sky ahead. "We'll be ramming."

Rose looked at him sharply. "And dying?"

Jack pointed at the mailbags and balloons laid out across the deck. "Bailing, not dying."

"One hopes," Rose sighed, strolling back to look at one mail array after another. Byfleet, Chertsey, Lightwater . . . "In my admittedly brief experience of derring-do thus far, things never seem to work out according to even the most cunning of plans. You, however, seem to be a better planner than mo—"

At that moment there was a queer thudding sound behind her, and she spun around in time to see Bleys Hardcastle sprawled senseless across several mailbags and the Iron Assassin charging from him straight at Tempest.

"Jack!" she shrieked, starting to sprint but already left behind by the man in the exoskeleton. God, but he was fast!

Tempest turned from the ship's wheel in time to face his creation—but that was all he had time to do before one of the hard fists that had felled Hardcastle struck his jaw with force enough to whip his head around and smash him clear off the deck.

He fell on his back on bulging mailbags, with the Assassin on top of him and raining solid punches. Rose didn't even have time to scream, let alone reach Steelforce, before Jack was lolling limp and senseless—and the man in the exoskeleton was turning and rising to clutch at Rose.

Fingers as cold and hard as iron brushed her throat as she twisted desperately aside, but that desperate evasion and the speed of her charge left her stumbling over mailbags and falling.

A hand closed around her right leg, just above her knee, dragged her, then lifted her as though she weighed nothing, turning her and setting her down face-to-face with Bentley Steelforce.

His face looked more like a skull than ever, only a few wisps of hair still clinging to the graying flesh. His *eyes* . . .

Heart in her throat, barely able to breathe, she stared at him.

He pointed at her bodice.

"S-sorry?" she gasped. He'd let go of her, but she stood within his reach, and there was nothing she could do against his strength. Nothing. She'd seen him fight his way through a hail of bullets . . .

He pointed at her bodice again.

"Y-you . . . you want me?" she whispered, reaching reluctantly for the thin fabric that covered her . . . her . . .

"*Key*," he growled at her, scowling.

"Oh," she almost moaned, and clawed down into her bodice for the little leather pouch. She fumbled the key forth, her fingers grazing the vial of pepper as she did so. But if she tried to use the pepper, what good would it do? They were on a canted deck in midair, and it wouldn't blind him forever . . .

She left the pepper where it was and held out the key. Her arm was trembling violently.

His hand came nearer, and nearer . . . Rose bit her lip to keep from screaming and fought to loosen her fingers, to let the little box Tempest had made shift from her palm to her fingertips . . . she would have to *touch* him . . .

His hand slid under hers and opened wide, like a great bowl.

"Drop the key," he growled. "Into it."

She did that, and his hand closed around it into a fist that shook briefly in a rippling spasm of crushing strength, and then opened again. Flattened fragments of key spilled from it.

He could tear her limb from limb at any moment, with casual ease . . .

He pointed at a mailbag.

She stared at him.

He pointed again.

"Sorry?" she whispered. "I don't understand."

"Sit," he growled at her, looming up over her. She sat.

"Don't move," he ordered, then thrust his face down close to hers and glowered. "Try *nothing*."

Rose managed to nod. "N-nothing," she echoed.

The Iron Assassin pointed at her eyes, then at himself, and then stalked to where Hardcastle lay. He tore open the nearest large mailbag, dumped its contents out into the wind, stuffed the unconscious man into it, tied its cord around one of his shoulders, then did the same with his other shoulder and another mailbag. Then he unclipped the rest of the mailbags from the balloons, turned the hooks that freed the whole assembly from the deck, carried Hardcastle to the nearest edge of the deck, planted one foot on the rail there, and tossed man and balloons into the sky.

Hardcastle fell away behind the *Windolphin*, hanging limply but descending slowly, not plummeting.

The Assassin stalked back to Tempest and repeated the process. He stared long and hard into his creator's slack face, and Rose feared he was about to do something to the man she . . . she . . .

But he didn't. Lurching into an abrupt turn, he went to the rail and gave Jack Straker to the sky.

Then the man in the exoskeleton came back to Rose and pointed again at the mailbag she was now sitting on.

"You mean to serve me . . . the same way?" she asked, unable to keep the fear entirely out of her voice.

He nodded.

"You won't . . . kill me?"

He gave her a look of disgust and shook his head.

She closed her eyes and gave into shuddering until she could breathe and think again. Whereupon she stood up, tried to smile, and said, "Then do it. I don't know what you're up to, but you deserve your freedom, after all Jack . . . and everyone else . . . has put you through. Godspeed."

They were nose to nose again. The Iron Assassin's sudden smile startled her. He bowed and extended a hand to her, as if to gallantly escort her.

Rose took it. His fingers were hard and ice-cold. She managed to suppress another shudder as he led her to a large mailbag, undid it, shook out its contents, and gestured to her to get inside.

Sinking down beside it, the Lady Harminster eyed the sack of thick, dirty canvas. It would only come up to about her waist, but she was slender and supple, and if she curled up . . . she clambered in, slid down, and curled up. Only her head and shoulders were out of the bag.

The Iron Assassin reached in and drew her right arm out, as tenderly as a mother might arrange a child, then tied the sack up around that shoulder. Then he guided her hand to the thick rope that led to the balloons, clasped it there, and patted it in a clear signal to keep holding on. Then he slid his other hand into the sack and felt around to make sure she could move her left hand.

"Guarding the Empire *your* work now," he growled.

And he bent and kissed her on the cheek.

She froze, and was still tense and fighting down fear as he carried her across the deck, adding into her ear, "Tell Straker I'm *grateful.*"

And dropped her over the side.

The *Windolphin* seemed to leap away from her as she sank. She was falling through the air, like Hardcastle and Tempest—where *was* he? Oh, there! But the balloons were slowing her descent to a gentle drift.

The Iron Assassin waved to her, then bent and busied himself along the deck. Cluster after cluster of mail joined her in the sky, a small flotilla of balloons descending in eerie silence.

The emptied and lightened mail ship rose a little and flew faster. She saw the Iron Assassin lurch to the helm and turn its nose into the sky.

It climbed swiftly, heading for . . . a distant, circling airship: a large freighter in the sky downriver, the other side of the Tower of London.

And from behind Rose's shoulder a great but graceful bulk swooped into view. The Lady Roodcannon's airship; she could see its distinctive bowsprit of mermaids. It raced after the mail ship, and its guns spat once, twice . . . and then fell silent, for the *Windolphin* was in line with the ship it was now rushing to meet, the freighter circling in the distance.

Men on the decks of the freighter, little larger than ants at this distance, were firing pistols at the speeding mail ship. Lady Roodcannon's huge airship was suddenly banking sharply to the left and climbing into the sky, seeming in desperate haste . . .

Leaving only two ships in Rose's view. Right in front of her, clear in the brightening morning sky.

She watched in the serene silence as the Iron Assassin flew the mail ship right into the freighter, turning it on edge at the last moment so that it seemed a gigantic arrowhead, streaking into the side of the larger—

The sky erupted into a huge ball of flame, hurling debris in all directions. The sound smote her ears like a hammer as the air slapped her across the face and flung her balloons across the sky.

The flames where the two ships had been spat out many smaller fireballs that arced in all directions, trailing smoke, like so many tentacles . . .

And Lady Rose Harminster found herself weeping.

Cold, hard stone bumped his elbow, leaving it burning. Then it bumped his hip, no more gently.

Then he slipped, or fell, and rope sawed at his shoulder . . . and Jack Straker, Lord Tempest, finally came awake.

His jaw ached like sin, and his chest and shoulders didn't feel much better. Exoskeletons were effective things, indeed.

He was . . .

He was dangling down the side of a curving wall of stone, huge old well-fitted blocks that fell away below him and continued a little way above him . . . a fortress tower.

He peered rather blearily around. Yonder was the White Tower, and *this* . . .

He looked, counted towers, and decided he was hanging from the top of the Lanthorn Tower. The collapsing balloons he was tied to were draped down its side, caught on something above him.

Gunfire promptly barked from windows just above him, punching out through the balloons into the dawn air. Which meant that the moment someone took a knife to the fabric, or opened a window below and aimed a pistol upwards with precision, the Empire was going to be one meddlesome tinkerer noble fewer.

Unless, of course, he did something about his present predicament. Somehow it *always* came down to Jack bloody Straker doing something.

He clawed his way up the balloon fabric, and when a gun barrel thrust out of a window, he grabbed it and pulled, hard.

A startled beagle came half out of the window, shouting, and Tempest punched him in the throat, good and hard. The man's shouts became strangling sobs, and then Tempest slid down the man's back and into the room.

There was another beagle in it, crouched over and reloading. "Keep your hair on, Anson," this worthy snarled, not looking up—which gave Tempest time to fish out one of the trusty small bags he'd brought from Foxden and club the man across the head and neck with it.

The man sagged, and Tempest gratefully relieved him of his knife, cut himself free of the mail harness, and got to the door just in time.

Half the heavy-booted members of the Constabulary in London seemed to be hurrying up the tower stairs. The foremost pair had pistols in their hands and anger on their faces and were raising their weapons to aim at him.

Loyal guards of the Queen, or traitors among the beagles? Well, the Order spread its Tentacles everywhere . . . and what were armed beagles doing here at the Tower anyway?

Tempest used the knife to slice the drawstring of his bag and poured its contents—oiled ball bearings of various sizes, the latest toys of advancing steam-driven technology—down the stone stairs.

The slick little metal spheres bounced and rolled underfoot, sending the beagles back down the stairs in helpless falls. The foremost man struggled for balance, pistol firing wildly into the ceiling—and Tempest sprang, grabbing the man by the throat and sending him over backward.

The man bounced with brutal force, the gun flying one way and his helmet the other, and Tempest clung to the unconscious result, riding that unfortunate beagle down the steps as a human toboggan.

Very like those he'd used as a boy on snowy slopes in the Dales—though none of those descents had been down interior stone stairs or involved crashing into fallen men and plunging over them and on, or bone-shattering meetings of a ridden man's limbs with walls while descending to lower levels.

Tempest's wild ride didn't end until they slid right out of an open door at ground level and out into the inner ward.

Where doors were banging open and orders were being shouted. Lying still atop his beagle, a little dazed—though he suspected the beagle was a long way beyond being dazed, perhaps forever past such things—Tempest listened to the familiar voice of Alston Drake bellowing orders that amounted to rearranging his men to assault the White Tower.

"Now that the planned grand crash of the fireship won't be happening, lads, we'll just have to do this the hard way!"

So Drake was part of it, and all of these beagles, too. That made Tempest feel a bit better about what he'd just done to a dozen of them on the tower stairs.

"Gregson, take your command around the—"

My, but Drake was in fine vocal form this morning!

The bellowing ended abruptly as three of the beagles standing beside Drake were smashed flat to the ground under the boots and elbows of an unconscious and unlooked-for Bleys Hardcastle, descending rapidly onto them out of the sky, trailing one balloon and the shrunken remnants of four more failed ones.

"Aerial assault!" Drake boomed, snatching out a pistol and looking up.

The first thing he saw was the Lady Rose Harminster drifting down in her balloon-escorted mail sack.

Drake gaped up at her for a moment, and Tempest, scrambling to his feet, saw the man's face change as he recognized her.

And then Drake's features hardened, and he raised his pistol to fire.

Tempest sprinted for him, second small bag in hand. Drake was taking careful aim at the descending noblewoman, but he heard or sensed Tempest behind him at the last moment and whirled around—so he got the bag of ball bearings right in his face.

Blood and teeth flew, and Tempest felt the man's jaw or nose break, or both, as he fell past.

Drake staggered, and Tempest rolled, came to his feet, turned—and pounced on the man from behind, slipping and falling but dragging Drake with him to the ground.

He was trying to get the gun out of Drake's hand before the man recovered enough to use it, but guns were firing all around, and it was Drake's body that stopped a flurry of bullets from his own men meant for Tempest.

Then fresh gunfire erupted from another direction, and Drake's men were falling.

Rose struggled to free herself as she came down to the ground, and Tempest furiously rolled Drake's dying weight off himself to try to get to her—and they both had a splendid view of the Prince Royal's men bursting out of the White Tower and shooting down Drake's men.

"Tempest!" someone roared from among them. "Keep back! The White Tower is crammed full of munitions and wired to explode!"

"Where's the Queen?" Tempest shouted back.

"The Prince has taken her down into the undercroft and the tunnels, for safety! This isn't done yet—there are traitors all over the towers and grounds!"

As if to prove those words, firing erupted from various windows and battlements, and Tempest hastened to throw himself atop the Lady Rose.

"Get *off* me, you ox!" she promptly hissed. "Hardcastle's yonder, and—"

The firing rose into a furious volley, then died away again just as quickly as everyone reached the need to reload.

Time that Rose and Tempest used to drag their friend Hardcastle back into the Lanthorn Tower.

Someone promptly fired at them out of the darkness—and Tempest cursed and clutched his shoulder, falling hard on that elbow on the steps.

The Lady Harminster snatched up a fallen pistol and fired wildly at where the shot had come from, awkwardly and two-handed, and was rewarded with a groan.

Which told her whoever it was still lived, so she ran to where she could see another pistol, scooped it up, and emptied it after the first.

Finding a third gun, Rose rushed fiercely into the tower, but found only dead and dying men, so she turned back to Tempest.

"Jack? *Jack!*"

"I'll live," he groaned. "See how Bleys is, will you?"

"I *was* sleeping peacefully," Hardcastle mumbled, "but someone started a war, and all the firing shook me awake. God, my head hurts. The head on the left, more than the head on the right. What happened?"

Rose looked at Tempest, and Tempest looked back at her, and they both grew wry grins.

"Oh, nothing much," Jack told his friend.

"A *lot*," the Lady Harminster corrected firmly, "but I'll tell you later. When fewer people are trying to kill us."

I see it's all gone wrong," Lady Roodcannon observed sharply, setting down her third glass of wine and reaching for the lever that worked the elevation vanes. "Must I do *everything* myself?"

She put *The Steel Kiss* into a dive, rang the bells that would send her crew scrambling to reload, aimed at the White Tower, and started firing.

As her great ship swept down, she kept her fingers firmly on the firing studs. Everyone down there was a target, every single running figure within the wards. She'd sacrifice any number of Order members to get the Prince Royal and to make the explosives in the Tower blow up and eliminate the Queen.

"Die!" she snarled. "Die! Die, damn you—*die!*"

She was still diving and firing when the world right in front of her burst into a wall of thunderous flame.

And *The Steel Kiss* plunged right into it.

I prefer to be known as 'Uncle.'"

Venetta Deleon's answering smile held only the slightest trace of mockery. "Very well, *Uncle*. I—"

The door behind her opened, bringing a frown to Uncle's face. He had given orders they were *not* to be disturbed, and—

The frown deepened when he saw who came through it. A man who should not be here: Grimstone, Lady Roodcannon's man.

"Forgive me," he said gravely, "but there are things you, sir, should know without any delay. Whipsnade and all of his men are imperiled by Lady Roodcannon and her airship, a battle is raging at the Tower of London, and the inventor Marlshrike has gone missing."

"Gone missing?" Uncle asked sharply. "What's this?"

"Packed and gone. An hour ago, if not less. No signs of any struggle."

"Well, *I* don't have him," Uncle scowled. "So what of the Queen? And the Prince Royal?"

Grimstone shrugged.

"Well," Uncle snapped, "we'll have to go in through the tunnels and find out." He got up from his chair and hurried to the door, pulling a bellpull—and then he turned, seemingly almost as an afterthought, and reached out to take Venetta Deleon's hand.

When she put her fingers in his, she felt a sharp jab.

And saw his cold smile as he lifted his hand to display that one of the rings he wore had a fang turned to the inside—a little point now slick and dark with her blood.

She reeled, feeling suddenly ice-cold, then burning hot.

Poison!

"What have you *done* to me?" she gasped, as the room seemed to darken.

She took a leaning, limp-limbed step sideways, like a drunkard—and then collapsed across Uncle's waiting arm, out cold.

"Put you to sleep, my dear," he told her. "I haven't time to attend to you now, but you'll bide here on my floor quite peacefully until this evening."

He looked at Grimstone, who had prudently moved back out of range, sighed, and said, "*You* needn't fear. I'm no dullard—and, lacking Whipsnade, I have need of you. Round up all the Tentacles you can find in the next ten minutes or so and meet me down below, at the Black Bird. Everyone should come armed—three weapons or more, each. There will be, as they say, unpleasantness. Not to mention bloody constraint."

The world was all raging, snarling fire, hot on her cheek and stinging her eyes and lungs—and then, quite suddenly, they were out of it and past.

Though the great airship beneath her was rocking and lurching, minor explosions buffeting her ears from various places beneath her. From above her was coming an ominous hissing, like a steam boiler slowly whistling up to its singing, kettle-boiling height.

The Steel Kiss shuddered as it flew on, the Tower of London far behind her but soon to come around again because she'd just put the helm hard over to send her ship into a tight turn.

It seemed to fight against the bank she was putting it into, wanting to list in the opposite direction—and it was definitely sinking, growing sluggish in the air.

Damn. Damn and *blast*.

Aye, blast was exactly what had befallen it. Stray ordnance flung out by the explosions within the White Tower—which had lost its roof and much of its upper floor, though there was no telling yet if any royal heads had been blown apart in that eruption—had obviously done some damage to her ship.

"What's *happened*?" she snarled, struggling with the controls, despite knowing the answer. Gunfire was coming at her from the Lanthorn Tower, and her ship was slowly but relentlessly sinking.

She sighed, turned the wheel hard over the other way, and departed the battlefield.

"Live to fight another day," she murmured, reaching for her wineglass again. "Constance may be my name, but to it should be added, 'And Everlasting Bloody Patience.'"

And she sailed away, trying to nurse her airship over the rest of London and out into the countryside before it sank low enough to start striking rooftops.

U ncle smiled. "We got here in time. They won't be getting out this way."

"Oh?" Whipsnade asked.

Uncle gestured. "Traitor's Gate was rebuilt long ago. Notice anything unusual about the inner gates?"

"Those fins?"

"Indeed. They're hulls. A dozen boats, concealed in the water gate itself—a means of escape the Queen and the Prince Royal can't use now, unless they want to be riddled with bullets."

"So we have them trapped?"

"They don't know it yet. They'll flee instead into the ancient Roman sewers that connect to the tunnels. Which is where we want them to go."

Whipsnade knew better than to ask why. The Masters of the Order liked their opportunities to gloat, and masters were best kept happy.

And after all, Uncle wouldn't be able to resist telling him soon enough.

That's Lord Winter!" Rose whispered, in Tempest's ear. "*What is going on?*"

"He's lighting a succession of torches and barring more than a few doors," the tinkerer murmured. "I'd say he's trying to guide or lure someone. And it almost has to be the Queen and the Prince, if they did come down here."

"So our play is?" Hardcastle rumbled, from behind them both.

"Watch, and follow, taking care not to be heard or seen. I'd say the Lion Throne stands in sore need of whatever aid we can give right now."

"And where are we all heading," Rose asked, "Winter and those with him and those he's trying to guide?"

"Somewhere under Whitechapel, by the looks of things." Tempest clutched his wounded shoulder for about the fortieth time and sighed. "Somehow I *always* end up in Whitechapel."

Tempest had to admit that the cellar where they all ended up— yes, somewhere under Whitechapel—looked impressive. Its groined ceiling, pillars, and walls were all slick with damp, which reflected back the lights of hundreds of thick white altar candles. Those candles threw off an almost-oppressive warmth.

There was even an altar. A huge rectangular ancient stone block of an altar with black hangings behind it, scores of rippling dark pleats across which wandered tentacles. Lots of tentacles.

A drawn and tired-looking Queen, a grim-faced Prince Royal, and two wounded and bleeding soldiers faced Uncle and Grimstone and seven other Order members—burly men, all—across the dancing candle flames.

Tempest, Rose, and Hardcastle lurked well back in the darkness behind the royal party, their presence hopefully not known to any of the others. Yet.

Uncle smiled his warmest smile. "Welcome to the lair of the Elder."

The Queen seemed unamused. "Lord Winter," she snapped, "what is the meaning of this?"

"The meaning of this," Uncle replied triumphantly, "is that the Ancient Order of Tentacles has two proper sacrifices in our grasp at last. And as our cause is right, we shall do what we must."

"Explain yourself, man," the Prince Royal said coldly.

Lord Winter's smile went smug. "You are about to learn the real secret of our Order. That those who serve long and well are chosen to receive the Deep Blessing."

The Prince sighed. "Why don't you gloatingly tell us what the Deep Blessing is?"

"*Thank* you," Lord Winter replied tartly. "I shall. The Deep Blessing is an alchemical concoction drunk from the Grail—yes, *that* Grail. The true Grail. Arthur's cup. Its keeping is the first duty of our Order, and in that sense we are far more the guardians of the Empire than you mere warmers of the Lion Throne. Only the Elders know how to brew the Deep Blessing, and to drink it is to join their ranks."

"And who are the Elders?"

Lord Winter gestured as grandly as any master of a music hall introducing a new act, and the dark tapestries swirled and parted.

What stepped through them walked like a man, but had the face of a *thing*. A mottled black and green snake-snouted hairless head above arms with fingers like the long, strong tentacles of a giant octopus. It wore an eternal, lipless smile, yet clearly conveyed gloating amusement as it stepped forward into the light, lidless eyes baleful, mighty arms crossed.

"By drinking the Deep Blessing," Lord Winter purred, "we gain eternal life, immunity to poisons, swift regeneration if we slay and take the life force of a creature when we are wounded—and powerful tentacles to slay with. Thus we become supreme over mere men, as the Elders are."

The Elder stopped behind the center of the altar, leaned forward, and uncrossed its arms, revealing what it had set on the altar.

An ancient, battered, leaning ruin of what had once been a large and grand goblet.

"Behold the Grail," Lord Winter said reverently. "The font of true kingship, the chalice that holds the life at the heart of all things. In it now the Elder has concocted the same potion that transformed him, long before any of us drew breath. He has waited long for the proper sacrifice to turn someone else into a fellow Elder. And now we have two."

"I think *not*," the Queen snapped.

"Oh, but a reigning queen is a fitting sacrifice, and, once made, her Prince as rightful successor is every bit as acceptable. The first candidate to be made an Elder is with us."

"And who might that be?" the Prince asked quietly.

"Mister Norbert Marlshrike."

The hangings parted again to reveal the smirking tinkerer.

"And the second candidate?"

"Is," Lord Winter gloated, "to be myself."

Unhurriedly, the Elder bent down behind the altar and lifted into view two huge, thick black candles, resting on their own metal tripods. Setting them at either end of the altar, he then produced a black altar cloth and smoothed it over the stone block as attentively as any parlor maid. As a shallow dish of beaten copper followed, the seven Order members advanced on the Queen and the Prince Royal.

Grimly, the two soldiers stepped in front of the royals, drawing belt knives, but two of the Tentacles drew pistols and casually shot them dead. The Queen stirred, as if to turn and run, but her son took her hand, and they calmly faced the altar as the Tentacle agents surrounded them.

The Elder produced a vial of clear oil and poured it into the copper dish, then pointed at Marlshrike and then at the hangings.

The tinkerer nodded and hurried back through the tapestries, only to reappear almost immediately with a candle lantern, which he passed to the Elder with reverence.

The Elder opened its shutter, removed the lit candle inside without apparent pain, and, with it, lit the two tall black candles.

They caught and blazed up smokily, emitting a strange spicy smell, and the Elder began a liquid, hissing chant of words Lady Rose had never heard before. Nor had Tempest, by his expression, or the royals. The Tentacles members all took up the chanting, though Rose noticed some of them pronounced the words very differently than the tentacled Elder. Awkwardly, that was the right word.

As they chanted, the Elder raised a wicked-looking knife, his movements as slow and deliberate as a priest conducting a long-memorized religious service at an altar; flourished it in the air; and then put it down again and lifted the Grail the same way.

That was the moment when Tempest chose to slice a small hole in another of his bags of ball bearings, to let some bearings escape when he threw it—and he hurled it, from the darkness behind the Order members clustered behind the Queen and the Lord Lion, right at the Elder's head.

It struck accurately and hard.

Dazed, the Elder staggered, the Grail clanging down against the altar and spilling the blessing—and ball bearings bounced everywhere.

Sending Marlshrike, Lord Winter, Grimstone, and Order members slipping, sliding, and falling.

"*Don't* move, Mother!" the Prince Royal told the Queen, wrapping his arms around her.

Nor did she. Like statues they stood amid spreading tumult. The black candles toppled, igniting the altar cloth and the oil in the copper dish.

Squalling, the Elder clawed at the flames, trying to put them out and to recover the Grail, which was now rolling lopsidedly across the floor. He was not helped in this endeavor by Order members, who kept helplessly falling onto him as ball bearings ruined their footing—in a spreading flood that Tempest reinforced with the contents of another slit-open and hurled bag that Hardcastle had just passed him. This bag exploded against the side of Lord Winter's head.

Tempest, Hardcastle, and Rose pounced on the Order members, keeping low so while they slipped often, they couldn't fall. Tempest wrapped his arms around one unwashed neck and jerked with all the strength the exoskeleton could lend him—and something broke, the man's head lolling sickeningly. He clawed at the Order tough's belt and pockets, recovered a cosh and some knives, and tossed them to Hardcastle and Rose.

The Lady Harminster let out a little shriek as that sharp steel came flashing at her in the candlelight, but clapped her forearms together and managed to field the knife an inch or so from her face.

Tempest gave her an apologetic grin and called, "Watch!" Then he tackled the next Order member, using a knife to slash open the man's jacket—and promptly pulling it up to shroud the man's head. He tied it there, then punched the blinded man into collapse.

Rose smiled, nodded, and did the same thing to the nearest Order member. As the man collapsed, she looked up to discover that Hardcastle was in his element. All this while, he'd been hammering Tentacle agents with the cosh—and grabbing everything flammable he could find, including their jackets, and hurling them onto the flames to keep the Elder busy.

Tempest was now peering all around the cellar. Hardcastle tore down some of the hangings to feed the flames, revealing a horizontal pipe studded with bulbous valves from which spoked metal wheels protruded and open-ended side pipes jutted. Tempest pointed at one and called, "Rose!"

The Lady Harminster saw where he was pointing, rushed to that wheel, and tugged on it.

Lord Winter and the Elder both struggled to rush at her.

"No!" Winter shouted. "Don't you *dare* touch that, woman!"

As he came around the altar, flames licking at his robes, the Elder was making shrill, squalling, burbling, wet sounds that might have been words. He threw the lit candle from the lantern at her, and then the knife.

Rose turned the wheel and told the onrushing lord angrily, "*That's* for the way Bentley Steelforce died."

The pipe jutting from the valve was a good three feet from her, but not far from Winter's face as he charged—and the candle bounced off his shoulder, spitting flames in all directions. The gas jetting forth from the pipe ignited with a roar, and Winter screamed as the Elder's knife struck him in the shoulder—and he vanished in the heart of a roaring flame.

The "Uncle" of the Ancient Order danced in agony amid the gas flame, managing to stay upright long enough to shield the Elder behind him from sharing his fate, but the tentacled thing seemed to have had enough.

Howling incoherently and trailing flames, it turned and fled from the cellar, its roars of pain echoing back to them from increasingly distant sewer tunnels.

The blazing Lord Winter staggered back, slipped on some ball bearings, and fell—right onto one of the black candles, impaling himself on its tripod spike. He shrieked once, then sagged, leaning over as he burned.

Rose shrank back from the sight in horror, only to find herself under attack from two grimly crawling Order members. She punched and kicked, as Tempest struggled forward through the ball bearings to the gas pipe, clawed his way up to turn the wheel she'd turned back again—and shut off the gas.

As the jet of flame died and Rose battered the last two Tentacles men into groaning immobility, Hardcastle ducked behind the rest of the hangings to make sure there were no more lurking foes.

He found himself staring at a ladder of rusty metal rungs set in one wall. The way Marlshrike must have come.

He climbed them, discovered they ended at a trapdoor, shoved it up and open, and found himself in a warehouse. The morning sun was flooding in through a nearby open loading-dock door, and a dozen or so curious-looking loaders were clustered near, behind two tense-looking beagles.

"Hold hard, there! Who are you, and what's going on down there?" the nearest one challenged him.

"Hardcastle's my name, and I'm trying to escape," Hardcastle replied, mustering what dignity he could.

"Who's been doing all the screaming?" the other beagle demanded.

By way of reply, he inquired, "Is Standish with you?"

"Wot?"

"Chief Inspector Theo Standish. Handsome fellow, about *yay* wide and—"

"That'll do, Hardcastle," Standish snapped, striding into view from behind the warehouse men. "Tell me, have you returned the mail ship you *borrowed*?"

"That you, Standish?" Tempest called, from the depths below. "There's something down here you should see."

"Oh? Such as?"

"The Queen and the Prince Royal, for a start. A little bruised, but—"

"Aye," Standish sighed, rolling his eyes. "If they're in *your* keeping, they would be."

The crash of *The Steel Kiss,* and the rolling explosions and rising tongues of flame that followed, were spectacular.

Lady Roodcannon watched from the tree that her lowered line had swung her into, smiled brightly at the spreading conflagration, and then shrugged.

"It's just a ship," she observed aloud. "I'll build others. And seize the Empire another day. After all, it's not *going* anywhere, is it?"

T he candles were all out, leaving behind a sharp reek and no small amount of smoke, but the cellars were brightly lit now by scores of beagle lanterns. Brisk constables were bustling everywhere, frowning as they snapped out queries and replies. The Queen and the Prince Royal were gone, taken to safety, but other disappearances were less acceptable. It seemed Marlshrike and Grimstone had slipped away unnoticed in the confusion of Lord Winter's grisly demise, and so had the Elder. Although they were pounding along miles of old tunnels and the nearest navigable sewers beyond, the beagles had as yet found no sign of those three persons.

And no wonder. London was a large place, and a proper flight of steps had been located a few rooms away from the altar-cellar that led up into the back room of a burnt-out public house. Now that there were beagles everywhere to stand escort, Tempest had sent Rose and Hardcastle away with the battered Grail in their keeping.

Which left him free to explain to a skeptical Standish what had occurred, in the heart of a throng of senior beagles who were examining the bodies.

"A tentacled man-thing?" the Chief Inspector growled. "That the *best* you can do? You'll be babbling of mermaids next!"

Jack Straker sighed in loud exasperation and gave Standish his best glare.

"Theo, I've *not* been drinking, and I'm not pulling your leg! I saw what I saw, and—"

"Where's Lord Winter? *Is* he dead? And has he said anything to anyone?"

Standish and Straker both turned. They knew that voice.

It was coming from behind two commanders and the Deputy Assistant Commissioner, who were all stepping into the lantern light in full uniform. Behind them stood a tall figure in a greatcoat, gloves, mask, and a top hat studded with a glittering column of diamonds.

Lord Staunton doffed that top hat, and his mask came with it. He handed it to the Deputy Assistant Commissioner as if the man was an underbutler and stepped forward.

"Yes, my Lord," Standish replied, "Lord Winter is dead. Caught in a gas flame, I understand. According to Lord Tempest here, he did say something about a Deep Blessing before he died."

He stepped aside and waved at what was left of Lord Winter.

Lord Staunton looked down at the sprawled bones and ashes, from which a few tardy wisps of smoke were still rising.

He gazed silently for a long time and then stepped back.

And nodded, seeming almost regretful. "The hunger," he murmured, "would have been almost unbearable."

Something in his tone made Standish look at him sharply.

As Lord Staunton took another step back, a twisted smile rose onto his face.

"You see," he said softly, as both hands came up with many-barreled guns in them, thrusting his coat open so they could see the tiny badge of many tentacles he wore, "I am one, too."

And then he started firing.

M ore tea?"

Lady Rathercoats was at her most motherly, her eyes sparkling with excitement. It wasn't often she had two fine men of noble rank in her parlor, and Lord Sefton and his son Algernon Hartworth seemed in no hurry to depart.

"I will, yes, thank you," Lord Sefton growled, and it was a mark of how shaken he was that he meant it, rather than shooting longing glances at the sideboard and wondering aloud if there was whisky to be had.

They'd been discussing the same thing the entire neighborhood seemed to be buzzing about—the exciting events of the preceding night. It seemed half the Tower of London had been destroyed, and most of an army of loyal soldiers of the Empire slaughtered—not to mention dozens of airships crashing together in the sky and falling in flames into the Thames. Dastardly traitors had sought the lives of the Queen and the Prince Royal, but failed.

"*This* time," Lady Rathercoats added darkly. "And what of that horrible walking dead man, that Bentley Roper?"

"Hadn't heard anything of him being involved," Lord Sefton growled, devouring another sandwich as he talked, "but it seems Lord Tempest and the man Hardcastle and Lady Harminster, too, were all in the thick of it and are due to be knighted, or decorated, or given silver punch bowls, or some such. Seems they rescued the Queen *and* the Prince."

"Some people have *all* the luck," Algernon observed gloomily. "Piloting airships, firing guns, shooting honest-to-God real masked bad men . . . why can't such things happen to *me*?"

"Oh!" Lady Rathercoats exclaimed, scandalized. "Lord Sefton! Did you just hear what your son *said*?"

"Yes," Lord Sefton replied gruffly, "and I'm rather proud of him."

Algernon turned and gaped at his father. The broad smile he saw on those gruff and usually frowning features reassured him of the truth even before his question left his lips. "You are?"

———

Standish swam back to consciousness to find himself staring at an unfamiliar ceiling with wandering cracks in its yellowed plaster. He felt weak indeed, emptied, and in a deuced amount of pain. Shoulder, ribs, head, left ear . . .

"What's left of me? And what happened to Staunton?"

"Escaped, I'm afraid," Lord Tempest told him cheerfully. "Thanks to the Commander and Deputy Assistant Commissioner traitors. As did the Lady Roodcannon. Dashed untidy mess your beagles have made of things, all told."

"What're you—*my* beagles?"

"Your beagles," Tempest said, checking his bandages. "You've lost most of an ear, but the rest of you should heal. You've been promoted to Assistant Commissioner by the Prince Royal. He expects a report, once you're well enough to go around and give it."

Standish groaned, shook his head, then closed his eyes and shook it harder. Yet when he opened them again, the ceiling hadn't gone away and he hadn't woken up from some dream. He *was* awake.

Assistant Commissioner?

"Where am I?" he demanded to know.

"Rented room at the Crown," Tempest replied, and waved at some decanters. "I ordered in some decent drinkables, but you can't have much until you're a little more healed."

Standish turned his head and blinked again. Among the gleaming glassware stood a battered, leaning metal goblet. Lady Rose Harminster and Mister Bleys Hardcastle were sitting behind it smiling at him.

"Oh, yes," Tempest added. "And you're in the presence of what might or might not be the Holy Grail, and esteemed individuals who are most definitely newly created *Lords* Investigator Royal— and the only Lady Investigator Royal in all the Empire. You lucky fellow. We'll have a drink on the strength of that now, I think."

And they did.